"It is his attention to style, to the extraordinary pull of places, to all the fleeting wisps of the past, that give this volume durability.... It is at the core a great deal more than 'reporting' ... it is the written geography of an imaginative artist.... The diminutive wizard with the savage tongue does not delude me.... The unbearable emotion is disciplined, but only barely; the feel for the word is his strength and his salvation.... *The Dogs Bark* suggests again that Capote is among our best, and surely the one who most defies a category."

—WILLIE MORRIS
in the *New Republic*

Truman Capote was born in New Orleans in 1924, was an office boy at *The New Yorker* at the age of 17, and won instant success with his first novel, *Other Voices, Other Rooms*, in 1948. Since then his work has included such fiction as *Breakfast at Tiffany's*; plays like *The Grass Harp* and *House of Flowers*; screenplays such as *Beat the Devil* and *The Innocents*; and a great variety of reportage, including the classic "nonfiction novel," *In Cold Blood* and his latest best-selling collection, *Music for Chameleons*.

The Dogs Bark

Public People
and
Private Places

Truman Capote

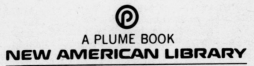

A PLUME BOOK
NEW AMERICAN LIBRARY
TIMES MIRROR
NEW YORK AND SCARBOROUGH, ONTARIO

NAL BOOKS ARE AVAILABLE AT QUANTITY DISCOUNTS WHEN USED TO
PROMOTE PRODUCTS OR SERVICES. FOR INFORMATION, PLEASE WRITE TO
PREMIUM MARKETING DIVISION, THE NEW AMERICAN LIBRARY, INC.,
1633 BROADWAY, NEW YORK, NEW YORK 10019.

Library of Congress Catalog Card Number: 73-3988

Portions of this book previously appeared in *Cosmopolitan, Harper's
Bazaar, Ladies Home Journal, Mademoiselle, The New Yorker,
Redbook, Saturday Evening Post,* and *Travel & Camera.*

ACKNOWLEDGMENTS

Grateful acknowledgment is made for permission to reprint the
following: Excerpts from *Observations* by Richard Avedon and
Truman Capote. Copyright © 1959 by Richard Avedon and
Truman Capote. Reprinted by permission of Simon and Schuster, Inc.
"New York," "Brooklyn," "Hollywood," "Haiti," "To Europe,"
"Tangier," Copyright 1947, 1948, 1949, 1950 by Truman Capote.
From *Local Color* by Truman Capote. "New Orleans," "Ischia,"
"A Ride Through Spain." Copyright 1946, 1950 by Truman Capote.
"A House on the Heights," Copyright © 1959 by The Curtis
Publishing Co. All from *Selected Writings of Truman Capote.*
Reprinted by permission of Random House, Inc., and Hamish
Hamilton, Ltd. "A Voice from a Cloud" from the twentieth-anniversary
edition of *Other Voices, Other Rooms* by Truman Capote. Copyright
© 1967 by Truman Capote. "The Muses Are Heard." Copyright ©
1956 by Truman Capote. Reprinted by permission of Random House
Inc., and William Heinemann, Ltd. *A Ride Through Spain,
The Duke in His Domain* and portions of *The Muses Are Heard,*
appeared originally in *The New Yorker.* "Cecil Beaton," Preface by
Truman Capote to *The Best of Beaton.* Reprinted by permission of
George Weidenfeld and Nicolson, Ltd.

PLUME TRADEMARK REG. U.S. PAT. OFF. AND FOREIGN COUNTRIES
REGISTERED TRADEMARK—MARCA REGISTRADA
HECHO EN WESTFORD, MASS., U.S.A.

SIGNET, SIGNET CLASSICS, MENTOR, PLUME, MERIDIAN
and NAL BOOKS are published *in the United States* by The New
American Library, Inc., 1633 Broadway, New York, New York 10019,
in Canada by The New American Library of Canada Limited,
81 Mack Avenue, Scarborough, Ontario M1L 1M8

First Plume Printing, October, 1977

3 4 5 6 7 8 9

PRINTED IN THE UNITED STATES OF AMERICA

For My Two Guardians
Joseph M. Fox
and
Alan U. Schwartz

"The dogs bark, but the caravan moves on."

—ARAB PROVERB

Contents

Preface

IT MUST HAVE BEEN the spring of 1950 or 1951, since I have lost my notebooks detailing those two years. It was a warm day late in February, which is high spring in Sicily, and I was talking to a very old man with a mongolian face who was wearing a black velvet Borsalino and, disregarding the balmy, almond-blossom-scented weather, a thick black cape.

The old man was André Gide, and we were seated together on a sea wall overlooking shifting fire-blue depths of ancient water.

The postman passed by. A friend of mine, he handed me several letters, one of them containing a literary article rather

* ix

unfriendly toward me (had it been friendly, of course no one would have sent it).

After listening to me grouse a bit about the piece, and the unwholesome nature of the critical mind in general, the great French master hunched, lowered his shoulders like a wise old . . . shall we say buzzard?, and said, "Ah, well. Keep in mind an Arab proverb: 'The dogs bark, but the caravan moves on.'"

I've often remembered that remark—occasionally in a gaga romantic way, thinking of myself as a planet wanderer, a Sahara tourist approaching through darkness desert tents and desert campfires where dangerous natives lurk listening to the warning barkings of their dogs. It seems to me that I've spent a great bit of time taming or eluding natives and dogs, and the contents of this book rather prove this. I think of them, these descriptive paragraphs, these silhouettes and souvenirs of places and persons, as a prose map, a written geography of my life over the last three decades, more or less from 1942 to 1972.

Everything herein is factual, which doesn't mean that it is the truth, but it is as nearly so as I can make it. Journalism, however, can never be altogether pure—nor can the camera, for after all, art is not distilled water: personal perceptions, prejudices, one's sense of selectivity pollute the purity of germless truth.

The earliest pieces in the present volume, youthful impressions of New Orleans and Tangier, Ischia, Hollywood, Spanish trains, Moroccan festivals, et al., were collected in *Local Color*, a slim limited edition published in 1951 and now long out-of-print. I use the present occasion to reissue its contents for two reasons: the first being nostalgia, a reminder of a time when my eye was less narrowed and more lyric;

the second, because these small impressions are the opening buds, the initial thrust of an interest in non-fiction writing, a genre I invaded in a more ambitious manner five years later with *The Muses Are Heard*, which also has appeared separately as a small book.

The Muses Are Heard is the one work of mine I can truly claim to have enjoyed writing, an activity I've seldom associated with pleasure. I imagined it as a brief comic novel; I wanted it to be very Russian, not in the sense of being reminiscent of Russian writing, but rather of some Czarist *objet*, a Fabergé contrivance, one of his music boxes, say, that trembled with some glittering, precise, mischievous melody.

Many in the cast of characters, Americans as well as Soviets, considered *The Muses Are Heard* just plain mischievous. However, in my journalistic experience it would seem that I've *never* described anyone to his or her satisfaction; or if, initially, some person was not unhappy with my revelations or small portraits, friends and relatives soon talked the subject into nit-picking misgivings.

Of all my sitters, the one most distressed was the subject of *The Duke in His Domain*, Marlon Brando. Though not claiming any inaccuracy, he apparently felt it was an unsympathetic, even treacherous intrusion upon the secret terrain of a suffering and intellectually awesome sensibility. My opinion? Just that it is a pretty good account, and a sympathetic one, of a wounded young man who is a genius, but not markedly intelligent.

However, the Brando profile interests me for literary reasons; indeed, that was why I wrote it—to accept a challenge and underline a literary point. It was my contention that reportage could be as groomed and elevated an art as any other prose form—the essay, short story, novel—a theory not so entrenched in 1956, the year the piece was printed, as it is today, when its acceptance has become perhaps a bit exaggerated. My thinking went: What is the lowest level of journalistic art, the one most difficult to turn from a sow's ear into a silk purse? The movie star "interview," *Silver Screen* stuff: surely nothing could be less easily elevated than that! After selecting Brando as the specimen for the experiment, I checked my equipment (the main ingredient of which is a talent for mentally recording lengthy conversations, an ability I had worked to achieve while researching *The Muses Are Heard*, for I devoutly believe that the taking of notes—much less the use of a *tape recorder*!—creates artifice and distorts or even destroys any naturalness that might exist between the observer and the observed, the nervous hummingbird and its would-be captor). It was a lot to remember, that long stretch of hours of Brando muttering and meandering, but I wrote it all out the morning after the "interview," then spent a month shaping it toward the ultimate result. What I learned most from it was how to control "static" writing, to reveal character and sustain mood unaided by a narrative line—the latter being, to a writer, what a rope and pickaxe are to a mountain climber.

In *The Dogs Bark* two pieces especially demonstrate the difference between narrative and "static" writing. *A Ride Through Spain* was a lark; buoyed along by its anecdotal nature, it skimmed off the end of a Black Wing pencil in a matter of hours. But something like *A House on the Heights*, where all the movement depends on the writing itself, is a matter of how the sentences sound, suspend, balance and tumble; a piece like that can be red hell, which is why I have more affection for it than *A Ride Through Spain*, even though I know the latter is better, or at least more effective.

Much of the substance of this book appeared over the years in various publications, but they have never before found shelter under one roof. One of them, *Lola*, has a curious history. Written to exorcise the ghost of a lost friend, it was bought by an American magazine, where for years it reposed unprinted because the magazine's editor decided he loathed it; he said he didn't know what it was about, and moreover, found it forbidding, black. I disagree; still, I can see what he meant, for instinctively he must have seen through the sentimental disguises of this true tale and realized, without altogether recognizing, what it in fact concerned: the perils, the dooms of not perceiving and accepting the limits of one's supposed identity, the classifications imposed by others—a bird that believes it is a dog, Van Gogh insisting that he was an artist, Emily Dickinson a poet. But without such misjudgments and such faiths, the seas would sleep, the eternal snows remain untracked.

TRUMAN CAPOTE

*

A Voice
from a Cloud

(1969)

❈

*O*ther Voices, Other Rooms (my own title: it is not a
quotation) was published in January, 1948. It took two years
to write and was not my first novel, but the second. The
first, a manuscript never submitted and now lost, was called
Summer Crossing—a spare, objective story with a New
York setting. Not bad, as I remember: technically accomplished, an interesting enough tale, but without intensity or
pain, without the qualities of a private vision, the anxieties
that then had control of my emotions and imagination.
Other Voices, Other Rooms was an attempt to exorcise
demons: an unconscious, altogether intuitive attempt, for I

was not aware, except for a few incidents and descriptions, of its being in any serious degree autobiographical. Rereading it now, I find such self-deception unpardonable.

Surely there were reasons for this adamant ignorance, no doubt protective ones: a fire curtain between the writer and the true source of his material. As I have lost contact with the troubled youth who wrote this book, since only a faded shadow of him is any longer contained inside myself, it is difficult to reconstruct his state of mind. However, I shall try.

At the time of the appearance of *Other Voices, Other Rooms*, critics, ranging from the warmest to the most hostile, remarked that obviously I was much influenced by such Southern literary artists as Faulkner and Welty and McCullers, three writers whose work I knew well and admired. Nevertheless, the gentlemen were mistaken, though understandably. The American writers who had been most valuable to me were, in no particular order, James, Twain, Poe, Cather, Hawthorne, Sarah Orne Jewett; and, overseas, Flaubert, Jane Austen, Dickens, Proust, Chekhov, Katherine Mansfield, E. M. Forster, Turgenev, De Maupassant and Emily Brontë. A collection more or less irrelevant to *Other Voices, Other Rooms*; for clearly no one of these writers, with the conceivable exception of Poe (who was by then a blurred childhood enthusiasm, like Dickens and Twain), was a necessary antecedent to this particular work. Rather, they *all* were, in the sense that each of them had contributed to my literary intelligence, such as it was. But the real progenitor was my difficult, subterranean self. The result was both a revelation and an escape: the book set me free, and, as in its prophetic final sentence, I stood there and looked back at the boy I had left behind.

I was born in New Orleans, an only child; my parents were divorced when I was four years old. It was a complicated divorce with much bitterness on either side, which is the main reason why I spent most of my childhood wandering among the homes of relatives in Louisiana, Mississippi and rural Alabama (off and on, I attended schools in New York City and Connecticut). The reading I did on my own was of greater importance than my official education, which was a waste and ended when I was seventeen, the age at which I applied for and received a job at *The New Yorker* magazine. Not a very grand job, for all it really involved was sorting cartoons and clipping newspapers. Still, I was fortunate to have it, especially since I was determined never to set a studious foot inside a college classroom. I felt that either one was or wasn't a writer, and no combination of professors could influence the outcome. I still think I was correct, at least in my own case; however, I now realize that most young writers have more to gain than not by attending college, if only because their teachers and classroom comrades provide a captive audience for their work; nothing is lonelier than to be an aspiring artist without some semblance of a sounding board.

I stayed two years at *The New Yorker*, and during this period published a number of short stories in small literary magazines. (Several of them were submitted to my employers, and none accepted, though once one was returned with the following comment: "Very good. But romantic in a way this magazine is not.") Also, I wrote *Summer Crossing*. Actually, it was in order to complete the book that I took courage, quit my job, left New York and settled with relatives, a cotton-growing family who lived in a remote part of

Alabama: cotton fields, cattle pastures, pinewoods, dirt roads, creeks and slow little rivers, jaybirds, owls, buzzards circling in empty skies, distant train whistles—and, five miles away, a small country town: the Noon City of the present volume.

It was early winter when I arrived there, and the atmosphere of the roomy farmhouse, entirely heated by stoves and fireplaces, was well suited to a fledgling novelist wanting quiet isolation. The household rose at four-thirty, breakfasted by electric light, and was off about its business as the sun ascended—leaving me alone and, increasingly, in a panic. For, more and more, *Summer Crossing* seemed to me thin, clever, unfelt. Another language, a secret spiritual geography, was burgeoning inside me, taking hold of my night-dream hours as well as my wakeful daydreams.

One frosty December afternoon I was far from home, walking in a forest along the bank of a mysterious, deep, very clear creek, a route that led eventually to a place called Hatter's Mill. The mill, which straddled the creek, had been abandoned long ago; it was a place where farmers had brought their corn to be ground into cornmeal. As a child, I'd often gone there with cousins to fish and swim; it was while exploring under the mill that I'd been bitten in the knee by a cottonmouth moccasin—precisely as happens to Joel Knox. And now as I came upon the forlorn mill with its sagging silver-gray timbers, the remembered shock of the snakebite returned; and other memories too—of Idabel, or rather the girl who was the counterpart of Idabel, and how we used to wade and swim in the pure waters, where fat speckled fish lolled in sunlit pools; Idabel was always trying to reach out and grab one.

Excitement—a variety of creative coma—overcame me. Walking home, I lost my way and moved in circles round the woods, for my mind was reeling with the whole book. Usually when a story comes to me, it arrives, or seems to, *in toto*: a long sustained streak of lightning that darkens the tangible, so-called real world, and leaves illuminated only this suddenly seen pseudo-imaginary landscape, a terrain alive with figures, voices, rooms, atmospheres, weather. And all of it, at birth, is like an angry, wrathful tiger cub; one must soothe and tame it. Which, of course, is an artist's principal task: to tame and shape the raw creative vision.

It was dark when I got home, and cold, but I didn't feel the cold because of the fire inside me. My Aunt Lucille said she had been worried about me, and was disappointed because I didn't want any supper. She wanted to know if I was sick; I said no. She said, "Well, you *look* sick. You're white as a ghost." I said good night, locked myself in my room, tossed the manuscript of *Summer Crossing* into a bottom bureau drawer, collected several sharp pencils and a fresh pad of yellow lined paper, got into bed fully clothed, and with pathetic optimism, wrote: *"Other Voices, Other Rooms*—a novel by Truman Capote." Then: "Now a traveller must make his way to Noon City by the best means he can . . ."

It is unusual, but occasionally it happens to almost every writer that the writing of some particular story seems outer-willed and effortless; it is as though one were a secretary transcribing the words of a voice from a cloud. The difficulty is maintaining contact with this spectral dictator. Eventually it developed that communication ran highest at night, as fevers are known to do after dusk. So I took to working all night and sleeping all day, a routine that distressed the household and caused constant disapproving comment: "But you've got everything turned upside down. You're ruining your health." That is why, in the spring of the year, I thanked my exasperated relatives for their generosity, their burdened patience, and bought a ticket on a Greyhound bus to New Orleans.

There I rented a bedroom in the crowded apartment of a Creole family who lived in the French Quarter on Royal Street. It was a small hot bedroom almost entirely occupied by a brass bed, and it was noisy as a steel mill. Streetcars racketed under the window, and the carousings of sightseers touring the Quarter, the boisterous whiskey brawlings of soldiers and sailors made for continuous pandemonium. Still, sticking to my night schedule, I progressed; by late autumn the book was half finished.

I need not have been as lonely as I was. New Orleans was my hometown and I had many friends there, but because I did not desire that familiar world and preferred to remain sealed off in the self-created universe of Zoo and Jesus Fever and the Cloud Hotel, I called none of my acquaintances. My only company was the Creole family, who were kindly working-class people (the father was a dock hand and his wife a seamstress), or encounters with drugstore clerks and café folk. Curiously, for New Orleans is not that sizable a town, I never saw a soul I knew. Except, by accident, my father. Which was ironic, considering that though I was unaware of it at the time, the central theme of *Other Voices, Other Rooms* was my search for the existence of this essentially imaginary person.

I seldom ate more than once a day, usually when I finished work. At that dawn hour I would walk through the humid, balconied streets, past St. Louis Cathedral and on to the French Market, a square crammed in the murky early morning with the trucks of vegetable farmers, Gulf Coast fishermen, meat vendors and flower growers. It smelled of earth, of herbs and exotic, gingery scents, and it rang, clanged, clogged the ears with the sounds of vivacious trading. I loved it.

The market's chief gathering place was a café that served only bitter-black chicory coffee and the crustiest, most delicious fresh-fried doughnuts. I had discovered the place when I was fifteen, and had become addicted. The proprietor of the café gave all its habitués a nickname; he called me the Jockey, a reference to my height and build. Every morning as I plowed into the coffee and the doughnuts, he would warn me with a sinister chuckle, "Better watch it, Jockey. You'll never make your weight."

It was in this café that five years earlier I'd met the prototype of Cousin Randolph. Actually, Cousin Randolph was suggested by two people. Once, when I was a very young child, I had spent a few summer weeks in an old house in Pass Christian, Mississippi. I don't remember much about it, except that there was an elderly man who lived there, an asthmatic invalid who smoked medicinal cigarettes and made remarkable scrap-quilts. He had been the captain of a fishing trawler, but illness had forced him to retire to a darkened room. His sister had taught him to sew; in consequence, he had found in himself a beautiful gift for designing cloth pictures. I often used to visit his room, where he would spread his tapestry-like quilts on the floor for me to admire: rose bouquets, ships in full sail, a bowl of apples.

The other Randolph, the character's spiritual ancestor, was the man I met in the café, a plump blond fellow who was said to be dying of leukemia. The proprietor called him the Sketcher, for he always sat alone in a corner drawing pictures of the clientele, the truckers and cattlemen, in a large loose-leaf notebook. One night it was obvious that I was his subject; after sketching for a while, he moseyed over to the counter where I was sitting and said, "You're a *Wunderkind*, aren't you? I can tell by your hands." I didn't know what it meant—*Wunderkind*; I thought that either he was joking or making a dubious overture. But then he defined the word, and I was pleased: it coincided with my own private opinion. We became friends; afterward I saw him not only at the café, but we also took lazy strolls along the levee. We did not have much conversation, for he was a monologist obsessed with death, betrayed passions and unfulfilled talent.

All this transpired during one summer. That autumn I went to school in the East, and when I returned in June and asked the proprietor about the Sketcher, he said, "Oh, he died. Saw it in the *Picayune*. Did you know he was rich? Uh-huh. Said so in the paper. Turned out his family owned half the land around Lake Pontchartrain. Imagine that. Well, you never know."

The book was completed in a setting far removed from the one in which it was begun. I wandered and worked in North Carolina, Saratoga Springs, New York City and, ultimately, in a rented cottage on Nantucket. It was there at a desk by a window with a view of sky and sand and arriving surf, that I wrote the last pages, finishing them with disbelief that the moment had come, a wonder simultaneously regretful and exhilarated.

I am not a keen rereader of my own books: what's done is done. Moreover, I am always afraid of finding that my harsher detractors are correct and that the work is not as good as I choose to think it. Until the subject of the present reissue arose, I never again really examined *Other Voices, Other Rooms*. Last week I read it straight through.

And? And, as I have already indicated, I was startled by its symbolic subterfuges. Also, while there are passages that seem to me accomplishments, others arouse uneasiness. On the whole, though, it was as if I were reading the fresh-minted manuscript of a total stranger. I was impressed by him. For what he had done has the enigmatic shine of a strangely colored prism held to the light—that, and a certain anguished, pleading intensity like the message of a ship-wrecked sailor stuffed into a bottle and thrown into the sea.

The White Rose

(1970)

A SILVERY JUNE AFTERNOON. A June afternoon in Paris twenty-three years ago. And I am standing in the courtyard of the Palais Royal scanning its tall windows and wondering which of them belong to the apartment of Colette, the *Grande Mademoiselle* of French letters. And I keep consulting my watch, for at four o'clock I have an appointment with this legendary artist, an invitation to tea obligingly obtained for me by Jean Cocteau after I had told him, with youthful maladroitness, that Colette was the only living French writer I entirely respected—and *that* included Gide, Genet, Camus and Montherlant, not to mention M. Cocteau.

Certainly, without the generous intervention of the latter, I would never have been invited to meet the great woman, for I was merely a young American writer who had published a single book, *Other Voices, Other Rooms*, of which she had never heard at all.

Now it was four o'clock and I hastened to present myself, for I'd been told not to be late, and not to stay long as my hostess was an elderly partial invalid who seldom left her bed.

She received me in her bedroom. I was astonished. Because she looked precisely as Colette ought to have looked. And that was astonishing indeed. Reddish, frizzly, rather African-looking hair; slanting, alley-cat eyes rimmed with kohl; a finely made face flexible as water . . . rouged cheeks . . . lips thin and tense as wire but painted a really brazen hussy scarlet.

And the room reflected the cloistered luxury of her worldlier work—say, *Chéri* and *The Last of Chéri*. Velvet curtains were drawn against the June light. One was aware of silken walls. Of warm, rosy light filtering out of lamps draped with pale, rosy scarves. A perfume—some combination of roses and oranges and limes and musk—hovered in the air like a mist, a haze.

So there she lay, propped up by layers of lace-edged pillows, her eyes liquid with life, with kindness, with malice. A cat of peculiar gray was stretched across her legs, rather like an additional comforter.

But the most stunning display in the room was neither the cat nor its mistress. Shyness, nerves, I don't know what it was, but after the first quick study I couldn't really look at Colette, and was somewhat tongue-tied to boot. Instead, I concentrated on what seemed to me a magical exhibition, some fragment of a dream. It was a collection of antique crystal paperweights.

There were perhaps a hundred of them covering two tables situated on either side of the bed: crystal spheres imprisoning green lizards, salamanders, *millefiori* bouquets, dragonflies, a basket of pears, butterflies alighted on a frond of fern, swirls of pink and white and blue and white, shimmering like fireworks, cobras coiled to strike, pretty little arrangements of pansies, magnificent poinsettias.

At last Madame Colette said, "Ah, I see my snowflakes interest you?"

Yes, I knew what she meant: these objects were rather like permanent snowflakes, dazzling patterns frozen forever. "Yes," I said. "Beautiful. Beautiful. But what are they?"

She explained that they were the utmost refinement of the crystal-maker's art: glass jewels contrived by the premier craftsmen of the greatest French crystal factories—Baccarat and St. Louis and Clichy. Selecting at random one of the weights, a big beauty exploding with thousand-flower colors, she showed where the date of creation, 1842, was concealed inside one of the tiny buds. "All the finest weights," she told me, "were made between 1840 and 1880. After that the whole art disintegrated. I started collecting them about forty years ago. They were out of fashion then and one could find great prizes in the flea market and pay very little for them. Now, of course, a first-class weight costs the earth. There are hundreds of collectors, and all in all only perhaps three or four thousand weights in existence worth a glance. This one, for instance." She handed me a piece of crystal about the size of a baseball. "It's a Baccarat weight. It's called the White Rose."

It was a faceted weight of marvelous, bubble-free purity

with a single decoration: a simple white rose with green leaves sunk dead-center.

"What does it remind you of? What thoughts run through your mind?" Madame Colette asked me.

"I don't know. I like the way it feels. Cool and peaceful."

"Peaceful. Yes, that's very true. I've often thought I would like to carry them with me in my coffin, like a pharaoh. But what *images* occur to you?"

I turned the weight this way and that in the dim, rosy light. "Young girls in their communion dresses."

She smiled. "Very charming. Very apt. Now I can see what Jean told me is true. He said. 'Don't be fooled, my dear. He looks like a ten-year-old angel. But he's ageless, and has a very wicked mind.' "

But not as wicked as my hostess, who tapped the weight in my hand and said, "Now I want you to keep that. As a souvenir."

By so doing she arranged for a financially ruinous destiny, for from that moment I became a "collector," and over the years, have done arduous duty searching out fine French weights everywhere from the opulent salesrooms at Sotheby's to obscure antiquaries in Copenhagen and Hong Kong. It is an expensive pastime (currently the cost of these *objets*, depending on quality and rarity, runs between $600 and $15,000), and in all the while that I have pursued it I have only found two bargains, but these both were staggering coups and more than compensated for many cruel disappointments.

The first was in a huge and dusty junkshop in Brooklyn. I was looking at a bunch of odds and bits in a dark glass cabinet when I saw a St. Louis flower weight with a tomato-colored porcelain overlay. When I sought out the proprietor and asked him about it, it was obvious he had no idea of what it was or what it was worth, which was about $4,000. He sold it to me for $20, and I did feel slightly crooked, but what the hell, it was the first and last time I ever got the best of a dealer.

My second great coup was at an auction in East Hampton on Long Island. I just happened to wander into it, not expecting much, and indeed it was mostly bad paintings and indifferent furniture culled from an old Long Island sea house But suddenly, just sitting there amid a lot of pottery and boring plates was an electrifying spectacle: an absolutely spectacular *millefiori* weight made in the form of an inkwell. I knew it was the real thing, and by searching carefully I found the date, 1840, and signature of the maker, J.C., deep inside the lower bouquet. It was about eleven o'clock in the morning when I made this discovery, and the inkwell did not appear on the auctioneer's podium until three that afternoon. While waiting, I walked around in a daze of anxiety, wondering if the auctioneer or any of his customers had any notion of the inkwell's rarity and value, which was enough to finance a pair of Siamese twins through college. If all this sounds rather unattractive, and I suppose it does, I can only say that that's what collecting does to you.

Anyway, the auctioneer opened the bidding on the ink-well-weight at $25, so I knew right away *he* didn't know what he was selling; the question was, did anyone in the audience? There were perhaps three hundred people there, a great many of them with very sophisticated eyes. As it turned out, there *was* one who had an inkling: a young dealer from New York who had come to bid on furniture and knew very little about paperweights, but was shrewd enough to realize this was something special. When we reached $300 the others in the auditorium began to whisper and stare; they couldn't fathom what it was that made this hunk of glass worth that kind of money. When we arrived at $600 the auctioneer was fairly excited himself, and my rival was sweating; he was having second thoughts, he wasn't really sure. In a faltering voice he bid $650 and I said $700, and that finished him. Afterward he came over and asked if I thought it worth $700, and I said, "No, seven thousand."

Some people, when traveling, carry with them photographs of friends and family, of loves; I do, too. But I also take along a small black bag that will hold six weights, each wrapped in flannel, for the weights, despite their seeming solidity, are quite fragile, and also, like a crowd of quarrelsome siblings, inimical; one of the easiest ways to chip or shatter a weight is to have it collide with another. So why do I cart them around on, say, a two-day trip to Chicago or Los Angeles? Because, when spread about, they can for me make the most sinisterly anonymous hotel room seem warm and personal and secure. And because, when it's a quarter to two and sleep hasn't come, a restfulness arises from contemplating a quiet white rose until the rose expands into the whiteness of sleep.

Occasionally I have given a weight as a gift to some very particular friend, and always it is from among those I treasure most, for as Colette said that long-ago afternoon, when I protested that I couldn't accept as a present something she so clearly adored, "My dear, really there is no point in giving a gift unless one also treasures it oneself."

Local Color

(1946–1950)

*

New Orleans

(*1946*)

❈

I N THE COURTYARD there was an angel of black stone, and its angel head rose above giant elephant leaves; the stark glass angel eyes, bright as the bleached blue of sailor eyes, stared upward. One observed the angel from an intricate green balcony—mine, this balcony, for I lived beyond in three old white rooms, rooms with elaborate wedding-cake ceilings, wide sliding doors, tall French windows. On warm evenings, with these windows open, conversation was pleasant there, tuneful, for wind rustled the interior like fan-breeze made by ancient ladies. And on such warm evenings the town is quiet. Only voices: family talk weaving on an ivy-curtained porch; a barefoot woman humming as she rocks a sidewalk chair, lulling to sleep a baby she nurses quite publicly; the complaining foreign tongue of an irritated lady who, sitting on her balcony, plucks a fryer, the loosened feathers floating from her hands, slipping into air, sliding lazily downward.

One morning—it was December, I think, a cold Sunday with a sad gray sun—I went up through the Quarter to the old market where at that time of year there are exquisite winter fruits, sweet satsumas, twenty cents a dozen, and winter flowers, Christmas poinsettia and snow japonica. New Orleans streets have long, lonesome perspectives; in empty hours their atmosphere is like Chirico, and things innocent, ordinarily (a face behind the slanted light of shutters, nuns moving in the distance, a fat dark arm lolling lopsidedly out some window, a lonely black boy squatting in an alley, blowing soap bubbles and watching sadly as they rise to burst), acquire qualities of violence. Now, on that morning, I stopped still in the middle of a block, for I'd caught out of the corner of my eye a tunnel-passage, an overgrown court-yard. A crazy-looking white hound stood stiffly in the green fern light shining at the tunnel's end, and compulsively I went toward it. Inside there was a fountain; water spilled delicately from a monkey-statue's bronze mouth and made on pool pebbles desolate bell-like sounds. He was hanging from a willow, a bandit-faced man with kinky platinum hair; he hung so limply, like the willow itself. There was terror in that silent suffocated garden. Closed windows looked on blindly; snail tracks glittered silver on elephant ears, nothing moved except his shadow. It swung a little, back and forth, yet there was no wind. A rhinestone ring he wore winked in the sun, and on his arm was tattooed a name, "Francy."

The hound lowered its head to drink in the fountain, and I ran. Francy—was it for her he'd killed himself? I do not know. N.O. is a secret place.

My rock angel's glass eyes were like sundials, for they told, by the amount of light focused on them, time: white at noon, they grew gradually dimmer, dark at dusk, black—nightfall eyes in a nightfall head.

The torn lips of golden-haired girls leer luridly on faded leaning house fronts: Drink Dr. Nutt, Dr. Pepper, NEHI, Grapeade, 7 Up, Koke, Coca-Cola. N.O., like every Southern town, is a city of soft-drink signs; the streets of forlorn neighborhoods are paved with Coca-Cola caps, and after rain, they glint in the dust like lost dimes. Posters peel away, lie mangled until storm wind blows them along the street, like desert sage—and there are those who think them beautiful; there are those who paper their walls with Dr. Nutt and Dr. Pepper, with Coca-Cola beauties who, smiling above tenement beds, are night guardians and saints of the morning. Signs everywhere, chalked, printed, painted: Madame Ortega —Readings, Love-potions, Magic Literature, C Me; If You Haven't Anything To Do . . . Don't Do It Here; Are You Ready To Meet Your Maker?; B Ware, Bad Dog; Pity The Poor Little Orphans; I Am A Deaf & Dumb Widow With 2 Mouths To Feed; Attention; Blue Wing Singers At Our Church Tonight (signed) The Reverend.

There was once this notice on a door in the Irish Channel district, "Come In And See Where Jesus Stood."

"And so?" said a woman who answered when I rang the bell. "I'd like to see where Jesus stood," I told her, and for a moment she looked blank; her face, cut in razorlike lines, was marshmallow-white; she had no eyebrows, no lashes, and she wore a calico kimono. "You too little, honey," she said, a jerky laugh bouncing her breasts, "you too damn little for to see where Jesus stood."

In my neighborhood there was a certain café no fun whatever, for it was the emptiest café around N.O., a regular funeral place. The proprietress, Mrs. Morris Otto Kunze, did not, however, seem to mind; she sat all day behind her bar, cooling herself with a palmetto fan, and seldom stirred except to swat flies. Now glued over an old cracked mirror backing the bar were seven little signs all alike: Don't Worry About Life . . . You'll Never Get Out Of It Alive.

July 3. An "at home" card last week from Miss Y., so I made a call this afternoon. She is delightful in her archaic way, amusing, too, though not by intent. The first time we met, I thought: Edna May Oliver; and there is a resemblance most certainly. Miss Y. speaks in premeditated tones but what she says is haphazard, and her sherry-colored eyes are forever searching the surroundings. Her posture is military, and she carries a man's Malacca cane, one of her legs being shorter than the other, a condition which gives her walk a penguin-like lilt. "It made me unhappy when I was your age; yes, I must say it did, for Papa had to squire me to all the balls, and there we sat on such pretty little gold chairs, and there we sat. None of the gentlemen ever asked Miss Y. to dance, indeed no, though a young man from Baltimore, a Mr. Jones, came here one winter, and gracious!—poor Mr. Jones—fell off a ladder, you know—broke his neck—died instantly."

My interest in Miss Y. is rather clinical, and I am not, I embarrassedly confess, quite the friend she believes, for one cannot feel close to Miss Y.: she is too much a fairy tale, someone real—and improbable. She is like the piano in her parlor—elegant, but a little out of tune. Her house, old even for N.O., is guarded by a black broken iron fence; it is a poor neighborhood she lives in, one sprayed with room-for-rent signs, gasoline stations, jukebox cafés. And yet, in the days when her family first lived here—that, of course, was long ago—there was in all N.O. no finer place. The house, smothered by slanting trees, has a graying exterior; but inside, the fantasy of Miss Y.'s heritage is everywhere visible: the tapping of her cane as she descends birdwing stairs trembles crystal; her face, a heart of wrinkled silk, reflects fumelike on ceiling-high mirrors; she lowers herself (notice, as this happens, how carefully she preserves the comfort of her bones) into father's father's father's chair, a wickedly severe receptacle with lion-head handrests. She is beautiful here in the cool dark of her house, and safe. These are the walls, the fence, the furniture of her childhood. "Some people are born to be old; I, for instance, was an atrocious child lacking any quality whatever. But I like being old. It makes me feel somehow more"—she paused, indicated with a gesture the dim parlor—"more suitable."

Miss Y. does not believe in the world beyond N.O.; at times her insularity results, as it did today, in rather chilling remarks. I had mentioned a recent trip to New York, whereupon she, arching an eyebrow, replied gently, "Oh? And how *are* things in the country?"

1. Why is it, I wonder, that all N.O. cabdrivers sound as though they were imported from Brooklyn?

2. One hears so much about food here, and it is probably true that such restaurants as Arnaud's and Kolb's are the best in America. There is an attractive, lazy atmosphere about these restaurants: the slow-wheeling fans, the enormous tables and lack of crowding, the silence, the casual but expert waiters who all look as though they were sons of the man-

agement. A friend of mine, discussing N.O. and New York, once pointed out that comparable meals in the East, aside from being considerably more expensive, would arrive elaborate with some chef's mannerisms, with all kinds of froufrou and false accessories. Like most good things, the quality of N.O. cookery derived, he thought, from its essential simplicity.

3. I am more or less disgusted by that persistent phrase "old charm." You will find it, I suppose, in the architecture here, and in the antique shops (where it rightly belongs), or in the minglings of dialect one hears around the French Market. But N.O. is no more charming than any other Southern city—less so, in fact, for it is the largest. The main portion of this city is made up of spiritual bottomland, streets and sections rather outside the tourist belt.

(From a letter to R.R.) There are new people in the apartment below, the third tenants in the last year; a transient place, this Quarter, hello and good-by. A real bona-fide scoundrel lived there when I first came. He was unscrupulous, unclean and crooked—a kind of dissipated satyr. Mr. Buddy, the one-man band. More than likely you have seen him—not here of course, but in some other city, for he keeps on the move, he and his old banjo, drum, harmonica. I used to come across him banging away on various street corners, a gang of loafers gathered round. Realizing he was my neighbor, these meetings always gave me rather a turn. Now, to tell the truth, he was not a bad musician—an extraordinary one, in fact, when, late of an afternoon, and for his own pleasure, he sang to his guitar, sang ghostly ballads in a grieving whiskey voice: how terrible it was for those in love.

"Hey, boy, you! You up there . . ." I was *you*, for he

never knew my name, and never showed much interest in finding it out. "Come on down and help me kill a couple."

His balcony, smaller than mine, was screened with sweet-smelling wisteria; as there was no furniture to speak of, we would sit on the floor in the green shade, drinking a brand of gin close kin to rubbing alcohol, and he would finger his guitar, its steady plaintive whine emphasizing the deep roll of his voice. "Been all over, been in and out, all around; sixty-five, and any woman takes up with me ain't got no use for nobody else; yessir, had myself a lota wives and a lota kids, but christamighty if I know what come of any of 'em—and don't give a hoot in hell—'cept maybe about Rhonda Kay. There was a woman, man, sweet as swamp honey, and was she hot on me! On fire all the time, and her married to a Baptist preacher, too, and her got four kids—five, countin' mine. Always kinda wondered what it was—boy or girl—boy, I spec. I always give 'em boys . . . Now that's all a long time ago, and it happened in Memphis, Tennessee. Yessir, been everywhere, been to the penitentiary, been in big fine houses like the Rockefellers' houses, been in and out, been all around."

And he could carry on this way until moonrise, his voice growing froggy, his words locking together to make a chant.

His face, stained and wrinkled, had a certain deceptive kindness, a childish twinkle, but his eyes slanted in an oriental manner, and he kept his fingernails long, knife-sharp and polished as a Chinaman's. "Good for scratching, and handy in a fight, too."

He always wore a kind of costume: black trousers, engine-red socks, tennis shoes with the toes slit for comfort, a morning coat, a gray velvet waistcoat which, he said, had belonged to his ancestor Benjamin Franklin, and a beret studded with

Vote for Roosevelt buttons. And there is no getting around it—he *did* have a good many lady friends—a different one each week, to be sure, but there was hardly ever a time when some woman wasn't cooking his meals; and on those occasions when I came to visit he would invariably, and in a most courtly fashion, say, "Meet Mrs. Buddy."

Late one night I woke with the feeling I was not alone; sure enough, there was someone in the room, and I could see him in the moonlight on my mirror. It was he, Mr. Buddy, furtively opening, closing bureau drawers, and suddenly my box of pennies splattered on the floor, rolled riotously in all directions. There was no use pretending then, so I turned on a lamp, and Mr. Buddy looked at me squarely, scarcely fazed, and grinned. "Listen," he said, and he was the most sober I'd ever seen him. "Listen, I've got to get out of here in a hurry."

I did not know what to say, and he looked down at the floor, his face turning slightly red. "Come on, be a good guy, have you got any money?"

I could only point to the spilt pennies; without another word he got down on his knees, gathered them and, walking very erectly, went out the door.

He was gone the next morning. Three women have come around asking for him, but I do not know his whereabouts. Maybe he is in Mobile. If you see him around there, R., won't you drop me a card, please?

I want a big fat mama, yes yes! Shotgun's fingers, long as bananas, thick as dill pickles, pound the keys, and his foot, pounding the floor, shakes the café. Shotgun! The biggest show in town! Can't sing worth a damn, but man, can he rattle that piano—listen: *She's cool in the summer and warm*

in the fall, she's a four-season mama and that ain't all . . .
There he goes, his fat mouth yawning like a crocodile's, his
wicked red tongue tasting the tune, loving it, making love to
it; jelly, Shotgun, jelly-jelly-jelly. Look at him laugh, that
black, crazy face all scarred with bullet-shot, all glistening
with sweat. Is there any human vice he doesn't know about?
A shame, though . . . Hardly any white folks ever see Shotgun, for this is a Negro café. Last year's dusty Christmas
decorations color the peeling arsenic walls; orange-green-
purple strips of fluted paper, dangling from naked light bulbs,
flutter in the wind of a tired fan; the proprietor, a handsome
quadroon with hooded milk-blue eyes, leans over the bar,
squalling, "Look here, what you think this is, some kinda
charity? Get up that two-bits, nigger, and mighty quick."

And tonight is Saturday. The room floats in cigarette
smoke and Saturday-night perfume. All the little greasy
wood tables have double rings of chairs, and everyone knows
everyone, and for a moment the world is this room, this dark,
jazzy, terrible room; our heartbeat is Shotgun's stamping
foot, every joyous element of our lives is focused in the
shine of his malicious eyes. *I want a big fat mama, yes yes!*
He rocks forward on his stool, and as he lifts his face to look
straight at us, a great riding holler goes up in the night: *I*
want a big fat mama with the meat shakin' on her, yes!

✳

New York

(*1946*)

❈

I T IS A MYTH, the city, the rooms and windows, the
steam-spitting streets; for anyone, everyone, a different
myth, an idol-head with traffic-light eyes winking a tender
green, a cynical red. This island, floating in river water like a
diamond iceberg, call it New York, name it whatever you
like; the name hardly matters because, entering from the
greater reality of elsewhere, one is only in search of a city, a
place to hide, to lose or discover oneself, to make a dream
wherein you prove that perhaps after all you are not an ugly
duckling, but wonderful, and worthy of love, as you thought

sitting on the stoop where the Fords went by; as you thought planning your search for a city.

Have seen Garbo twice in the last week, once at the theatre, where she sat in the next seat, and again at a Third Avenue antique shop. When I was twelve I had a tiresome series of mishaps, and so stayed a good deal in bed, spending most of my time in the writing of a play that was to star the most beautiful woman in the world, which is how I described Miss Garbo in the letter accompanying my script. But neither play nor letter was ever acknowledged, and for a long time I bore a desperate grudge, one which was indeed not dispelled until the other night when, with an absolute turning over of the heart, I identified the woman in the adjoining seat. It was surprising to find her so small, and so vividly colored: as Loren MacIver pointed out, along with those lines one scarcely expects color, too.

Someone asked, "Do you suppose she is at all intelligent?" which seems to me an outrageous question; really, who cares whether or not she is intelligent? Surely it is enough that such a face could even exist, though Garbo herself must have come to regret the rather tragic responsibility of owning it. Nor is it any joke about her wanting to be alone; of course she does. I imagine it is the only time she does not feel alone: if you walk a singular path, you carry always a certain grief, and one does not mourn in public.

Yesterday, at the antique store, she roamed around, quite intent about everything, not really interested in anything, and for one mad moment I thought I might speak to her, just to hear her voice, you know; the moment passed, thank heaven, and presently she was out the door. I went to the window and watched her hurrying along the blue dusk street with that long, loping step. At the corner she hesitated, as if uncertain which direction she wanted. The street lights went on, and a trick of glare created suddenly on the avenue a blank white wall: wind lashing her coat, and alone, Garbo, still the most beautiful woman in the world, Garbo, a symbol, walked directly toward it.

Lunch today with M. Whatever is one to do about her? She says the money is gone finally, and unless she goes home, her family refuse absolutely to help. Cruel, I suppose, but I told her I did not see the alternative. On one level, to be sure, I do not think going home possible for her. She belongs to that sect most swiftly, irrevocably trapped by New York, the talented untalented; too acute to accept a more provincial climate, yet not quite acute enough to breathe freely within the one so desired, they go along neurotically feeding upon the fringes of the New York scene.

Only success, and that at a perilous peak, can give relief, but for artists without an art, it is always tension without release, irritation with no resulting pearl. Possibly there would be if the pressure to succeed were not so tremendous. They feel compelled to prove something, because middle-class America, from which they mostly spring, has withering words for its men of feeling, for its young of experimental intelligence, who do not show immediately that these endeavors pay off on a cash basis. But if a civilization falls, is it cash the inheritors find among the ruins? Or is it a statue, a poem, a play?

Which is not to say that the world owes M., or anyone, a living; alas, the way things are with her, she most likely could not make a poem, a good one, that is; still she is important, her values are balanced by more than the usual measure of truth, she deserves a finer destiny than to pass from belated adolescence to premature middle age with no intervening period, and nothing to show.

Down the street there is a radio-repair shop run by an elderly Italian, Joe Vitale. Early in the summer there appeared across the front of his store a strange sign: *The Black Wido*. And in smaller lettering: WATCH THIS WINDOW FOR NEWS OF THE BLACK WIDO. So our neighborhood wondered, waited. A few days later two yellowed photographs were added to the display; these, taken some twenty years before, showed Mr. Vitale as a husky man dressed in a black knee-length bathing suit, a black swimming cap and a mask. Typed captions below the pictures explained that Joe Vitale, whom we'd all known only as a stoop-shouldered, sad-eyed radio-repair man, had once been, in a more supreme incarnation, a champion swimmer and a lifeguard at Rockaway Beach.

We were warned to continue watching the windows; our reward came the following week: in a bold streamer, Mr. Vitale announced that The Black Wido was about to resume his career. There was a poem in the window, and the poem was called "The Dream of Joe Vitale"; it told of how he'd dreamed of again breasting the waves, conquering the sea.

On the next day appeared a final notice; it was an invitation, really, one which said we were all welcome to come to Rockaway on August 20, for this day he planned to swim from that beach to Jones Beach, a far piece. Through the intervening summer days, Mr. Vitale sat outside his store on a camp stool, observing the reactions of passers-by to his various declarations, sat there, dreamy and detached, nodding, smiling politely when neighbors stopped to wish him luck. A smart-aleck kid asked him why he'd left out the last letter of Wido, and he answered very gently that widow with a *w* is for ladies.

For a while nothing more happened. Then one morning the world woke up and laughed at the dream of Joe Vitale. His story was in every paper; the tabloids put his picture on the front pages. And sorry pictures they were, too, for here he was, in a moment not of triumph, but agony, here he was standing on the beach at Rockaway with policemen on either side. And in their accounts this is the attitude most of the papers took: once upon a time there was a mad silly old man who rubbed himself with grease and trotted down to the sea, but when the lifeguards saw him out swimming so far, they put to their boats and brought him to shore; such a shy one, this comical old man, for the instant their backs were turned, he was off again, and so out the lifeguards rowed once more, and The Black Wido, forced upon the beach like a half-dead shark, returned to hear not the mermaids singing, but curses, catcalls, police whistles.

The proper thing to do would be to go and tell Joe Vitale how sorry you are, how brave you think him, and say, well, whatever you can; the death of a dream is no less sad than death, and, indeed, demands of those who have lost as deep a mourning. But his radio store is closed; it has been for a long time; there is no sign of him anywhere, and his poem has slipped from place, has fallen beyond view.

Hilary said to come and have tea before the other guests arrived. Even though he had an extravagant cold, he insisted on going ahead with the party; naturally, why not? Playing host is his cure-all. No matter whose house you may be in, if Hilary is there, it is his house, you are his guest. Some think this a too high-handed attitude, but the real hosts are always pleased, for Hilary, with his large, spectacular appearance and roaring, giggling monologues, gives even the dreariest occasions a bubbling glamour. Hilary so wants everyone to be glamorous, to be a story-book creature; somehow he persuades himself that the grayest folk are coated with legend-making glitter; what is more, he persuades them, too, and that in part accounts for the tenderness with which a usually not soft-hearted public refers to him.

Another appealing point is that Hilary is always the same; always making you laugh when you damn well want to cry; and there is this curious feeling that after you have gone, he does your crying for you. Hilary with a velvet lap robe spread over his knees, a telephone in one hand, a book in the other, a radio, a music box, another telephone and a phonograph all sounding in surrounding rooms.

When I arrived for tea, Hilary was propped up in bed, from which he intended to conduct his party. The walls of this room are papered with photographs, almost everyone he has ever known: maiden ladies, debutantes, somebody's secretary, film stars, college professors, chorus girls, circus freaks, Westchester couples, businessmen: they may part with him, but he cannot bear to lose anyone; or anything. Books are piled in the corners, are sagging on shelves, among them his old school texts, and ancient theatre programs, mounds of sea shells, broken records, dead flowers, amusement-park souvenirs turn the apartment into a wonderland attic.

A time may come when there is no Hilary; it would be easy to destroy him—it may be that some one will. Could it be that the transition from innocence to wisdom happens in that moment when we discover not all the world loves us? Most of us learn this too early. But Hilary does not know it yet. I hope he never does, for I should hate it if suddenly he saw he was playing in a playground all alone, and spending love upon an audience that had never been there.

August. Although the morning papers said simply fair and warm, it was apparent by noon that something exceptional was happening, and office workers, drifting back from lunch with the dazed, desperate expression of children being bullied, began to dial Weather. Toward midafternoon, as the heat closed in like a hand over a murder victim's mouth, the city thrashed and twisted, but with its outcry muffled, its hurry hampered, its ambitions hindered, it was like a dry fountain, some useless monument, and so sank into a coma. The steaming willow-limp stretches of Central Park were like a battlefield where many have fallen: rows of exhausted casualties lay crumpled in the dead-still shade, while newspaper photographers, documenting the disaster, moved sepulchrally among them. At night, hot weather opens the skull of a city, exposing its white brain and its central nerves, which sizzle like the inside of an electric-light bulb.

I should probably get a good deal more work done if I left New York. However, more than likely that is not true either. Until one is a certain age, the country seems a bore; and anyway, I like nature not in general, but in particular. Nevertheless, unless one is in love, or satisfied, or ambition-driven, or without curiosity, or reconciled (which appears to be the modern synonym for happiness), the city is like a monumental machine restlessly devised for wasting time, devouring illusions. After a little, the search, the exploration, can become sinisterly hurried, sweatingly anxious, a race over hurdles of Benzedrine and Nembutal. Where is what you were looking for? And by the way, what *are* you looking for? It is misery to refuse an invitation; one is always declining them, only to put in a surprise appearance; after all, it is difficult to stay away when whispers eerily persist to suggest that in keeping to yourself, you've let love fly out the window, denied your answer, forever lost what you were looking for: oh to think! all this awaits a mere ten blocks away: hurry, put on your hat, don't bother with the bus, grab a taxi, there now, hurry, ring the doorbell: hello, sucker, April fool.

Today is my birthday and, as always, Selma remembered: her customary offering, a dime carefully wadded in a sheet of john paper, arrived with the morning mail. In both time and age, Selma is my oldest friend; for eighty-three years she has lived in the same small Alabama town; a hooked little woman with parched cinder-dark skin and spicy, hooded eyes, she was for forty-seven years a cook in the house of my three aunts; but now that they are dead, she has moved to her daughter's farm, just, as she says, to sit quiet and take her ease. But accompanying her gift there was a sort of note, and in it she said to make ready, for any day now she was going to take a Greyhound bus for that "grandus city." It does not mean anything; she will never come; but she has been threatening to for as long as memory. The summer before I first saw New York, and that was fourteen years ago, we used to sit talking in the kitchen, our voices strumming away the whole lazy day; and what we talked about mostly was the city where I was soon to go. It was her understanding that there were no trees there, nor flowers, and she'd heard it said that most of the people lived underground or, if not underground, in the sky. Furthermore, there were "no nourishin' vittles," no good butterbeans, black-eyes, okra, yams, sausage—like we had at home. And it's cold, she said, yessireebobtail, go on up in that cold country, time we see you again your nose will have freeze and fall off.

But then Mrs. Bobby Lee Kettle brought over some picture slides of New York, and after that Selma began telling her friends that when I went North she was going with me. The town seemed to her suddenly shriveled and mean. And so my aunts bought her a round-trip ticket, the idea being that she should ride up with me, turn around and go back. Everything was fine until we reached the depot; and there Selma began to cry, and say that she couldn't go, that she would die so far from home.

It was a sad winter, inside and out. For a child the city is a joyless place. Later on, when one is older and in love, it is the double vision of sharing with your beloved which gives experience texture, shape, significance. To travel alone is to journey through a wasteland. But if you love enough, sometimes you can see for yourself, and for another, too. That is the way it was with Selma. I saw twice over everything: the first snow, and skaters skimming in the park, the fine fur coats of the funny cold country children, the Chute-the-Chute at Coney, subway chewing-gum machines, the magical Automat, the islands in the river and the glitter upon the twilight bridge, the blue upward floating of a Paramount band, the men who came in the courtyard day after day and sang the same ragged, hoarse songs, the magnificent fairy tale of a ten-cent store where one went after school to steal things; I watched, listened, storing up for the quiet kitchen-hours when Selma would say, as she did, "Tell stories about that place, true stories now, none of them lies." But mostly they were lies I told; it wasn't my fault, I couldn't remember, because it was as though I'd been to one of those supernatural castles visited by characters in legends: once away, you do not remember, all that is left is the ghostly echo of haunting wonder.

Brooklyn

(1946)

❖

A N ABANDONED CHURCH, a For Rent sign defacing its baroque façade, towers black and broken at the corner of this lost square; sparrows nest among the stone flowers carved above its chalked-up door (Kilroy Was Here, Seymour Loves Betty, You Stink!); inside, where sunlight falls on shattered pews, all manner of stray beasts have found a home: one sees misty cats watching from its windows, hears queer animal cries, and neighborhood children, who dare each other to enter there, come forth toting bones they claim as human (yeah, they is so! I'm tellin' yuh; the guy was kilt). Definitive in its ugliness, the church for me symbolizes some elements of Brooklyn: if a similar structure were destroyed, I have the uneasy premonition that another, equally old and monstrous, would swiftly be erected, for Brooklyn, or the chain of cities so-called, has, unlike Manhattan, no interest in architectural change. Nor is it lenient toward the individual: in despair one views the quite endless stretches of look-alike bungalows, gingerbread and brownstones, the inevitable empty, ashy lot where the sad, sweet, violent children, gathering leaves and tenement-wood, make October bonfires, the sad, sweet children chasing down these glassy August streets to Kill the Kike! Kill the Wop! Kill the Dinge!—a custom of this country where the mental architecture, like the houses, is changeless.

Manhattan friends, unwilling to cope with the elaborately dismal subway trip (Oh, B., do come, I swear to you it takes only forty minutes, and honest, you don't have to change trains but three times) say so-sorry to any invitation. For this reason I've often daydreamed of leasing and renovating the church: who could resist visiting so curious a residence? As matters stand I have two rooms in a brownstone duplicated by twenty others on the square; the interior of the house is a grimy jungle of Victoriana: lily-pale, plump-faced ladies garbed in rotting Grecian veils prance tribally on wallpaper; in the hall an empty, tarnished bowl for calling cards and a hat tree gnarled like a spruce glimpsed on the coast of Brittany are elegant mementos from Brooklyn's less blighted days; the parlor bulges with dusty fringed furniture, a family history in daguerreotype parades across an old untuned piano, everywhere antimacassars are like little crocheted flags declaring a state of Respectability, and when a draught goes through this room beaded lamps tinkle oriental tunes.

However, there are telephones: two upstairs, three down,

and 125 in the basement; for it is in the basement that my
landladies are more or less locked to a switchboard: Mrs. Q.,
a waddling, stunted woman with a red bulldog face, knobby
lavender eyes and bright orange, unbelievable hair which,
like her daughter Miss Q., she wears wild and waist-length,
is a suspicious person, and her suspicion is the sort that goes
with those who, despising everything, are looking for a reason. Poor Miss Q. is simply tired; soft and honeyed, she
labors under what is essentially a birth-to-death fatigue, and
at times I wonder whether she is really Miss Q. or Zasu Pitts.
Nevertheless, there is established between us an agreeable
rapport. It is based principally on the fact that we are both
harassed by hair-raising headaches. Almost every day she
sneaks upstairs, and giggling at her naughty daring, begs an
aspirin; her mother, a devotee of Bernarr MacFadden, forbids
aspirin and all medicine as "stew from the devil's stove."
Their story is an old story: Mr. Q., "a very decidedly prominent mortician," just "passed away with no word of warning
while reading the *New York Sun*," leaving his wife and
spinster daughter to "go on living with no visible means of
doing so," because "a crook got Papa to invest all his money
in a factory to make artificial funeral wreathes." So she and
her mother set up a telephone-answering service in the basement. Day and night for ten years they'd alternated inter-
cepting calls for persons out-of-town or not at home. "Oh,
it's a misery," says Miss Q. with counterfeit despondency,
for this career-woman role is the realest illusion of her illu-
sioned life. "I tell you God's truth, I couldn't count the years
since I've had a straight hour's rest. Mama's right there on the
job, too, bless her soul, but Mama's got a good many com-
plaints, you know, and I just have to practically tie her in the
bed. Sometimes when it's late at night and my head starts to

hurt—why, I look at the switchboard, and suddenly it's like all those long wires were arms and fingers squeezing me to death." Upon occasion Mrs. Q. has been known to visit a Turkish bath near Borough Hall, but her tired daughter's isolation is absolute; if one is to believe her, she has left the basement only once in eight years, and on this holiday she went with her mother to watch Mr. MacFadden do calisthenics on the stage of Carnegie Hall.

In dread I some nights listen as Mrs. Q. comes heaving up the stairs, presently to present herself at my door; standing there, shrouded in a sleazy sateen kimono, her sunset-colored hair falling Viking-fashion, she regards me with a baleful glitter. "Two more," she says, her hairy baritone voice suggesting fire and brimstone. "We saw them from the window, two whole families riding by in moving vans."

When she has squeezed dry the lemon of her sourness, I ask, "Families of what, Mrs. Q.?"

"Africans," she announces with a righteous owl-like blink, "the whole neighborhood's turning into a black nightmare; first Jews, now this; robbers and thieves, all of them—makes my blood run cold."

Though I suspect Mrs. Q. herself does not realize it, this is not a performance, she is seriously frightened: what is going on outside corresponds with nothing she has known; the husband whose mind she fed upon is gone, and she herself, having possessed merely borrowed attitudes, has never owned an idea. She has had fixed on every door an abnormal number of catches and locks, a few of the windows are barred, there is a mongrel with an ear-splitting bark: someone without, some shapeless someone, desires to be within. Each step remarks her weight as she descends the stairs; below, an image, her own, is groping on the mirror: not recognizing Mrs. Q., she pauses, her breath coming heavy as she wonders who is waiting there: a chill starts in her bones: two more today, more tomorrow, a flood is rising, her Brooklyn is the lost Atlantis, even her reflection on the mirror (a wedding present, remember? forty years: oh, what has happened, tell me, God?) even it is someone, something. "Good night," she calls. The locks go clink-clunk, the gates are closed; 125 telephones are singing in the dark, the Grecian ladies dance in shadow, the house sighs, settles. Outside, wind brings the sweet cookie smell of a bakery blocks away; sailors, bound for Sands Street, cross the lamplit square, and look up at the skeleton church to meet the yellow knowledge of cold cat-eyes. "Good night, Mrs. Q."

I heard a cock crow. Strange at first, it seemed less so remembering the secret unseen city, the continent of back-yard lots, nowhere more flourishing than here: ribbon-clerk and shoe-salesman, tillers of the soil: "Our own radishes, you know." Recently a Flatbush woman was arrested for keeping hogs in her backyard. Envy doubtless drove her neighbors to complain. In the evening, arriving from Manhattan, it is somewhat unnerving to see a sky where real stars are really shining, to mosey down leaf-strewn streets where the smoky autumn smells drift undiluted, and the voices of children, roller-skating in the twilight, bring on the silence homecom-ing messages: "Look, Myrtle, it's a moon—like a Hallowe'en pumpkin!" Underneath, the subway seethes; above, neon cuts the night, yes, still I heard a cock crow.

As a group, Brooklynites form a persecuted minority; the uninventive persistence of not very urbane clowns has made any mention of their homeland a signal for compulsory guf-faws; their dialect, appearance and manners have become, by way of such side-splitting propaganda, synonymous with the crudest, most vulgar aspects of contemporary life. All this, which perhaps began good-naturedly enough, has turned the razory road toward malice: an address in Brooklyn is now not altogether respectable. A peculiar irony, to be sure, for in this unfortunate region the average man, being on the edge of an outcast order, guards averageness with morbid intensity; he does, in fact, make of respectability a religion; still, insecurity makes for hypocrisy, and so he greets The Big Joke with the loudest hee-haw of all: "Yaaah, ain't Brooklyn a kick—talk about funny!" Terribly funny, yes, but Brooklyn is also sad brutal provincial lonesome human silent sprawling raucous lost passionate subtle bitter immature innocent perverse tender mysterious, a place where Crane and Whitman found poems, a mythical dominion against whose shores the Coney Island sea laps a wintry lament. Here, scarcely anyone can give directions; nobody knows where anything is, even the oldest taxi driver seems uncertain; luckily, I've earned my degree in subway travel, though learning to ride these rails, which, buried in the stone, are like the veins found on fossilized fern, requires fiercer application, I'm sure, than working toward a master's. Rocking through the sunless, starless tunnels is an outward-bound feeling: the train, hurtling below unlikely land, seems destined for fog and mist, only the flash-by of familiar stations revealing our identities. Once, thundering under the river, I saw a girl, she was sixteen or so and being initiated into some sorority, I suspect, who carried a basket filled with little hearts cut from scarlet paper. "Buy a lonely heart," she wailed, passing through the car. "Buy a lonely heart." But the pale, expressionless passengers, none of whom needed one, merely flipped the pages of their *Daily News.*

Several nights a week I have dinner at the Cherokee Hotel.

It is an apartment hotel, and exceedingly antique, both in décor and clientele: the youngest Cherokee, as they call themselves, is sixty-six, and the oldest, ninety-eight; females, of course, predominate, but there is a skin-and-bone assortment of widowers, too. Now and then war breaks out between the sexes, and it is easy to deduce when this has happened, for the general sitting room will be deserted; there is a men's parlor and a ladies' parlor, and to these respective sanctuaries the embattled retire, the ladies in a pouting huff, the men, as always, silent, grim. Both parlors, along with a lot of depressing statuary, sport radios, and when a war is on, the ladies, who ordinarily are not in the least interested, turn the volume of theirs as loud as it will go, trying, as it were, to drown out the men's after-dinner news. You can hear the boom three blocks away, and Mr. Littlelow, the proprietor, a nervous young man to begin with, scampers back and forth threatening to abolish the radios altogether, or, worse still, call in his guests' relatives. From time to time he has to resort to this last-mentioned measure; for instance, take the case of Mr. Gilbert Crocker, who sins so constantly poor Littlelow had at last to send for his grandson, and together they reprimanded the old man publicly. "A perpetual center of dissension," accused Littlelow, a finger lifted toward the culprit, "he spreads vicious rumors about the management, says we read his mail, says we have a percentage deal with the Cascades Funeral Home, told Miss Brockton the seventh floor is closed because we've rented it to a fugitive from the law (an ax murderess, he said) when everybody knows the water pipes have burst. Scared Miss Brockton out of her wits; her heart-flutter is ever so much worse. We were willing to overlook all this, but when he started dropping light bulbs from the windows, we thought: well really, the time has come!"

"Why did you drop light bulbs, Grandfather?" said the grandson, glancing anxiously at his watch and obviously wishing the old man had met his Maker.

"Not light bulbs, son," corrected Mr. Crocker patiently. "They were bombs."

"Yes, certainly, Grandfather. And why did you drop the bombs?"

Mr. Crocker surveyed the assemblage of fellow Cherokees; then, with a saturnine smile, bobbed his head in the direction of Miss Brockton. "Her—" he said, "I wanted to blow her up. She's a stinking pig; she and Cook have it fixed up between them never to give me any chocolate sauce so she can gobble it all her big fat self."

Promptly the ladies gathered around his intended victim, whose heart-flutter seemed suddenly on the verge of flying her to the ceiling; above their outraged clucking, Mrs. Allen T. Bonaparte's *non sequiturs* carried clearest: "Murder dear Miss Brockton, imagine, did you ever visit the waxworks in London? You know the ones I mean: look alike, don't they?" And it was understood the radios that night would set every window trembling.

Now, among the tenants there is one so formidable she gives pause even to Littlelow. Very grand is Mrs. T. T. Huett-Smith, and when she appears in the dining room, twinkling with yellowed musty diamonds, her entrance lacks only musical fanfare: with stuttering steps she advances toward her table (the one with a rose, the only one with a rose: paper, at that), accepting, in passage, the homage of the socially ambitious: she is the last souvenir they have of those faraway days when Brooklyn, too, supported an altitudinous society. But like most things which have lingered beyond their valid bloom, Mrs. T. T. has turned decadent, has become a tragi-comic exaggeration: lipstick and rouge, of which she uses an inordinate quantity, look rancid on her narrow, shriveled face, and her pleasures are perverse: she enjoys nothing so much as making some sadistic revelations. When Mrs. Bonaparte first moved into the hotel, Mrs. T. T., seeing her enter the dining room, announced vociferously, "I remember that creature when her mother was a scrub-woman in the *lowest* bath in Coney Island." The shy and silent Webster sisters are another target: "Damned old maids, my husband always called them."

I know a secret about Mrs. T. T. She is a thief. For years she has been slipping the Cherokee's dime-store silverware into her embroidered handbag, and one day, during what was doubtless a mental blackout, she appeared at the desk asking to have her collection locked safely in the hotel safe. "But my dear Mrs. Huett-Smith," said Littlelow, rising above his astonishment, "this can hardly belong to you; after all, it isn't your pattern." Mrs. T. T. examined the knives and forks with a puzzled frown: "Of course not," she said, "no, of course not: we always had the best."

Weeks have gone by since I was last at the Cherokee. I had a dream. I dreamt one of Mr. Crocker's bombs blew them all away; to tell the truth, I'm rather afraid to go and see.

December 28. A blue crystal day, too exquisite for the stuffy precincts of Mrs. Q.'s, and so with a friend I went for a walk on Brooklyn Heights; Boston's Beacon Hill and Charleston, these alone of places I have known, can project a comparable sense of the past (the *vieux carré* of New

Orleans is exempt because its quality is too directly foreign); and of the three, Brooklyn Heights seems the less contrived, and certainly the least exploited. It is condemned, of course; even now a tunnel is coming through, a highway is planned; steel-teethed machines are eating at its palisades, many of the old mansions wait in derelict darkness for the demolition crew; the red newness of *Danger! Men Working* signs glitter in the sober shade of dwarfed Dickensian streets: Cranberry, Pineapple, Willow, Middagh. The dust of dynamited stone hangs its sentence in the air. As it was getting dusk we bought a pecan pie; we sat down on a bench and watched the honeycomb of lights go on in the towers across the river. Wind whipped whitecaps on the cold water, sang through the harplike bridge, swept crying gulls in looping patterns. Eating my portion of the pie, I sat looking at Manhattan and wondering what sort of ruins it would make: as for Brooklyn, archaeologists of another civilization, like taxi drivers of our own, will never decipher the secret of its streets, their destination, their meaning.

Hollywood

(1947)

❈

Approaching Los Angeles, at least by air, is like, I should imagine, crossing the surface of the moon: prehistoric shapes, looming in stone ripples and corroded, leer upward, and paleozoic fish swim in the shadowy pools between desert mountains: burned and frozen, there is no living thing, only rock that was once a bird, bones that are sand, ferns turned to fiery stone. At last a welcoming fleet of clouds: we have crept between a sorcerer's passage, snow is on the mountains, yet flowers color the land, a summer sun juxtaposes December's winter sea, down, down, the plane splits through plumed, gold, incredible air. Oh, moaned Thelma, I can't stand it, she said, and poured a cascade of Chiclets into her mouth. Thelma had boarded the plane in Chicago; she was a young Negro girl, rather pretty, beautifully dressed, and it was the most wonderful thing that would ever happen to her, this trip to California. "I know it, it's going just to be grand. Three years I've been ushering at the Lola Theatre on State Street just to save the fare. My auntie tells the cards, and she said—Thelma, honey, head for Hollywood 'cause there's a job as private secretary to a movie actress just waiting for you. She didn't say what actress, though. I hope it's not Esther Williams. I don't like swimming much."

Later on she asked if I was trying for film work, and because the idea seemed to please her, I said yes. On the whole she was very encouraging, and assured me that as soon as she was established as a private secretary, thereby having access to the ears of the great, she would not forget me, would indeed give me every assistance.

At the airport I helped with her luggage, and eventually we shared a taxi. It came about then that she had no place specific to go, she simply wanted the driver to let her off in the "middle" of Hollywood. It was a long drive, and she sat all the way on the edge of the seat, unbearably watchful. But there was not so much to see as she'd imagined. "It don't look correct," she said finally, quite as if we'd been played a wretched trick, for here again, though in disguise, was the surface of the moon, the noplace of everywhere; but how very correct, after all, that here at continent's end we should find only a dumping ground for all that is most exploitedly American: oil pumps pounding like the heartbeat of demons, avenues of used-car lots, supermarkets, motels, the gee dad I never knew a Chevrolet gee dad gee mom gee whiz wham of publicity, the biggest, broadest, best, sprawled and helplessly etherized by immaculate sunshine and sound of sea and unearthly sweetness of flowers blooming in December.

During the drive the sky had grown ash-colored, and as we turned into the laundered sparkle of Wilshire Boulevard, Thelma, giving her delicate feathered hat a protective touch, grumbled at the possibility of rain. Not a chance, said the driver, just wind blowing in dust from the desert. These words were not out of his mouth before the palm trees shivered under a violent downpour. But Thelma had no place to go, except into the street, so we left her standing there, rain pulling her costume apart. When a traffic light stopped us at the corner, she ran up and stuck her head in the window. "Look here, honey, remember what I say, you get hungry or anything you just find where I'm at." Then, with a lovely smile, "And listen, honey, lotsa luck!"

December 3. Today, through the efforts of a mutual friend, Nora Parker, I was asked to lunch by the fabled Miss C. There is a fortress wall surrounding her place, and at the entrance gate we were more or less frisked by a guard who then telephoned ahead to announce our arrival. All this was very satisfying; it was nice to know that at least someone was living the way a famous actress should. At the door we were met by a red-faced, overly nourished child with a gooey pink ribbon trailing from her hair. "Mummy thinks I should entertain you till she comes down," she said apathetically, then led us into a large and, now that I think about it, preposterous room: it looked as though some rich old rascal had personally decorated himself a lavish hideaway: sly, low-slung couches, piles of lecherous velvet pillows and lamps with sinuous, undulating shapes. "Would you like to see Mummy's things?" said the little girl.

Her first exhibit was an illuminated bibelot cabinet. "This," she said, pointing to a bit of Chinese porcelain, "is Mummy's ancient vase she paid Gump's three thousand dollars for. And that's her gold cocktail shaker and gold cups. I forget how much they cost, an awful lot, maybe five thousand dollars. And you see that old teapot? You wouldn't believe what it's worth . . ."

It was a monstrous recital, and toward the end of it, Nora, looking dazedly round the room for a change of topic, said, "Such lovely flowers. Are they from your own garden?"

"Heavens, no," replied the little girl disdainfully. "Mummy orders them every day from the most expensive florist in Beverly Hills."

"Oh?" said Nora, wincing. "And what is your favorite flower?"

"Orchids."

"Now really. I don't believe orchids could be your favorite flower. A little girl like you."

She thought a moment. "Well, as a matter of fact, they aren't. But Mummy says they are the most expensive."

Just then there was a rustling at the door; Miss C. skipped like a schoolgirl across the room: her famous face was without make-up; hairpins dangled loosely. She was wearing a very ordinary flannel housecoat. "Nora, darling," she called, her arms outstretched, "do forgive my being so long. I've been upstairs making the beds."

Yesterday, feeling greedy, I remembered ravishing displays of fruit outside a large emporium I'd driven admiringly past a number of times. Mammoth oranges, grapes big as ping-pong balls, apples piled in rosy pyramids. There is a sleight of hand about distances here, nothing is so near as you supposed, and it is not unusual to travel ten miles for a package of cigarettes. It was a two-mile walk before I even caught sight of the fruit store. The long counters were tilted so that from quite far away you could see the splendid wares, apples, pears. I reached for one of these extraordinary apples, but it seemed to be glued into its case. A salesgirl giggled. "Plaster," she said, and I laughed too, a little feverishly perhaps, then wearily followed her into the deeper regions of the store where I bought six small, rather mealy apples, and six small, rather mealy pears.

It is Christmas week. And it is evening now a long time. Below the window a lake of light bulbs electrifies the valley. From the haunting impermanence of their hilltop homes impermanent eyes are watching them, almost as if suddenly they might go out, like candles at last consumed.

Earlier today I took a bus all the way from Beverly Hills into downtown Los Angeles. The streets are strung with garlands, we passed a motorized sleigh that was spinning along spilling a wake of white cornflakes, at corners sweating woolly men rustle bells under the shade of prefabricated trees; carols, hurled from lamppost loudspeakers, pour their syrup on the air, and tinsel, twinkling in twenty-four-karat sunshine, hangs everywhere like swamp moss. It could not be more Christmas, or less so. I once knew a woman who imported a pink villa stone by stone from Italy and had it reconstructed on a demure Connecticut meadow: Christmas is as out of place in Hollywood as the villa was in Connecticut. And what is Christmas without children, on whom so much of the point depends? Last week I met a man who concluded a set of observations by saying, "And of course you know this is the childless city."

For five days I have been testing his remark, casually at first, now with morbid alarm; preposterous, I know, but since commencing this mysterious campaign I have seen less than half a dozen children. But first, a relevant point: a primary complaint here is overpopulation; old-guard natives tell me the terrain is bulging with "undesirable" elements, hordes of ex-soldiers, workers who moved here during the war, and those spiritual Okies, the young and footloose; yet walking around I sometimes have the feeling of one who awakened some eerie morning into a hushed, deserted world where overnight, like sailors aboard the *Marie Celeste*, all souls had disappeared. There is an air of Sunday vacancy; here where no one walks cars glide in a constant shiny silent stream, my shadow, moving down the stark white street, is like the one living element of a Chirico. It is not the comfortable silence felt in small American towns, though the physical atmosphere of stoops and yards and hedges is very often the same; the difference is that in real towns you can be pretty sure what sorts of people there are hiding beyond those numbered doors, but here, where all seems transient, ephemeral, there is no general pattern to the population, and nothing is intended—this street, that house, mushrooms of accident, and a crack in the wall, which might somewhere else have charm, only strikes an ugly note prophesying doom.

1. A teacher here recently gave a vocabulary test in which she asked her students to provide the antonym of *youth*. Over half the class answered *death*.

2. No stylish Hollywood home is thought quite sanitary without a brace of modern masters to brighten up the walls. One producer has what amounts to a small gallery; he refers

to paintings merely as good investments. His wife is less modest: "Sure we know about art. We've been to Greece, haven't we? California is just like Greece. Exactly. You'd be surprised. Go over there and talk to my husband about Picasso; he can give you the real low-down."

The day I saw their famous collection I had a picture that I was taking to a framer, a small colored Klee lithograph. "Pleasant," said the producer's wife cautiously. "Paint it yourself?"

Waiting for a bus, I ran into P., of whom I am rather admiring. She has the sort of wit that excludes malice, and, what is more uncommon, she has managed thirty years of Hollywood with humor and dignity. Naturally, she is not very rich. At the moment she is living above a garage. It is interesting, because by local standards she is a failure, which along with age, is unforgivable; even so, success pays her homage, and her Sunday coffee sessions are quite luminously attended, for above that garage she contrives a momentary sense of security, and for all a feeling of having roots. She is an inexhaustible scrapbook, too, the time sequence of her conversation shifting, sliding, until, as she fixes you with her cornflower eyes, Valentino passes lightly brushing your arm, the young Garbo hovers at the window, John Gilbert appears on the lawn, stands there like a twilight statue, the senior Fairbanks roars up the driveway, two mastiffs baying in the rumble seat.

P. offered to drive me home. We went by way of Santa Monica, in order that she could drop off a present for A., that sad, jittery lady who once, after the departure of her third husband, threw an Oscar into the ocean.

The thing about A. which most intrigued me was the way

she applied make-up—such a brutally objective performance; cold-eyed, calculating, she wields her paints and powders altogether as if the face belongs to someone else, managing, in the process, to smooth away whatever time has given her.

As we were leaving, the maid came out to say that A.'s father would like to see us. We found him in a garden facing the ocean; a knotty, phlegmatic old man with blue-white hair and skin browner than iodine, he was slumped in a patch of sunshine, his eyes closed, no sound to disturb him but the slumbering slap of waves, the dozy singing of bees. Old people love California; they close their eyes, and the wind through the winter flowers says sleep, the sea says sleep: it is a preview of heaven. From daybreak to dark A.'s father follows the sun around his garden, and on rainy days he whiles away the time by making bracelets of beer-bottle caps. He gave each of us one of these bracelets, and in a voice that hardly carried through the honeyed, blowing air, said, "A merry Christmas, children."

Haiti

(*1948*)

To look at, Hyppolite is perhaps an ugly man: monkey-thin, gaunt-faced, quite dark, he looks (through silver school-marm spectacles), listens with the steadiest, most gracious precision, his eyes echoing a subtle and basic understanding. One feels with him a certain safety; there is created between you that too uncommon circumstance, no sense of isolation.

This morning I heard that during the night his daughter died, a daughter eight months old; there are other children, he has been married many times, five or six; even so, how hard it must be, for he is not young. No one has told me, I wonder if there is a wake. In Haiti they are extravagant, these wakes, and excessively stylized: the mourners, strangers in large part, claw air, drum their heads on the ground, in unison moan a low doglike grief. Heard at night, or seen suddenly on a country road, it seems so alien the heart shivers, and then one realizes that in essence these are mimes.

Because he is the most popular of Haiti's primitive painters, Hyppolite could afford a running-water house, real beds, electricity; as it is, he lives by lamp, by candle, and all the neighbors, old withered coconut-headed ladies and handsome sailor boys and hunched sandal makers, can see into his affairs as he can see into theirs. Once, some while back, a friend took it upon himself to rent Hyppolite another house, a sturdy sort of place with concrete floors and walls behind which one could hide, but of course he was not happy there, he has no need for secrecy or comfort. It is for this reason that I find Hyppolite admirable, for there is nothing in his art that has been slyly transposed, he is using what lives within himself, and that is his country's spiritual history, its singings and worships.

Displayed prominently in the room where he paints is an enormous trumpet-shaped shell; pink and elaborately curled, it is like some ocean flower, an underwater rose, and if you blow through it, there comes forth a howl hoarse and lonesome, a windlike sound: it is for sailors a magic horn that calls the wind, and Hyppolite, who plans an around-the-world voyage aboard his own red-sailed ship, practices upon it regularly. Most of his energy and all his money go into the building of this ship; there is about his dedication the quality frequently seen in those who supervise the plotting of their own funerals, the building of their own tombs. Once he sets sail and is out of land's sight I wonder if again anyone will ever see him.

From the terrace where in the mornings I sit reading or writing, I can see the mountains sliding blue and bluer down to the harbor bay. Below there is the whole of Port-au-Prince, a town whose colors are paled into peeling historical pastels by centuries of sun: sky-gray cathedral, hyacinth fountain, green-rust fence. To the left, and like a city within this other, there is a great chalk garden of baroque stone; here is the cemetery, this is where, amid flat metal light and monuments like bird cages, they will bring his daughter: they will bring her up the hill, a dozen of them dressed in straw hats and black, sweet peas heavy on the air.

1. Tell me, why are there so many dogs? to whom do they belong, and for what purpose? Mangy, hurt-eyed, they pad along the streets in little herds like persecuted Christians, all innocuous enough by day, but come night how their vanity and their voices exaggerate! First one, another, then all, through the hours you can hear their enraged, embittered, moon-imploring tirades. S. says it is like a reversed alarm clock, for as soon as the dogs commence, and that indeed is early, it is time to go to bed. You might as well; the town has drawn shutters by ten, except, that is, on rahrah weekends, when drums and drunks drown out the dogs. But I like hearing a morning multitude of cock-crows; they set blowing a windfall of reverberations. On the other hand, what is more irritating than the racket of car horns? Haitians who own cars seem so to adore honking their horns; one begins to suspect this activity of political and/or sexual significance.

2. If it were possible I should like to make a film here; except for incidental music it would be soundless, nothing but a camera brilliantly framing architecture, objects. There is a flying kite, on the kite there is a crayon eye, now the eye

is loose and blowing in the wind, it snags on a fence and we, the eye, the camera, see a house (like M. Rigaud's). This is a tall, brittle, somewhat absurd structure representing no particular period, but seeming rather to be of an infinitely bastard lineage: the French influence, and England in somber Victorian garb; there is an oriental quality, too, touches that suggest a lantern of frilled paper. It is a carved house, its turrets, towers, porticoes are laced with angel heads, snow-flake shapes, valentine hearts: as the camera traces each of these we hear a tantalizing sub-musical tap-rap of bamboo rods. A window, very sudden; a sugar-white meringue of curtains, and a lumplike eye, and then a face, a woman like an old pressed flower, jet at her throat and jet combs in her hair; we pass through her, and into the room, two green chameleons race over the chifforobe mirror where her image shines. Like dissonant piano notes, the camera shifts with swift sharp jabs, and we are aware of the happenings our eyes never notice: a rose leaf falling, a picture tilting crooked. Now we have begun.

3. Comparatively few tourists come to Haiti, and a fair number of those who do, especially the average American couple, sit around in their hotels in a superior sulk. It is unfortunate, for of all the West Indies, Haiti is quite the most interesting; still, when one considers the objectives of these vacationers their attitude is not without reason: the nearest beach is a three-hour drive, night life is unimpressive, there is no restaurant whose menu is very distinguished. Aside from the hotels, there are only a few public places where late of an evening one can go for a rum soda; among the pleasanter of these are the whorehouses set back among the foliage along the Bizonton Road. All the houses have names, rather egotistical ones: the Paradise, for example.

And they are uncompromisingly respectable, perfect parlor decorum is observed: the girls, most of whom are from the Dominican Republic, sit on the front porch rocking in rocking chairs, fanning themselves with cardboard pictures of Jesus and conversing in a gentle, gossipy, laughing way; it is like any American summer scene. Beer, not whiskey or even champagne, is considered *de rigueur*, and if one wants to make an impression, it is the drink to order. One girl I know can down thirty bottles; she is older than the others, wears lavender lipstick, is rumba-hipped and viper-tongued, all of which makes her a popular lady indeed, though she herself says she will never feel like a success until she can afford to have every tooth in her head converted into solid gold.

4. The Estimé government has passed a law which forbids promenading in the streets sans shoes: this is a hard, uneconomical ruling, and an uncomfortable one as well, especially for those peasants who must bring their produce to market afoot. But the government, now anxious to make the country more of a tourist attraction, feels that shoeless Haitians might depress this potential trade, that the poorness of the people should not be overt. By and large, however, Haitians *are* poor, but about this poverty there is none of that vicious, mean atmosphere which surrounds the poverty that demands a keeping-up of appearances. It always makes me rather wretched when some popular platitude proves true; still, it is a fact, I suppose, that the most generous of us are those that have the least to be generous with. Almost any Haitian who comes to call will conclude his visit by presenting you with a small, usually odd gift: a can of sardines, a spool of thread; but these gifts are given with such dignity and tenderness that, ah! the sardines have swallowed pearls, the thread is purest silver.

5. This is R.'s story. A few days ago he went out into the country to sketch; suddenly, coming to the bottom of a hill, he saw a tall, slant-eyed, ragged girl. She was tied to the trunk of a tree, wire and rope binding her there. At first, because she laughed at him, he thought it was a joke, but when he tried to let her loose several children appeared and began to poke at him with sticks; he asked them why the girl was tied to the tree, but they giggled and shouted and would not give an answer. Presently an old man joined them; he was carrying a gourd filled with water. When R. asked again about the girl, the old man, tears misting his eyes, said, "She is bad, monsieur, there is no use she is so bad," and shook his head. R. started back up the hill; then, turning, he saw the man was letting her drink from the gourd, and as she took a last swallow she spat into his face; with a gentle patience the old man wiped himself and walked away.

6. I like Estelle, and I must say I have come to care less for S. because he doesn't: there is no brand of intolerance so tiresome as that which results in condemning characteristics you yourself possess: in the opinion of S., Estelle is lusty, vulgar, a fraud; S., to be sure, and except for the first mentioned, is not without these qualities himself. In any event, it shows a finer nature to be unconsciously vulgar than to be consciously virtuous. But of course S. is very much "in" with the American colony here, and their views, with a few isolated exceptions, are often gray and always severe. Estelle isn't cherished by any group. "Who gives a damn?" says she. "Listen, egghead, there's nothing wrong with me but the fact that I'm so almighty good-looking, and when a girl's as good-looking as me and she won't let a lot of crumbs crawl all over, well, thumbs down, get it?"

Estelle is one of the tallest girls I've ever seen, an easy six feet; her face is strong and bony, in the Swedish manner, her hair rosy, her eyes cat-green: somehow there is always an aura about her which suggests that she has just been tossed about in a hurricane. She is several Estelles, actually. One of them is the heroine of a not-too-good novel: here today— gone tomorrow, hello, you heartache of a world, that school of antics. Another Estelle is a big puppy of a girl dizzy for love: she is always quite sure the most improbable people have the most honorable intentions. A third Estelle is not so much shady as she is shadowy: who is Estelle? what is she doing here? how long does she intend to stay? what is it that makes her get up in the morning? Now and then this third element of the multiple Miss E. will refer to her "work." But the nature of her work is never labeled. Most of the time she sits in a café on the Champ de Mars and, at a cost of ten cents a round, drinks rum punches. The bartender is always asleep, and whenever she wants anything she swaggers over and thumps his head as though it were a ripe watermelon. There is a crazy little lop-eared dog that follows her everywhere, and usually she has some human crony with her, too. Her favorite is a pale, prim man who might be a Bible salesman; as it happens, he is a traveling entertainer who hops from island to island with a suitcase full of puppets and a head full of nonsense. On clear evenings Estelle sets up head-quarters at a table on the sidewalk outside the café; many of the young native girls bring their love problems here to this table: about other people's love she is serious and sad. Once she herself was married, when or to whom I do not know, she is so altogether vague, but, and even though she is only twenty-five, it must have been a very long time ago. Last night I passed by the café, and as usual she was sitting at her sidewalk table. But there was a difference. She was wearing make-up, which she seldom does, and a neat, conventional dress; there were two pink carnations burning in her hair, the sort of decoration of which I'd thought her incapable. Also, I'd never seen her really drunk before. "Egghead, hello, is it you? Yesyesyes," she said, tapping me on the chest, "listen, kid, I'm going to give you proof positive, I'm going to show you it's a fact, it's a fact that when you love somebody that somebody can make you eat *any* goddam thing. Look now"—and she yanked a carnation from her hair— "he's nuts about me," she said, thrusting the flower at the little dog crouched at her feet, "he'll eat it just because I say to, damn if he won't."

But the dog merely sniffed.

The last few weekends here have been devoted to the rahrahs preceding carnival, and carnival, which began yesterday, continues for three days. Rahrahs are miniature previews of carnival itself; Saturday, sometime past noon, the drums commence, separately at first, one high in the hills, another nearer town, back and forth these signals run, insinuating, insistent, until there is established a pervasive vibration which shimmers the surface of silence, ripples like heat waves, and here where I am, alone in this arsenic-colored room, all action seems to stem from their sound: doom die doom, over there, look: light quivers in the water jar, a crystal bubble, set in motion, rolls across a table, shatters on the floor, wind, catching curtains, curling Bible leaves, tells doom die doom. By dusk the island takes the expanding shape of a sound of drums. Small bands carouse the streets; these are made of family groups, or secret societies, all singing different songs which sound the same; the leader of each band wears feathers in his hair, a spangled crazy-quilt suit, and each has a pair of cheap dark glasses; while the others sing and stamp their feet he spins around, grinds his hips, cocks his head from side to side like an evil parrot: everybody laughs, and some couples join together, dancing with their heads thrown back, their lips ajar, doom die doom, the rhythm rotates their haunches, their eyes are rich moons, doom die doom.

Last night R. took me into the midst of the carnival. We were going to see the ceremony of a young *houngan*, that is to say, Voodou priest, this one an extraordinary boy whose name I never heard. It was held at a distance from the city, and so we had to take an autobus, a small wagon which can inconveniently carry ten passengers; but there were almost double that number, some of them in costume, including a dwarf wearing a cap of bells and an old man with a mask like raven wings; R. sat next to the old man, who at one point said, "Do you understand the sky? Yes, I thought you would, but it was I who made it."

To which R. answered, "I suppose you made the moon, too?"

The man nodded. "And the stars, they are my grandchildren."

A rowdy woman clapped her hands and announced that the old man was crazy. "But, dear lady," he replied, "if I am crazy, then how could I have done these beautiful things?"

It was a slow trip; the autobus stalled, crowds surged around, faces concealed behind masks dangled in the dark, archaic light of candle torches showering them like some eccentric yellow rain.

When we reached the *houngan's*, which is above the town, a quiet place shrill only with the night noises of insects, the ceremony had already begun, although the *houngan* himself had not yet appeared. Surrounding the temple, a long thatch-roofed shed with altar rooms at either end (the doors to these rooms were closed, for beyond one the *houngan* awaited his entrance), were perhaps a hundred silent, solemn Haitians. In the open clearing between the rooms seven or eight barefoot girls, all dressed in white with white bandannas wrapped around their heads, moved in a snaking circle, smacking their sides and singing a chant that two drummers echoed. A kerosene lamp cast smoky, horizontal shadows of the dancers, and the drummers, both intent, both froglike, wavered on the walls. Suddenly the drums stopped, the girls made an aisle leading to an altar door. It was so quiet one could almost identify the various species of serenading insect. R. asked for a cigarette, but I would not give it to him: who smokes in church? and Voodou after all is a real, very complex religion, one which is nevertheless frowned on by the Haitian bourgeoisie, who, when they are anything, are Catholics, and that is why, as a compromise you might think, so much Catholicism has seeped into Voodou: a picture of the Virgin Mary, for example, and an image of the Infant Jesus, who is represented sometimes by a homemade doll, will be found adorning the altar of almost any *houngan*. And the primary functions of Voodou do not seem to me basically different from those of other religions: appeals to certain gods, symbols, appease the pressures of evil, man is weak but God protects him, there is magic abroad, the gods own it, they can provide a man's wife with child or allow the sun to burn his crops, steal the breath from his body but reward him with a soul. In Voodou, however, there is no boundary between the countries of the living and the dead; the dead rise and walk among the living.

Now again the drums began, the voices of the girls spac-

ing every slow, dramatic beat, and then the door to the altar
opened: three boys came out, each carrying a plate filled
with a different substance—ashes, cornmeal, black powder—
and candles, like those for a birthday cake, burned in the
center of these materials; balancing the plates on a rounded
stone, the boys knelt facing the door. The drums grew softer,
there began a nervous rhythmical rattling, this made by a
gourd encasing snake vertebrae, and swiftly, like a spirit that
has unexpectedly solidified, the *houngan* glided airy as a bird
through the column of girls and around the room, his feet,
the ankles tinkling with silver bracelets, seeming not at all to
touch the floor, and his loose silk scarlet robes rustling wing-
like. There was a caul of red velvet draped around his head,
a pearl gleamed in his ear. Here and there he paused, like a
hummingbird, and clasped the hands of a worshiper: he took
mine, and I looked into his face, an amazing, androgynous
face, beautiful, really, a troubling combination of blue-black
skin and Caucasian features; he could not have been more
than twenty, still, there was something about him unaccount-
ably old, asleep, transfixed.

At last, taking a handful of cornmeal and ashes, he started
drawing on the ground a *verver*; there are in Voodou hundreds of *ververs*, which are intricate, somewhat surrealist
designs whose every detail has implications, and to execute
them demands not only the sort of academic memory
required of a pianist who would, say, play an entire program of Bach, but also unusually deft technique, artistry.
While the drums grew explosively fast he stooped about,
deep in his art, like a red spider that, instead of silk, spills
forth an ashy, ferocious web of crowns, crisscrosses, snakes,
phallic shapes, eyes, fishtails. Then, the *verver* completed,
he went back to the altar room, and reappeared wearing

green, in his hands a great iron ball; as he stood there the ball caught fire, holy blue wrapping it like the atmospheres of earth; still carrying it, he fell to his knees, crawled, chants and shouts applauding him, and when the flames cooled he arose, stretching his unburned palms upward. A tremor swept his body, as if an unknown wind passed through him, his eyes rolled into his skull, the spirit (god and demon) opened like a seed and flowered in his flesh: unsexed, unidentifiable, he gathered in his arms man and woman. Whoever his partner, they whirled over the snakes and eyes of the *verver*, mysteriously never quite disturbing them, and when he changed to another, the castoff partner flung himself, as it were, into infinity, tore his breast, screamed. And the young *houngan*, shining with sweat, his pearl earring loosened, ran smash into the farthest, unopened door: singing, crying, he beat his hands upon it until they left blood prints. It was as if he were a moth, the door the bright enormity of an electric bulb, for beyond this obstacle, immediately beyond it, there was magic: truth's secret, pure peace. And if the door had opened, as it never will, would he have found it, this unobtainable? That he believed so is all that matters.

*

To Europe

(*1948*)

✤

STANDING VERY STILL you could hear a harp. We climbed the wall, and there, among the burning rain-drenched flowers of the castle's garden, sat four mysterious figures, a young man who thumbed a hand harp and three rusted old men who were dressed in patched-together black: how stark they were against the storm-green air. And they were eating figs, those Italian figs so fat the juice ran out of their mouths. At the garden's edge lay the marble shore of Lago di Garda, its waters swarming in the wind, and I knew then I would be always afraid to swim there, for, like distortions beyond the beauty of ivy-glass, Gothic creatures must move in the depths of water so ominously clear. One of the old men tossed too far a fig peel, and a trio of swans, thus disturbed, rustled the reeds of the waterway.

D. jumped off the wall and gestured for me to join him; but I couldn't, not quite then: because suddenly it was true and I wanted the trueness of it to last a moment longer—I could never feel it so absolutely again, even the movement of a leaf and it would be lost, precisely as a cough would for-ever ruin Tourel's high note. And what was this truth? Only the truth of justification: a castle, swans and a boy with a harp, for all the world out of a childhood storybook—before the prince has entered or the witch has cast her spell.

It was right that I had gone to Europe, if only because I could look again with wonder. Past certain ages or certain wisdoms it is very difficult to look with wonder; it is best done when one is a child; after that, and if you are lucky, you will find a bridge of childhood and walk across it. Going to Europe was like that. It was a bridge of childhood, one that led over the seas and through the forests straight into my imagination's earliest landscapes. One way or another I had gone to a good many places, from Mexico to Maine—and then to think I had to go all the way to Europe to go back to my hometown, my fire and room where stories and legends seemed always to live beyond the limits of our town. And that is where the legends were: in the harp, the castle, the rustling of the swans.

A rather mad bus ride that day had brought us from Venice to Sirmione, an enchanted, infinitesimal village on the tip of a peninsula jutting into Lago di Garda, bluest, saddest, most silent, most beautiful of Italian lakes. Had it not been for the gruesome circumstance of Lucia, I doubt that we should have left Venice. I was perfectly happy there, except of course that it is incredibly noisy: not ordinary city noise, but ceaseless argument of human voices, scudding oars, running feet. It was once suggested that Oscar Wilde retire there from the world. "And become a monument for tourists?" he asked.

It was an excellent advice, however, and others than Oscar have taken it: in the palazzos along the Grand Canal there are colonies of persons who haven't shown themselves publicly in a number of decades. Most intriguing of these was a Swedish countess whose servants fetched fruit for her in a black gondola trimmed with silver bells; their tinkling made a music atmospheric but eerie. Still, Lucia so persecuted us we were forced to flee. A muscular girl, exceptionally tall for an Italian and smelling always of wretched condiment oils, she was the leader of a band of juvenile gangsters, displaced roaming youths who had flocked north for the Venetian season. They could be delightful, some of them, even though they sold cigarettes that contained more hay than tobacco, even though they would short-circuit you on a currency exchange. The business with Lucia began one day in the Piazza San Marco.

She came up and asked us for a cigarette; whereupon D., whose heart doesn't know that we are off the gold standard, gave her a whole package of Chesterfields. Never were two people more completely adopted. Which at first was quite pleasant; Lucia shadowed us wherever we went, abundantly giving us the benefits of her wisdom and protection. But there were frequent embarrassments; for one thing, we were always being turned out of the more elegant shops because of her overwrought haggling with the proprietors; then, too, she was so excessively jealous that it was impossible for us to have any contact with anyone else whatever: we chanced once to meet in the piazza a harmless and respectable young woman who had been with us in the carriage from Milan. "Attention!" said Lucia in that hoarse voice of hers, "Attention!" and proceeded almost to persuade us that this was a lady of infamous past and shameless future. On another occasion D. gave one of her cohorts a dollar watch which he had much admired. Lucia was furious; the next time we saw her she had the watch suspended on a cord around her neck, and it was said the young man had left overnight for Trieste.

Lucia had a habit of appearing in our hotel at any hour that pleased her (she lived no place that we could divine); scarcely sixteen, she would sit herself down, drain a whole bottle of Strega, smoke all the cigarettes she could lay hold of, then fall into an exhausted sleep; only when she slept did her face resemble a child's. But then one dreadful day the hotel manager stopped her in the lobby and told her that she could no longer visit our rooms. It was, he said, an insupportable scandal. So Lucia, rounding up a dozen of her more brutish companions, laid such siege to the hotel that it was necessary to bring down iron shutters over the doors and call the carabinieri. After that we did our best to avoid her.

But to avoid anyone in Venice is much the same as playing hide-and-seek in a one-room apartment, for there was never a city more compactly composed. It is like a museum with carnivalesque overtones, a vast palace that seems to have no doors, all things connected, one leading into another. Over and over in a day the same faces repeat like prepositions in a long sentence: turn a corner, and there was Lucia, the dollar watch dangling between her breasts. She was so in love with D. But presently she turned on us with that intensity of the wounded; perhaps we deserved it, but it was unendura-

ble: like clouds of gnats her gang would trail us across the
piazza spitting invective; if we sat down for a drink they
would gather in the dark beyond the table and shout outrageous jokes. Half the time we didn't know what they were
saying, though it was apparent that everyone else did. Lucia
herself did not overtly contribute to this persecution; she
remained aloof, directing her operations at a distance. So at
last we decided to leave Venice. Lucia knew this. Her spies
were everywhere. The morning we left it was raining; just
as our gondola slipped into the water, a little crazy-eyed boy
appeared and threw at us a bundle wrapped in newspaper.
D. pulled the paper apart. Inside there was a dead yellow
cat, and around its throat there was tied the dollar watch. It
gave you a feeling of endless falling. And then suddenly we
saw her, Lucia; she was standing alone on one of the little
canal bridges, and she was so far hunched over the railing it
looked as if she were going to fall. *"Perdonami,"* she cried,
"ma t'amo" (forgive me, but I love you).

In London a young artist said to me, "How wonderful it
must be for an American traveling in Europe the first time;
you can never be a part of it, so none of the pain is yours, you
will never have to endure it—yes, for you there is only the
beauty."

Not understanding what he meant, I resented this; but
later, after some months in France and Italy, I saw that he
was right: I was not a part of Europe, I never would be. Safe,
I could leave when I wanted to, and for me there was only
the honeyed, hallowed air of beauty. But it was not so wonderful as the young man had imagined; it was desperate to
feel that one could never be a part of moments so moving,
that always one would be isolated from this landscape and

these people; and then gradually I realized I did not have to be a part of it: rather, it could be a part of me. The sudden garden, opera night, wild children snatching flowers and running up a darkening street, a wreath for the dead and nuns in noon light, music from the piazza, a Paris pianola and fireworks on La Grande Nuit, the heart-shaking surprise of mountain visions and water views (lakes like green wine in the chalice of volcanoes, the Mediterranean flickering at the bottoms of cliffs), forsaken far-off towers falling in twilight and candles igniting the jeweled corpse of St. Zeno of Verona —all a part of me, elements for the making of my own perspective.

When we left Sirmione, D. returned to Rome and I went back to Paris. Mine was a curious journey. First off, I'd engaged through a dizzy Italian ticket agent a *wagonlit* aboard the Orient Express, but when I reached Milan, I discovered the arrangement had been entirely spurious and that there were no such accommodations for me; in fact, if I hadn't stepped on a few toes, I doubt that I should have got on the train at all, for everything was holiday-jammed. As it was, I managed to squeeze myself into an airless, August-hot compartment along with six other people. The name of the Orient Express evoked for me the most spine-tingling expectations: think of the extraordinary things that have occurred on that train, at least if one is to believe Miss Agatha Christie or Mr. Graham Greene. But I was not at all prepared for what happened actually.

In the compartment there were a pair of dreary Swiss businessmen, a somewhat more exotic businessman traveling from Istanbul, an American teacher and two elegant snow-headed Italian ladies with haughty eyes and features as delicate as fishbones. They were dressed like twins, these ladies; flowing black and wisps of lace caught at the throat with pearl-studded amethysts. They sat with their gloved hands clasped together and never spoke except when exchanging a box of expensive chocolates. Their only luggage appeared to be a huge bird cage; inside this cage, though it was partially covered by a silk shawl, you could see scuttling around a moldy green parrot. Now and then the parrot would let forth a burst of demented laughter; whenever this happened the two ladies would smile at each other. The American teacher asked them if the parrot could speak, and one of the ladies, with the slightest nod, replied yes, but that the parrot's grammar was very poor. As we neared the Italian-Swiss frontier, customs and passport officials began their tiresome little duties. We thought they were finished with our compartment, but presently they returned, several of them, and stood outside the glass door looking in at the aristocratic ladies. It seemed they were having quite a discussion about them. Everyone in the compartment grew quite still, except the parrot, who laughed in an unearthly way. The old ladies paid no attention whatever. Other men in uniform joined those already in the corridor. Then one of the ladies, plucking at her amethyst brooch, turned to the rest of us and, first in Italian, then German, then English, said, "We have done nothing wrong."

But at that moment the door slid open and two of the officials entered. They did not look at the old ladies but went straight to the bird cage and stripped away its covering shawl. "*Basta, basta,*" screamed the parrot.

With a lurch the train came to a halt in the mountain darkness. The abruptness of this toppled the cage, and the parrot, suddenly free, flew laughingly from wall to wall of the compartment while the ladies, flurried and flying themselves, grasped for it. The customs men went on taking the cage apart; in the feed tray were a hundred or so papers of heroin wrapped like headache powders, and in the brass ball atop the cage there were still more. The discovery did not seem to irritate the ladies at all; it was the loss of their parrot that upset them. For all at once it had flown out the lowered window, and the desperate ladies stood calling after it, "Tokyo, you will freeze, little Tokyo, come back! Come back!"

He was laughing somewhere in the dark. There was a cold Northern moon, and for an instant we saw him flying flat and dark against its brilliance. They turned then and faced the door; it was crowded now with onlookers. Poised, disdainful, the ladies stepped forward to meet faces they seemed not to see, and voices they certainly never heard.

Ischia

(1949)

I FORGET WHY WE CAME HERE: Ischia. It was being very much talked about, though few people seemed actually to have seen it—except, perhaps, as a jagged blue shadow glimpsed across the water from the heights of its celebrated neighbor, Capri. Some people advised against Ischia and, as I remember, they gave rather spooky reasons: You realize that there is an active volcano? And do you know about the plane? A plane, flying a regular flight between Cairo and Rome, crashed on top an Ischian mountain; there were three survivors, but no one ever saw them alive, for they were stoned to death by goatherds intent on looting the wreckage.

Consequently, we watched the chalky façade of Naples fade with mixed anticipation. It was a classic day, a little cold for southern Italy in March, but crisp and lofty as a kite, and the *Princepessa* spanked across the bay like a sassy dolphin. It is a small civilized boat with a tiny bar and a somewhat outré clientele: convicts on their way to the prison island of Procida or, at the opposite extreme, young men about to enter the monastery on Ischia. Of course, there are less dramatic passengers: islanders who have been shopping in Naples; here and there a foreigner—extraordinarily few, however: Capri is the tourist catch-all.

Islands are like ships at permanent anchor. To set foot on one is like starting up a gangplank: one is seized by the same feeling of charmed suspension—it seems nothing unkind or vulgar can happen to you; and as the *Princepessa* eased into the covelike harbor of Porto d'Ischia it seemed, seeing the pale, peeling ice-cream colors of the waterfront, as intimate and satisfying as one's own heartbeat. In the wrangle of disembarking, I dropped and broke my watch—an outrageous bit of symbolism, too pointed: at a glance it was plain that Ischia was no place for the rush of hours, islands never are.

I suppose you might say that Porto is the capital of Ischia; at any rate, it is the largest town and even rather fashionable. Most people who visit the island seldom stray from there, for there are several superior hotels, excellent beaches and, perched in the offing like a giant hawk, the Renaissance castle of Vittoria Colonna. The three other fair-sized towns are more rugged. These are: Lacco Ameno, Cassamiciola and, at the farthest end of the island, Forio. It was in Forio that we planned to settle.

We drove there through a green twilight and under a sky

of early stars. The road passed high above the sea, where fishing boats, lighted with torches, crawled below like brilliant water-spiders. Furry little bats skimmed in the dusk; *buena séra, buena séra*, dim evening voices called along the way, and herds of goats, jogging up the hills, bleated like rusty flutes; the carriage spun through a village square—there was no electricity, and in the cafés the tricky light of candles and kerosene lamps smoked the faces of masculine company. Two children chased after us into the darkness beyond the village. They clung panting to the carriage as we began a steep careening climb, and our horse, nearing the crest, breathed back on the chilled air a stream of mist. The driver flecked his whip, the horse swayed, the children pointed: look. It was there, Forio, distant, moon-white, the sea simmering at its edges, a faint sound of vesper bells rising off it like a whirl of birds. *Multo bella?* said the driver. *Multo bella?* said the children.

When one rereads a journal it is usually the less ambitious jottings, the haphazard, accidental notations that, seen again, plow a furrow through your memory. For example: "Today Gioconda left in the room assorted slips of colored paper. Are they presents? Because I gave her the bottle of cologne? They will make delightful bookmarks." This reverberates. First, Gioconda. She is a beautiful girl, though her beauty depends upon her mood: when she is feeling glum, and this seems too often the case, she looks like a bowl of cold oatmeal; you are likely to forget the richness of her hair and the mildness of her Mediterranean eyes. Heaven knows, she is overworked: here at the *pensione*, where she is both chambermaid and waitress, she gets up before dawn and is kept on the run sometimes until midnight. To be truthful, she is lucky to have the job, for employment is the island's major problem; most girls here would like nothing better than to supplant her. Considering that there is no running water (with all that that implies), Gioconda makes us remarkably comfortable. It is the pleasantest *pensione* in Forio, an interesting bargain, too: we have two huge rooms with great expanses of tiled floor and tall shutter-doors which lead onto little iron balconies overlooking the sea; the food is good, and there is rather too much of it—five courses with wine at lunch and dinner. All included, this costs each of us about one hundred dollars a month. Gioconda speaks no English, and my Italian is—well, never mind. Nevertheless, we are confidantes. With pantomime and extravagant use of a bilingual dictionary we manage to convey an astonishing lot —which is why the cakes are always a flop: on gloomy days when there is nothing else to do we sit in the patio-kitchen experimenting with recipes for American pastries ("Toll House, what is?"), but these are never a success because we are too busy thumbing through the dictionary to give our baking much attention. Gioconda: "Last year, in the room where you are, there was a man from Rome. Is Rome like he said, so wonderful? He said I should come and visit him in Rome, and that it would be all right because he was a veteran of three wars. First World War, Second, and Ethiopia. You can see how old he was. No, I have never seen Rome. I have friends who have been there, and who have sent me postcards. You know the woman who works at the *posta*? Of course you believe in the evil eye? She has one. It is known, yes. That is why my letter never comes from Argentina."

Not receiving this Argentine letter is the real cause of Gioconda's misery. A faithless lover? I have no idea; she refuses to discuss it. So many young Italians have migrated to South America looking for work; there are wives here who have waited five years for their husbands to send them passage. Each day, when I come bringing the mail, Gioconda rushes to meet me.

Collecting the mail is a self-appointed chore. It is the first time during the day that I see the other Americans living here: there are four at the moment and we meet at Maria's café in the piazza (from the journal: "We all know that Maria waters her drinks. But does she water them with water? God, I feel awful!"). With the sun warming you, and Maria's bamboo curtains tinkling in the breeze, there is no nicer place to wait for the postman. Maria is a sawed-off woman with a gypsy face and a shrugging, cynical nature; if there is anything you want around here, from a house to a package of American cigarettes, she can arrange it; some people claim she is the richest person in Forio. There are never any women in her café; I doubt that she would allow it. As noon heightens, the village converges in the piazza: like blackbirds schoolchildren in capes and wooden sandals flock and sing in the alleys, and squadrons of unemployed men lounge under the trees laughing roughly—women passing them lower their eyes. When the mailman comes he gives me the letters for our *pensione*; then I must go down the hill to face Gioconda. Sometimes she looks at me as though it were my fault that the letter never comes, as though the evil eye were mine. One day she warned me not to come home empty-handed; and so I brought her a bottle of cologne.

But the slips of gaudy paper that I found in my room were not, as I had supposed, a present in return. It was intended that we should shower these upon a statue of the Virgin which, newly arrived on the island, was being toured through

most of the villages. The day the Virgin was to visit here
every balcony was draped with fine laces, finer linens—an
old bedspread if the family had nothing better; woven
flowers garlanded the cramped streets, old ladies brought out
their longest shawls, men combed their mustaches, someone
put the town idiot into a clean shirt, and the children, dressed
all in white, had angel-wings of golden cardboard strapped to
their shoulders. The procession was supposed to enter town
and pass below our balcony at about four o'cock. Alerted by
Gioconda, we were at our station on time, ready to throw the
pretty papers and shout, as instructed, *"Viva La Vergenie
Immocalata."* A drizzling dull rain began; at six it was getting dark, but like the street-tightening crowd that waited
below, we remained steadfast. A priest, scowling with annoyance, and his black skirts flapping, roared off on a motor-
cycle—he'd been sent to hurry along the procession. It was
night, then, and a flare-path of kerosene was spilled along the
route the procession was to follow. Suddenly, incongruously,
the stirring *ratata* of a military band sounded and, with a
scary crackle, the flare-path leapt alive as if to salute the
arriving Virgin: swaying on a flower-filled litter, Her face
shrouded in a black veil, and followed by half the island, she
was laden with gold and silver watches, and as she passed, a
hush surrounding her immediate presence, there was only
the enchanting, surrealistic noise of these offerings, the
watches: *tickticktick.* Later, Gioconda was very put out to
discover us still clutching the bits of bright paper which in
our excitement we'd forgotten to throw.

"April 5. A long, perilous walk. We discovered a new
beach." Ischia is stony, a stark island that suggests Greece or
the coast of Africa. There are orange trees, lemon trees and,
terracing the mountains, silvery-green grape arbors: the wine

of Ischia is highly considered, and it is here that they make Lachrimae Christi. When you walk beyond the town you soon come upon the branching paths that climb through the grape fields where bees are like a blizzard and lizards burn greenly on the budding leaves. The peasants are brown and thick as earthenware, and they are horizon-eyed, like sailors. For the sea is always with them. The path by the sea runs along straight-dropping volcanic cliffs; there are junctures when it is best just to close your eyes: it would make a long fall, and the rocks below are like sleeping dinosaurs. One day, walking on the cliffs, we found a poppy, then another; they were growing singly among the somber stones, like Chinese bells strung on a stretching string. Presently the trail of poppies led us down a path to a strange and hidden beach. It was enclosed by the cliffs, and the water was so clear you could observe sea-flowers and the dagger movements of fish; not far from shore, flat, exposed rocks were like swimming rafts, and we paddled from one to another: hauling ourselves into the sun, we could look back above the cliffs and see the green grape terraces and a cloudy mountain. Into one rock the sea had carved a chair, and it was the greatest pleasure to sit there and let the waves rush up and over you.

But it is not hard to find a private beach on Ischia. I know of at least three that no one ever goes to. The town beach in Forio is strewn with fishing nets and overturned boats. It was on this beach that I first encountered the Mussolini family. The late dictator's widow and three of their children live here in what I presume to be a quiet self-imposed exile. Something about them is sad and sympathetic. The daughter is young, blond, lame and apparently witty: the local boys who talk with her on the beach seem always to be laughing. Like any of the island's plain women, Signora Mussolini is

often to be seen dressed in shabby black and trudging up a
hill with the weight of a shopping bag lopsiding her figure.
She is quite expressionless, but once I saw her smile. There
was a man passing through town with a parrot who plucked
printed fortunes out of a glass jar, and Signora Mussolini,
pausing to consult him, read her future with a shadowy, Da
Vincian curling of her lips.

"June 5. The afternoon is a white midnight." Now that
hot weather is here the afternoons are like white midnights;
shutters are drawn, sleep stalks the streets. At five the shops
will open again, a crowd will gather in the harbor to welcome the *Princepessa*, and later everyone will promenade in
the piazza, where someone will be playing a banjo, a harmonica, a guitar. But now it is siesta, and there is only the blue
unbroken sky, the crowing of a cock. There are two idiots
in the town, and they are friends. One is always carrying a
bouquet of flowers which, when he meets his friend, he
divides into equal parts. In the silent shadowless afternoons
they alone are seen in the streets. Hand in hand, and holding
their flowers, they stroll across the beach and out along the
stone wall that juts far into the water. From my balcony I
can see them there, sitting among the fishnets and the slowly
rocking boats, their shaved heads glinting in the sun, their
eyes pale as space. The white midnight is meant for them; it
is then that the island is theirs.

We have followed spring. In the four months since we
came here the nights have warmed, the sea has grown softer,
the green, still wintry water of March has turned in June to
blue, and the grape vines, once gray and barren on their
twisting stalks, are fat with their first green bunches. There
is a hatching of butterflies, and on the mountain there are
many sweet things for the bees; in the garden, after a rainfall,

you can faintly, yes, hear the breaking of new blooms. And we are waking earlier, a sign of summer, and stay lingering out late in the evening, which is a sign, too. But it is hard to bring yourself indoors these nights: the moon is drawing nearer, it winks on the water with a frightful brightness; and on the parapet of the fishermen's church, which points to sea like the prow of a ship, the young whispering people wander back and forth and through the piazza and into some secret dark. Gioconda says it has been the longest spring she can remember: the longest is the loveliest.

Tangier

(*1950*)

❈

TANGIER? It is two days by boat from Marseille, a charming trip that takes you along the coast of Spain, and if you are someone escaping from the police, or merely someone escaping, then by all means come here: hemmed with hills, confronted by the sea, and looking like a white cape draped on the shores of Africa, it is an international city with an excellent climate eight months of the year, roughly March to November. There are magnificent beaches, really extraordinary stretches of sugar-soft sand and surf; and if you have a mind for that sort of thing, the nightlife, though neither particularly innocent nor especially varied, is dark to dawn, which, when you consider that most people nap all afternoon, and that very few dine before ten or eleven, is not too unusual. Almost everything else in Tangier is unusual, however, and before coming here you should do three things: be inoculated for typhoid, withdraw your savings from the bank, say good-by to your friends—heaven knows you may never see them again. This advice is quite serious, for it is alarming, the number of travelers who have landed here on a brief holiday, then settled down and let the years go by. Because Tangier is a basin that holds you, a timeless place; the days slide by less noticed than foam in a waterfall; this, I imagine, is the way time passes in a monastery, unobtrusive and on slippered feet; for that matter, these two institutions, a monastery and Tangier, have another common denominator: self-containment. The average Arab, for example, thinks Europe and America are the same thing and in the same place, wherever that may be—in any event, he doesn't care; and frequently Europeans, hypnotized by the tinkling of an oud and the swarming drama around them, come to agree.

One spends a great lot of time sitting in the Petit Soko, a café-cluttered square at the foot of the Casbah. Offhand, it seems to be a miniature version of the Galleria in Naples, but on closer acquaintance it assumes a character so grotesquely individual you cannot fairly compare it with any other place in the world. At no hour of the day or night is the Petit Soko not crowded; Broadway, Piccadilly, all these places have their off moments, but the little Soko booms around the clock. Twenty steps away, and you are swallowed in the mists of the Casbah; the apparitions drifting out of these mists into the hurdy-gurdy clamor of the Soko make a lively show: it is a display ground for prostitutes, a depot for drug-peddlers, a spy center; it is also the place where some simpler folk drink their evening *apéritif.*

The Soko has its own celebrities, but it is a precarious honor, one is so likely at any second to be cut down and cast away, for the Soko audience, having seen just about everything, is excessively fickle. Currently, however, they are starring Estelle, a beautiful girl who walks like a rope unwinding. She is half-Chinese and half-Negro, and she works in a bordello called the Black Cat. Rumor has it that she once was a Paris model, and that she arrived here on a private yacht, planning, of course, to leave by the same means; but it appears that the gentleman to whom the yacht belonged sailed away one fine morning, leaving Estelle stranded. For a while there Maumi was giving her rather a race; the Soko appreciated Maumi's talents, both as a *flamenco* dancer and as a conversationalist: wherever he sat, there were always loud bursts of laughter. Alas, poor Maumi, an exotic young man given to cooling his face with a lacy fan, was stabbed in a bar the other night, and is now out of the running. Less heralded, but to me more intriguing, are Lady Warbanks and her two hangers-on, a curious trio that arrive each morning and have their breakfast at one of the sidewalk tables: this breakfast is unvarying—a bowl of fried octopus and a bottle of Pernod. Someone who ought really to know says that at one time the now very *déclassé* Lady Warbanks was considered the greatest beauty in London; probably it is true, her features are finely made and she has, despite the tight sailor suits she lumps herself into, a peculiar innate style. But her morals are not all they might be, and the same may be said of her companions. About these two: one is a sassy-faced, busy youth whose tongue is like a ladle stirring in a cauldron of scandal—he knows everything; and the other friend is a tough Spanish girl with brief, slippery hair and leather-colored eyes. She is called Sunny, and I am told that financed by Lady Warbanks, she is on her way to becoming the only female in Morocco with an organized gang of smugglers: smuggling is a high-powered profession here, employing hundreds, and Sunny, it appears, has a boat and crew that nightly runs the Straits to Spain. The precise relation of these three to each other is not altogether printable; suffice to say that between them they combine every known vice. But this does not interest the Soko, for the Soko is concerned by quite another angle: how soon will Lady Warbanks be murdered, and which of the two will do it, the young man or Sunny? She is very rich, the Englishwoman, and if it is greed, as so obviously it is, that holds her companions, then clearly violence is indicated. Everyone is waiting. Meanwhile, Lady Warbanks sits innocently nibbling octopus and sipping her morning Pernod.

The Soko is also something of a fashion center, a proving ground for the latest fads. One innovation that has got off to a popular start among the flashier types are shoes with ribbon laces that wind right up to the knee. They are unbecoming, but not nearly so regrettable as the passion for dark glasses that has developed among Arab women, whose eyes, peering just above their veiling, have been always so provocative. Now all one sees are these great black lenses imbedded like coal-hunks in a snowball of cloth.

Of an evening at seven the Soko reaches its height. It is the crowded *apéritif* hour, some twenty nationalities are rubbing elbows in the tiny square, and the hum of their voices is like the singing of giant mosquitoes. Once, when we were sitting there, a sudden silence fell: an Arab orchestra, trumpeting in

a gay style, moved along up the street past the bright cafés—
it was the only cheerful Moorish music I've ever heard, all
the rest sounds like a sad and fragmentary wailing. But death,
it would seem, is not an unhappy event among Arabs, for this
orchestra proved to be the vanguard of a funeral procession
that then came joyfully winding through the throng. Presently the corpse, a half-naked man carried on an open litter,
wobbled past, and a rhinestone lady, leaning from her table,
sentimentally saluted him with a glass of Tio Pepe: a moment
later she was laughing gold-toothed laughter, plotting, planning. And so was the little Soko.

"If you are going to write something about Tangier," said
a person to whom I applied for certain information, "please
leave out the riffraff; we have a lot of nice people here, and
it's hard on us that the town has such a bad reputation."

Well, and though I'm not at all sure our definitions coin-
cide, there are at least three people I think eminently nice.
Jonny Winner, for instance. A sweet, funny girl, Jonny
Winner. She is very young, very American, and you would
never believe, looking at her clouded, wistful face, that she is
able to take care of herself: to tell the truth, I don't think
she is. Nevertheless, she has lived here two years, been across
Morocco and to the Sahara alone. Why Jonny Winner wants
to spend the rest of her life in Tangier is of course her own
business; obviously she is in love: "But don't you love it, too?
to wake up and know that you're here, and know that you
can always be yourself, never be anyone that isn't you? And
always to have flowers, and to look out your window and see
the hills getting dark and the lights in the harbor? Don't you
love it, too?" On the other hand, she and the town are always
at war; whenever you meet her she is undergoing a new

crise: "Have you heard? the most awful mess: some fool in the Casbah painted his house yellow, and now everybody's doing it—I'm just on my way to see if I can't put a stop to the whole thing."

The Casbah, traditionally blue and white, like snow at twilight, would be hideous painted yellow, and I hope Jonny gets her way—though certainly she has had no success in her campaign to keep them from clearing the Grand Soko, a heartrending business that has reduced her to prowling the streets, in tears. The Grand Soko is the great Arab market square: Berbers, down from the mountains with their goat-skins and baskets, squat in circles under the trees listening to storytellers, flute players, magicians; cornucopia stalls spill over with flowers and fruit; hashish fume and the minty scent of *thé Arabe* cling to the air; vivid spices burn in the sun. All this is to be moved elsewhere, presumably to make way for a park, and Jonny is wringing her hands: "Why shouldn't I be upset? I feel as though Tangier were my house, and how would you like it if somebody came into your house and started moving the furniture around?"

So she has been out saving the Soko in four languages, French, Spanish, English and Arabic; though she speaks all of these exceedingly well, the closest she has come to official sympathy is the doorman at the Dutch Consulate, and her only real emotional support has been an Arab taxi driver, who thinks her not the least mad and drives her around free of charge. One late afternoon a few days ago we saw Jonny dragging along through her beloved, dissolving Grand Soko; she looked absolutely done in, and she was carrying a mangy, sore-covered kitten. Jonny has a way of launching right into what she wants to say, and she said, "I was feeling just as though I couldn't go on living, and then I found Monroe.

This is Monroe"—she patted the kitten— "and he's made me ashamed: he's so interested in living, and if he can be, why shouldn't I?"

Looking at them, Jonny and the kitten, both so bedraggled and bruised, you knew that somehow something would see them through: if not common sense, then their interest in life.

Ferida Green has plenty of common sense. When Jonny spoke to her about the situation in the Grand Soko, Miss Green said, "Oh, my dear, you mustn't worry. They are always tearing down the Soko, but it never really happens; I remember in 1906 they wanted to make it into a whaling center: imagine the odor!"

Miss Ferida is one of the three great Green ladies of Tangier, which includes her cousin, Miss Jessie, and her sister-in-law, Mrs. Ada Green; between them they manage more often than not to have the last say here. All three are past seventy: Mrs. Ada Green is famous for her chic, Miss Jessie for her wit, and Miss Ferida, the oldest, for her wisdom. She has not visited her native England in over fifty years; even so, observing the straw skimmer skewered to her hair and the black ribbon trailing from her pince-nez, one knows she goes out in the noonday sun and has never given up tea at five. Every Friday in her life there is a ritual known as Flour Morning. Seated at a table at the foot of her garden, and judging each case as it is presented, she rations flour to Arab applicants, usually old women who otherwise would starve: from the flour they make a paste which must last them until the next Friday. There is much joking and laughter, for the Arabs adore Miss Ferida, and for her, all these old women, such anonymous bundles of laundry to the rest of us, are friends whose personalities she comments on in a large ledger. "Fathma has a bad temper but is not bad," she writes of one, and of another: "Halima is a good girl. One can take her at face value."

And that, I suppose, is what you would have to say about Miss Ferida.

Anyone in Tangier longer than overnight is bound to hear about Nysa: how at the edge of twelve she was taken off the streets by an Australian who, in true Pygmalion fashion, created out of this raggedy Arab child an accomplished, extremely elegant personage. Nysa is, as far as I know, the only example in Tangier of a Europeanized Arab woman, a fact which, strangely, no one quite forgives her, neither the Europeans, nor the Arabs, who are avowedly bitter and who, because she lives in the Casbah, have constant opportunity to vent their malice: women send their children to scrawl obscenities on her door, men do not hesitate to spit at her on the street—for in their eyes she has committed the gravest sin possible: become a Christian. Such a situation must make for terrible resentment, but Nysa, at least as far as surface appearances go, never seems aware that there is anything to resent. She is a charming, calm girl of twenty-three; it is in itself an entertainment just to sit quietly and marvel over her beauty, the tilted eyes and the flowerlike hands. She does not see many people; like the princess in a storybook, she stays behind the walls and in the shade of her patio, reading, playing with her cats and a large white cockatoo who mimics whatever she does: sometimes the cockatoo flares forward and kisses her on the lips. The Australian lives with her; since he found her as a child she has never for a moment been separated from him; if something should happen to him, there really would be no way for Nysa to turn: she could not ever be an Arab again, and it isn't likely that she could pass completely into a European world. But the Australian is an old man now. One day I rang Nysa's bell; no one came to answer. There is a grillwork at the top of the door; peering, I saw her through a veil of vine and leaves standing in the shadows of her patio. When I rang again she remained dark and still as a statue. Later I heard that during the night the Australian had had a stroke.

At the end of June, and with the start of a new moon, *Ramadan* begins. For the Arabs, *Ramadan* is a month of abstinence. As dark comes on, a colored string is stretched in the air, and when the string grows invisible, conch horns signal the Arabs to the food and drink that during the day they cannot touch. These dark-night feasts emanate a festive spirit that lasts until dawn. From distant towers oboe players serenade before prayers; drums, hidden but heard, tom-tom behind closed doors, and the voices of men, singsonging the Koran, carry out of the mosques into the narrow, moon-bright streets. Even high on the mountain above Tangier you can hear the oboe player wailing in the far-off dark, a solemn thread of melody winding across Africa from here to Mecca and back.

Sidi Kacem is a limitless, Sahara-like beach bordered by olive groves; at the end of *Ramadan*, Arabs from all over Morocco arrive at Sidi Kacem in trucks, astride donkeys, on foot: for three days a city appears there, a fragile dream city of colored lights and cafés under lantern-lighted trees. We drove out there around midnight; the first glimpse of the city was like seeing a birthday cake blazing in a darkened room, and it filled you with the same exciting awe: you knew you could not blow out all the candles. Right away we got sepa-

rated from the people we'd come with, but in the surge and
sway it was impossible to stay together, and after the first
few frightened moments we never bothered looking for
them; the night caught us in its hand and there was nothing
to do but become another of the masked, ecstatic faces flashing in the torch-flare. Everywhere little orchestras played.
Voices, sweet and sultry as *kif* smoke, chanted over drums,
and somewhere, stumbling through the silver, floating trees,
we got smothered in a crowd of dancers: a circle of old
bearded men beat the rhythm, and the dancers, so concentrated you could put a pin in them, rippled as though wind
were moving them around. According to the Arab calendar
this is the year 1370; seeing a shadow through the silk of a
tent, watching a family fry honeycakes on a flat twig fire,
moving among the dancers and hearing the trill of a lonely
flute on the beach, it was simple to believe that one was living
in 1370 and that time would never move forward.

Occasionally we had to rest; there were straw mats under
the olive trees, and if you sat on one of these a man would
bring you a glass of hot mint tea. It was while we were
drinking tea that we saw a curious line of men file past. They
wore beautiful robes, and the man in front, old like a piece
of ivory, carried a bowl of rose water which, to the accompaniment of bagpipes, he sprinkled from side to side. We got
up to follow them, and they took us out of the grove onto
the beach. The sand was as cold as the moon; humped dunes
of it drifted toward the water, and flickers of light burst in
the dark like fallen stars. At last the priest and his followers
went into a temple which it was forbidden us to enter, and so
we wandered down across the beach. J. said, "Look, a shooting star"; and then we counted the shooting stars, there were
so many. Wind whispered on the sand like the sound of the

seas; cutthroat figures outlined themselves against the kneeling orange moon, and the beach was as cold as a snowfield, but J. said, "Oh, I can't keep my eyes open any longer."

We woke up in a blue, almost dawn light. We were high on a dune, and there below us, spread along the shore, were all the celebrants, their brilliant clothes fluttering in the morning breeze. Just as the sun touched the horizon a great roar went up, and two horsemen, riding bareback, splashed through the surf and swept down the beach. Like a lifting curtain sunrise crept toward us across the sand, and we shuddered at its coming, knowing that when it reached us we would be back in our own century.

*

A Ride
Through Spain

(1950)

❖

CERTAINLY THE TRAIN WAS OLD. The seats sagged like
the jowls of a bulldog, windows were out and strips of ad-
hesive held together those that were left; in the corridor a
prowling cat appeared to be hunting mice, and it was not
unreasonable to assume his search would be rewarded.

Slowly, as though the engine were harnessed to elderly
coolies, we crept out of Granada. The southern sky was as
white and burning as a desert; there was one cloud, and it
drifted like a traveling oasis.

We were going to Algeciras, a Spanish seaport facing the
coast of Africa. In our compartment there was a middle-aged

Australian wearing a soiled linen suit; he had tobacco-colored teeth and his fingernails were unsanitary. Presently he informed us that he was a ship's doctor. It seemed curious, there on the dry, dour plains of Spain, to meet someone connected with the sea. Seated next to him there were two women, a mother and daughter. The mother was an overstuffed, dusty woman with sluggish, disapproving eyes and a faint mustache. The focus for her disapproval fluctuated; first, she eyed me rather strongly because as the sunlight fanned brighter, waves of heat blew through the broken windows and I had removed my jacket—which she considered, perhaps rightly, discourteous. Later on, she took a dislike to the young soldier who also occupied our compartment. The soldier, and the woman's not very discreet daughter, a buxom girl with the scrappy features of a prizefighter, seemed to have agreed to flirt. Whenever the wandering cat appeared at our door, the daughter pretended to be frightened, and the soldier would gallantly shoo the cat into the corridor: this by-play gave them frequent opportunity to touch each other.

The young soldier was one of many on the train. With their tasseled caps set at snappy angles, they hung about in the corridors smoking sweet black cigarettes and laughing confidentially. They seemed to be enjoying themselves, which apparently was wrong of them, for whenever an officer appeared the soldiers would stare fixedly out the windows, as though enraptured by the landslides of red rock, the olive fields and stern stone mountains. Their officers were dressed for a parade, many ribbons, much brass; and some wore gleaming, improbable swords strapped to their sides. They did not mix with the soldiers, but sat together in a first-class compartment, looking bored and rather like unemployed actors. It was a blessing, I suppose, that something finally happened to give them a chance at rattling their swords.

The compartment directly ahead was taken over by one family: a delicate, attenuated, exceptionally elegant man with a mourning ribbon sewn around his sleeve, and traveling with him, six thin, summery girls, presumably his daughters. They were beautiful, the father and his children, all of them, and in the same way: hair that had a dark shine, lips the color of pimientos, eyes like sherry. The soldiers would glance into their compartment, then look away. It was as if they had seen straight into the sun.

Whenever the train stopped, the man's two youngest daughters would descend from the carriage and stroll under the shade of parasols. They enjoyed many lengthy promenades, for the train spent the greatest part of our journey standing still. No one appeared to be exasperated by this except myself. Several passengers seemed to have friends at every station with whom they could sit around a fountain and gossip long and lazily. One old woman was met by different little groups in a dozen-odd towns—between these encounters she wept with such abandon that the Australian doctor became alarmed: why no, she said, there was nothing he could do, it was just that seeing all her relatives made her so happy.

At each stop cyclones of barefooted women and somewhat naked children ran beside the train sloshing earthen jars of water and furrily squalling *Agua! Agua!* For two pesetas you could buy a whole basket of dark runny figs, and there were trays of curious white-coated candy doughnuts that looked as though they should be eaten by young girls wearing Communion dresses. Toward noon, having collected a bottle of wine, a loaf of bread, a sausage and a cheese, we were prepared for lunch. Our companions in the compartment were hungry, too. Packages were produced, wine uncorked, and for a while there was a pleasant, almost graceful festiveness. The soldier shared a pomegranate with the girl, the Australian told an amusing story, the witch-eyed mother pulled a paper-wrapped fish from between her bosoms and ate it with a glum relish.

Afterward everyone was sleepy; the doctor went so solidly to sleep that a fly meandered undisturbed over his open-mouthed face. Stillness etherized the whole train; in the next compartment the lovely girls leaned loosely, like six exhausted geraniums; even the cat had ceased to prowl, and lay dreaming in the corridor. We had climbed higher, the train moseyed across a plateau of rough yellow wheat, then between the granite walls of deep ravines where wind, moving down from the mountains, quivered in strange, thorny trees. Once, at a parting in the trees, there was something I'd wanted to see, a castle on a hill, and it sat there like a crown.

It was a landscape for bandits. Earlier in the summer, a young Englishman I know (rather, know of) had been motoring through this part of Spain when, on the lonely side of a mountain, his car was surrounded by swarthy scoundrels. They robbed him, then tied him to a tree and tickled his throat with the blade of a knife. I was thinking of this when without preface a spatter of bullet fire strafed the dozy silence.

It was a machine gun. Bullets rained in the trees like the rattle of castanets, and the train, with a wounded creak, slowed to a halt. For a moment there was no sound except the machine gun's cough. Then, "Bandits!" I said in a loud, dreadful voice.

"*Bandidos!*" screamed the daughter.

"*Bandidos!*" echoed her mother, and the terrible word swept through the train like something drummed on a tom-tom. The result was slapstick in a grim key. We collapsed on the floor, one cringing heap of arms and legs. Only the mother seemed to keep her head; standing up, she began systematically to stash away her treasures. She stuck a ring into the buns of her hair and without shame hiked up her skirts and dropped a pearl-studded comb into her bloomers. Like the cryings of birds at twilight, airy twitterings of distress came from the charming girls in the next compartment. In the corridor the officers bumped about yapping orders and knocking into each other.

Suddenly, silence. Outside, there was the murmur of wind in leaves, of voices. Just as the weight of the doctor's body was becoming too much for me, the outer door of our compartment swung open, and a young man stood there. He did not look clever enough to be a bandit.

"*Hay un médico en el tren?*" he said, smiling.

The Australian, removing the pressure of his elbow from my stomach, climbed to his feet. "I'm a doctor," he admitted, dusting himself. "Has someone been wounded?"

"*Si, Señor*. An old man. He is hurt in the head," said the Spaniard, who was not a bandit: alas, merely another passenger. Settling back in our seats, we listened, expressionless with embarrassment, to what had happened. It seemed that for the last several hours an old man had been stealing a ride by clinging to the rear of the train. Just now he'd lost his hold, and a soldier, seeing him fall, had started firing a machine gun as a signal for the engineer to stop the train.

My only hope was that no one remembered who had first mentioned bandits. They did not seem to. After acquiring a clean shirt of mine which he intended to use as a bandage, the doctor went off to his patient, and the mother, turning her back with sour prudery, reclaimed her pearl comb. Her daughter and the soldier followed after us as we got out of the carriage and strolled under the trees, where many passengers had gathered to discuss the incident.

Two soldiers appeared carrying the old man. My shirt was wrapped around his head. They propped him under a tree and all the women clustered about vying with each other to lend him their rosary; someone brought a bottle of wine, which pleased him more. He seemed quite happy, and moaned a great deal. The children who had been on the train circled around him, giggling.

We were in a small wood that smelled of oranges. There was a path, and it led to a shaded promontory; from here, one looked across a valley where sweeping stretches of scorched golden grass shivered as though the earth were trembling. Admiring the valley, and the shadowy changes of light on the hills beyond, the six sisters, escorted by their elegant father, sat with their parasols raised above them like guests at a *fête champêtre.* The soldiers moved around them in a vague, ambitious manner; they did not quite dare to approach, though one brash, sassy fellow went to the edge of the promontory and called, *"Yo te quiero mucho."* The words returned with the hollow sub-music of a perfect echo, and the sisters, blushing, looked more deeply into the valley.

A cloud, somber as the rocky hills, had massed in the sky, and the grass below stirred like the sea before a storm. Someone said he thought it would rain. But no one wanted to go: not the injured man, who was well on his way through a second bottle of wine, nor the children who, having discovered the echo, stood happily caroling into the valley. It was like a party, and we all drifted back to the train as though each of us wished to be the last to leave. The old man, with my shirt like a grand turban on his head, was put into a first-class carriage and several eager ladies were left to attend him.

In our compartment, the dark, dusty mother sat just as we had left her. She had not seen fit to join the party. She gave me a long, glittering look. "*Bandidos*," she said with a surly, unnecessary vigor.

The train moved away so slowly butterflies blew in and out the windows.

Fontana Vecchia

(*1951*)

FONTANA VECCHIA, OLD FOUNTAIN. So the house is called. *Pace*, peace: this word is carved into the stone doorstep. There is no fountain; there has been, I think, something rather like peace. It is a rose-colored house dominating a valley of almond and olive trees that sinks into the sea. Across the water there is a view on clear days of Italy's tip end, the peninsula of Calabria. Back of us, a stony, wavering path, traveled mostly by farming peasants, their donkeys and goats, leads along the side of the mountain into the town of Taormina. It is very like living in an airplane, or a ship trembling on the peak of a tidal wave: there is a momentous feeling each time one looks from the windows, steps onto the terrace, a feeling of being suspended, like the white reeling doves, between the mountains and above the sea. This vastness reduces to an intimate size particulars of the landscape—the cypress trees are small as green pen quills; each passing ship could be held in the palm of your hand.

Before dawn, when drooping stars drift at the bedroom window fat as owls, a racket begins along the steep, at moments perilous, path that descends from the mountains. It is the farm families on their way to the marketplace in Taormina. Loose rocks scatter under the stumbling hoofs of overloaded donkeys; there are swells of laughter, a sway of lanterns: it is as though the lanterns were signaling to the far-below night fishermen, who just then are hauling in their nets. Later, in the market, the farmers and the fishermen meet: a small people, not unlike the Japanese, but brawny; indeed there is something almost lush about their lean walnut-hardness. If you question the freshness of a fish, the ripeness of a fig, they are great showmen. *Si, buono:* your head is pushed down to smell the fish; you are told, with an ecstatic and threatening roll of eyes, how delicious it is. I am always intimidated; not so the villagers, who poke stonily among the tiny jewel tomatoes and never hesitate to sniff a fish or bruise a melon. Shopping, and the arranging of meals, is universally a problem, I know; but after a few months in Sicily even the most skilled householder might consider the noose—no, I exaggerate: the fruit, at least when first it comes into season, is more than excellent; the fish is always good, the *pasta*, too. I'm told you can find edible meat; I've never been so fortunate. Also, there is not much choice of vegetables; in winter, eggs are rare. But of course the real trouble is we can't cook; neither, I'm afraid, can our cook. She is a spirited girl, very charming, a little superstitious: our gas bill, for instance, is sometimes astronomical, as she is fond of melting immense pots of lead on the stove, then twisting the lead into carven images. As long as she keeps to simple Sicilian dishes, really simple and really Sicilian, they are, well, something to eat.

But let me tell about the chicken. Not long ago Cecil Beaton, in Sicily on a holiday, came to stay with us. After a few days he was beginning to look a bit peaked: we saw that a more proper effort toward feeding him would have to be made. We sent for a chicken; it appeared, quite alive, and accompanied by the cagey peasant woman who lives slightly higher on the mountain. It was a great black bird—I said it must be very old. No, said the woman, not old, just large. Its neck was wrung and G., the cook, put it to boil. Around twelve she came to say the chicken was still *troppo duro*—in other words, hard as nails. We advised her to keep trying, and settling on the terrace with glasses of wine, prepared to wait. Several hours, several wine liters later, I went out to the kitchen to find G. in a critical condition: after boiling the chicken, she had roasted it, then fried it, and now, in desperation, was giving it another boil. Though there was nothing else to eat, it should never have been brought to the table, for when it was set before us we had to avert our eyes: crowning this steaming heap was the poor bird's severed head, its withered eyes gazing at us, its blackened cockscomb still attached. That evening Cecil, who previously had been staying with other friends on the island, informed us, quite suddenly, that he must return to them.

When first we leased Fontana Vecchia—this was in the

spring, April—the valley was high with wheat green as the lizards racing among its stalks. It begins in January, the Sicilian spring, and accumulates into a kingly bouquet, a wizard's garden where all things have bloomed: the creek sprouts mint; dead trees are wreathed in wild clamber roses; even the brutal cactus shoots tender blossoms. April, Eliot writes, is the cruelest month: not here. It is bright as the snows on Etna's summit. Children climb along the mountain-side filling sacks of petals in preparation for a Saint's Day, and fishermen, passing with their baskets of pearl-colored *pesce*, have geraniums tucked behind their ears. May, and the spring is in its twilight: the sun enlarges; you remember that Africa is only eighty miles away; like a bronze shadow autumn color falls across the land. By June the wheat was ready to harvest. We listened with a certain melancholy to the scythes swinging in the golden field. When the work was over, our landlord, to whom the crop belonged, gave a party for the harvesters. There were only two women—a young girl who sat nursing a baby, and an old woman, the girl's grandmother. The old woman loved to dance; barefooted, she whirled with all the men—no one could make her take a rest, she would spring up in the middle of a tune to grab herself a partner. The men, who took turns playing the accordion, all danced together, which is a rural custom in Sicily. It was the best kind of party: too much dancing, far too much wine. Later, as I went exhaustedly to bed, I thought of the old woman. After working all day in the field and dancing all evening, she had now to start on a five-mile upward climb to her house in the mountains.

It is a walk to the beach, or beaches; there are several, all of them pebbly, and only one of them, Mazzaro, especially inhabited. The most attractive, Isola Bella, a guarded cove with water clear as barrel rain, is a mile and a half straight down; getting up again is the trick. A few times we have walked into Taormina and taken the bus, or a taxi. But mostly we go on foot. You can swim from March until Christmas (so the hearty souls say), but I confess I was not too enthusiastic until we bought the water mask. The mask had a round glass viewing plate, and a breathing tube that closes when you dive. Swimming silently among the rocks it is as though one had discovered a new visual dimension: in the underwater dusk a red phosphorescent fish looms at alarming proximity; your shadow drifts over a field of ermine-colored grass; blue, silver bubbles rise from some long-legged sleeping thing lying in a field of blowing sea flowers, and it is as if a wind of music were moving them: the sea flowers, the Javanese tendrils of purple jelly. Coming to shore, how static, gross, the upper world seems.

If we do not go to the beach, then there is only one other reason for leaving the house: to shop in Taormina, and have an *apéritif* in the piazza. Taormina, really an extension of Naxos, the earliest Greek city in Sicily, has had a continuous existence since 396 B.C. Goethe explored here in 1787; he describes it thus: "Now sitting at the spot where formerly sat the uppermost spectators, you confess at once that never did any audience, in any theatre, have before it such a spectacle as you there behold. On the right, and on high rocks at the side, castles tower in the air; farther on, the city lies below you, and although all of its buildings are of a modern date, still similar ones, no doubt, stood of old on the same site. After this the eye falls on the whole of the long range of Aetna, then on the left it catches a view of the seashore as far as Catania, and even Syracuse, and then the wide and extensive view is closed by the immense smoking volcano, but not horribly, for the atmosphere, with its softening effect, makes it look more distant and milder than it really is." Goethe's vantage point was, I gather, the Greek theatre, a superb cliff-top ruin where even today plays and concerts are occasionally given.

Taormina is as scenically extravagant as Goethe claims; but it is a curious town. During the war it was the head-quarters of Kesselring, the German general; consequently, it came in for a share of Allied bombing. The damage was slight. Nevertheless, the war has been the town's undoing. Up until 1940 it was, with the exception of Capri, the most successful Mediterranean resort south of the French Riviera. Though Americans have never come here, at least in any quantity, it had considerable reputation among English and Germans. (A guidebook to Sicily, written by an Englishman, and published in 1905, remarks: "Taormina is flooded with Germans. At some hotels they have separate tables for them, because the other nations do not like sitting with Germans.") Now, of course, the Germans are in no position to travel; due to currency restrictions, neither are the English. Last year the San Domenico, an old convent that late in the nine-teenth century was converted into a most luxurious hotel, was never more than a quarter filled; before the war it was necessary to have your reservations a year in advance. This winter, as perhaps a frantic last measure, the town, in the hope that it will attract the international audience, is open-ing a gambling casino. I wish them luck: it is imperative that someone come along and buy all those hand-woven hats, handbags, that junk up the shops along the Corso. For myself,

Taormina suits me the way it is; it has the comforts of a tourist center (running water, a shop with foreign newspapers, a bar where you can buy a good martini) without the tourists.

The town, not large, is contained between two gates; near the first of these, the Porto Messina, there is a small tree-shaded square with a fountain and a stone wall along which village idlers are arranged like birds on a telephone wire. Taking one of my first walks through Taormina, I was startled to see perched upon this wall an old man wearing velvet trousers and wrapped in a black cape; his hat, an olive fedora, had been dented into a peaked tricorne crown, and the brim threw a shadow over his broad, yellowed, somewhat Mongolian face. It was a surprisingly theatrical appearance, merely that, until looking closely I realized it was André Gide. Through the spring and early summer I often saw him there, either sitting unnoticed on the wall, apparently only another of the old men, or browsing about the fountain where, with his cape drawn about him in a Shakespearean manner, he seemed to be observing in the water his own reflection: *si jeunesse savait, si vieillesse pouvait.*

Beneath the excess trappings Taormina is an ordinary town, and its people have ordinary ambitions, occupations. However, many of them, the young men in particular, possess what I think of as the mentality of hotel-children, children who have spent their lives in hotels, and who know that all things are transient, that the heart must never be involved, for friendship is a matter of days. These young men live, as it were, "outside" the town; they are interested in foreigners, not so much for gainful reasons as the distinction they believe it bestows upon them to have English and American acquaintances, and as most of them have a primitive way with several languages, they spend their days at piazza cafés courteously, artificially, chattering with travelers.

It is a beautiful piazza centering around a promontory with a view of Etna and the sea. Toy Sardinian donkeys, attached to delicately carved carts, go prancing past, their bells jangling, their carts filled with bananas and oranges. On Sunday afternoons, while the town band plays an eccentric but catchy concert, there is a grand promenade, and if I am there I always look out for the butcher's daughter, a stout, beefy girl who all week swings a meat ax with the ferocity of any two men; but on Sunday, coiffed and scented, careening on two-inch heels, and accompanied by her fiancé, a slender boy rising not quite to her shoulder, there is about her a romance, an atmosphere of triumph that stalls the satiric tongue: hers is the haughtiness, the belief in oneself, that should be the spirit of a promenade. Occasionally traveling entertainers appear in the piazza: goatlike mountain boys who play on hair-covered bagpipes haunting, yodelerlike tunes; or, as in the spring, a singer, a child whose family supported themselves by each year touring him around the island: his stage was the limb of a tree, and there, his head thrown back and his throat trembling with heart-bursts of soprano song, he sang until his voice tired to the saddest whisper.

When shopping, the *tabacchi* is my last stop before starting out into the country. In Sicily all tobacconists are irritable fellows. Their places are usually crowded, but few of the customers buy more than three or four loose cigarettes: with a pinched solemnity the weathered men put down their ragged lire, then minutely examine the cigarettes, the poky cigars that have been doled out to them—it seems the most important moment of their day, this visit to the *tabacchi;* perhaps that is why they are so reluctant to give up their place in line. There are possibly twenty different Sicilian newspapers; great garlands of them are strung in front of the tobacconist shop. One afternoon as I walked into town it started to rain. It was not a serious rainfall; still, the streets were deserted, not a soul about until I came alongside the *tabacchi*—a crowd was gathered where the newspapers, shriekingly headlined, fluttered in the rain. Young boys, bareheaded, unmindful, stood with their heads leaning together, while an older boy, his finger pointing to an enormous photograph of a man stretched in a pool of blood, read aloud to them: Giuliano, dead, shot in Castelvetrano. *Triste, triste,* a shame, a pity, the older people said; the young ones said nothing, but two girls went into the shop and came out with copies of *La Sicilia,* a paper whose front page was taken up by a giant portrait of the slain bandit; protecting their papers against the rain, the girls ran hand in hand skidding along the shining street.

Then it was August; we felt the sun before it had risen. Strangely, here on the open mountain, the days were cooler than the nights, for more often than not a booming breeze blew off the water; at sunset the wind turned, plowed seaward, south, toward Greece, Africa. It was a month of silent leaves, shooting stars, red moons, a season of gorgeous moths, sleeping lizards. Figs split, plums swelled, the almonds hardened. One morning I woke to hear in the almond trees the rattle of bamboo canes. In the valley, off on the hills, hundreds of peasants, working in family groups, were knocking down the almonds, then gathering them off the ground; and they sang to each other, one voice leading the rest, Moorish, flamenco-like voices whose songs began nowhere, ended nowhere, and yet contained the marrow of work, heat, a harvest. They were a week bringing in the almonds, and each day the singing reached a not quite sane intensity. I could not think for it; there was in me such an overriding sense of extra-life. At the end, during the mad last days, the fierce fine voices seemed to rise from the sea, the almond roots; it was as if one were lost in a cave of echoes, and when darkness came, and stillness, even so I could hear, at the edge of sleep, the sound of singing, and it seemed, though one tried to push it back, about to tell a pitiful, painful story, about to impart some terrible knowledge.

We do not have many visitors at Fontana Vecchia; it is too far a walk for casual callers, and days go by when no one knocks at the door except the ice boy. Blond, witty, the ice boy is a scholarly-looking child of eleven. He has a beautiful young aunt, surely one of the most attractive girls I've ever known, and I often talk to him about her. Why, I wanted to know, does A., the aunt, have no beau? Why is she always alone, never at the dances or the Sunday promenade? The ice boy says it is because his aunt has no use for the local men, that she is very unhappy and longs only to go to America. Perhaps. But it is my own theory that the men in her family are so jealous of her that no one dares come too near. Sicilian males have quite a lot to say about what their women do or don't; heaven knows, the women seem to like it. For instance our cook, G., who is nineteen, has a somewhat older brother. One morning she appeared with a split lip, black-ened eyes, a knife gash in her arm, and bruised yellow-green top to toe. It was astonishing; she should have been in a hospital. Smiling lopsidedly, G. said, Well, her brother had beat her up; they'd quarreled because he felt she went too often to the beach. Of course, we thought that an odd objection; when did she go to the beach—at night? I told her to pay no attention to her brother, that he was *brute*, ugly. Her reply, in effect, was that I should mind my own business; she said her brother was a fine man. "He is good-looking and has many friends—only to me is he *brute*." Nevertheless, I went to our landlord and complained that G.'s brother must be warned that we would not tolerate his sister's coming to work in this kind of condition. He seemed mystified: why should I blame the brother? After all, a brother is entitled to reprimand his sister. When I spoke of it to the ice boy he agreed with the landlord, and stated firmly that if he had a sister who didn't do what he said he would beat her up too. One evening in August, when the moons were so preposterous, the ice boy and I had a small but chilling exchange. He asked, What do you think of the werewolf? Are you afraid to go out after dark? As it happened, I'd just that day heard of the werewolf scare: a boy walking home late at night claimed to have been set upon by a howling animal, a human on all fours. But I laughed. You don't believe in werewolves, do you? Oh yes. "There used to be many werewolves in Taormina," he said, his gray eyes regarding me steadily; then, with a disdainful shrug, "Now there are only two or three."

And so autumn came, is here at this moment, a tambourine wind, a ghost of smoke moving between the yellow trees. It has been a good year for grapes; sweet in the air is the smell of fallen grapes in the mould of leaves, new wine. The stars are out at six; still, it is not too chilly to have a cocktail on the terrace and watch, in the bright starlight, the sheep with their Buster Keaton faces coming down from pasture, and the goats, whose herd-movement makes a sound like the dragging of dry branches. Yesterday men brought us a wagon-load of wood. So I am not afraid of winter's coming: what better prospect than to sit by a fire and wait for spring?

Lola

(*1964*)

Y ES, IT SEEMED in every respect a curious gift. An appalling one, really. For I had already a sufficiency of pets: two dogs, an English bulldog and a Kerry blue terrier. Moreover, I have never been partial to birds; indeed, I've had always rather an aversion to them: when, on a beach, sea gulls swoop and dive, I am (for example) very liable to panic and run. Once when I was five or six, a sparrow, having flown through the window of my room, became trapped there: flew about till I was almost faint from an emotion in which pity figured but fear predominated. And so it was with some dismay that

I received Graziella's Christmas present: an ugly young raven with wings cruelly clipped.

Now more than twelve years have gone by, for that was Christmas morning, 1952. I was living then in Sicily on a mountainside; the house, placed amid a silvery olive orchard, was made of pale pink stone; it had many rooms, and a terrace with a view of Etna's snowcapped summit. Far below one saw, on sunlit days, a sea blue as a peacock's eye. It was a beautiful house, though not very comfortable, especially in winter when north winds sang, shouted, when one drank wine for warmth and even so the touch of the stone floors was cold as a dead man's kiss. Whatever the weather, winter-withered or sun-scorched, the house would not have been quite habitable without Graziella, a servant girl from the village who appeared early each morning and stayed until after supper. She was seventeen, a stocky young lady too sturdily built: she had the legs of a Japanese wrestler—slightly bowed, with bulging calves. Her face, however, was pretty as could be: eyes brown and gold as the local home-brewed brandy; rosy cheeks; rosier lips; a fine dark brow; and black hair brushed smooth to the skull, then secured in that austere position by a little pair of Spanish combs. She had a hard life, and in an amused, uncomplaining fashion, complained of it constantly: a father who was the village drunk, at any rate one of them; her mother, a religious hysteric; and Paolo, her elder brother —she adored him, though he every week beat her and robbed her of her wages. We were good friends, Graziella and I, and it was natural that at Christmas we should exchange gifts. I gave her a sweater, a scarf and a necklace of green beads. And she, to repeat, presented me with a raven.

I have said it was ugly. It was. An object both dreadful and pathetic. No matter the risk of outraging Graziella, I would have set it free at once had it been capable of fending for itself. But the wings had been very closely cut and it could not fly; it could only wobble about, its black beak agape like the jaws of an idiot, its eyes flat and bleak. Graziella, having climbed high into the dour volcanic slopes above Bronte, had captured it in a ravine where ravens thrive, a valley of stones and thorns and deformed trees. She said, "I caught it with a fishing net. I ran among the birds. When I threw the net in the air two of them tangled. One I let go. The other, this one, I put in a shoebox. I took it home and cut its wings. Ravens are very clever. Smarter than parrots. Or horses. If we split its tongue, we can teach it to talk." It was not that Graziella was unkind; she simply shared the indifference of Mediterraneans to the sufferings of animals. She grew quite cross when I refused to let her mutilate the bird's tongue; in fact, she lost all interest in the poor creature, the well-being of which now became my own unhappy burden.

I kept it shut away in a spare, unfurnished room; kept it locked there like a mad relative. I thought, Well, its wings will soon grow out, then it can go away. But the New Year came and went, weeks passed, and presently Graziella confessed it would be six months before my Christmas gift could once again ascend the skies.

I loathed it. I loathed visiting it; the room was the coldest in the cold house, and the bird so forlorn, so impeccably sad a sight. Yet awareness of its loneliness forced me there— though at the start it seemed to enjoy my visits rather less than I did: it would stalk into a corner and turn its back on me, a silent prisoner hunched between a bowl of water and a bowl of food. In time, however, I came to feel my presence was not unwelcome; it ceased to avoid me, it stared me in the eye and, in a rough, unmusical voice, produced friendly-seeming noises: muted cawings. We began to make discoveries concerning one another: I found it liked to have its head scratched, it realized how much its playful peckings amused me. Soon it learned to balance on the rim of my hand, then to sit upon my shoulder. It grew fond of kissing me—that is, gently, with its beak nipping at my chin, cheeks, an earlobe. Nevertheless, I remained, or imagined I did, somewhat repelled by it: the funereal coloring, the bird-feel of its feathers—distasteful (to me) as fish skin, snake hide.

One morning—it was late January, but spring comes early to Sicily, and the almond trees were in flower: a mist of scent and bloom drifting across the landscape—one morning I arrived to find the raven had absconded. The room in which it lived contained French doors leading into a garden; during the night the doors had somehow come undone; perhaps the sirocco, which was blowing then (bringing with it gritty bits of African desert), had pushed them open. The bird, anyway, was gone. I combed the garden; Graziella climbed the mountainside. The morning ended, and the afternoon. By nightfall we had searched "everywhere": the prickly interior of a wild cactus grove, among the graves of a cemetery close by, inside a cave reeking of bat urine. Gradually, in the course of our pursuit, a certain fact at last penetrated: I very much liked—Lola. Lola! The name emerged like the new moon overhead, unbidden but inevitable; until then I'd not wanted to give her a name: to do so, I felt, would be to admit she was a permanent belonging.

"Lola?"

I called to her from my window. Finally I went to bed.

Of course I could not sleep. Visions intervened: Lola, her neck clasped between cat teeth; a red tom racing with her toward the feasting hall of some bloodstained, feather-strewn lair. Or Lola, earthbound and helpless, somewhere hiding until hunger and thirst felled her forever.

"Lo-o-o-la-a-a?"

We had not looked through the house. Possibly she had never left it, or departed by one door and reentered by another. I lighted a candle (our electricity seldom functioned); I traveled from room to room; and in one, an unused parlor, the candlelight illuminated a familiar pair of eyes.

"Ah, Lola."

She stepped aboard my hand; back in the bedroom I transferred her to the foot-railing of a brass bed. She clutched it with her claws and tucked a tired head under one of her disfigured wings. Soon she was asleep, so was I, so were the dogs (curled together in front of a fireplace vaguely aglow with the aromatic flames of a eucalyptus fire).

The dogs had never met Lola, and it was with some anxiety that I next morning introduced them, for they both, and particularly the Kerry blue, were capable of cranky behavior. But if she meant to make her home with us, it must be done. I put her on the floor. The bulldog sniffed at her with his squashed, trufflelike nose, then yawned, not from boredom but embarrassment; all dogs yawn when they are embarrassed. Clearly he did not know what she was. Food? A plaything? The Kerry decided Lola was the latter. He tapped her with his paw. He chased her into a corner. She fought back, pecked his snout; her cawings were coarse and violent as the harshest curse words. It frightened the bulldog; he ran from the room. Even the Kerry retreated—sat down and gazed at her, marveling.

From then on, the dogs had great respect for Lola. They showed her every consideration; she showed them very few. She used their water bowl as a splash bath; at mealtimes, never content with her own dish, she always raided theirs, taking what she pleased. The bulldog she turned into a private mount; perched on his broad rump, she trotted around the garden like a bareback circus rider. At night, camping by the hearth, she huddled between the dogs, and if they threatened to stir, or otherwise disturb her comfort, she stabbed them with her beak.

Lola must have been very young when Graziella caught her—hardly more than a fledgling. By June she had tripled in size, grown big as a chicken. Her wings had come back, or almost. But still she did not fly. Indeed, she refused to. She preferred to walk. When the dogs went for a hike she hopped along beside them. One day it occurred to me that Lola did not know she was a bird. She thought she was a dog. Graziella agreed with me, and we both laughed; we considered it a delightful quirk, neither one foreseeing that Lola's misconception was certain to end in tragedy: the doom that awaits all of us who reject our own natures and insist on being something else than ourselves.

Lola was a thief; otherwise she might never have used her wings at all. However, the sort of articles she was fond of stealing—shiny things, grapes and fountain pens, cigarettes —were situated usually in elevated areas; so, to reach a table-top, she occasionally took a (quite literally) flying jump. Once she stole a set of false teeth. The teeth belonged to a guest, a difficult and elderly friend, a lady. She said she thought it not the least funny and burst into tears. Alas, we did not know where Lola hid her loot (according to Graziella, all ravens are robbers and invariably keep a secret storage den for stolen treasure). The only sensible course was to try to trick Lola into revealing where she had taken the teeth. She admired gold: a gold ring I sometimes wore constantly excited her greedy gaze. We (Graziella and I) therefore baited our trap with the ring: left it on the luncheon table, where Lola was cleaning up crumbs, and hid behind a door. The instant she imagined herself unobserved, she snatched the ring and rushed out of the dining room and along a hall to the "library"—a small, gloomy room stuffed with cheap paperback editions of the classics, the property of a former tenant. She leaped from floor to chair to bookshelf; then, as though it were a cleft in a mountainside leading to an Ali Baba's cavern, she squeezed between two books and disappeared behind them: evaporated, rather like Alice through the looking glass. *The Complete Jane Austen* concealed her cache, which, when we found it, consisted in addition to the purloined dentures, of the long-lost keys to my car (I'd not blamed Lola: I thought I'd lost them myself), a mass of paper money—thousands of lire torn into tiny scraps, as though intended for some future nest, old letters, my best cuff links, rubber bands, yards of string, the first page of a short story I'd stopped writing because I couldn't find the first page, an American penny, a dry rose, a crystal button—

Early that summer Graziella announced her engagement to a young man named Luchino, a slim-waisted waiter with oily, curly hair and a film-star profile. He spoke a little English, a little German; he wore green suede shoes and drove his own Vespa. Graziella had reason to think him a formidable catch; still, I was not happy about it. I felt she was too plain and healthy, simply too nice, for a sharp fellow like Luchino (who had a reputation as a semiprofessional gigolo catering to solitary tourists: Swedish spinsters, German widows and widowers), though, to be fair, such activities were far from uncommon among the village youth.

But Graziella's joy was difficult to resist. She pinned photographs of Luchino all over the kitchen, above the stove, above the sink, inside the icebox door and even on the trunk of a tree that grew outside the kitchen window. Romance, of course, interfered with her care of me: now, in the Sicilian fashion, she had her fiancé's socks to mend, laundry to do (and such a lot of it!), not to mention the hours she spent preparing a trousseau, embroidering underwear, fitting a wedding veil. Often at lunch I was handed a plate of ice-hard spaghetti, then given cold fried eggs for supper. Or perhaps nothing at all; she was forever hurrying off to meet her lover in the piazza for a twilight promenade. Yet in retrospect I do not begrudge her that happiness: it was but the prelude to the bitterest bad luck.

One August night her father (much beloved despite his drunkenness) was offered (by an American tourist) a tall glass of straight gin, told to drink it at one go, did so and underwent a stroke that left him paralyzed. And the very next day even starker misfortune struck; Luchino, streaking along a country road aboard his Vespa, rounded a corner, ran into and instantly killed a three-year-old girl. I drove Luchino and Graziella to the child's funeral; afterward, on the way home, Luchino was dry-eyed but Graziella moaned and wept as though her heart had been halved: I assumed she was grieving for the dead baby. No, it was for herself, the dark prospect before her: Luchino faced possible imprisonment and certainly a huge indemnity payment—there would be no marriage now, not for years (if ever).

The poor girl was prostrated. A doctor confined her to bed. One day I went to see how she was getting on. I took Lola with me, meaning to cheer the invalid. Instead, the sight of the bird horrified her; she screamed. She said Lola was a witch, she said Lola had the *malocchio*, the evil eye, and that the double tragedy, her father's stroke and Luchino's accident, was Lola's work, a punishment inflicted for having caught her and clipped her wings. She said, Yes, yes, it's true: every child knows ravens are the embodiment of black and wicked spirits. And, "I will never come to your house again."

Nor did she. Nor did any other servant girl. For out of Graziella's accusations, a myth grew that mine was a house of the evil eye: that not merely Lola, but I myself, possessed a potent *malocchio*. Nothing worse can be said of one in Sicily. Moreover, it is a charge against which there is no defense. In the beginning I joked about it, though it was not in the least a humorous adventure. Persons meeting me in the street crossed themselves; or, as soon as I had passed, arranged one hand in the shape of a bull's head with horns —a dark-magic gesture meant to dispel the power of my malevolent, spell-casting, tortoise-shell-rimmed eye.

I woke one night around midnight and decided (snap!) to clear out. Leave before dawn. Rather a decision, for I'd lived there two years, and did not altogether relish being suddenly homeless. Homeless with two large dogs and an uncaged, peculiar bird. Nevertheless, I stuffed the car: it looked like a rolling cornucopia: shoes and books and fishing

gear spilling out the windows; with a few rough shoves I contrived to fit the dogs inside. But there was no room left for
Lola. She had to sit on my shoulder, which was not ideal, for
she was a nervous passenger, and any abrupt twist or turn
made her either squawk or relieve herself.

Across the Straits of Messina, across Calabria, on to
Naples and Rome. It is a journey pleasant to look back
upon: sometimes, when balanced on the edge of sleep, I see
pictures of it slide past. A picnic in the Calabrian mountains:
a hard blue sky, a herd of goats below, the thin sweet pipings
of the goatherder on a bamboo whistle—and Lola gobbling
bread crumbs soaked in red wine. Or Cape Palinuro, a remote, forest-fringed Calabrian beach where we all were
sunning ourselves under a still-warm October sun when a
wild pig charged out of the woods and raced toward us, as
though to attack. I was the only one intimidated: I ran into
the sea. The dogs stood their ground and Lola stood with
them, flapped about, shouting encouragements in her rusty
voice; together, in concert, they chased the pig back into the
forest. The evening of the same day we traveled as far as the
ruins at Paestum: a brilliant evening, the sky like another sea,
the half-moon like an achored ship rocking in a surf of stars,
and all around us the moon-brightened marble, the broken
temples of a distant time. We slept on the beach that borders
the ruins; or they did—Lola and the dogs: I was tormented
by mosquitoes and thoughts of mortality.

We settled for the winter in Rome, first at a hotel (the
management of which expelled us after five days, and it was
not even a first-class establishment), then in an apartment at
33 Via Margutta, a narrow street often painted by bad paint-

ers and renowned for the number of cats who dwell there, unowned cats sheltering in the overgrown patios and existing on the charity of half-mad elderly women, crones who every day tour the cat jungles with sacks of scrap food.

Our apartment was a penthouse: to reach it one climbed six flights of steep dark stairs. We had three rooms and a balcony. It was because of the balcony that I rented it; after the vastness of the view from the Sicilian terrace, the balcony offered, in contrast, a miniature scene tranquil and perfect as firelight: several Roman rooftops, faded orange, faded ocher, and a few across-the-way windows (behind which episodes of family life could be observed). Lola loved the balcony. She was scarcely ever off it. She liked to sit perched on the edge of the stone balustrade and study the traffic on the cobbled street below: the old ladies feeding the Margutta cats; a street musician who came each afternoon and played bagpipes, until, feeling throughly blackmailed, one tossed him a coin; a handsome knife-grinder advertising his services with a song sung in the most bull-like of baritones (housewives hurried!).

When the sun was out Lola always took her bath on the balcony balustrade. Her tub was a silver soup dish; after a moment of sprightly immersion in the shallow water, she would spring up and out, and as though casting off a crystal cloak, shake herself, swell her feathers; later, for long, bliss-saturated hours, she drowsed in the sun, her head tilted back, her beak ajar, her eyes shut. To watch her was a soothing experience.

Signor Fioli seemed to think so. He sat at his window, which was exactly opposite the balcony, and played attentive audience to Lola as long as she was visible. Signor Fioli interested me. I had taken the trouble to learn his name and something of his story. He was ninety-three years old, and in his ninetieth year he had lost the ability to speak: whenever he wished to attract the attention of his family (a widowed granddaughter and five grown great-grandsons), he rang a small supper bell. Otherwise, and even though he never left his bedroom, he appeared to be in complete command of himself. His eyesight was excellent: he saw everything Lola did, and if she did anything especially foolish or lovely, a smile sweetened his sour, very virile old face. He had been a cabinetmaker, and the business he had founded still operated on the ground floor of the building in which he lived; three of his great-grandchildren worked there.

One morning—it was the week before Christmas, almost a year to the day that Lola had entered my life—I filled Lola's soup bowl with mineral water (she preferred to bathe in mineral water, the bubblier the better), carried it out to her on the balcony, waved at Signor Fioli (who, as usual, was settled at his window waiting to attend Lola's toilette), then went inside, sat down at my desk and started to write letters.

Presently I heard the summoning tinkle of Signor Fioli's supper bell: a well-known noise, one heard it twenty times a day; but it had never sounded just like this: a ringing rapid as the beat of an excited heart. I wondered why, and went to see, and saw: Lola, a stupefied sun worshiper squatting on the balustrade—and behind her an immense ginger cat, a cat that had crept across the rooftops and was now crawling on its belly along the balustrade, green eyes aglitter.

Signor Fioli shook his bell. I shouted. The cat leaped, claws unfurled. But it was as if at the last moment Lola sensed her peril. She jumped off the balustrade, fell outward into space. The disgruntled cat, Signor Fioli and I watched her extraordinary descent.

"Lola! Fly, Lola, fly!"

Her wings, though spread, remained motionless. Slowly, gravely, as though attached to a parachute, she drifted downward; down and down.

A small pickup truck was passing in the street below. At first I thought Lola would fall in front of it: that seemed dangerous enough. But what happened was worse, was eerie and awful: she landed on top of some sacks stacked on the back of the truck. And stayed there. And the truck kept going: turned the corner and drove out of the Via Margutta.

"Come back, Lola! Lola!"

I ran after her; skidded down the six flights of slippery stone stairs; fell; skinned my knees; lost my glasses (they flew off and smashed against a wall). Outside, I ran to the corner where the truck had turned. Far off, through a haze compounded of myopia plus tears of pain, I saw the little truck stopped at a traffic light. But before I could reach it, long before, the light changed and the truck, bearing Lola away, taking her forever from me, blurred into the traffic swirling about the Piazza di Spagna.

Not many minutes had elapsed since the cat had lunged, only four or five. Yet it took an hour to retrace my route, climb the stairs, pick up and pocket the broken glasses. And all the while Signor Fioli had been sitting at his window, waiting there with an expression of grieved astonishment. When he saw that I had returned he rang his bell, calling me to the balcony.

I told him, "She thought she was something else."

He frowned.

"A dog."
The frown thickened.
"She's gone."
That he understood. He bowed his head. We both did.

A House
on the Heights

(1959)

I LIVE IN BROOKLYN. By choice.

Those ignorant of its allures are entitled to wonder why. For, taken as a whole, it *is* an uninviting community. A veritable veldt of tawdriness where even the *noms des quartiers* aggravate: Flatbush and Flushing Avenue, Bushwick, Brownsville, Red Hook. Yet, in the greenless grime-gray, oases do occur, splendid contradictions, hearty echoes of healthier days. Of these seeming mirages, the purest example is the neighborhood in which I am situated, an area known as Brooklyn Heights. Heights, because it stands atop a cliff that secures a sea-gull's view of the Manhattan and Brooklyn bridges, of lower Manhattan's tall dazzle and the ship-lane waters, breeding river to bay to ocean, that encircle and seethe past posturing Miss Liberty.

I'm not much acquainted with the proper history of the Heights. However, I *believe* (but please don't trust me) that the oldest house, the oldest still extant and functioning, belongs to our backyard neighbors, Mr. and Mrs. Philip Broughton. A silvery-gray, shingle-wood Colonial shaded by trees robustly leafed, it was built in 1790, the home of a sea captain. Period prints, dated 1830, depict the Heights area as a cozy port bustling with billowed sails; and, indeed, many of the section's finer houses, particularly those of Federal design, were first intended to shelter the families of shipmasters. Cheerfully austere, as elegant and other-era as formal calling cards, these houses bespeak an age of able servants and solid fireside ease; of horses in musical harness (old rosebrick carriage houses abound hereabouts; all now, naturally, transformed into pleasant, if rather doll-pretty, dwellings); invoke specters of bearded seafaring fathers and bonneted stay-at-home wives: devoted parents to great broods of future bankers and fashionable brides. For a century or so that is how it must have been: a time of tree-shrouded streets, lanes limp with willow, August gardens brimming with bumblebees and herbaceous scent, of ship horns on the river, sails in the wind, and a country-green meadow sloping down to the harbor, a cow-grazing, butterflied meadow where children sprawled away breezy summer afternoons, where the slap of sleds resounded on December snows.

Is that how it was? Conceivably I take too Valentine a view. However it be, my Valentine assumes the stricter aspect of a steel engraving as we mosey, hand in hand, with Henry Ward Beecher, whose church once dominated the spiritual life of the Heights through the latter half of the last century. The great Bridge, opened in 1883, now balanced above the river; and the port, each year expanding, becoming a more raucous, big-business matter, chased the children out of the meadow, withered it, entirely whacked it away to make room for black palace-huge warehouses tickly with imported tarantulas and reeking of rotten bananas.

By 1910 the neighborhood, which comprises sly alleys and tucked-away courts and streets that sometimes run straight but also dwindle and bend, had undergone fiercer vicissitudes. Descendants of the Reverend Beecher's stiff-collared flock had begun removing themselves to other pastures; and immigrant tribes, who had first ringed the vicinity, at once infiltrated en masse. Whereupon a majority of what remained of genteel old stock, the sediment in the bottom of the bottle, poured forth from their homes, leaving them to be demolished or converted into eyesore-seedy rooming establishments.

So that, in 1925, Edmund Wilson, allowing a paragraph to what he considered the dead and dying Heights, disgustedly reported: "The pleasant red and pink brick houses still worthily represent the generation of Henry Ward Beecher; but an eternal Sunday is on them now; they seem sunk in a final silence. In the streets one may catch a glimpse of a solitary well-dressed old gentleman moving slowly a long way off; but in general the respectable have disappeared and only the vulgar survive. The empty quiet is broken by the shouts of shrill Italian children and by incessant mechanical pianos in dingy apartment houses, accompanied by human voices that seem almost as mechanical as they. At night, along unlighted streets, one gives a wide berth to drunkards that sprawl out across the pavement from the shadow of darkened doors; and I have known a dead horse to be left in the road—two blocks from the principal post office and not much more from Borough Hall—with no effort made to remove it, for nearly three weeks."

Gothic as this glimpse is, the neighborhood nevertheless continued to possess, cheap rents aside, some certain appeal that brigades of the gifted—artists, writers—began to discover. Among those riding in on the initial wave was Hart Crane, whose poet's eye, focusing on his window view, produced *The Bridge*. Later, soon after the success of *Look Homeward, Angel*, Thomas Wolfe, noted prowler of the Brooklyn night, took quarters: an apartment, equipped with the most publicized icebox in literature's archives, which he maintained until his "overgrowed carcass" was carried home to the hills of Carolina. At one time, a stretch of years in the early forties, a single, heaven knows singular, house on Middagh Street boasted a roll call of residents that read: W. H. Auden, Richard Wright, Carson McCullers, Paul and Jane Bowles, the British composer Benjamin Britten, impresario and stage designer Oliver Smith, an authoress of murder entertainments—Miss Gypsy Rose Lee, and a Chimpanzee accompanied by Trainer. Each of the tenants in this ivory-tower boarding house contributed to its upkeep, lights, heat, the wages of a general cook (a former Cotton Club chorine), and all were present at the invitation of the owner, that very original editor, writer, *fantaisiste*, a gentleman with a guillotine tongue, yet benevolent and butter-hearted, the late, the justly lamented George Davis.

Now George is gone, and his house too; the necessities of some absurd civic project caused it to be torn down during the war. Indeed, the war years saw the neighborhood slide to its nadir. Many of the more substantial old houses were

requisitioned by the military, as lodgings, as jukebox can-
teens, and their rural-reared, piney-woods personnel treated
them quite as Sherman did those Dixie mansions. Not that it
mattered; not that anyone gave a damn. No one did; until,
soon after the war, the Heights commenced attracting a
bright new clientele, brave pioneers bringing brooms and
buckets of paint: urban, ambitious young couples, by and
large mid-rung in their Doctor-Lawyer-Wall Street-What-
ever careers, eager to restore to the Heights its shattered
qualities of circumspect, comfortable charm.

For them, the section had much to offer: roomy big houses
ready to be reconverted into private homes suitable for families of old-fashioned size; and such families are what these
young people either had made or were making at stepladder
rates. A good place to raise children, too, this neighborhood
where the traffic is cautious and the air has clarity, a seaside
tartness; where there are gardens for games, quiet stoops for
amusing; and where, above all, there is the Esplanade to
roller-skate upon. (Forbidden: still the brats do it.) While
far from being a butterflied meadow, the Esplanade, a wide
terrace-like walk overlooking the harbor, does its contemporary best to approximate that playing pasture of long-gone
girls and their brothers.

So, for a decade and longer, the experiment of reviving
the Heights has proceeded: to the point where one is tempted
to term it a *fait accompli*. Window boxes bloom with geraniums; according to the season, green foliated light falls
through the trees or gathered autumn leaves burn at the corner; flower-loaded wagons wheel by while the flower seller
sings his wares; in the dawn one occasionally hears a cock
crow, for there is a lady with a garden who keeps hens and
a rooster. On winter nights, when the wind brings the fare-

well callings of boats outward bound and carries across roof-tops the chimney smoke of evening fires, there is a sense, evanescent but authentic as the firelight's flicker, of time come circle, of ago's sweeter glimmerings recaptured.

Though I'd long been acquainted with the neighborhood, having now and then visited there, my closer association began two years ago when a friend bought a house on Willow Street. One mild May evening he asked me over to inspect it. I was most impressed; exceedingly envious. There were twenty-eight rooms, high-ceilinged, well proportioned, and twenty-eight workable marble-manteled fireplaces. There was a beautiful staircase floating upward in white, swan-simple curves to a skylight of sunny amber-gold glass. The floors were fine, the real thing, hard lustrous timber; and the walls! In 1820, when the house was built, men knew how to make walls—thick as a buffalo, immune to the mightiest cold, the meanest heat.

French doors led to a spacious rear porch reminiscent of Louisiana. A porch canopied, completely submerged, as though under a lake of leaves, by an ancient but admirably vigorous vine weighty with grapelike bunches of wisteria. Beyond, a garden: a tulip tree, a blossoming pear, a perched black-and-red bird bending a feathery branch of forsythia.

In the twilight, we talked, my friend and I. We sat on the porch consulting martinis—I urged him to have one more, another. It got to be quite late, he began to see my point: Yes, twenty-eight rooms *were* rather a lot; and yes, it seemed only *fair* that I should have some of them.

That is how I came to live in the yellow brick house on Willow Street.

Often a week passes without my "going to town," or "crossing the bridge," as neighbors call a trip to Manhattan.

Mystified friends, suspecting provincial stagnation, inquire, "But what do you *do* over there?" Let me tell you, life can be pretty exciting around here. Remember Colonel Rudolf Abel, the Russian secret agent, the biggest spy ever caught in America, head of the whole damned apparatus? Know where they nabbed him? Right here! smack on Fulton Street! Trapped him in a building between David Semple's fine-foods store and Frank Gambuzza's television-repair shop. Frank, grinning as though he'd done the job himself had his picture in *Life*; so did the waitress at the Music Box Bar, the colonel's favorite watering hole. A peevish few of us couldn't fathom why our pictures weren't in *Life* too. Frank, the Music Box Bar girl—they weren't the only people who knew the colonel. Such a gentleman-like gentleman: one would never have *supposed* ...

I confess, we don't catch spies every day. But most days are supplied with stimulants: in the harbor some exotic freighter to investigate; a bird of strange plumage resting among the wisteria; or, and how exhilarating an occurrence it is, a newly arrived shipment at Knapp's. Knapp's is a set of shops, really a series of storerooms resembling caverns, clustered together on Fulton near Pineapple Street. The proprietor—that is too modest a designation for so commanding a figure—the czar, the Aga Khan of these paradisaic emporiums is Mr. George Knapp, known to his friends as Father.

Father is a world traveler. Cards arrive: he is in Seville, now Copenhagen, now Milan, next week Manchester, everywhere and all the while on a gaudy spending spree. Buying: blue crockery from a Danish castle. Pink apothecary jars from an old London pharmacy. English brass, Barcelona lamps, Battersea boxes, French paperweights, Italian witch balls, Greek icons, Venetian blackamoors, Spanish saints,

Korean cabinets; and junk, glorious junk, a jumble of ragged dolls, broken buttons, a stuffed kangaroo, an aviary of owls under a great glass bell, the playing pieces of obsolete games, the paper moneys of defunct governments, an ivory umbrella cane *sans* umbrella, crested chamber pots and mustache mugs and irreparable clocks, cracked violins, a sundial that weighs seven hundred pounds, skulls, snake vertebrae, elephants' hoofs, sleigh bells and Eskimo carvings and mounted swordfish, medieval milkmaid stools, rusted firearms and flaking waltz-age mirrors.

Then Father comes home to Brooklyn, his treasures trailing after him. Uncrated, added to the already perilous clutter, the blackamoors prance in the marvelous gloom, the swordfish glide through the store's Atlantic-depth dusk. Eventually they will go: fancier *antiquaries*, and anonymous mere beauty lovers, will come, cart them away. Meanwhile, poke around. You're certain to find a plum; and it may be a peach. That paperweight—the one imprisoning a Baccarat dragonfly. If you want it, take it now: tomorrow, assuredly the day after, will see it on Fifty-seventh Street at quintuple the tariff.

Father has a partner, his wife Florence. She is from Panama, is handsome, fresh-colored and tall, trim enough to look well in the trousers she affects, a woman of proud posture and, vis-à-vis customers, of nearly eccentric curtness, take-it-or-go disdain—but then, poor soul, she is under the discipline of not being herself permitted to sell, even quote a price. Only Father, with his Macaulayan memory, his dazzling ability to immediately lay hold of any item in the dizzying maze, is so allowed. Brooklyn-born, waterfront-bred, always hatted and usually wearing a wet cold cigar, a stout, short, round powerhouse with one arm, with a strutting

walk, a rough-guy voice, shy nervous sensitive eyes that
blink when irritation makes him stutter, Father is nevertheless an aesthete. A tough aesthete who takes no guff, will not
quibble over his evaluations, just declares; "Put it down!"
and, "Get it Manhattan half the money, I give it yuh free."
They are an excellent couple, the Knapps. I explore their
museum several times a week, and toward October, when a
Franklin stove in the shape of a witch hut warms the air and
Florence serves cider accompanied by a damp delicious date-
nut bread she bakes in discarded coffee cans, never miss a day.
Occasionally, on these festive afternoons, Father will gaze
about him, blink-blink his eyes with vague disbelief, then, as
though his romantic accumulations were closing round him
in a manner menacing, observe: "I got to be crazy. Putting
my heart in a fruitcake business like this. And the *investment*.
The money alone! Honest, in your honest opinion, wouldn't
you say I'm crazy?"

Certainly not. If, however, Mrs. Cornelius Oosthuizen
were to beg the question—

It seems improbable that someone of Mrs. Oosthuizen's
elevation should have condescended to distinguish me with
her acquaintance. I owe it all to a pound of dog meat. What
happened was: the butcher's boy delivered a purchase of
mine which, by error, included hamburger meant to go to
Mrs. O. Recognizing her name on the order slip, and having
often remarked her house, a garnet-colored château in mood
remindful of the old Schwab mansion on Manhattan's River-
side Drive, I thought of taking round the package myself, not
dreaming to meet the fine lady, but, at most, ambitious for a
moment's glance into her fortunate preserve. Fortunate, for
it boasted, so I'd had confided to me, a butler and staff of six.
Not that this is the Height's sole *maison de luxe*: we are

blessed with several exponents of limousine life—but unarguably, Mrs. O. is *la regina di tutti*.

Approaching her property, I noticed a person in Persian lamb very vexedly punching the bell, pounding a brass knocker. "God damn you, Mabel," she said to the door; then turned, glared at me as I climbed the steps—a tall, intimidating replica of frail unforbidding Miss Marianne Moore (who, it may be recalled, is a Brooklyn lady too). Pale lashless eyes, razor lips, hair a silver fuzz. "Ah, *you*. I know you," she accused me, as behind her the door was opened by an Irish crone wearing an ankle-length apron. "So. I suppose you've come to sign the petition? Very good of you, I'm sure." Mumbling an explanation, muttering servile civilities, I conveyed the butcher's parcel from my hands to hers; she, as though I'd tossed her a rather rotten fish, dangled it gingerly until the maid remarked, "Ma'am, 'tis Miss Mary's meat the good lad's brought."

"Indeed. Then don't stand there, Mabel. Take it." And, regarding me with a lessening astonishment that I could not, in her behalf, reciprocate: "Wipe your boots, come in. We will discuss the petition. Mabel, send Murphy with some Bristol and biscuit. . . . Oh? At the dentist's! When I *asked* him *not* to tamper with that tooth. What hellish nonsense," she swore as we passed into a hatrack-vestibule. "Why didn't he go to the hypnotist, as I told him? Mary! Mary! Mary," she said when now appeared a friendly nice dog of cruel pedigree: a spaniel *cum* chow attached to the legs of a dachshund, "I believe Mabel has your lunch. Mabel, take Miss Mary to the kitchen. And we will have our biscuits in the Red Room."

The room, in which red could be discerned only in a bowl

of porcelain roses and a basket of marzipan strawberries, contained velvet-swagged windows that commanded a pulse-quickening prospect: sky, skyline, far away a wooded slice of Staten Island. In other respects, the room, a heavy confection, cumbersome, humorless, a hunk of Beidermeier pastry, did not recommend itself. "It was my grandmother's bedroom; my father preferred it as a parlor. Cornelius, Mr. Oosthuizen, died here. Very suddenly: while listening at the radio to the Roosevelt person. An attack. Brought on by anger and cigars. I'm sure you won't ask permission to smoke. Sit down . . . Not there. There, by the window. Now here, it *should* be here, somewhere, in this drawer? Could it be upstairs? Damn Murphy, horrid man always meddling with my— No, I have it: the petition."

The document stated, and objected to, the plans of a certain minor religious sect that had acquired a half-block of houses on the Heights which they planned to flatten and replace with a dormitory building for the benefit of their Believers. Appended to it were some dozen protesting signatures; the Misses Seeley had signed, and Mr. Arthur Veere Vinson, Mrs. K. Mackaye Brownlowe—descendants of the children in the meadow, the old-guard survivors of *their* neighborhood's evilest hours, those happy few who regularly attended Mrs. O.'s black-tie-sit-downs. She wasted no eloquence on the considerable merit of their complaint; simply, "Sign it," she ordered, a Lady Catherine de Bourgh instructing a Mr. Collins.

Sherry came; and with it an assembly of cats. Scarred battlers with leprous fur and punch-drunk eyes. Mrs. O., motioning toward the least respectable of these, a tiger-striped marauder, told me, "This is the one you may take home. He's been with us a month, we've put him in splendid condition, I'm sure you'll be devoted. Dogs? What *sort* of dogs have you? Well, I don't approve the pure breeds. Anyone will give *them* a home. I took Miss Mary off the street. And Lovely Louise, Mouse and Sweet William—my dogs, all my cats, too, came off the streets. Look below, there in the garden. Under the heaven tree. Those markings: graves are what you see, some as old as my childhood. The seashells are goldfish. The yellow coral, canaries. That white stone is a rabbit; that cross of pebbles: my favorite, the first Mary—angel girl, went bathing in the river and caught a fatal chill. I used to tease Cornelius, Mr. Oosthuizen, told him, ha-ha, told him I planned to put him there with the rest of my darlings. Ha-ha, he wasn't amused, not at all. So, I mean to say, your having dogs doesn't signify: Billy here has such spirit, *he* can hold his own. No, I insist you have him. For I can't keep him much longer, he's a disturbing influence; and if I let him loose, he'll run back to his bad old life in the St. George alley. I wouldn't want *that* on my conscience if I were you."

Her persuasions failed; in consequence our parting was cool. Yet at Christmas she sent me a card, a Cartier engraving of the heaven tree protecting the bones in its sad care. And once, encountering her at the bakery, where we both were buying brownies, we discussed the impudent disregard her petition had received: alas, the wreckers had wrecked, the brethren were building. On the same occasion, she shame-on-you informed me that Billy the cat, released from her patronage, had indeed returned to the sinful ways of the St. George alley.

The St. George alley, adjoining a small cinema, is a shad-

owy shelter for vagrants: wino derelicts wandered over the
bridge from Chinatown and the Bowery share it with other
orphaned, gone-wild creatures; cats, as many as minnows in
a stream, who gather in their greatest numbers toward nightfall; for then, as darkness happens, strange-eyed women, not
unlike those black-clothed fanatics who haunt the cat arenas
in Rome, go stealing through the alley with caressing hisses
and sacks of crumbled salmon. (Which isn't to suggest that
Mrs. O. is one who indulges in this somehow unhealthy
hobby: regarding animals, her actions, while perhaps a bit
overboard, are kindly meant, and not untypical of the
Heights, where a high percentage of the pet population has
been adopted off the streets. Astonishing, really, the amount
of lost strays who roam their way into the neighborhood, as
though instinct informed them they'd find someone here who
couldn't abide being followed through the rain, but would,
instead, lead them home, boil milk and call Dr. Wasserman,
Bernie, our smart-as-they-come young vet whose immaculate hospital resounds with the music of Bach concertos and
the barkings of mending beasts.)

Just now, in connection with these notes, I was hunting
through a hieroglyphic shambles I call my journal. Odd,
indeed the oddest, jottings—a majority of which conceal
from me their meanings. God knows what "Thunder on
Cobra Street" refers to. Or "A diarrhea of platitudes in seventeen tongues." Unless it is intended to describe a most tiresome local person, a linguist terribly talkative in many
languages though articulate in none. However, "Took T&G
to G&T" does make sense.

The first initials represent two friends, the latter a restaurant not far away. You must have heard of it, Gage &

Tollner. Like Kolb's and Antoine's in New Orleans, Gage &
Tollner is a last-century enterprise that has kept in large
degree its founding character. The shaky dance of its gaslight
chandeliers is not a period-piece hoax; nor do the good plain
marble-topped tables, the magnificent array of gold-edged
mirrors, seem sentimental affectations—rather, it is a testa-
ment to the seriousness of the proprietors, who have obliged
us by letting the place stay much as it was that opening day in
1874. One mightn't suppose it, for in the atmosphere there is
none of the briny falderal familiar to such aquariums, but the
specialty is sea food. The best. Chowders the doughtiest
down-Easter must approve. Lobsters that would appease
Nero. Myself, I am a soft-shelled-crab *aficionado*: a plate of
sautéed crabs, a halved lemon, a glass of chilled Chablis—
most satisfactory. The waiters, too, dignified but swift-to-
smile Negroes who take pride in their work, contribute to
the goodness of Gage & Tollner; on the sleeves of their very
laundered jackets they sport military-style chevrons awarded
according to the number of years each has served; and, *were*
this the Army, some would be generals.

Nearby, there is another restaurant, a fraction less distinguished, but of similar vintage and virtually the same menu:
Joe's—Joe being, by the way, an attractive young lady. On
the far fringes of the Heights, just before Brooklyn becomes
Brooklyn again, there is a street of Gypsies, with Gypsy
cafés (have your future foretold and be tattooed while sipping tankards of Moorish tea); there is also an Arab-Arme-
nian quarter sprinkled with spice-saturated restaurants where
one can buy, hot from the oven, a crusty sort of pancake
frosted with sesame seed—once in a while I carry mine down
to the waterfront, intending to share with the gulls; but gob-

bling as I go, none is ever left. On a summer's evening a stroll across the bridge, with cool winds singing through the steel shrouds, with stars moving about above and ships below, can be intoxicating, particularly if you are headed toward the roasting-pork, sweet-and-sour aromas of Chinatown.

Another journal notation reads: "At last a face in the ghost hotel!" Which means: after months of observation, in all climates at all hours, I'd sighted someone in a window of a haunted-seeming riverfront building that stands on Water Street at the foot of the Heights. A lonely hotel I often make the destination of my walks: because I think it romantic, in aggravated moments imagine retiring there, for it is as secluded as Mt. Athos, remoter than the Krak Chevalier in the mountains of wildest Syria. Daytimes the location, a dead-end Chiricoesque piazza facing the river, is little disturbed; at night, not at all: not a sound, except foghorns and a distant traffic whisper from the bridge which bulks above. Peace, and the shivering glow of gliding-by tugs and ferries.

The hotel is three-storied. Sunstruck scraps of reflected river-shine, and broken, jigsaw images of the bridge waver across the windows; but beyond the glass nothing stirs: the rooms, despite contradictory evidence, milk bottles on sills, a hat on a hook, unmade beds and burning bulbs, appear unoccupied: never a soul to be seen. Like the sailors of the *Marie Celeste*, the guests, hearing a knock, must have opened their doors to a stranger who swallowed them whole. Could it be, perhaps it *was*, the stranger himself that I saw?—"At last a face in the ghost hotel!" I glimpsed him just the once, one April afternoon one cloudless blue day; and he, a balding man in an undershirt, hurled up a window, flexed hairy arms, yawned hugely, hugely inhaled the river breeze—was gone.

No, on careful second thought, I will never set foot in that hotel. For I should either be devoured or have my mystery dispelled. As children we are sensitive to mystery: locked boxes, whisperings behind closed doors, the what-thing that lurks yonder in the trees, waits in every stretch between street lamps; but as we grow older all is too explainable, the capacity to invent pleasurable alarm recedes: too bad, a pity—throughout our lives we ought to believe in ghost hotels.

Close by the hotel begins a road that leads along the river. Silent miles of warehouses with shuttered wooden windows, docks resting on the water like sea spiders. From May through September, *la saison pour la plage*, these docks are diving boards for husky ragamuffins—while perfumed apes, potentates of the waterfront but once dock-divers themselves, cruise by steering two-toned (banana-tomato) car concoctions. Crane-carried tractors and cotton bales and unhappy cattle sway above the holds of ships bound for Bahia, for Bremen, for ports spelling their names in oriental calligraphy. Provided one has made waterfront friends, it is sometimes possible to board the freighters, carouse and sun yourself: you may even be asked to lunch—and I, for one, am always quick to accept, embarrassingly so if the hosts are Scandinavian: they always set a superior table from larders brimming with smoked "taste thrills" and iced aquavit. Avoid the Greek ships, however: very poor cuisine, no liquor served except ouzo, a sickly licorice syrup; and, at least in the opinion of this panhandler, the grub on French freighters by no means meets the standards one might reasonably expect.

The tugboat people are usually good for a cup of coffee, and in wintry weather, when the river is tossing surf, what joy to take refuge in a stove-heated tug cabin and thaw out with a mug of the blackest Java. Now and again along the route minuscule beaches occur, and once, it was around sunset on a quiet Sunday, I saw on one of them something that made me look twice, and twice more: still it seemed a vision. Every kind of sailor is common enough here, even saronged East Indians, even the giant Senegalese, their onyx arms afire with blue, with yellow tattooed flowers, with saucy torsos and garish *graffiti* (Je t'aime, Hard Luck, Mimi Chang, Adios Amigo). Runty Russians, too—one sees them about, flap-flapping in their pajama-like costumes. But the barefooted sailors on the beach, the three I saw reclining there, profiles set against the sundown, seemed mythical as mermen: more exactly, mermaids—for their hair, striped with albino streaks, was lady-length, a savage fiber falling to their shoulders; and in their ears gold rings glinted. Whether plenipotentiaries from the pearl-floored palace of Poseidon or mariners merely, Viking-tressed seamen out of the Gothic North languishing after a long and barberless voyage, they are included permanently in my memory's curio cabinet: an object to be revolved in the light that way and this, like those crystal lozenges with secretive carvings sealed inside.

After consideration, "Thunder on Cobra Street" does become decipherable. On the Heights there is no Cobra Street, though a street exists that suits the name, a steep downhill incline leading to a dark sector of the dockyards. Not a true part of the Heights neighborhood, it lies, like a serpent at the gates, on the outmost periphery. Seedy hangouts, beer-sour bars and bitter candy stores mingle among the eroding houses, the multifamily dwellings that architecturally range from time-blackened brownstone to magnified concepts of Mississippi privy.

Here, the gutters are acrawl with Cobras; that is, a gang

of "juvenile" delinquents: COBRA, the word is stamped on their sweat shirts, painted, sometimes in letters that shine with a fearful phosphorescence, across the backs of their leather jackets. The steep street is within their ugly estate, a bit of their "turf," as they term it; an infinitesimal bit, for the Cobras, a powerful cabala, cast owning eyes on acres of metropolitan terrain. I am not brave—*au contraire*; quite frankly, these fellows, may they be twelve years old or twenty, set my heart thumping like a sinner's at Sunday meeting. Nevertheless, when it has been a matter of convenience to pass through this section of their domain, I've compelled my nerves to accept the challenge.

On the last venture, and perhaps it will remain the last, I was carrying a good camera. The sun was unseen in a sky that ought to either rumble or rain. Rackety children played skip-rope, while a lamppost-lot of idle elders looked on, dull-faced and drooping: a denim-painted, cowboy-booted gathering of Cobras. Their eyes, their asleep sick insolent eyes, swerved on me as I climbed the street. I crossed to the opposite curb; then *knew*, without needing to verify it, that the Cobras had uncoiled and were sliding toward me. I heard them whistling; and the children hushed, the skip-rope ceased swishing. Someone—a pimpled purple-birthmark bandit-masked the lower half of his face—said, "Hey yuh, Whitey, lemmeseeduhcamra." Quicken one's step? Pretend not to hear? But every alternative seemed explosive. "Hey, Whitey, hey yuh, takemuhpitchawantcha?"

Thunder salvaged the moment. Thunder that rolled, crashed down the street like a truck out of control. We all looked up, a sky ripe for storm stared back. I shouted, "Rain! Rain!" and ran. Ran for the Heights, that safe citadel, that bourgeois bastion. Tore along the Esplanade—where the nice young mothers were racing their carriages against the coming disaster. Caught my breath under the thrashing leaves of troubled elms, rushed on: saw the flower-wagon man struggling with his thunder-frightened horse. Saw, twenty yards ahead, then ten, five, then none, the yellow house on Willow Street. Home! And happy to be.

Greek Paragraphs

(1968)

A FEW SUMMERS AGO ITALIAN FRIENDS invited me on a cruise through the Greek Islands aboard an especially graceful sailing yacht. We were to depart from Piraeus on a morning in July. The sea was calm, the ship sparkled, the captain and his crew awaited us in uniforms as white as the churches of Mykonos; and I was there, oh yes. Unfortunately, a sudden tragedy, a death in the family, had detained my hosts; but, though unable to meet me, they insisted I should proceed with the cruise. Just imagine!—a whole yacht at the disposal of one passenger. Only the nuttiest, richest, most selfish person could deliberately conceive such an adventure. However, as it had happened by accident, I felt neither guilt nor hesitation. *Avanti.*

Herewith, some notes from the voyage.

PEACHES

I dislike Greek wines; however, there is one unresinated white wine that is as dry and light as the best Italian soaves. It's called King Minos, and just now, sitting under the starlight on the afterdeck, I drank a half bottle of it while eating two enormous peaches. Peaches the size of cantaloupes and the color of cantaloupe meat. Peaches of a deliciously yielding texture and a juicy liqueur-like sweetness. And to think they are the product of a Greek island, these mountainous bits of sea-surrounded desert. One would not have thought they could grow such peaches in the greenest Persian garden, much less here on these sun-seared rocks. Yet it is true, for the cook bought them at Santorin, where we are harbored for the night.

The crew have gone ashore: up Up UP to Santorin village. Quite a climb, a matter of several thousand steps and dizzying views. I made it there this afternoon astride one of these fragile and courageous little fly-pestered donkeys, bless its put-upon heart. Felt very ashamed of myself, also was rump-sore, so returned afoot.

The sky, a bonfire of stars—as ablaze as the skies above the Sahara. The sway of caiques. The sway of moored caiques. Music from a harbor café. An ouzo-scented old man dancing in front of the café. The cool King Minos warming my veins, the taste of peaches lingering, the perfume of peach skins saturating the soft, salt-tart air.

MELTEMI

That cursed wind, the meltemi. Yesterday we were caught in one, an inevitable event on the summer seas of Greece, for the damn thing blasts about the whole of July and August. Some years ago I spent a summer in the Cyclades on the island of Paros, which is surely the meltemi's favored haunt: indeed, it seldom departs, but hurls around the island howling like the spectral voices of drowned sailors, centuries of sailors smashed against its shores.

It *is* an evil wind, scratchy, nerve-twisting. And look what it does to the economy, the diet of the islanders: when fishermen can't fish, as they can't when the meltemi roars, an islander's already sufficiently meager menu is reduced by half.

April is the finest month to visit here: fields of wild flowers, wild anemones, white violets, and the water, green as spring buds, is just warm enough for a brisk swim. April . . . or late September, when the water is still warm enough (if you don't object to sharing it with migrating geese who abruptly plunge from the heavens and swim along beside you), and the meltemi has stopped prowling.

But until yesterday I had never experienced one at sea. I was below when it arrived; even so I could hear it approaching across the water—a dark rippling feathery noise. The ship lurched, spun, fish peered into the portholes; it seemed the mast must crack: how close we all come to joining that complaining choir of drowned mariners! At dusk it died and we hurried to hide in a cove.

A TERRIBLE TALE

There are Yugoslavs in the crew, Greeks, mostly Italians. The captain is Italian. He doesn't much like the yacht because he doesn't like sailing yachts, not even that black pearl of the Aegean, Niarchos' *Creole*. He says they are romantic but too much work for the crew. He speaks English, speaks it well, and is a rather youngish man with dramatic eyes and a dark-toned voice; he might easily have been an actor, and all actors are liars, I've never met one that wasn't. But perhaps the captain is not a liar. Anyway, this morning we passed Delos, not stopping because I'd been there twice before, and a glimpse of the marble ruins drifting by in a shimmering lavender haze reminded him of a story. At lunch he told it to me. He swore it was true.

"This happened when I was a boy of seventeen, and in the crew of a yacht owned by an Englishman, Lord Sickle. Now, Lord Sickle often chartered his yacht, and in August of that year he chartered it to a beautiful Englishwoman: a widow, I would say forty, very tall, a tiny waist, so elegant. She had a son, a lad sixteen or so and also very beautiful and elegant. Crippled, however: a withered leg in a brace, and he walked with two canes. But a genius, this boy. A scholar. It was for his sake that the mother undertook a Greek cruise; he wanted to see the places he knew so well from his studies.

"They came aboard accompanied by a maid and a man-servant; otherwise they were alone, and I've often thought what a pity that was. Perhaps it wouldn't have happened if they had had friends with them.

"There was a strange island the boy wanted to visit. North of Delos. Yes, north. I can't remember precisely. It was an island of only a few acres and all but unknown; still, he knew of it and spoke of a well-preserved temple there.

"We arrived *aprés midi*, and because of the shallows, had to anchor more than a mile offshore. The boy was very excited. He had made up his mind to pack a supper and spend the night alone with his mother on the island; he wanted to see the temple by moonlight and sleep on the shore. The mother loved him very much. Too much. She laughed and ordered a picnic.

"It was I who rowed them there, set them ashore; and it was I who returned at dawn to collect them. The boy was dead, stripped to a skeleton; and the mother, whom I found wading in the water, was unrecognizable—fearfully muti-lated, half mad.

"Only months later, months spent in an Athens hospital, was she able to tell a court of inquiry what had happened. She said, 'At first it was very peaceful and lovely. We wan-dered around the temple until twilight, then spread our supper on a flight of steps; my son Eric said oh, look, it's going to be a full moon. We could see the lights of the yacht riding far out—I wished we had kept the sailor with us. Because, as the moon thickened, brightened, somehow I mistrusted the landscape. And gradually I became aware of a sound. Claws. An icy scuttling. And a huge brown rat, another and another, leapt with tearing teeth into our pic-nic. A horde of rats pouring out of the temple, hundreds flailing in the moonlight. Eric screamed; he tried to run and fell, and I had to drag him by the arms, but the rats were at us, all over us, they even swam after us into the water, pulled

Eric back onto the beach, and no one heard me the whole
night I bled and screamed and cried there in the sea.' "

The captain lit a cigar. "This woman is still alive. She lives
in Nice. I've seen her—sitting in a chaise on the promenade.
She wears a full veil. I'm told she never speaks to anyone."

OBSERVATIONS

1) Numerous educated Greek men share a snobbish affec-
tation—obsessed by their fingernails, they pamper them
ceaselessly, letting the nails on either little finger grow to
Dragon Lady length. This is to let the lesser folk know that
they work with their heads, not their hands. 2) Greek businessmen also share an eccentric hobby: playing with ropes
of amber or ivory beads, their nervous fingers twitching
from bead to bead, rubbing, counting. This conduct is said
to relieve the pressure of affairs and prevent ulcers. 3) And
what most Greeks, male or female, have in common are
medical superstitions. The humblest village has a vendor
who sells small replicas, stamped from sheets of polished tin,
of hands, hearts, feet, ears, eyes. If, say, you are recovering
from a coronary, why, you simply acquire a tin heart, carry
it on your person, and presently the actual ailing organ will
have magically healed itself. The True Believers are not
limited to peasants and middle-class housewives, but includes
many intellectuals. Once, when I was living on Paros, I
mentioned to a Professor Calliope, a linguist of great renown,
that my father was virtually blind and that I myself had a
considerable fear of failing eyesight. He bought me a pair of
tin eyes, and insisted we walk, through curtains of quivering
August heat, to a nunnery in the mountains where there

resided a remarkable abbess endowed with witch-powers: once she had blessed my medals, my worries were over. At the monastery I was made to feel like a missionary captive in some perilous Hottentot village: the nuns, very unused to visitors, gathered around me, all giggling and poking and pinching—really pinching, as if to judge how juicy I'd be when put to boil. But soon the professor had them calmed down and we were served cool water and a crystal candy that smelled of roses and contained inside each piece a roseleaf. As for the abbess—we were too late: she had died the week before.

A BLUE COVE

The only scenery that bores me is any that I can't imagine purchasing a part of: usually, if a place provides the slightest uplift, I instantly consider buying or building a house. The hundreds of properties I've constructed mentally! But now something serious has occurred. For the past few days we've been cruising around Rhodes, lingering a lot at the perfect little bay of Lindos. An American acquaintance who has a house above Lindos took me to see something he thinks I should own. I think so too. It is a small stone farmhouse situated inside a horseshoe-shaped cove; the beach is a sandy confection, and the water, being entirely protected, tranquil as a sapphire winking in a jeweler's window. It could be mine for three thousand dollars: an investment of another five or six would put the house in delicious order. It is a prospect that sizzles the imagination.

At night I think, Yes I will, but in the morning I recall—politics, old mortality, inconvenient emotional commitments, the impossibilities of the Greek tongue, a trillion difficulties. Still, I ought to have the courage; I'll never again find anything quite as ideal as that.

AT A CAFÉ

I left the yacht at Rhodes, and this morning flew to Athens. Now at not quite midnight am sitting alone in an outdoor café on Constitution Square. There are not many patrons, though I recognize one of them as someone I'd seen years ago in Tangier, where she was quite the Queen of the Casbah (Southern Belle Version): Eugenia Bankhead, Tallulah's even more voluble sister. She is arguing with a Negro companion.

Come to consider, many of the world-trampers who used to hang around Tangier now frequent Athens. Across the street from where I sit I see every conceivable breed of hustler, from muscled dockhands to plump Egyptian lovelies wearing wavy platinum wigs.

It is very hot, and the ubiquitous white dust of Athens mists the air, coats the street and my tabletop like the pale rough crust on a bilious tongue. I am remembering the stone house in the blue cove, But that is all I will ever do, Remember it.

The Muses
Are Heard

(1956)

When the Cannons
Are Silent

(*Part 1*)

❖

ON SATURDAY, THE SEVENTEENTH OF DECEMBER, 1955, a foggy wet day in West Berlin, the cast of the American production of *Porgy and Bess* and others associated with the company, a total of ninety-four persons, were asked to assemble at the company's rehearsal hall for a "briefing" to be conducted by Mr. Walter N. Walmsley, Jr., and Mr. Roye L. Lowry, respectively Counsel and Second Secretary of the American Embassy in Moscow. Mr. Walmsley and Mr. Lowry had traveled from Moscow expressly to advise and answer any questions members of the production might have concerning their forthcoming appearance in Leningrad and Moscow.

This trip to Russia, the first of its kind ever attempted by an American theatrical group, was to be the culmination of a four-year world tour for *Porgy and Bess*. It had come about after many months of complicated, in some areas still beclouded, negotiation between the U.S.S.R. and the producers of the Gershwin opera, Robert Breen and Blevins Davis, who operate under the name Everyman Opera, Incorporated.

Although the Russians had not yet delivered their actual visas, the enormous troupe, consisting of fifty-eight actors, seven backstage personnel, two conductors, assorted wives and office workers, six children and their schoolteacher, three journalists, two dogs and one psychiatrist, were all set to depart within the next forty-eight hours, traveling by train from East Berlin via Warsaw and Moscow to Leningrad, a distance of some eleven hundred miles, yet requiring, apparently, three days and nights.

On my way to the diplomatic briefing, I shared a taxi with Mrs. Ira Gershwin and a square-cut, muscular man called Jerry Laws, who was formerly a boxer and is presently a singer. Mrs. Gershwin is of course the wife of the lyricist, who, aside from being the brother of its composer, is himself co-author of *Porgy and Bess*. Periodically, for the past four years, she has left her husband at home in Beverly Hills to accompany the opera on its around-the-world wanderings: "Ira's such a stick-in-the-mud. He hates to go from one room to the next. But I'm a gypsy, darling. I love wheels." Known to her friends as Lee, an abbreviation of Lenore, she is a small and fragile woman devoted to diamonds, and wears them, quite a few, at both breakfast and dinner. She has sun-streaked hair and a heart-shaped face. The flighty fragments of her conversation, delivered in a girlish voice that rushes along in an unsecretive whisper, are pasted together with terms of endearment.

"Oh, love," she said, as we rode through the dark drizzle along the Kurfurstendam, "have you heard about the Christmas tree? The Russians are giving us a Christmas tree. In Leningrad. I think that's so sweet of them. Since they don't *believe* in Christmas. They don't—do they, darling? Anyway, their Christmas comes much later. Because they have a different calendar. Darling, do you think it's true?"

"About whether they believe in Christmas?" said Jerry Laws.

"*No*, love," said Mrs. Gershwin impatiently. "About the microphones. And the photographs."

For several days there had been speculation among the company on the subject of personal privacy in Russia. It was based on the rumor that their letters would be censored, their hotel rooms wired and the walls encrusted with concealed cameras.

After a thoughtful moment, Laws said, "I believe it."

"Oh, darling, you don't!" Mrs. Gershwin protested. "It can't be true! After all, *where* are we going to gossip? Unless we simply stand in the bathroom and keep flushing. As for the cameras—"

"I believe that, too," said Laws.

Mrs. Gershwin settled into a musing silence until we reached the street where the rehearsal hall was located. Then, rather wistfully, she said, "I *still* think it's nice about the Christmas tree."

We were five minutes late, and had difficulty in finding seats among the folding chairs that had been set up at one end of the mirrored rehearsal hall. It was crowded and the room was well heated; nevertheless many of those present, as though they could feel already the cold winds of the steppes, sat bundled in the paraphernalia, the scarves and woolly coats, they'd specially acquired for their Russian journey. A competitive spirit had pervaded the purchasing of these outfits, of which more than several had a certain Eskimo-look.

The meeting was called to order by Robert Breen. In addition to being the co-producer of *Porgy and Bess*, he is also its director. After he'd introduced the representatives from the Moscow Embassy, Mr. Walmsley and Mr. Lowry, who were seated behind a table facing us, Mr. Walmsley, a stocky middle-aged man with a Mencken-style haircut and a dry, drawling manner, began by speaking of the "unique opportunity" the proposed tour offered and congratulating the company in advance on the "great success" he was sure they would have behind the iron curtain.

"Since nothing happens in the Soviet Union that isn't planned, and since it is *planned* that you should have a success there, I feel perfectly safe in congratulating you now."

As though sensing a faultiness in his colleague's presumed compliment, Mr. Lowry, a youngish man with the strait-laced façade of a schoolmaster, interposed to suggest that while what Mr. Walmsley had said was perfectly correct, it was also true that there was "a genuine excitement in Russia about your coming there. They know the Gershwin music. In fact, a Russian acquaintance of mine told me he was at a party the other night where three friends of his sang 'Bess, You Is My Woman Now' all the way through."

The cast smiled appreciatively, and Mr. Walmsley resumed. "Yes, there are some nice Russians. Very nice people. But they have a bad government," he said, in slow spelling-it-out tones. "You must always bear in mind that their system of government is basically hostile to our own. It is a system, with rules and regulations, such as you have never experienced before. Certainly in my experience, which is a long one, I've never encountered anything like it."

A member of the cast, John McCurry, raised his hand to ask a question. McCurry plays the villainous part of Crown, and is, in his own appearance, high and heavy and somewhat forbidding, as befits the role. He wanted to know, "Suppose some of these people invite us into their home? See, most places we go, people do that. Now, is it all right for us to go?"

The two diplomats exchanged an amused glance. "As you may well imagine," said Mr. Walmsley, "we at the Embassy have never been bothered with that problem. We're never invited *any*where. Except officially. I can't say *you* won't be. And if so, by all means take advantage of the opportunity. From what I understand," he continued, "your hosts plan an extensive program of entertainment. Something every minute. Enough to wear you out."

Some of the youngsters smacked their lips at this prospect, but one of them complained, "I don't touch a drop of nothing. So when they're making all these toasts we've heard about, how do I get out of it gracefully?"

Mr. Walmsley shrugged. "You don't have to drink if you don't want to."

"Sure, man," the worried one was advised by a friend, "nobody's got to drink what they don't want to. And what you don't want, you hand to me."

Now the questions came quickly. The parents, for instance, were concerned about their children. Would there be pasteurized milk? Yes. Still, Mr. Lowry thought it advisable to take a supply of Starlac, which is what he fed his own two children. And the water, was it fit to drink? Perfectly safe.

Mr. Walmsley often drank it from the tap. How does one address a Soviet citizen? "Well," said Mr. Walmsley, "I *wouldn't* call them Comrade. Mr. and Mrs. will do." What about shopping, was it expensive? "Outrageously," but it hardly mattered, since there was nothing much to buy anyway. How cold did it get? Oh, it *could* occasionally go to thirty-two below zero. In that case, would their hotel room be warm? Yes, indeed. Overheated, actually.

When these fundamentals had been gone through, a voice from the back raised itself to say, "There's been so much myth talk around here. We heard we're going to be trailed all the time."

"Trailed?" Mr. Walmsley smiled. "Perhaps. Though not in the manner you're thinking of. If they assign anyone to follow you, it will be for your own protection. You must, you see, expect to attract extraordinary attention, crowds wherever you go. It won't be like walking down a street in Berlin. For that reason you may be followed, yes."

"After all," said Mr. Lowry, "the Ministry of Culture has been so anxious to have you come there that you will probably receive very generous treatment, free of the niggling-naggling that a stray foreign visitor might expect."

The voice from the back persisted, somewhat in a key of disappointment, "We heard they were going to trail us. And open our letters."

"Ah," said Mr. Walmsley, "*that* is another matter. Something you take for granted. I always assume my letters have been opened."

His audience shifted in their chairs, their eyes swerving with I-told-you-so's. Robert Breen's secretary, Nancy Ryan, stood up. Miss Ryan (Radcliffe '52) had been with the company three months, having taken the job because of an interest in the theatre. A New Yorker, she is blond, very blue-eyed, tall, just under six feet in fact, and bears considerable resemblance to her mother, an often-photographed and celebrated beauty, Mrs. William Rhinelander Stewart. She wanted to make a suggestion. "Mr. Walmsley, if it's true our letters will be censored, then wouldn't it be better to do all our correspondence on postcards? I mean, if they didn't have to open it to read it, wouldn't that cause less of a delay in outgoing mail?"

Mr. Walmsley seemed not to think Miss Ryan's plan had much merit, as either a time-saving or trouble-saving device. Meanwhile, Mrs. Gershwin had been urging Jerry Laws into action. "Go on, darling. Ask him about the microphones."

Laws caught the diplomat's attention. "A lot of us," he said, "we've been worried about the possibility of wire-tapping in our rooms."

Mr. Walmsley nodded. "I should say it's more than a possibility. Again, it's the sort of thing you should assume. Of course, no one really *knows*."

There was a silent pause, during which Mrs. Gershwin, plucking at a diamond brooch, seemed to wait for Jerry Laws to bring up the matter of concealed cameras, but he hadn't the chance before McCurry regained the floor.

McCurry leaned forward, hunching his burly shoulders. He said he thought it was about time they stopped beating around the bush and came to grips with "the big problem. The big problem is, now what do we say when they ask us political stuff? I'm speaking of the Negro situation."

McCurry's deep voice made the question ride across the room like a wave, collecting as it went the complete interest of the audience. Mr. Walmsley hesitated, as though uncertain whether to ride over it or swim under; at all events, he seemed not prepared to meet it head on.

"You don't have to answer political questions, any more than they would answer questions of that nature put to them by you." Walmsley cleared his throat, and added, "It's all dangerous ground. Treading on eggs."

Mutterings in the audience indicated that they felt the diplomat's advice was inadequate. Lowry whispered in Walmsley's ear, and McCurry consulted his wife, a melancholy woman who was sitting beside him with their three-year-old daughter on her lap. Then McCurry said, "But they're bound to ask us about the Negro situation. They always do. Last year we were in Yugoslavia, and all the time we were there—"

"Yes, I know," said Walmsley peremptorily. "That's what this whole thing is about. That's the point, isn't it?"

Walmsley's statement, or possibly the manner in which it was made, seemed to rub several people the wrong way; and Jerry Laws, a legend in the company for his fighting quick temper, jumped to his feet, his body stiff with tension. "Then how do we handle it? Should we answer it the way it is? Tell the truth? Or do you want us to gloss it over?"

Walmsley blinked. He took off a pair of hornrimmed glasses and polished them with a handkerchief. "Why, tell the truth," he said. "Believe me, sir, the Russians know as much about the Negro situation as you do. And they don't give a damn one way or another. Except for statements, propaganda, anything they can turn to their own interests. I think you ought to keep in mind that any interviews you give will be picked up by the American press and reprinted in your home-town newspapers."

A woman, the first who had spoken, rose from her seat in the front row. "We all know there's discrimination back home," she said in a shy voice to which everyone listened respectfully. "But in the last eight years Negroes have made a lot of progress. We've come a long way and that's the truth. We can point with pride to our scientists, artists. If we did that [in Russia], it might do a lot of good."

Others agreed, and addressed the group in a similar vein. Willem Van Loon, a Russian-speaking son of the late historian, and one of the persons handling publicity for Everyman Opera, announced that he was "very, very glad this matter is being gone into so thoroughly. The other day I had a couple of the cast taping an interview for the American Service stations here in Germany, and touching on this point, this racial question, I knew we had to be very, very careful, because of being so near to East Berlin and the possibility of our being monitored—"

"Of course," said Walmsley, quietly interrupting. "I suppose you realize that we're being monitored right now."

Clearly Van Loon had not, nor had anyone else, to judge from the general consternation and gazing-round to see who could be the cause of Walmsley's remark. But any evidence, at least in the shape of mysterious strangers, was not apparent. Van Loon, however, didn't finish what he'd intended saying. His voice trailed away, as did the meeting itself, which shortly came to a meandering conclusion. Both of the diplomats blushed when the company thanked them with applause.

"Thank you," said Walmsley. "It's been a great pleasure to talk to you. Mr. Lowry and I don't often get into contact with the atmosphere of grease paint."

The director, Robert Breen, then called his cast to

rehearsal, but before it began, there was much milling about and swapping of opinions on the "briefing." Jerry Laws restricted himself to one word, "Uninformative." Mrs. Gershwin, on the contrary, seemed to have found it too informative. "I'm stunned, darling. Think of living like that! Always assuming. Never *knowing*. Seriously, darling, where are we going to gossip?"

Downstairs, I was offered a return ride to the hotel by Warner Watson, production assistant to Mr. Breen. He introduced me to Dr. Fabian Schupper, who also shared the taxi. Dr. Schupper is an American student at the German Psychoanalytic Institute. I was told he'd been invited on the Russian tour to counteract any "stresses" members of the company might experience. At the last moment, much to his disappointment, Dr. Schupper did not actually go, the management having decided that a psychiatrist was perhaps, after all, not necessary; though the fact that psychoanalysis and its practitioners are not welcome in the Soviet Union may well have been a contributing cause. But at the moment, in the taxi, he was advising Warner Watson to "relax."

Watson, lighting a cigarette with hands that trembled noticeably, said, "Relaxed people do *not* get productions like this played on the samovar circuit."

Watson is in his late thirties. He has a graying crew-cut, and timid, resigned brown eyes. There is about his face, and his manner too, a blurred gentleness, a beyond-his-years fatigue. At one time an actor, he has been associated with Everyman Opera since its inception in 1952. In his job, he is primarily concerned with what he calls "fencing things in." During the past two weeks in Berlin, he'd very nearly taken up residence at the Soviet Embassy, attempting to get a few things fenced in. Despite these efforts, there remained a

multiplicity of matters that had escaped corralling. Among
them, there was the situation over the company's passports,
which, at this late date, were still lurking in Russian hands
waiting to be visaed. Then, too, Watson was encountering
trouble on the subject of the train by which the troupe was
to travel to Leningrad. The production had requested four
sleeping cars. The Russians had replied, quite flatly, that
they could only supply three second-class cars with "soft-
bed" (the Russian term for sleeping berth) accommodations.
These, together with a baggage car and a car for the show's
scenery, would be attached to The Blue Express, a regularly
scheduled Soviet train running between East Berlin and Moscow. Watson's difficulty was that he could not obtain from
the Russians a plan of the "soft-bed" cars, and so was unable
to chart out sleeping arrangements. He therefore imagined
on the train a slapstick *Walpurgisnacht:* "More bodies than
berths." He'd also not been able to learn at what hotels in
either Leningrad or Moscow the troupe would be staying,
and other details of that nature. "They'll never tell you the
whole thing about anything. Not all at once. If they tell you
A, they *might* tell you B, but between the two there's a long,
long wait."

Apparently, though, the Russians themselves did not practice the same patience they required of others. Some hours
earlier a cable had arrived from Moscow that Watson counted
among the causes for his trembling hands. UNLESS ORCHESTRA-
TIONS DELIVERED EMBASSY BERLIN TONIGHT WILL POSTPONE
LENINGRAD OPENING REDUCE FEE. The Soviets had for weeks
been demanding the orchestrations because they wanted
their musicians to rehearse in advance of the company's
arrival. Breen, fearing the orchestrations, his only copy,
might be lost in transit, had refused to comply. But this ulti-

matum cable, with its two dire last words, seemed to have changed his mind, and now Watson was on his way to deliver the orchestrations to the Soviet Embassy.

"Don't worry," said Watson, wiping beads of moisture from his upper lip. "*I'm* not worried. We're going to get all this fenced in."

"Relax," said Dr. Schupper.

Back at my hotel, the Kempenski, where many of the company were staying, I stopped by Breen's suite to see his wife, Wilva. She'd just returned from an overnight flight to Brussels, where she'd gone to consult a doctor. For some while twinges of appendicitis had been troubling her, and when, the day before, she'd flown to Brussels, it was with the knowledge that she might have to undergo an immediate operation, thereby canceling her part in the trip to Russia. The previous October she'd spent ten days in Moscow discussing arrangements for the tour with the Ministry of Culture, a "fascinating" experience that had made her anxious to return.

"It's all right, the doctor says I can go. I didn't know how much I wanted to until I thought I couldn't," she said, smiling the smile that seems less an expression than a circumstance of her eager, her anxious-to-please personality. Mrs. Breen has dimples and large brown eyes. Her hair, a maple color, is worn upswept and held in place by huge pins that could serve as weapons. At the moment she was wearing a dress of purple wool, the color that dominates her wardrobe: "Robert's mad for purple." She and Breen met at the University of Minnesota, where both were graduate students in the drama department. They have been married eighteen years. Though Mrs. Breen has played professionally on the stage, once as Shakespeare's Juliet, her real devotions, in the words of one of their associates, are to "Robert and Robert's career. If she could find enough paper, she'd wrap up the world and hand it to him."

On the surface of it, a shortage of paper would not appear to be one of Mrs. Breen's problems, for she lives with a traveling mountain of letters and clippings and files. The international correspondence for Everyman Opera is among her principal responsibilities; that, and seeing that the company is "kept happy." In the latter role, she'd brought back from Brussels a parcel of toys to be distributed among the children of the cast at Christmas time in Leningrad. "*If* I can get them away from Robert long enough to pack them again," she said, pointing to a bathroom where an armada of mechanical boats floated in a filled tub. "Robert's mad for toys. Really," she sighed, "it's dreadful to think of getting all *this* into suitcases." Several of the objects on view, in the bedroom and in the living room which doubled as an office, presented obvious packing difficulties, especially a large see-saw-like apparatus known as a Relaxer Board. "I don't see why I can't take it to Russia. I've taken it everywhere else. It does me a world of good."

Mrs. Breen asked if I were looking forward to boarding The Blue Express, and was exaggeratedly pleased to hear that I was. "Oh, Robert and I wouldn't miss this train ride for the world! Everybody in the cast is so darling. I know it's going to be the kind of fun you'll never stop talking about. But," she said, with a sudden sorrow in her voice that sounded not altogether sincere, "Robert and I have decided to go by plane. Of course we'll see you off at the station here —and be right there on the platform when you pull into Leningrad. At least I *hope* we will. Only I can't believe it.

That it's really going to happen." She paused; for an instant a frown marred her immaculate enthusiasm. "Someday I'll tell you the real story behind it all. The people who didn't want this to happen! Oh, we've had such blows." She struck her breast. "Real body blows. And they're still coming. Right up to the last minute," she said, glancing at a sheaf of cables on a desk.

A few of the Breens' tribulations were already common knowledge. For instance, it seemed an accepted fact, in the rumor and publicity surrounding the Soviet venture, that the Russians had, on their own initiative, and out of a Geneva-spirit impulse, invited *Porgy and Bess* to tour their country. The truth of the matter is, Everyman Opera had invited itself. Breen, having long considered a trip to Russia the logical extension of his company's "good will" travels, sat down and wrote a letter to the Soviet Premier, Marshal Bulganin, saying, in effect, that *Porgy and Bess* would be pleased to undertake the journey if the U.S.S.R. was willing to have them. The appeal must have impressed Bulganin favorably, for he forwarded the letter to the Ministry of Culture, the government monopoly which, under the direction of Nikolai Mikhailov, controls every facet of artistic life inside the Soviet Union. Theatre, music, films, publishing, painting, each of these activities comes under the specific, not always lenient, supervision of the Ministry of Culture, whose headquarters are in Moscow. Therefore, with the implied blessings of Bulganin, the Ministry began negotiations with Everyman Opera, though to do so could not have been a casual decision. Casual, say, as the decisions might have been in the case of the Comédie Française, whose company had appeared in Moscow a year earlier, or a British production of *Hamlet*, which had been given a Moscow première in the autumn of 1955. Both of these troupes had enjoyed whole-hearted success. But from any point of view, whether that of the visiting artists or their hosts, the risks involved were merely aesthetic. Molière and Shakespeare do not lend themselves to the intentions of modern political propaganda.

The same cannot be said of *Porgy and Bess*. Here, either side of the curtain, American or Soviet, had much to concern them, for the Gershwin opera, when slipped under the dialectical microscope, proves a test tube brimming with the kind of bacteria to which the present Russian regime is most allergic. It is extremely erotic, a serious cause for dismay in a nation with laws so prim, persons can be arrested for kissing in public. It is God-fearing; over and again it stresses the necessity of faith in a world above the stars rather than below, demonstrates in song and dialogue the comforts to be derived from religious belief ("the opium of the people"). Furthermore, it discourses, in an uncritical vein, on the subject of superstition, i.e., "The Buzzard Song." As if this weren't anathema enough, it also sings out loud that people can be happy with plenty of nothin', an unwelcome message indeed.

Certainly the Ministry of Culture must have taken these drawbacks into account, and then reflected that, though the pill was definitely there, at least it was sugar-coated. After all, and despite its accent on folkish fun, the situation of the American Negro as depicted in *Porgy and Bess*, an exploited race at the mercy of ruthless Southern whites, poverty-pinched and segregated in the ghetto of Catfish Row, could not be more agreeably imagined if the Ministry of Culture had assigned one of their own writers to the job. And so, midsummer of 1955, the Ministry informed Everyman Opera they were prepared to roll out the red carpet.

Assured of a welcome in Russia, Breen then faced the problem of getting there, and that required money, an estimated $150,000. The first newspaper announcements of the Russian "invitation" to *Porgy and Bess* more or less suggested that the American State Department would not only be the spiritual heart of this "unprecedented project," as Breen occasionally called it, but would also provide its financial backbone. Breen believed so, and with good reason. Over the last several years the State Department had received universal praise for its moral and financial sponsoring of *Porgy and Bess*, which *The New York Times*, among others, frequently summarized as the "best ambassador" the State Department had ever sent abroad. But Breen soon discovered, after a series of pleading trips to Washington, that he could no longer rely on the patronage of his Potomac friends. Apparently they thought his project too unprecedented, or, in their own phrase, "politically premature." In other words, not one cent.

In New York, theatrical circles theorized that the State Department had withdrawn its support because they feared the opera too vulnerable to the purposes of Soviet propaganda. Defenders of the enterprise considered this attitude nonsensical. In their opinion, the fact that such social-critical aspects as the opera contained could be freely presented in the American theatre counteracted the possibilities of effective propaganda on that score. A further argument was that in Russia the very presence of the Negro cast, their affluent appearance, their so obviously unoppressed outspokenness, their educated, even worldly manner ("Why," said Mrs. Breen, "some of our cast speak three and four languages. Perfectly") would impress on the Russian people a different image of the American Negro from the stereotype that continues to make Harriet Beecher Stowe one of the Soviet's best-selling authors.

Variety, the theatrical trade paper, reported as rumor a more straightforward explanation for the State Department's reversal. According to them, the International Exchange Program, a branch of the American National Theatre and Academy (ANTA), whose advice on theatrical matters carries great weight in Washington, had registered opposition on the grounds that the State Department had already spent enough money on *Porgy and Bess*, and that the funds at their disposal should be more evenly spread to allow a larger catalogue of events in cultural exchange.

Nonetheless, ANTA and the State Department wished Everyman Opera the best of luck. They were not disowning, simply disinheriting. But well-wishers added little to Breen's bank account, and as he pondered the possibilities of raising the needed amount of private subscription, there was an unexpected development. The Russians stepped forward and offered to pick up the tab themselves. While the feeblest linguist could translate the meaning of this gesture, designed, as it was, to embarrass the State Department, American partisans of Breen's venture welcomed it for the very reason it was offered. They felt it would shame Washington into taking a less miserly position. They were mistaken.

Consequently, with time growing short, Breen had the choice of abandoning his plan or permitting the Soviet to capitalize it. A contract, dated December 3, 1955, was drawn up in Moscow between the Ministry of Culture of the U.S.S.R. ("designated hereinafter under the name of the 'Ministry' ") and Everyman Opera, Inc. ("hereinafter under the name of the 'Company' "). The contract consists of three and a half closely typed pages, and contains several quaint items—the Ministry agrees to supply a Russian member of the cast, namely, "one domesticated she-goat." But the burden of it is set forth in Article 5. When the writhings of language in this long clause are disentangled, it emerges that during their stay in the Soviet Union, the company would receive weekly payments of $16,000, a figure quite below their customary fee, especially so since the payments were to be made half "in U. S. Dollars in a bank check in New York, the remainder in cash Rubles at the official rate." (As everyone knows, the official rate is an arbitrary four rubles to the dollar. Opinion wavers on what a fair exchange would be, but on the Moscow black market it is possible to get ten to one, and if a person were willing to take a chance on transporting currency out of the country, thereby risking Siberian detention, he could obtain in Switzerland only one dollar for every fifteen rubles.) In addition to these monetary agreements Article 5 also promised that the Ministry would supply the Company with: "Free lodging and food in first-class hotels or, when traveling, with sleeper accommodations and food in a dining car. Furthermore, it is understood and agreed that the Ministry pay all expenses for traveling of all members of the Company and the transportation of its scenic equipment to and through the Soviet Union and back to a European border of the Soviet Union."

All told, the Russians were investing approximately $150,000. This should not be construed as cultural philanthropy. Actually, for them it was a sound business proposition. If every performance sold out, as was almost certain to happen, the Ministry would double its investment, that is, have a total box-office gross the equivalent of $300,000. Whereas, on the basis of the Ministry-Company contract, and by applying the laws of income versus operating cost, it could be calculated that Everyman Opera would lose around $4,000 a week. Presumably Breen had devised a formula for sustaining such a loss. "But don't ask *me* what it is, darling," said Mrs. Gershwin. "It's an absolute mystery."

While Mrs. Breen was still on the theme of "body blows," her husband returned from the studio where he'd been rehearsing the cast after the diplomatic briefing. She asked him if he'd like a drink. He said he would, very much. Straight brandy, please.

Breen is around forty-five, a man of medium height. He has an excellent figure, and one is kept aware of it by the fit of his clothes, for he is partial to trim Eisenhower jackets and those close-cut, narrow-legged trousers known as frontier pants. He wears custom-made shirts, preferably in the colors black and purple. He has thinning blond hair and is seldom indoors or out without a black beret. Depending on the expression, whether solemn or smiling, his face, pale and with a smoothly gaunt bone structure, suggests altogether opposite personalities. In the solemn moments, which can last hours, his face presents a mask of brooding aloofness, as though he were posing for a photographer who had warned him not to move a muscle. Inevitably, one is reminded that Breen, like his wife, has acted Shakespeare—and that the part was Hamlet, which he played in a production that, soon after the war, toured Europe and was even staged at Elsinore itself. But when Breen relaxes, or when something succeeds in catching his interest, he has a complete physical altering in the direction of extreme liveliness and boyish grinning good humor. A shyness, a vulnerable, gullible look replaces the remote and seeming self-assurance. The dual nature of Breen's appearance may explain why an Everyman Opera employee could complain in one breath, "You never know where you stand with Mr. Breen," and say in the next, "Anybody can take advantage of him. He's just too kind."

Breen took a swallow of brandy and beckoned me into the bathroom, where he wanted to demonstrate how one of the toy boats operated. It was a tin canoe with a windup Indian that paddled. "Isn't that wonderful?" he said, as the Indian paddled back and forth across the tub. "Did you ever see anything like that?" He has an actor's trained voice, "placed" in a register so very deep that it makes for automatic pomposity, and as he speaks his manicured hands move with his words, not in an excitable, Latin style, but in a gracefully slow ritualistic manner, rather as though he were saying Mass. Indeed, Breen's earliest ambitions *were* ecclesiastical. Before his interest turned toward the stage, he spent a year training to become a priest.

I asked him how the rehearsal had gone. "Well, it's a good cast," he said. "But they're a little spoiled, they take it too much for granted. Curtain calls and ovations. Rave reviews. I keep telling them, I want them to understand going to Russia isn't just another engagement. We've got to be the best we've ever been."

If Breen expected the wish contained in this last sentence to come true, then, in the estimation of some observers, he had his work cut out for him. In 1952, when Breen and his co-producer, Blevins Davis, revived the Gershwin opera, which had been a box-office and somewhat of a critical failure in its original (1935) Theatre Guild presentation, the program listed William Warfield as Porgy, Leontyne Price as Bess, and Cab Calloway in the role of Sportin' Life. Since then, these stars had been replaced, and even their replacements replaced, not always with artists of comparable quality. To maintain a high level in performance of any long-run production, doubly so if the show is on tour where the strain of overnight hops, the dreamlike flow of rooms and restaurants, the electric emotional climate surrounding groups who continuously live and work together, are factors creating an accumulative fatigue that the show often reflects. Horst Kuegler, a Berlin theatre critic who, when he'd reviewed *Porgy and Bess* three years earlier (it was then appearing in Germany as part of the Berlin Music Festival), had been so enthusiastic he'd gone to see it five times, now felt, seeing it again, that it was "still full of energy and charm, though the production has deteriorated greatly." For the past week, Breen had rehearsed his cast to the limit Actors Equity permits; but whether or not the show could be whipped into prime shape, Breen had no qualms about its reception at the Leningrad première. It was going to be a "bombshell"! The Russians would be "stunned"! And, what was an unarguable prediction, "They'll never have seen anything like it!"

As Breen was finishing his brandy, his wife called from the next room, "You'd better get ready, Robert. They'll be here at six, and I've reserved a private dining room."

"Four Russians from the Embassy," Breen explained, showing me to the door. "They're coming over for dinner. You know, get friendly. It's friendship that counts."

When I arrived back in my own room in the Kempenski, I found waiting on my bed a large package wrapped in plain brown paper. My name was on it, the name of the hotel and the number of my room, but nothing to identify the sender. Inside, there were half a dozen thick anti-Communist pamphlets, and a handwritten card, without signature, which said, *Dear Sir—You can be saved.* Saved, one presumed, from the fates described in the accompanying literature, most of which purported to be the case histories of individuals, primarily Germans, who had gone behind the iron curtain, either voluntarily or as the result of force, and had not been heard from again. It was absorbing, as only case histories can be, and I would have read through the lot uninterruptedly if the telephone hadn't rung.

The caller was Breen's secretary, Nancy Ryan. "Listen," she said, "how would you like to sleep with me? On the train, I mean. The way it works out, there are going to be four in a compartment, so I'm afraid we'll have to do as the Russians do. They always put boys and girls together. *Anyway*, I'm helping assign the berths, and what with all the affections and frictions and those who want to be together and those who definitely do *not*, well, really, it's *frightening*. So it would simplify the situation if you and I shared a compartment with the lovebirds."

The so-called "lovebirds" were Earl Bruce Jackson, one of three alternates in the role of Sportin' Life, and Helen Thigpen, a soprano who plays the part of Serena. Jackson and Miss Thigpen had been engaged for many months. According to Everyman Opera's publicity releases, they planned to be married in Moscow.

I told Miss Ryan the arrangement sounded satisfactory. "That's brilliant," she said. "Well, see you on the train. If our visas ever come through . . ."

On Monday, the nineteenth of December, passports and visas were still in abeyance. Regardless, around three o'clock that afternoon a trio of chartered buses began circling through Berlin to collect, from the hotels and pensions where they were staying, the personnel of Everyman Opera and transport them to the railway station in East Berlin where the Soviet train, The Blue Express, was scheduled to depart at four or six or midnight, no one seemed to know for certain.

A small group, spoken of by Warner Watson as "our distinguished guests," waited together in the lobby of the Hotel Kempenski. The distinguished quests were persons who had no direct connection with *Porgy and Bess*, but had, nevertheless, been invited by the management to travel with the troupe into Russia. They amounted to: Herman Sartorius, a New York financier and close friend of Breen's; a newspaper columnist, Leonard Lyons, who was described to the Soviets in Everyman Opera's official dossier as "Company Historian," neglecting to mention that he would be mailing his history to the *New York Post*; another journalist, a Pulitzer Prize winner, Ira Wolfert, accompanied by his wife, Helen. Mr. Wolfert is on the staff of the *Reader's Digest*, and the Breens, who keep extensive scrapbooks, hoped he would do an article on their Russian adventures for that publication. Mrs. Wolfert is also an author, a poet. "A *modern* poet," she emphasized.

Mr. Lyons paced the lobby, impatient for the bus to arrive. "I'm excited. I can't sleep. Just before I left New York, Abe Burrows called me up. We live in the same building. He said you know how cold it is in Moscow? He heard on the radio it was forty below. That was day before yesterday. You got on your long underwear?" He hiked up his trouser leg to flash a stretch of red wool. Ordinarily a trim-looking man of average size, Lyon had so well prepared himself for the cold that, resplendent in a fur hat and fur-lined coat and gloves and shoes, he seemed to bulge like a shoplifter. "My wife, Sylvia, bought me three pairs of these. From Saks. They don't itch."

The financier, Herman Sartorius, attired in a conservative

topcoat and business suit, as though he were setting off for Wall Street, said that no, he was not wearing long underwear. "I didn't have time to buy anything. Except a map. Did you ever try to buy a road map of Russia? Well, it's the damnedest thing. Had to turn New York upside down before I found one. Good to have on the train. Know where we are."

Lyons agreed. "But," he said, lowering his voice, and with his alert black eyes snapping from side to side, "better keep it out of sight. They might not like it. A map."

"Hmn," said Sartorius, as though he could not quite follow the drift of Lyons' thought. "Yes, well, I'll keep that in mind." Sartorius has gray hair, a height, a weight, a gentlemanly reserve that inspire the kind of confidence desirable in a financier.

"I had a letter from a friend," continued Lyons. "President Truman. He wrote me I'd better be careful in Russia because he was no longer in any position to bail me out. Russia! What a dateline!" he said, glancing around as if hunting some evidence that his elation was shared by the others.

Mrs. Wolfert said, "I'm hungry."

Her husband patted her on the shoulder. The Wolferts, who are the parents of grown children, resemble each other in that both have pink cheeks and silvering hair, a long-married, settled-down calm. "That's all right, Helen," he said, between puffs on a pipe. "Soon as we get on the train, we'll go right to the dining car."

"Sure," said Lyons. "Caviar and vodka."

Nancy Ryan came racing through the lobby, her blond hair flying, her coat flapping. "Don't stop me! There's a crisis!" She stopped, of course; and, rather as though she enjoyed imparting the bad news, said, "*Now* they tell us! Ten minutes before we leave! That there *isn't* a dining car on the train. And there *won't* be, not until we reach the Russian border. Thirty hours!"

"I'm hungry," said Mrs. Wolfert plaintively.

Miss Ryan hurried onward. "We're doing the best we can." By which she meant the management of Everyman Opera were out scouring the delicatessens of Berlin.

It was turning dark, a rain-mist was sifting through the streets when the bus arrived, and with a joking, shouting full load of passengers, rumbled off through West Berlin toward the Brandenburg Gate, where the Communist world begins.

In the bus I sat behind a couple, a young pretty member of the cast and an emaciated youth who was supposed to be a West German journalist. They had met in a Berlin jazz cellar, presumably he had fallen in love, at any rate he was now seeing her off, amid whispers and tears and soft laughter. As we neared the Brandenburg Gate, he protested that he must get off the bus. "It would be dangerous for me to go into East Berlin." Which, in retrospect, was an interesting remark. Because several weeks later who should turn up in Russia, grinning and swaggering and with no plausible explanation of how he'd got there, but this selfsame young man, still claiming to be a West German and a journalist and in love.

Beyond the Brandenburg Gate, we rode for forty minutes through the blackened acres of bombed-out East Berlin. The two additional buses, with the rest of the company, had arrived at the station before us. We joined the others on the platform where The Blue Express waited. Mrs. Gershwin was there, supervising the loading of her luggage onto the train. She was wearing a nutria coat and, over her arm, carried a mink coat zippered into a plastic bag. "Oh, the mink's

for Russia, darling. Darling," he said, "why do they call it
The Blue Express? When it's not blue at all?"

It was green, a sleek collection of dark green cars hitched
to a diesel engine. The letters CCCP were painted in yellow
on the side of each car, and below them, in different languages, the train's cities of destination: Berlin-Warsaw-
Moscow. Soviet train officers, elegantly turned out in black
Persian lamb hats and flaring princess-cut coats, were stationed at the entrances to every car. Sleeping-car attendants,
more humbly dressed, stood beside them. Both the officers
and the attendants were smoking cigarettes in long vamp-
style holders. As they watched the confusion around them,
the excited milling about of the troupe, they managed to
preserve a stony uninterest despite the bold attentions of
those Americans who approached and stared at them as
though amazed, and rather peeved, to discover Russians had
two eyes correctly located.

A man from the cast walked over to one of the officers.
"Tell me something, kid," he said, indicating the lettering on
the side of the train, "what's that mean, CCCP?"

The Russian pointed his cigarette holder at the man.
Frowning, he said, "*Sie sind Deutsch?*"

The actor laughed. "I'd make a kind of funny-looking
German. Seems to me I would."

A second Russian, a car attendant, spoke up. "*Sind sie nicht
Deutsch?*"

"Man," said the actor, "let's us settle this misery." He
glanced down the platform and beckoned to Robin Joachim,
a young Russian-speaking New Yorker whom Everyman
Opera had hired to go along on the trip as a translator.

The two Russians smiled with pleasure when Joachim began to talk to them in their own language; pleasure gave way to astonishment as he explained that the passengers boarding their train were not Germans, but "Amerikansky" on their way to perform an opera in Leningrad and Moscow.

"Isn't that peculiar?" said Joachim, turning to a group of listeners that included Leonard Lyons. "Nobody told them a thing about us being on the train. They never heard of *Porgy and Bess*."

Lyons, the first of the Americans to recover from the shock of this news, whipped out a notebook and pencil. "Well, what do they think? What's their reaction?"

"Oh," said Joachim, "they couldn't be happier. They're delirious with joy."

It was true that the Russians were nodding and laughing. The officer gave the attendant a hearty slap on the back and shouted an order.

"What did he say?" asked Lyons, pencil poised.

Joachim said, "He told him to go put some tea on the samovar."

A station clock said six-five. There were signs of departure, whistle sounds, a clanging of doors. In the corridors of the train a radio began blaring martial music, and the company, now all aboard, were hanging out the windows waving at dispirited German luggage porters, none of whom had received the "capitalist insult," as we'd been warned the People's Democracies consider it, of a tip. Suddenly, at every window, a cheer went up. It was for the Breens, Robert and Wilva, who were plunging along the platform, followed by a wagonload of food supplies, cardboard cases of beer and wine, frankfurters, rolls and sweet buns, cold cuts, apples and oranges. There was only time to carry the cases onto the train before the radio's military fanfare reached a crescendo, and the Breens, watching with brave parental smiles, saw their "unprecedented project" slide away from them into the night.

The space to which I'd been assigned was in Car 2, Compartment 6. It seemed larger than an ordinary *wagon-lit* compartment, and had a certain prettiness about it, despite the presence of a radio loudspeaker that could not be completely turned off, and a blue light bulb, burning in a blue ceiling, that could never be extinguished. The walls were blue, the window was framed with blue plush curtains which matched the seat upholstery. There was a small table between the seats, and on it a lamp with a rosy silk shade.

Miss Ryan introduced me to our companions in Compartment 6, Earl Bruce Jackson and his fiancée, Helen Thigpen, whom I'd not met before.

Jackson is tall and lean, a live-wire with slanting eyes and a saturnine face. He affects a chin goatee, and his hands are radiant with rings, diamonds and sapphires and rubies. We shook hands. "Peace, brother, peace. That's the word," he said, and resumed peeling an orange, letting the hulls drop on the floor.

"No, Earl," said Miss Ryan, "that's *not* the word. The word is, keep things tidy. Put your orange hulls in the ashtray. After all," she said, looking out the window where the lonely last lights of East Berlin were fading, "this is going to be our home for a hell-uva long time."

"That's right, Earl. Our home," said Miss Thigpen.

"Peace, brother, peace. That's the word. Tell the boys back in New York," said Jackson, and spit out some seed.

Miss Ryan began to distribute part of the last-minute picnic the Breens had provided. With a sigh, Miss Thigpen
refused a bottle of beer and a salami sandwich. "I don't know
what I'll eat. There's nothing goes with my diet. Since I met
Earl, I went on a diet and lost fifty-six pounds. Five table-
spoons of caviar add up to one hundred calories."

"*This* isn't caviar. For God's sake," said Miss Ryan, her
mouth full of salami sandwich.

"I'm thinking of the future," said Miss Thigpen glumly.
She yawned. "Anybody object if I slip into my negligee?
Might as well make ourselves comfortable."

Miss Thigpen, a concert artist before she joined *Porgy and
Bess* four years ago, is a small, plump woman, lavishly pow-
dered. She wears the highest heels, the tallest hats, and generous sprinklings of Joy ("The World's Costliest Perfume").

"Hi there, good-lookin'," said Jackson, admiring his
fiancée's efforts to make herself comfortable. "The number
to play is seven seven three, and peace is the word.
Ooble-ee-do!"

Miss Thigpen ignored these compliments. "Earl," she said,
"it *was* São Paulo, honey?"

"Was what?"

"Was where we got engaged."

"Yeah. São Paulo. Brazil."

Miss Thigpen seemed relieved. "That's what I told Mr.
Lyons. He wanted to know. He's the one writes for the
paper. You met him?"

"Yeah," said Jackson. "I rubbed palms with that cat."

"Maybe you heard?" said Miss Thigpen, looking at me.
"About us being married in Moscow. 'Twas Earl's idea. I
didn't even know we were engaged. I lost fifty-six pounds,

but I didn't know we were engaged until Earl had this idea about us being married in Moscow."

"Bound to be a big story," said Jackson, and though he snapped his glittering fingers, his tone was serious, slow, as though thinking long throughts. "The first couple of Negro Americans married in Moscow. That's front page. That's TV." He turned to Miss Thigpen. "And I don't want you to go telling that cat Lyons anything about it. Not till we're sure the magnetic vibrations are right. With a big thing like this, you got to feel the right vibrations."

Miss Thigpen said, "You ought to see Earl's wedding suit. He had it made in Munich."

"Crazy, man, crazy," said Jackson. "Brown tails with champagne satin lapels. Shoes to match, natch. And on top of that, I've got a brand-new overcoat with a—how d'ya call it —Persian lamb collar. But man, nobody's going to see *none* of it, not till The Day."

I asked when that would be, and Jackson admitted that no exact date had been set. "Mr. Breen's handling all the arrangements. He's talking to the Russians. It'll be a big thing for them, too."

"Sure," said Miss Ryan, retrieving orange hulls off the floor. "Put Russia on the map."

Miss Thigpen stretched out in her negligee and prepared to study a musical score; but she seemed troubled, unable to concentrate. "What bothers me, it won't be legal. Back home, in several states, they don't consider it legal, people married in Russia."

"*What* states?" said Jackson, as though resuming with her a tedious argument.

Miss Thigpen thought. "Several," she said finally.

"It's legal in Washington, D.C.," he told her. "And that's your hometown. So if it's legal in your hometown, what have you got to worry about?"

"Earl," said Miss Thigpen wearily, "why don't you go find your friends and have a game of Tonk?"

Tonk, popular with some elements among the cast, is a five-card variation of ordinary rummy. Jackson complained that it was useless for him to try getting up a game. "There's nowhere for us to play. All the sharps [gamblers] are bunked in with a lot of squares [non-gamblers]."

The door of our compartment was open, and Ducky James, a boyish, blond Englishman who is prop man for the production, passed by, announcing, in his Cockney accent, "Anybody wants a drink, we've set up a bar in our place. Martinis . . . Manhattans . . . Scotch . . ."

"That Ducky!" said Miss Thigpen. "If *he's* not the lucky one! I don't wonder he's handing out drinks. You know what happened to him? Just before we got on the train along comes this telegram. His aunt died. Leaving him ninety thousand pounds."

Jackson whistled. "How much is that in real money?"

"Two hundred and seventy thousand dollars, thereabouts," said Miss Thigpen. Then, as her future husband stood up to leave the compartment, "Where you going, Earl?"

"Just thought I'd find out if Ducky plays Tonk."

Presently we had a visit from Twerp, an all-white boxer puppy who gaily trotted into the compartment and promptly proved herself unhousebroken. She belonged to the company's wardrobe mistress, a young woman from Brooklyn named Marilyn Putnam. Miss Putnam appeared, calling,

"Twerp! Twerp! Oh, *there* you are, you little bitch. Isn't she a little bitch?"

"Yes," said Miss Ryan, down on her hands and knees scrubbing at the carpet with wadded newspaper. "We have to live in here. For God's sake."

"The Russians don't mind," said Miss Putnam defensively. She scooped up her puppy and kissed its forehead. "Twerp's been being naughty up and down the corridor—haven't you, angel? The Russians just smile. *They* understand she's only a baby." She turned to leave and almost collided at the door with a girl who stood there crying. "Why, Delirious," she said to the girl, "darling, what's the matter—are you sick?"

The girl shook her head. Her chin trembled, her large eyes quivered with fresh tears.

"Delirious, honey, don't take on so," said Miss Thigpen. "Sit down. Say what's wrong."

The girl sat down. Her name was Dolores Swann; but like many of the cast, she had acquired a nickname, in this case the descriptive Delirious. A singer in the chorus, she has red poodle-cut hair. Her pale gold face is as round as her eyes, and has the same quality of show-girl innocence. She swallowed and wailed, "I lost both my coats. Both of them. My fur coat and the blue one, too. I left them back there in the station. Not insured or anything."

Miss Thigpen clucked her tongue. "Only *you* could do a thing like that, Delirious."

"But it wasn't my fault," said Miss Swann. "I was so scared. You see, I got left behind. I missed the bus. And it was terrible, running around trying to find a taxi to take me to the station. Because none of them wanted to go to *East* Berlin. Well, finally this man spoke English and he felt sorry for me and he said he would. Well, it was terrible. Because police kept stopping us and asking questions and wanting to see papers and, oh—I was sure I was going to be left there in the pitch-black with police and Communists and what-all. I was sure I'd never see any of you again."

The reliving of her ordeal brought on more tears. Miss Ryan poured her a brandy, and Miss Thigpen squeezed her hand, saying, "It's all right, honey."

"But you can imagine how I felt, how relieved I was when I got to the station—and there everybody was. You hadn't left without me. I wanted to hug everybody. I put down my coats to hug Ducky. I hugged Ducky and forgot about my coats. Until just now."

"Think of it like this, Delirious," said Miss Thigpen, as though searching for a comforting phrase, "just remember, you're the only person who ever went to Russia without a coat."

"I know a more unique claim that we can *all* make," said Miss Ryan. "Not only unique, but nuts. I mean, here we are —rattling off to Russia without our passports. No passports, no visa, no nothin'."

Half an hour later Miss Ryan's claim became less valid, for when the train stopped at Frankfurt-am-Oder, which marks the German-Polish border, a delegation of officials boarded the train and, quite literally, dumped the company's long-absent passports into Warner Watson's lap.

"I don't understand it," said Watson, parading through the train delivering the passports to their individual owners. "This very morning the Russian Embassy told me the passports had gone to Moscow. Now they suddenly turn up at the Polish border."

Miss Ryan quickly riffled through her passport and found blankness on those pages where the Russian visa should have been stamped. "For God's sake, Warner. There's nothing here."

"They've issued a collective visa. They have, or they're going to, don't ask me which," said Watson, his timid, tired voice skidding to a hoarse whisper. His skin was gray, and under his eyes purple bruises of fatigue were prominent as paint.

"But Warner . . ."

Watson held up a protesting hand. "I'm not human," he said. "I've got to go to bed. I'm going to go to bed and stay there until we get to Leningrad."

"Well, it's a pity," said Miss Ryan as Watson fled, "a damned shame we can't have a stamp in our passports. I like souvenirs."

The train was scheduled to stay at the border forty minutes. I decided to get off and look around. At the end of the car, I found the exit door open and started down the small iron steps leading onto the tracks. Far ahead I could see the lights of a station, and a misty red lantern swinging back and forth. But it was dark where I was, except for the yellow squares cast by the train's windows. I walked along the tracks, liking the fresh feel of the cold and wondering whether I was in Germany or Poland. Suddenly I noticed figures running toward me, a set of shadows that, drawing nearer, turned into three soldiers, pale flat-faced men with awkward ankle-length coats and bayoneted rifles strapped to their shoulders. They stared at me in silence. Then one of them pointed to the train; he grunted and motioned for me to get back on it. We marched along together, the four of us, and I said in English that I was sorry, I hadn't realized passengers were not allowed off the train. There was no response, merely another grunt and an urging forward. I climbed the train steps and turned to wave at them. They didn't wave back.

"Darling, you haven't been *out*," said Mrs. Gershwin, whose compartment I passed in returning. "Well, you shouldn't. It isn't safe." Mrs. Gershwin was one of the two people occupying compartments to themselves. (The other was Leonard Lyons, who had obtained privacy by threatening to leave the train unless his erstwhile roommates, Herman Sartorius and Warner Watson, were removed. "It's nothing personal," he said, "but I'm a working man. I've got to turn out a thousand words a day. I can't write with a lot of characters sitting around." Sartorius and Watson had therefore been forced to move in with the Ira Wolferts. As for Mrs. Gershwin, she'd been allotted her solo status because, in the view of the management, "She deserves it. She's a Gershwin.") Without discarding her diamonds, Mrs. Gershwin had changed into slacks and a sweater; she'd tied ribbons in her hair and slippered her feet in bits of fluff. "It must have been freezing out there. I see snow on the ground. You ought to have some hot tea. Mmmmm, it's lovely," she said, sipping dark, almost black tea from a tall glass set in a silver holder with a silver handle. "That darling little man is brewing it on his samovar."

I went to look for the tea-maker, who was the attendant for Car 2; but when I found him, at the end of the corridor, he was contending with more than a blazing samovar. Twerp, the boxer puppy, was yapping between his legs and snapping at his trousers. Moreover, he was undergoing an intense interview, Lyons asking the questions and Robin Joachim acting as translator. Small and haggard, the Russian had a pushed-in, Pekingese face creased with wrinkles that seemed to indicate nutritional defects rather than age. His mouth was studded with steel teeth, and his eyelids drooped, as though he were on the verge of sleep. Between dispensing tea and fending off Twerp, he answered Lyons' quick-fire queries like a wilted housewife talking to the censor. He said he was from Smolensk. He said his feet hurt him, his back hurt him, that he always had a headache from overwork. He said he only made two hundred rubles a month ($50, but much less in actual buying power) and considered himself underpaid. He said yes, he'd very much appreciate a tip.

Lyons paused in his note-taking and said, "I didn't know they were allowed to complain like this. The way it sounds, I get the impression this guy is a discontent."

The attendant gave me my tea, and at the same time offered me, from a crumpled pack, one of his own cigarettes. It was two-thirds filter and one-third tobacco, good for seven or eight harsh puffs, though I didn't enjoy that many, for as I started back to my compartment the train lurched forward with an abruptness that sent both tea and cigarette flying.

Marilyn Putnam poked her head into the corridor. "Holy mackerel," she said, surveying the wreckage, "did *Twerp* do that?"

In Compartment 6 the berths had been made for the night, indeed for the whole journey, since they were never remade. Clean coarse linen, a crunchy pillow that smelled of hay, a single thin blanket. Miss Ryan and Miss Thigpen had gone to bed to read, having first turned the radio as low as it would go and opened the window a finger's width.

Miss Thigpen yawned, and asked me, "Did you see Earl, honey?"

I told her that I had. "He's teaching Ducky to play Tonk."

"Oh," said Miss Thigpen, giggling sleepily, "that means Earl won't be home till dawn."

I kicked off my shoes, and lay down in my berth, thinking in a moment I'd finish undressing. Overhead, in the berth above mine, I could hear Miss Ryan muttering to herself, as though she were reading aloud. It developed that she was studying Russian, using for the purpose an old English-Russian phrase book the U. S. Army had issued during the war for the benefit of American soldiers who might come in contact with Russians.

"Nancy," said Miss Thigpen, like a child asking for a bedtime story, "Nancy, say us something in Russian."

"The only thing I've learned is *Awr-ga-nih-ya raneen . . .*" Miss Ryan faltered. She took a deep breath ". . . *V-pa-lavih-yee*. Wow! I only wanted to learn the alphabet. So I can read street signs."

"But that was nice, Nancy. What does it mean?"

"It means, 'I have been wounded in the privates.' "

"Really, Nancy," said Miss Thigpen, bewildered, "why on earth would you care to memorize something like that?"

"Go to sleep," said Miss Ryan, turning off her reading light.

Miss Thigpen yawned again. She pulled the covers up to her chin. "I'm about ready to."

Soon, lying there, I had a sense of stillness traveling

through the train, seeping through the cars like the wintry color of the blue light bulb. Frost was spreading at the corners of the window; it seemed like a web-weaving in reverse. On the muted radio an orchestra of balalaikas made shivery music; like an odd and lonely counterpoint, someone somewhere nearby was playing a harmonica.

"Listen," whispered Miss Thigpen, calling attention to the harmonica. "That's Junior," she said, meaning Junior Mignatt, a member of the cast still in his teens. "Don't you know that boy is lonesome? He's from Panama. He's never seen snow before."

"Go to sleep," said Miss Ryan. The northern roar of wind at the window seemed to echo her command. The train shrieked into a tunnel. For me, fallen asleep fully clothed, the tunnel lasted all night long.

Coldness woke me. Snow was blowing through the window's opening. Enough had settled at the foot of my berth to scoop into a snowball. I got up, glad I'd gone to bed with my clothes on, and closed the window. It was blurred with ice. I rubbed a part of it until I could peer out. There were hints of sunrise on the rim of the sky, yet it was skill dark, and the traces of morning color were like goldfish swimming in ink. We were on the outskirts of a city. Rural lamplighted houses gave way to cement blocks of forlorn, lookalike apartment dwellings. The train rumbled over a bridge that spanned a street; below, a frail streetcar, jammed with people on their way to work, careened round a curve like a rickety bobsled. Moments later we pulled into a station, which by now I realized must be Warsaw. On a dim, snowdeep platform gangs of men stood clustered together stamping their feet and slapping their ears. I noticed our car attendant, the tea-maker, join one of the groups. He gestured toward the train and said something that made them laugh. An explosion of breath-smoke filled the air. Still laughing, several of the men approached the train. I slipped back into bed, for it was obvious that they intended to peek in the windows. One after another, distorted faces mashed themselves against the glass. Presently I heard a short scream. It came from a compartment further ahead and sounded like Dolores Swann. Screams were understandable if she'd wakened to see, looming at the window, one of these frosty masks. Though it roused none of my own companions, I waited, expecting a commotion in the car, but quietness resumed, except for Twerp, who started barking with a regular rhythm that sent me off to sleep again.

At ten, when I opened my eyes, we were in a wild, crystal world of frozen rivers and snowfields. Here and there, like printing on paper, stretches of fir trees interrupted the whiteness. Flights of crows seemed to skate on a sky hard and shiny as ice.

"Man," said Earl Bruce Jackson, just awake and sleepily scratching himself as he stared out the window. "I'm telling you. They don't grow oranges here."

The washroom in Car 2 was a bleak, unheated chamber. There was a rusty washbasin with the customary two faucets, hot and cold. Unfortunately, they both leaked a frigid trickle. That first morning a long queue of men waited at the washroom door, toothbrushes in one hand, shaving tackle in the other. Ducky James had the notion of asking the attendant, who was busily stoking the little coal fire under his samovar, to part with some of his tea water and "give us blokes a chance at a decent shave." Everyone thought this a splendid idea except the Russian, for when the request was translated to him, he looked at his samovar as though it were bubbling with melted diamonds. Then he did a curious thing.

He stepped up to each man and brushed his fingertips against their cheeks, examining their beard stubble. There was a tenderness in the action that made it memorable. "Boy," said Ducky James, "he sure is affectionate."

But the attendant concluded his researches with a head-shake. Absolute no, *nyet*, he would not give away his hot water. The condition of the gentlemen's beards did not justify such a sacrifice, and besides, when traveling, the "realistic" man should expect to go unshaven. "My water is for tea," he said. "Hot and sweet and good for the spirit."

A steaming glass of it went with me into the washroom. I used it for brushing my teeth, and then, combining it with soap, transformed it into a shaving cream. Rather sticky, but not bad at all.

Afterwards, feeling spruce, I commenced a round of visits. The occupant of Compartment 1, Leonard Lyons, was having a professional tête-à-tête with Earl Bruce Jackson. Clearly Jackson had overcome his fear that Lyons might not possess the "right vibrations," for he was describing to him the details of his forthcoming Moscow marriage.

"That's great. Just great, Earl," said Lyons, scribbling away. "Brown tails. Champagne satin lapels. Now—who's going to be your best man?"

Jackson told him he'd invited Warner Watson to serve in that capacity. Lyons seemed reluctant to approve the choice. "Listen," he said, tapping Jackson on the knee, "did you ever think of asking somebody, well, important?"

"Like you, you mean?"

"Like *Khrushchev*," said Lyons. "Like *Bulganin*."

Jackson's eyes narrowed, as though he couldn't decide whether Lyons' suggestion was serious or a leg pull. "But I already ask Warner. But maybe, under that kind of circumstance . . ."

"Sure," said Lyons, "Warner would understand."

Still, Jackson had one last vestige of doubt. "You think Mr. Breen can arrange it, to get me one of those cats?"

"He could try," said Lyons. "And just trying, see, that could land you on the front page."

"*C'est* ooble-ee-do," said Jackson, gazing at Lyons with perfect admiration. "Really crazy, man. Gone."

Further along the corridor, I called on the Wolferts, who were sharing their compartment with Herman Sartorius and Warner Watson, the pair Lyons had evicted, the latter in more ways than one. But Watson was still asleep, unaware of his impending dismissal as Jackson's best man. Sartorius and Ira Wolfert were sitting with an immense map spread across their collective lap, and Mrs. Wolfert, bundled in a fur coat, was hunched over a manuscript. I asked if she were keeping a journal.

"I *do*. Only this is a poem. I've been working on it since last January. I thought I might finish it on the train. But the way I feel . . ." she said dismally. "I didn't sleep a wink last night. My hands are cold. My head's whirling with impressions. I don't know where I am."

Sartorius placed a fastidious finger on his map. "I'll tell you where we are. We've passed Lidice. Now we've got about five more hours of Poland before Brest Litovsk."

Brest Litovsk was to be the first stop in Russia. A good deal was scheduled to happen there. The wheels of the train would be changed to fit Russia's wide-gauge tracks; a dining car would be attached, and, most importantly, representatives from the Ministry of Culture were to meet the company and travel on with them to Leningrad.

"Know what this reminds me of," said Ira Wolfert, pointing a pipe at the severe landscape. "Parts of America. The West."

Sartorius nodded. "Wyoming in the winter."

Returning to the corridor, I encountered Miss Ryan, still wearing her bed costume, a red flannel nightshirt. She was hopping on one foot, her other foot having made contact with a sample of Twerp's misbehavior.

I said, "Good morning."

She said, "*Don't speak to me*," and hopped away toward the washroom.

Next, I went to Car 3, where the family groups, children and their parents, were installed. School had just let out; that is, the children had finished their morning lessons and were consequently in sportive spirit. Paper planes sailed through the air. Caricatures were being finger-drawn on the frosted windows. The Russian attendant, who looked even more mournful and harassed than his colleague in Car 2, was kept at such a hop protecting Soviet property that he hadn't noticed what was happening to his samovar. Two little boys had taken it over and were roasting hot dogs. One of them, Davy Bey, offered me a bite. "Good, huh?" I told him it was indeed. Well, he said, if I liked it that much, then I could have the rest of it; he'd already eaten fifteen.

"You see the wolves?" he asked.

An older friend, Gail Barnes, told him, "Stop making stories, Davy. They weren't wolves. They were plain dogs."

"Was wolves," said Davy, who has a snub nose and a wicked tilt to his eyes. "Everybody saw them. Out the window. They *looked* like dogs. Police dogs, only littler. And what they were up to, they were chasing each other round and round in the snow. Like they were having a grand time. I coulda killed one dead. Woooooolves," he howled, and poked me in the stomach with a cowboy pistol.

Gail said that she hoped I understood. "Davy's only a child." Gail, whose father, Irving Barnes, alternates in the role of Porgy, is eleven, the oldest of the company's six children, most of whom play minor parts in the show. Because of her seniority, she has developed a sense of big-sister responsibility toward all the children, and handles them with mature good nature, a firm politeness that could set any governess an example. "Excuse me," she said, glancing down the corridor where several of her charges, by managing to open a window, were letting in blasts of Arctic wind. "I'm afraid I'll have to put a stop to that."

But before she had completed her mission, Gail herself was swept away into being a child again. "Oh, look," she cried, hanging out the very window she'd gone to close. "Look, kids . . . *People!*"

The people were two small children ice-skating on a long ribbon of pond at the edge of a white wood. They skated fast as they could, trying to keep up with the train, and as it sped beyond them they stretched out their arms, as though to catch the shouted greetings, the blown kisses of Gail and her friends.

Meanwhile, the Russian attendant had discovered smoke billowing from his samovar. He snatched charred hot dogs off the fire, and tossed them on the floor. Then, sucking blistered fingers and employing a vocabulary that must have been, to judge from its tone, on the blistery side itself, he rushed to pry the children away from the window and slam it shut.

"Aw, don't be a sorehead," Davy told him. "We're just having a grand time."

The remnants of a cheese and fruit lunch were scattered on the table (and the carpet) of Compartment 6. Midafternoon sunlight sparkled in a glass of Chianti Miss Ryan was revolving in her hand. "I adore wine," she said fervently. "I began drinking it when I was twelve. Heavily. It's a wonder I'm not a wino." She sipped and sighed with a contentment that reflected the general mood. Miss Thigpen and her fiancé, who'd had their share of Chianti, were nestled together in a corner of their seat, her head resting on his shoulder. The drowsy, dreaming spell was broken by a knock at the door, and someone saying, "This is it. Russia."

"Places, please," said Miss Ryan. "Curtain going up."

The first signs of an approaching frontier came into view: stark wooden guard towers, not unsimilar to those that encircle Southern convict farms. Spread at wide intervals, they marched across the wastes like giant telephone poles. In the nearest of them I could see a man watching the train through binoculars. The train slowed round a curve and slackened to a stop. We were in a switch yard, surrounded by a maze of tracks and halted freight cars. It was the Soviet border, forty minutes from Brest Litovsk.

Along the tracks, herds of women with shawl-wrapped heads, like a woolly version of purdah, were swinging picks, shoveling snow, pausing only to blow their noses into naked, raw-red hands. The few who even glanced at The Blue

Express risked sharp looks from various militiamen lounging about with their hands stuffed in their coat pockets.

"If that's not a *shame*," said Miss Thigpen. "Ladies doing all the work, while the men just stand around. How disgraceful!"

"That's what it is here, honey," said Jackson, puffing on one of his ruby rings, and polishing it against his lapel. "Every man a Sportin' Life."

"I'd like to see somebody treat *me* that way," replied Miss Thigpen, warningly.

"But I must say," said Miss Ryan, "the men are pretty divine." Her interest was fixed on a pair of officers pacing below the window, tall-strong-silent types with thin lips and rugged, windburned faces. One of them looked up and, catching sight of Miss Ryan's blue eyes and long golden hair, lost step with his partner. Miss Ryan whimpered, "Oh, wouldn't it be awful!"

"Awful what, honey?" said Miss Thigpen.

"If I fell in love with a Russian," said Miss Ryan. "Wouldn't that be the absolute *fin?* Actually, my mother's afraid that I might. She said if I fell in love with any Russians I needn't bother coming home. But," she added, her gaze again drifting toward the officer, "if they're all like *that* . . ."

Quite suddenly Miss Ryan's admirer had no time for flirtation. He became part of a small Russian army chasing round the yard after Robin Joachim. Joachim, an overly avid photographer, had broken the rules by getting off the train, then compounded that error by attempting to take pictures. Now he was racing zigzag across the tracks, narrowly avoiding the wrathful swipe of a woman worker's shovel, barely eluding the grasp of a guard.

"I hope they catch him," said Miss Ryan coldly. "Him and his goddam cameras. I knew he'd get us into trouble."

Joachim, however, turned out to be a resourceful young man. Slipping past his pursuers, he hurled himself onto the train, rushed into a compartment, threw his coat, his camera and cap under the seat, and to further alter his appearance, whipped off his horn-rimmed glasses. Seconds later, when the angry Soviets came aboard, he calmly assumed his role of company translator and helped them hunt the culprit, a search that included every compartment. Warner Watson, roused from his slumbers, was the person least amused by the situation. He promised Joachim a good talking to. "This," he said, "is *not* the way to begin a cultural exchange."

The incident caused the train to be delayed forty-five minutes and had other repercussions as well, one of them involving Twerp, for the Russians, in the course of their search, had been appalled by certain condtions in Car 2 attributable to the puppy. Twerp's owner, Marilyn Putnam, said later, "I put it to them straight. I said, since we're never allowed off the train, what the hell do you expect? That shut 'em up."

We reached Brest Litovsk in a luminous twilight. Statues of political heroes, painted cheap-silver like those souvenir figures sold at Woolworth's, saluted us along the last mile of track leading to the station. The station was on high ground that afforded a partial view of the city dim and blue and dominated, far-off, by an Orthodox cathedral, whose onion-domes and mosaic towers still projected, despite the failing light, their oriental colors.

Among the company it had been rumored that we would be allowed off the train here, and perhaps, while the wheels were changed and the dining car added, permitted to tour the city. Leonard Lyons was most anxious that this should happen. "I can't write a thousand words a day just sitting on a train. I need action." Lyons had gone so far as to discuss with the cast the kind of action he would like. He wanted them to traipse around Brest Litovsk singing spirituals. "It's a good story and it's a good showmanship. I'm surprised Breen didn't think of it." When the train stopped, the doors opened all right, but were immediately closed again, after admitting a five-man delegation from Moscow's Ministry of Culture.

One of these emissaries was a middle-aged woman with straying dishwater hair and, except for her eyes, what seemed a kind, motherly face. The eyes, dull gray and flecked with dots of milky white, had an embalmed glaze that did not blend with the cheerful contours of her expression. She wore a black cloth coat and a rusty black dress that sagged at the breasts from the weight of an ivory rose. In introducing herself and her colleagues, she ran the names together so that it sounded like a patter song. "You will please to meet Sascha-MenashaTiomkenKerinskyIvorsIvanovichNikolaiSavchenko-PlesitskyaGrutchenkoRickiSomanenko . . ."

In due time, the Americans were to sort and simplify these names until their owners became familiar as Miss Lydia. Henry, Sascha and Igor, the latter young underlings from the Ministry who, like the middle-aged Miss Lydia, had been assigned to the company as translators. But the fifth member of the quintet, Nikolai Savchenko, was not the man you call Nick. An important official in the Ministry, Savchenko was in charge of the *Porgy and Bess* tour.

The victim of a slightly receding chin, mildly bulging eyes and a tendency toward fat, he was nevertheless a formidable figure—well over six feet, with a stern, no-nonsense attitude and a handshake like a nutcracker. Beside him, his young assistants looked like sickly children, though two of them, Sascha and Igor, were strapping boys whose shoulders were too broad for their fur-collared coats; and Henry, a spidery mite with huge ears so red they were purple, made up by personal vividness what he lacked in stature.

It seemed natural that Miss Lydia and the young men should react awkwardly to this, their first encounter with Westerners; understandable that they should hesitate to test their English, so tediously learned at Moscow's Institute of Foreign Languages but never before practiced on bona-fide foreigners; forgivable that they should, instead, stare as though the Americans represented pawns in a chess problem. But Savchenko also gave an impression of being ill at ease, of preferring, in fact, a stretch in Lubyanka to his present chores. Which was excusable, too; though rather odd when you consider that for two years during the war he served as Counsel at the Soviet Embassy in Washington. Even so, he seemed to find Americans such a tongue-tying novelty that for the moment he affected not to speak English. He delivered a small speech of welcome in gruff Russian, then had it translated by Miss Lydia. "We hope each and all have had a pleasant journey. Too bad you see us in the winter. It is not the good time of year. But we have the saying, Better now than never. Your visit is a step forward in the march toward peace. When the cannons are heard, the muses are silent; when the cannons are silent, the muses are heard."

The muse-cannon metaphor, which was to prove a Savchenko favorite, the starring sentence of all future speeches, was an instant hit with his listeners ("A beautiful thing." "Just great, Mr. Savchenko." "That's cool cookin', man."), and Savchenko, warmed by success and beginning to relax, decided there was perhaps no reason to keep the company cooped up in the train. Why not step out on the platform and watch the changing of the wheels?

Outside, Lyons canvassed the group, trying to work up a song fest. But the temperature, ten below zero, was not conducive to a musical mood. Moreover, a large percentage of those who had been grateful to escape The Blue Express were, after the briefest exposure, shoving each other to get back in. The hearties who remained watched in the nightfall as workers of both sexes uncoupled the cars and jacked them to the height of a man. The old wheels, spraying sparks, were then rolled from under the train, while from the opposite direction the new wide-gauge wheels came gliding into place. Ira Wolfert called the operation "very efficient"; Herman Sartorius considered it "most impressive"; but Miss Ryan thought it was a "damned bore" and said that if I'd follow her into the station, she would buy me a vodka.

No one stopped us. We crossed a hundred yards of track, walked down a dirt lane between warehouses, and arrived at what appeared to be a combination of a parking lot and a marketplace. Brightly lighted kiosks circled it like candles burning on a cake. It was puzzling to discover that each of the kiosks sold the same products: cans of Red Star salmon, Red Star sardines, dusty bottles of Kremlin perfume, dusty boxes of Kremlin candy, pickled tomatoes, hairy slabs of raw bacon slapped between thick slices of grime-colored bread, weird liqueurs, cross buns (without the cross) that one somehow felt had been baked last July. And though the kiosks were attracting a brisk trade, the most sought-after item was not on sale at any of them. It was in the private hands of a peddler, an elderly Chinese who carried a tray of apples. The apples were as shriveled and miniature as himself, but his waiting line of customers appeared disconsolate when the last of them evaporated. At the far end of the area a flight of steps led to the main entrance of the station, and the Chinese, folding his empty tray, wandered over to them and sat down next to a friend. The friend was a beggar bundled in an old army coat and with a pair of crutches sprawled beside him like the wings of a wounded bird. Every third or fourth person going by dropped a coin into his hand. The Chinese gave him something, too. An apple. He'd saved one for the beggar, and one for himself. The two friends gnawed their apples and leaned against each other in the cutting cold.

The constant wailing of a train whistle seemed to fuse the apple-eaters and the kiosks and the batlike passings of fur-shrouded faces into a smoky, single image of its woeful sound. "I've never been homesick. Never in my life," Miss Ryan informed me. "But sometimes, for God's sake. Sometimes," she said, running up the steps and pushing open the doors of the station, "you do feel a long *way* from home."

Since Brest Litovsk is one of Russia's most strategic railroad centers, its station is among the country's largest. Looking for somewhere to buy a drink, we explored lofty corridors and a series of waiting rooms, the principal one furnished with handsome oak benches occupied by many passengers with very few suitcases. Children and paper bundles filled their laps. The stone floors, soggy with black slush, made slippery walking, and there was an odor in the air, a saturation so heavy it seemed less a smell than a pressure. Travelers to Venice often remark on the vivid scents of that city. The public places of Russia, terminals and department stores, restaurants and theatres, also have a reek instantly recognizable. And Miss Ryan, taking her first sniff of it, said,

"Boy, I wouldn't want a bottle of this. Old socks and a million yawns."

In the search for a bar, we began opening doors at random. Miss Ryan sailed through one and out again. It was a men's room. Then, spotting a pair of dead-drunks as they emerged from behind a small red door, she decided, "That's the place we're looking for." The red door led into an extraordinary restaurant. The size of a gymnasium, it looked as if it had been done over for a school prom by a decorating committee with Victorian tastes. Plush crimson draperies were looped along the walls. Other-era chandeliers distributed a tropic glare that beat down on a jungle of borscht-stained table-cloths and withering rubber plants. The maître d'hôtel seemed appropriate to this atmosphere of grandeur gone to seed. He was at least eighty years old, a white-bearded patri-arch with ferocious eyes that peered at us, through a sailor's-dive haze of cigarette smoke, as though questioning our right to be there.

Miss Ryan smiled at him and said, "Vodka, *pjolista*." The old man stared at her with more hostility then comprehen-sion. She tried varying pronunciations, "Woedka . . . Wadka . . . Woodka," and even performed a bottoms-up pantomime. "The poor thing's deaf," she said, and shouted, "*Vodka*. For God's sake."

Although his expression remained unenlightened, the old man beckoned us forward and, following the Russian cus-tom of seating strangers together, put us at a table with two men. They both were drinking beer, and the old man pointed at it, as if asking if this was what we wanted. Miss Ryan, resigning herself, nodded.

Our companions at the table were two very different

specimens. One, a beefy boy with a shaved head and wearing some sort of faded uniform, was well on his way to being drunk, a condition shared by a surprising lot of the restaurant's clientele, most of whom were male, many of them either boisterous or slumped across their tables mumbling to themselves. The second man was an enigma. In appearance he might have been a Wall Street partner of Herman Sartorius, the kind of person better imagined dining at the Pavillon than sipping beer in Brest Litovsk. His suit was pressed, and one could see that he hadn't sewn it himself. There were gold cuff links in his shirt, and he was the only man in the room sporting a tie.

After a moment the shaven-headed soldier spoke to Miss Ryan. "I'm afraid I don't speak Russian," she told him. "We're Americans. *Amerikansky.*" Her declaration had a somewhat sobering effect. His reddened eyes slowly came into semifocus. He turned to the well-dressed man and made a long statement, at the end of which the man answered him with several chiseled, cold-sounding sentences. There followed between them a sharp repartee, then the soldier took his beer and stalked to another table, where he sat glowering. "Well," said Miss Ryan, glowering back, "not *all* the men are attractive, that's for sure." However, she considered our apparent defender, the well-dressed man: "Very attractive. Sort of Otto Kruger. Funny, I've always liked older men. Stop staring. He'll know we're talking about him. Listen," she said, after calling attention to his shirt, his cuff links, his clean fingernails, "do you suppose there's such a thing as a Russian millionaire?"

The beer arrived. A quart bottle and two glasses. The maître d'hôtel poured an inch of beer into my glass, then waited expectantly. Miss Ryan saw the point before I did.

"He wants you to *taste* it, like wine." Lifting the glass, I wondered if beer-tasting was a Soviet commonplace, or if it was a ceremony, some confused champagne-memory of Czarist elegance that the old man had revived to impress us. I sipped, nodded, and the old man proudly filled our glasses with a warm and foamless brew. But Miss Ryan said suddenly, "Don't touch it. It's dreadful!" I told her I didn't think it was that bad. "I mean, we're in dreadful trouble," she said. "I mean, my God, we can't pay for this. I completely forgot. We haven't any rubles."

"Please, won't you be my guests?" inquired a soft voice in beautifully accented English. It was the well-dressed man who had spoken, and though his face was perfectly straight, his eyes, a bright Nordic blue, wrinkled with an amusement that took full measure of our discomfort. "I am not a Russian millionaire. They *do* exist—I know quite a few—but it would give me pleasure to pay for your drink. No, please, there is no cause to apologize," he said, in response to Miss Ryan's stammered efforts, and openly smiling, "It's been the keenest enjoyment. Very unusual. Very unusual to run across Americans in this part of the world. Are you Communists?"

After disabusing him of that notion, Miss Ryan told him where we were going, and why. "You are fortunate that you go to Leningrad first. A lovely city," he said, "very quiet, really European, the one place in Russia I could imagine living, not that I do, but still . . . Yes, I like Leningrad. It's not the least like Moscow. I'm on my way to Warsaw, but I've just been two weeks in Moscow. That's equal to two months anywhere else." He told us that he was Norwegian, and that his business, lumber, had required him to visit the Soviet Union several weeks of every year, except for a gap during the war, since 1931. "I speak the language quite well, and among my friends I don't mind passing as a Russian authority. But to be honest, I can't say I understand much more about it now than I did in 1931. Whenever I go to your country—I've been there, oh, I guess a half dozen times—it always strikes me that Americans are the only people who remind me of Russians. You don't object to my saying that? Americans are so generous. Energetic. And underneath all that brag they have such a wishing to be loved, they want to be petted, like dogs and children, and told that they are just as good and even better than the rest of us. Well, Europeans are inclined to agree with them. But they simply won't believe it. They go right on feeling inferior and far away. Alone. Like Russians. Precisely."

Miss Ryan wanted to know the substance of his dialogue with the soldier who had left the table. "Oh, silly rot," he said. "Alcoholic bravado. For some foozled reason he thought you had insulted him. I told him he was being *nye kulturni*. Remember that: *nye kulturni*. You'll find it extremely useful, because when these chaps are rude and you feel obliged to tick them off, it means not a whit to call them a bastard, a son of a dog, but to tell him he's *uncultured*, that really strikes home."

Miss Ryan was growing anxious about the time. We shook hands with the gentleman and thanked him for the beer. "You've been very *kulturni*," she said. "And by the way, I think you're *more* attractive than Otto Kruger."

"I shall certainly tell my wife," he said, grinning. "*Dazvedanya*. Good luck."

An hour out of Brest Litovsk, the first call to the dining car was announced. It was an event the company had looked

forward to with appetites excited by both genuine hunger
and the conviction that the Soviet hosts were bound to make
this, the company's first Russian meal, a "real spread"; or,
as another of the cast forthrightly phrased it, "a bust-gut."

Miss Thigpen's desires were the most modest. "Five spoons
of caviar and a piece of dry toast. That's one hundred and
thirty calories." Calories were Mrs. Gershwin's last concern.
"Don't think I'm not going to tear into the cavy, darling. It
cost thirty-five dollars a pound in Beverly Hills." The dreams
of Leonard Lyons centered around hot borscht and sour
cream. Earl Bruce Jackson planned to "stone" himself with
vodka and "slay" himself with shashlik. Marilyn Putnam
hoped that everyone would save little tidbits for Twerp.

The first sitting, fifty strong, marched into the dining car
and took their places at linen-covered tables, each seating
four, that ran down either side of the aisle. The tables were
set with white crockery and smoothly worn silver. The
diner itself seemed as old as the silver, and the smell of cooking, a half-century's worth, hung in the air like a visible
steam. Savchenko was absent, but Miss Lydia and the three
young men from the Ministry played host at different tables.
The young men kept gazing round, as though silently calling
to each other from separate islands of exile and misery.

Miss Lydia shared a table with Lyons, Miss Ryan and myself. One sensed that for this middle-aged woman, who said
that her ordinary life was translating articles and living in a
room in Moscow, the unique experience, the one that
brought such a flush to her cheeks, was not that she was talking to foreigners, but that she was sitting in a dining car riding on a train. Something about the silver and the clean cloth
and a little basket of puckered apples, like those the Chinese
man had sold, made her fuss with her ivory rose and tuck up

the straying ends of her hair. "Ah, we eat!" she said, her eyes shifting toward a quartet of chunky waitresses who came waddling down the aisle with trayloads of the first coarse.

Those whose palates had been anticipating iced caviar and chilled carafes of vodka were a bit chagrined to see, set before them, yogurt accompanied by bottles of raspberry soda. Miss Thigpen, seated behind me, was the sole voice expressing enthusiasm: "I just could kiss them! More proteins than a steak and only half the calories." But across the aisle, Mrs. Gershwin warned Miss Putnam not to ruin her appetite by eating it. "Don't, darling, I'm sure the cavy will come along next." The next course, however, consisted of stiff noodles lying like sunken logs in a watery broth. The entree that followed featured breaded veal cutlets, boiled potatoes, and peas that rattled on the plate like gunshot; to wash this down, there were further provisions of raspberry soda. Miss Putnam said to Mrs. Gershwin, "It's not *my* stomach I'm worried about. It's Twerp's," and Mrs. Gershwin, sawing at her cutlet, said, "Do you suppose they could be saving the cavy for dessert? You know, with little pancakes?"

Miss Lydia's cheeks bulged, her eyes popped, her jaws pumped like pistons, a trickle of sweat ran down her neck. "Eat, eat," she urged, "it's good, yes?" Miss Ryan told her it was wonderful, and Miss Lydia, swabbing her plate with a quarter loaf of black bread, nodded vehemently: "You will not obtain better in Moscow itself."

During the lull between entree and dessert, she went to work on the basket of apples; as the cores piled up she paused occasionally to answer questions. Lyons was anxious to learn at what hotel the company would be staying in Leningrad. Miss Lydia was startled that he didn't know. "The Astoria. For weeks the rooms have been reserved," she said, and went on to describe the Astoria as "very old-fashion but exquisite." "Well," said Lyons, "what about the night life in Leningrad, any action there?" Miss Lydia replied by saying that perhaps her English was not all it should be, and proceeded, from her Muscovite point of view, to discuss Leningrad rather as a New Yorker might Philadelphia; it was "old-fashion," it was "provincial," it was "not the same like Moscow." At the end of this recital, Lyons said glumly, "Sounds like a two-day town to me." Miss Ryan thought to ask when was the last time Miss Lydia had visited Leningrad. Miss Lydia blinked. "The last time? Never. I have never been there. It will be interesting to see, yes?"

Presently she had a question of her own. "I would appreciate you to explain to me. Why is Paul Robeson not in with the players? *He* is a colored person, yes?"

"Yes," said Miss Ryan; and so, she added, were sixteen million other Americans. Surely Miss Lydia didn't expect *Porgy and Bess* to employ them all?

Miss Lydia leaned back in her chair with a cunning, I'm-no-fool expression. "It is because *you*," she said, smiling at Miss Ryan, "*you* do not permit him his passport."

The dessert arrived. It was vanilla ice cream, and it was excellent. Behind me, Miss Thigpen said to her fiancé, "Earl, honey, I wouldn't touch it. Maybe it's not pasteurized." Across the aisle, Mrs. Gershwin observed to Miss Putnam, "It's my theory they send it all to California. It cost thirty-five dollars a pound in Beverly Hills."

Coffee followed, and with it an altercation. Jackson and several of his friends had taken over a table and were dealing out a game of Tonk. The two huskiest of the Ministry's young men, Sascha and Igor, converged on the card players and informed them, their voices struggling to sound firm, that "gambling" was illegal in the Soviet Union. "Man," said one of the players, "nobody's gambling here. We got to do *something*. We don't have a friendly game, we blow our stacks." Sascha insisted, "It's illegal. Not allowed." The men threw down their cards, and Jackson, tucking them into a case, said, "Old Squareville. Home for dead cats. The number to play is zero. Tell the boys back in New York."

"They are unhappy. We regret," said Miss Lydia. "But we must remember our restaurant workers." Her stubby-fingered hand motioned elegantly toward the waitresses, whose blear-eyed, solid faces glistened with perspiration as they shambled down the aisle balancing a hundred pounds of dirty dishes. "You understand. It would not look well for them to see the laws disenforced." She gathered the last few apples, and stuffed them into a cloth handbag. "Now," she said cheerfully, "we go to dream. We unravel the sleeve of care."

On the morning of December 21, The Blue Express was twenty-four hours from Leningrad, another day and night, though the difference between the two seemed, as the train crawled deeper into Russia, tenuous indeed, so little did the sun, a gray ghost rising at ten and returned to its grave by three, help to divide them. The fragile span of daylight continued to reveal winter at its uncrackable hardest: birches, their branches broken from the weight of snow; a log-cabin village, not a soul in sight and the roofs hung with icicles heavy as elephant tusks. Once, a village cemetery, poor plain wooden crosses, wind-bent and all but buried. But here and there haystacks, standing in deserted fields, were evidence that even this harsh ground could, in distant spring, grow green again.

Aboard, among the passengers, the emotional pendulum had settled at that nirvana point between the strains of depar-

ture and the tensions of arrival. An on and on timeless nowhere that one accepted as perhaps lasting forever, like the
wind that swept white cauldrons of snow-spray against the
train. At last, even Warner Watson relaxed. "Well," he said,
lighting a cigarette with hands that scarcely trembled, "I
guess maybe I've got my nerves fenced in." Twerp snoozed in
the corridor, pink stomach upturned, paws awry. In Compartment 6, by now a welter of unmade berths, orange
peelings, spilled face powder and cigarette butts floating in
cold tea, Jackson practiced card-shuffling while his fiancée
buffed her nails, and Miss Ryan, pursuing her Russian studies,
memorized a new phrase out of the old army textbook;
"SLOO-*sha eess-ya ee-lee ya* BOO-*doo streel*-YAHT! Obey or
I'll fire!" Lyons alone stayed faithful to the pressures of a
workaday world. "Nobody gets in my tax bracket looking at
scenery," he said, sternly typing the heading for a new column: "*Showtrain to Leningrad.*"

At seven that evening, when the others had gone off to the
day's third round of yogurt and raspberry soda, I stayed in
the compartment and dined on a Hershey chocolate bar. I
thought Twerp and I had the car to ourselves until I noticed
one of the Ministry's interpreters, Henry, the child-sized
young man with the large ears, pass my door, then pass again,
each time giving me a glance that quivered with curiosity. It
was as though he wanted to speak but caution and timidity
prevented him. When finally, after another reconnoiter, he
did come into the compartment, the approach he'd designed
was official.

"Give me your passport," he said, with that bluntness shy
people often assume.

He sat on Miss Thigpen's berth, and studied the passport

through a pair of spectacles that kept sliding to the tip of his nose; like everything he wore, from his shiny black suit with its bell-bottom trousers to his brown worn-down shoes, they were much too big for him. I said if he would tell me what he was looking for, possibly I could help him. "It is necessary," he mumbled, his red ears burning like hot coals. The train must have traveled several miles while he fingered through the passport like a boy poring over a stamp album; and though he carefully examined the mementos left on its pages by immigration authorities, his attention lingered longest on the data that states one's occupation, height and color, date of birth.

"Here is correct?" he said, pointing to my birth date. I told him it was. "We are three years apart," he said. "I am youngest—*younger?*—I am younger, thank you. But you have seen much. So. I have seen Moscow." I asked him if he would like to travel. His anger began as a physical action, a queer sequence of shrugs and flutterings, shrinking inside his fat man's suit that seemed to mean yes and no, perhaps. He pushed up his spectacles, and said, "I have not the time. I am a worker like him and him. Three years, it could also happen my passport has many imprimaturs. But I am content with the scenic—no, *scenery*—scenery of the mind. The world is the same, but here," he tapped his forehead, struck it really, "*here*," he spread a hand over his heart, "are changefuls. Which is correct; chang*ings* or change*fuls*?" I said either one; as used, they both made sense.

The effort of shaping these sentences, and an excess of feeling behind them, had left him breathless. He leaned on his elbow and rested a spell before suddenly observing, "You resemble Shostakovich. That is correct?" I told him I wouldn't have thought so, not from the photographs of Shostakovich that I'd seen. "We have discuss it. Mr. Savchenko has also the opinion," he said, as though this were final, for who were we, either of us, to challenge Savchenko? Shostakovich's name led to mention of David Oistrakh, the great Soviet violinist who had recently played concerts in New York and Philadelphia. He listened to my report of Oistrakh's American triumphs as if I were praising him, Henry; his hunched shoulders straightened, all at once he seemed to fill out his flapping suit, and the heels of his shoes, dangling over the side of the berth, swung together and clicked, clicked and swung, as though he were dancing a jig. I asked him if he thought *Porgy and Bess* would have a success in Russia comparable to Oistrakh's American reception. "It is not my ability to say. But we at the Ministry hope more than you hope. A real man's job for us, that *Porgy-Bess*." He told me that although he'd worked at the Ministry for five years, this was the only time his job had taken him outside Moscow. Usually, he said, he spent six days a week at a desk in the Ministry ("I have my own telephone"), and on Sundays he stayed home reading ("Among your writers, the powerful one is A. J. Cronin. But Sholikov is more powerful, yes?"). Home was an apartment on the outskirts of Moscow, where he lived with his family and, as he was unmarried ("My stipend is not yet equal to the aspiration"), shared a bedroom with his brother.

The conversation moved with an increasing ease; he ate a piece of Hershey, he laughed, his heels clicked; and then I offered him some books. They were stacked on the table, and his eyes continually strayed toward them, a gaudy collection of twenty-five-cent thrillers mixed in with Edmund

Wilson's *To the Finland Station*, a history of the rise of Socialism, and Nancy Mitford's biography, *Madame de Pompadour*. I told him he could have them, if he liked.

At first, he was pleased. Then, as he reached for the books, his hands hesitated, withdrew, and his personal tic started; more shrugs, shrinkings, until he was swallowed again in the looseness of his clothes. "I have not the time," he said regretfully. Afterward there seemed nothing left to say. He informed me that my passport was in order, and left.

Between midnight and two in the morning, The Blue Express stood still in a railroad siding near Moscow. The exterior coldness had stolen into the cars, forming lenses of ice on the inside surface of the windowpanes; looking out, one saw merely spectral diffusions, as if your vision were deformed by cataracts. As soon as the train left Moscow, a restless mood rippled through the compartments; those who had been asleep wakened, began to flutter about like chickens tricked by a false dawn. The stay-ups poured another drink and breathed a second wind. Already the pendulum was swinging toward the tensions of arrival.

Miss Thigpen woke up, calling, "Earl! Earl!" as though she'd had a bad dream.

"Gone," said Miss Ryan, who was curled in her berth nursing a brandy and reading Mickey Spillane. "He's out defying the law. Somebody's running a bootleg Tonk in the next car."

"That's no way to do. Earl ought to be getting his rest," said Miss Thigpen grouchily.

"Give him hell," Miss Ryan advised her. "He's *got* to marry you."

"Nancy, *quelle heure est-il?*"

"Twenty to four." At four Miss Thigpen again inquired the time; and again at ten past. "For God's sake, Helen. Either get a watch or take an *Oblivon*."

Miss Thigpen kicked back her covers. "No sense trying. I'm better off dressed." It took her an hour and twenty-five minutes to select her costume and apply the right proportions of cosmetics and perfume. At five thirty-five she put on a feathered hat with a veil and sat down on her berth, completely clothed except for stockings and shoes. "I'm worried sick what to wear on my legs. I don't want to be poisoned," she said. Her fear was founded on a memo the Russians had issued to the ladies of the company on the subject of nylon hosiery. In conditions of severe cold, nylon, they announced, had a tendency to disintegrate, which might cause nylon poisoning. Miss Thigpen rubbed her naked legs and groaned. "What kind of place *is* this we're going? Where a lady's stockings fall to pieces on the street and maybe kill her?"

"Forget it," said Miss Ryan.

"But the Russians . . ."

"How the hell would they know? They don't have any nylons. That's why they say it."

It was eight in the morning before Jackson returned from his Tonk game. "Earl," said Miss Thigpen, "is this how you're going to do after we're married?"

"Sweet-girl," he said, wearily climbing into his berth, "the cat has howled his last. He's zero point zero. Ooble-ee-dood out."

Miss Thigpen was unsympathetic. "Earl, don't you dare go to sleep now. We're almost there. Go to sleep for such a little bit and you'll wake up an ugly mess."

Jackson muttered and drew a blanket over his head.

"Earl," said Miss Ryan softly, "I suppose you know they're going to make newsreels at the station?"

Very shortly afterward, Jackson had shaved, changed shirts and arrayed himself in a caramel-colored fur coat. He owned a hat of the same fur that he'd had "custom-made" fedora-style. While working his hands into a pair of gloves with holes along the fingers to reveal his rings, he gave his fiancée instructions on how to handle the expected cameras: "See, honey, we don't want to get stuck with a lot of still-men. That's a waste of time when they're busting out the flicker stuff." He scratched at the window with his jeweled fist, and squinted out; it was nine-five and still pitch-black, not the ideal color for photography. But half an hour later the darkness had turned to steel-gray mist and one could see the blueness of lightly falling snow.

One of the Ministry's representatives, Sascha, passed through the car, knocking at compartment doors. "Ladies and gentlemen, in twenty minutes we are arriving Leningrad."

I finished dressing and squeezed my way into the crowded corridor, where an excitement was moment by moment accelerating like the wheels of the train. Even Twerp, shawl-wrapped and hugged in Miss Putnam's arms, was prepared to disembark. Mrs. Gershwin was more prepared than Twerp. She bristled with mink, was frosted with diamonds and her curls peeked charmingly from under a rich soft sable hat. "The hat, darling? I bought it in California. I've been saving it for a surprise. You do, love? How sweet of you, darling. *Darling* . . ." she said, an abrupt silence adding volume to her voice, "we're *there!*"

A stunned instant of disbelief, then a collective pushing

toward the vestibule. The sad-eyed car attendant, stationed there to receive his tips, found himself not only ignored but also crushed against the wall. Alert as horses at the starting gate, Jackson and John McCurry jockeyed by the exit for position. McCurry is the heftier of the two, and when the door opened, he was the first man out.

He stepped straight into a gray throng, and a flash bulb's pop. "Bless you," said McCurry, as women vied to thrust bouquets into his hand. "Bless your little pointed heads."

"As we arrived, there were many birds flying about— black and white," wrote Warner Watson, as he later recorded the scene in his diary. "The white ones are *sakaros*. I write it down for my bird-watching friends. We were greeted by many friendly Russians. The women and men (of the company) were given bouquets of flowers. I wonder where they got them this time of year. Pathetic little bouquets like those made by a child."

Miss Ryan, also the keeper of a diary, wrote: "Official welcoming party of giant men and shabby ladies dressed more to meet a coffin than a theatrical company (black clothes, gray faces) but perhaps that's what they *were* doing. My useless plastic galoshes kept falling off, making it impossible to elbow efficiently through the press of microphones, cameras, and those battling to get at them. The Breens were on hand, Robert still half asleep but Wilva smile-smiling. At the head of the quay, dull brass letters spelled out LENINGRAD—and then I knew it was true."

The poet, Helen Wolfert, composed for her journal a lengthy description. Here is an excerpt: "As we advanced along the platform to the exit, two columns of people stood on either side applauding. When we reached the street a

press of spectators closed in on us. Policemen pushed them
away to let us pass but the people in return pushed them
with equal vigor. The actors responded to the warmth and
bustle and welcome with grace, graciousness, expansiveness
and flair. If the Russian people fell in love with them, they
weren't alone. I fell in love with them myself."

Perhaps a few footnotes should be added to these entries.
The persons Miss Ryan refers to as "giant men and shabby
ladies" were a hundred or more of Leningrad's leading
theatrical artists who had been organized to meet the train.
Remarkably, none of them had known in advance that
Porgy and Bess had a Negro cast, and before the committee
could rearrange their bewildered faces into expressions of
positive welcome, the company were halfway out of the station. The "press of spectators" noted by Mrs. Wolfert consisted of ordinary citizens whose presence was the result of
an item printed in the local edition of the previous day's
Izvestia. "A touring American opera company will arrive
by train tomorrow morning in Leningrad. It is expected
they will perform here." These two lines were, by the way,
the first publicity the Soviet press had given Breen's venture; but despite its meager detail, the announcement had
proved sufficiently intriguing to attract the at least one thousand Leningraders who lined the length of the station, cas-
caded down a flight of stairs and spilled into the street. I
was less aware of the "warmth and bustle" that impressed
Mrs. Wolfert. Except for light sprinklings of applause, the
crowd, so it seemed to me, watched the exiting cast with immense silence, an almost catatonic demeanor that provided
few clues as to what they thought of the American parade—
Mrs. Gershwin, loaded with more bouquets than a bride;
small Davy Bey, dancing an impromptu Suzy-Q; Jackson,

dispensing royal waves, and John McCurry, walking with his hands clenched above his head like a prize fighter.

While the Russian reaction may have been inscrutable, the official Company Historian, Leonard Lyons, had a very definite opinion of his own. Taking professional note of the scene, he shook his head. "It hasn't been handled right. No showmanship. Why, if Breen knew his business," he said, passing through the door of the station, "we would've come out singing!"

The Muses
Are Heard

(Part II)

✵

THE LENINGRAD PREMIÈRE of *Porgy and Bess*, an event expected to reap international publicity, was planned for the evening of Monday, December 26, which gave the company five days to prepare and rehearse, a sufficient time considering that the show had been touring the world nearly four years. But Robert Breen, the production's director, was determined that the audience at the Leningrad première would see the finest possible rendering of the Negro opera. Breen and his energetic partner-wife, Wilva, and their chief assistant, the gentle, yet highly strung Warner Watson, were confident that the Russians would be "stunned" by the musical folk tale, that they would "never have seen anything like it." Several observers, though sympathetic, were not as sure. However looked at, by the Americans or by their Russian sponsors, the opening night promised to be one of the most suspenseful in theatrical annals. But that event was, on the morning of arrival, over a hundred hours away; and after the company had been driven in chartered buses from the Leningrad terminal to the Hotel Astoria, their feelings of suspense were centered around room accommodations.

The Astoria, situated on the impressive expanse of St. Isaac's Square, is an Intourist hotel, which means that it is run by the Soviet agency in control of all hotels where foreigners are permitted to stay. The Astoria justifiably claims to be the best hotel in Leningrad. Some think it the Ritz of all Russia. But it contains few concessions to Western ideas of a deluxe establishment. Of these, one is a room off the lobby that advertises itself as an *Institut De Beauté*, where guests may obtain *Pedicure*, and *Coiffeur pour Madame*. The *Institut*, with its mottled whiteness, its painful appurtenances, resembles a charity clinic supervised by not too sanitary nurses, and the coiffure that Madame receives there is liable to leave her hair with a texture excellent for scouring pans. There is also on the lobby floor a trio of restaurants, each leading into the other, cavernous affairs cheerful as airplane hangars. The center one is Leningrad's smartest restaurant, and in the evenings, from eight till midnight, an orchestra plays Russian jazz for a local *haut monde* who seldom dance but sit morosely counting the bubbles in syrupy glasses of Georgian champagne. The hotel's Intourist office is located behind a low counter in the main lobby; its dozen desks are so arranged that the employees have a broad view, which simplifies their task of keeping tabs on the comings and goings of the guests. It is a job they have made still simpler, or foolproof, by stationing dormitory matrons on each of the residential floors, vigilantes who are on duty from dawn to dawn, never allowing anyone to leave his room without giving him the key, and constantly, like human punch-clocks, recording ins and outs in a bulky ledger. Perhaps Houdini could've eluded them, but it is hard to see how, since they sit at desks that face both the staircase and the elevator, an ancient bird cage that creaks on its cables.

Actually, there is a rear, unguarded staircase connecting the upper floors with a remote side-lobby; and for the clandestine visitor, or the resident wishing to depart unnoticed, this would make the ideal route. Would, except that it is barricaded top to bottom with wooden fences reinforced by old settees and armoires. It might be that the management can find nowhere else to stash these pieces of furniture. Certainly there is no more room in the rooms. For the average Astoria abode is like the annex in a Victorian attic where some poor relation lives buried among the family discards: a miasma of romantic marble statuary, weak-bulbed lamps with tulle shades like ballerina skirts, tables, several of them, covered with oriental carpeting, chairs galore, plush settees, armoires that could store steamer trunks, flower-papered walls kaleidoscopic with gilt-framed paintings of fruit and country idylls, beds concealed in cavelike alcoves behind dank velvet curtains: all this crammed into a tomb-dark, unventilated area (you can't open the windows in winter, and wouldn't want to if you could) quadruple the size of a train compartment. The hotel has grander quarters, of course, suites with five and six rooms, but the effect of the décor is the same, merely more abundantly so.

Nevertheless, the majority of the *Porgy and Bess* company were most approving of the Astoria, many because they had anticipated "something so much *worse*" and, instead, found their rooms "cozy," "kind of atmospheric" or, as the production's sophisticated publicist, Willem Van Loon, put it, "Full of art-nouveau charms. Really me!" But when the troupe first entered the lobby of the hotel, already milling with Chinese dignitaries and high-booted Cossacks, actual occupancy of these rooms was, in some instances, distant and debatable.

The Astoria's assigning of the rooms and, particularly, the suites seemed to be governed by a protocol, or lack of one, that embittered rather a few. Nancy Ryan volunteered a theory that the Russians had arrived at their system of room distribution by consulting Everyman Opera's payroll: "The less you get the more they give you." Whatever the reason, several of the leading players and prominent personalities, who were traveling as guests of the company, thought it "grotesque" and "crazy, man, crazy" that stagehands and wardrobe mistresses, carpenters and electricians were being led straight-away to the V.I.P. apartments, while they, the "real people," were supposed to content themselves with the hotel's backwater leftovers. "Are they kidding?" said Leonard Lyons. Another company guest, the New York financier, Herman Sartorius, had valid cause to complain; he'd been assigned no room at all. Nor had Mrs. Gershwin, who sat on her luggage in the lobby being soothed by Wilva Breen and Warner Watson.

"Don't you worry, baby," said Mrs. Breen, who had arrived the night before by plane and was ensconced with her husband in six rooms of Astorian splendor. "The Russians may be slow, they may get things a little mixed up, but everything comes out straight in the end. Look what happened when I went to Moscow," she added, referring to a visit she had made to Moscow the previous October in connection with the present tour. "It took me nine days to do two hours' work. But everything came out fine in the end."

"Sure, Lee," said Warner Watson, brushing down his graying crew-cut with an agitated hand. "Sure, honey, we'll get this room business fenced in."

"Darling, I'm perfectly happy, darling," Mrs. Gershwin assured them. "I just think it's so wonderful *being* here."

"To think we really made it," said Mrs. Breen, beaming round her. "And what sweet, kind, adorable people. Wasn't that adorable when the train arrived?"

"Adorable," said Mrs. Gershwin, glancing at the mass of wilting bouquets that had been given her at the station.

"And the hotel's simply beautiful, isn't it?"

"Yes, Wilva," said Mrs. Gershwin blankly, as though her friend's enthusiasm was beginning to tire her.

"You'll have a beautiful room, Lee," said Mrs. Breen, and Warner Watson added, "If you don't like it, you can change it. Anything you want, Lee, we'll get it fenced in."

"Darling, please. It's not important, Not the tiniest bit. If they'll just put me *some*where, I wouldn't dream of moving," said Mrs. Gershwin, who was destined, in the course of the next few days, to insist on changing her accommodations three times.

The Ministry of Culture's delegation, headed by Nikolai Savchenko, the businesslike, formidable six-footer, were now in a whirl of pacifying, rectifying, promising everyone they would get the rooms they deserved. "Patience," pleaded one of them, the middle-aged Russian interpreter called Miss Lydia. "Do not contribute to the misery. We have plenty rooms. No one will stride the streets." Nancy Ryan said she wouldn't mind striding the streets, and suggested to me that we escape the confusion in the lobby by taking a walk.

St. Isaac's Square is hemmed on one side by a canal stemming from the Neva, a river that in winter threads through the city like a frozen Seine, and on the other by St. Isaac's Cathedral, which is now an antireligious museum. We walked toward the canal. The sky was sunless gray, and there was snow in the air, buoyant motes, playthings that seethed and floated like the toy flakes inside a crystal. It was noon, but there was no modern traffic on the square except for a car or two and a bus with its headlights burning. Now and then, though, horse-drawn sleds slithered across the snowy pavement. Along the embankments of the Neva, men on skis silently passed, and mothers aired their babies, dragging them in small sleds. Everywhere, like darting blackbirds, black-furred schoolchildren ice-skated on the sidewalks. Two of these children stopped to inspect us. They were twins, girls of nine or ten, and they wore gray rabbit coats and blue velvet bonnets. They had divided a pair of skates between them, but by holding hands and pushing together, they managed very well on one skate apiece. They looked at us with pretty brown puzzled eyes, as though wondering what made us different: Our clothes? Miss Ryan's lipstick? The soft waves in her loose blond hair? Most foreigners in Russia soon become accustomed to this: the slight frown of the passer-by who is disturbed by something about you that he can't at once put his finger on, and who stops, stares, keeps glancing back, even quite often feels compelled to follow you. The twins followed us onto a footbridge that crossed the Neva, and watched while we paused to look at the view.

The canal, no more than a snow ditch, was a sporting ground for children whose laughing shrillness combined with a ringing of bells, both sounds carrying on the strong, shivery winds that blow from the Bay of Finland. Skeleton trees, sheathed in ice, glittered against the austere fronts of palaces that lined the embankments and stretched to the distant Nevsky Prospekt. Leningrad, presently a city of four million, the Soviet Union's second largest and northernmost metropolis, was built to the taste of the Czars, and Czarist taste ran to French and Italian architecture, which accounts not only for the style but also for the coloring of the palaces along the Neva and in other old quarters. Parisian blacks and grays predominate, but suddenly, here and there, the hot Italian palette intervenes: a palace of bitter green, of brilliant ocher, pale blue, orange. A few of the palaces have been converted into apartments, most are used for offices. Peter the Great, who is given high marks by the current regime because he introduced the sciences to Russia, would probably approve the myriad television aerials that have settled like a swarm of metal insects on the roofs of his once imperial city.

We crossed the bridge and wandered through opened iron gates into the deserted courtyard of a blue palace. It was the beginning of a labyrinth, an arctic Casbah where one courtyard led into another via arcades and tunnels and across narrow streets snow-hushed and silent except for sleigh horses stamping their hooves, a drifting sound of bells, an occasional giggle from the twins, still trailing behind us.

The cold was like an anesthetic; gradually I felt numb enough to undergo major surgery. But Miss Ryan refused to turn back. She said, "This is St. Petersburg, for God's

sake. We're not just walking anywhere. I want to see as
much as I can. And I'd better. From now on, you know
where *I'll* be? Locked in a room typing a lot of nonsense
for the Breens." But I saw that she couldn't last much
longer, her face was drunkard-red, a frostbite spot whitened
the tip of her nose. Minutes later, feeling its first sting, she
was ready to seek the Astoria.

The trouble was, we were lost. It amused the twins
greatly to see us rotating round the same streets and court-
yards. They screeched and hugged each other with laughter
when we came on an old man chopping wood and begged
him for directions by swinging our arms like compass
needles and shouting, *Astoria! Astoria!* The woodchopper
didn't understand; he put down his ax and accompanied
us to a street corner, where we were required to repeat our
pantomime for three swarthy friends of his, none of whom
got the point, but nevertheless beckoned us up another street.
On the way, out of curiosity, we were joined by a gangly
boy carrying a violin case, and a woman who must have
been a butcher, for over her coat she was wearing an apron
splattered with blood. The Russians babbled and argued;
we decided they were taking us to a police station, and
neither of us cared, as long as it was heated. By now the
moisture in my nose had frozen, my eyes were unfocused
with cold. Still, I could see well enough to know that abruptly
we were back at the Neva Canal footbridge. I wanted to
grab Miss Ryan's hand and run. But she felt our entourage
had been so faithful they deserved to see the mystery solved.
From woodchopper to violinist, the procession, led by the
twins who skated ahead like pied pipers, convoyed us across
the square and straight to the Astoria's entrance. While they
surrounded one of the Intourist limousines that stay parked

in front of the hotel, and began to question its chauffeur about us, we rushed inside, collapsed on a bench and sucked the warm air like divers who have been too long under-water.

Leonard Lyons walked by. "Looks like you've been out," he said. Miss Ryan nodded, and Lyons, lowering his voice, asked, "Anybody follow you?"

"Yes," said Miss Ryan, "*crowds.*"

A company bulletin board had been installed in the lobby. Attached to it were announcements concerning the company's rehearsal schedule, and a list of entertainments their Soviet hosts had planned for them, which included, in the days before the première, ballet and opera perform-ances, a ride on the new Leningrad subway, a visit to the Hermitage Museum and a Christmas party. Under the head-ing PROMPTLY, the dining hours had also been posted, and these, influenced by the fact that in the Russian theatre matinées start at noon and evening performances at eight, were listed as: Breakfast 9:30 A.M., Lunch 11:00 A.M., Din-ner 5 P.M., Evening snack 11:30 P.M.

But at five on that first evening, I was enjoying a hot tub too much to bother about dinner. The bathroom, which belonged to the third-floor room assigned to me, had peeling sulphur walls, a cold radiator, and a broken toilet that rumbled like a mountain brook. The tub itself, circa 1900, was splotched with rust stains, and the water that poured from its taps was brown as iodine; but it was warm, it made a wonderful steam, and I basked in it, idly won-dering if downstairs in the bleak dining room the company were at last being treated to caviar and vodka, shashlik, blinis and sour cream. (Ironically, as I learned later, they

were receiving the same menu that had been served at
every meal on the train: yogurt and raspberry soda, broth,
breaded veal cutlets, carrots and peas.) My water-logged
drowsing was interrupted when the telephone rang in the
outer room. I let it go awhile, the way you might if you
were sitting in a bath at home. Then I realized I wasn't
home, remembered that, looking at the telephone earlier,
I'd thought what a dead object it was to me in Russia, as
useless as if the wires were cut. Naked and dripping, I
picked up the receiver to hear the interpreter, Miss Lydia,
telling me I had a call from Moscow. The telephone was
on a desk next to the window. In the street below, a regiment of soldiers marched by singing a military song, and
when Moscow came through I could hardly hear for the
robust boom of their voices. The caller was someone I'd
never met, Henry Shapiro, a United Press correspondent.
He said, "What's going on there? Anything'd make a story?"
He told me he'd been intending to travel to Leningrad
for "the big story," the *Porgy and Bess* première, but now he
couldn't, because he had to cover "another opening," the
Supreme Soviet, which was happening in Moscow the same
night. He would therefore appreciate it if he could call
again on Monday after the première and have me report
to him "how it went, what really happened." I said all
right, I'd try.

The call, and the shock of standing unclothed in a cold
room, had brought me back to life. The company were expected to attend a ballet, and I started to get dressed for
it. There was a problem here. The Breens had decreed
that the men should wear black-tie, and the ladies short
evening dresses. "It's more respectful," said Mrs. Breen,
"and besides, Robert and I like everything to be gala."

There was an opposing clique who felt that the Breens' pronouncement would, if obeyed, make them look "ridiculous" in a country where no one dressed formally for any occasion whatever. I compromised by putting on a gray flannel suit *and* a black tie. While dressing, I moved around the room straightening some of the fruit and flower paintings that clotted the walls. They were rather atilt, owing to an inspective visit from Leonard Lyons, who was convinced the Astoria's rooms were wired for sound. Lyons' theories were shared by most of the company, which was not remarkable, considering that the two American diplomats from the Moscow Embassy had told them at a briefing in Berlin that during their Russian visit, they should "assume" their rooms would be wired and their letters opened. Even Breen, who called the diplomatic advice "a lot of blah," had unwittingly encouraged the company's suspicions by declaring that regardless of what anyone might individually feel, he hoped in correspondence they simply would write how "interesting" Russia was and what a "good time" they were having; this, some pointed out, was a contradiction, for why would Breen make such a request if he, too, didn't believe they were living in an atmosphere of microphones and steam kettles?

On my way out, I stopped at the floor desk and handed my key to the guardian, a plump pale woman with a Kewpie-doll smile who wrote in her ledger *224-1900*: the number of my room and hour of departure.

Downstairs, there was a row in progress. The company, dressed and ready to leave for the ballet, stood around the lobby like mortified figures in a tableau, while one of the cast, John McCurry, a husky bull-like man, stomped about yelling, "Goddam if I will. I'm not gonna pay any goddam crooked somebody seven bucks fifty to baby-sit any-body." McCurry was complaining of the price a Russian baby-sitter was charging to stay with his four-year-old daughter while he and his wife went to the ballet. At a cost of thirty rubles per sitter, Intourist had supplied a batch to all the parents of the troupe's six children; they had even arranged one for Twerp, the boxer puppy belonging to the production's wardrobe mistress. Thirty rubles, at the exchange of four to one, amounts to $7.50, a stiff tariff; but actually, to the Russian, thirty rubles has a buying power equivalent to $1.70, and the Russians, who had only this modest fee in mind, couldn't fathom why McCurry was causing such a scene. Savchenko, head man from the Ministry of Culture, was rosy with indignation, Miss Lydia white. Breen spoke sharply to McCurry, and McCurry's wife, a shy woman whose eyes are usually downcast, told him if he would please be quiet she would remain home with the child. Warner Watson and Miss Ryan hustled everyone out of the lobby and onto the two buses that had been chartered for the duration of their Leningrad stay.

Later, Breen apologized to Savchenko for the "conduct" of a few members of the company. The apology was intended to cover more than the McCurry incident. Free liquor was not included in the contract that had been drawn up between the Ministry of Culture and Everyman Opera, Inc. Savchenko was distressed because several persons had ordered drinks brought to their rooms and refused to pay for them, fought and insulted the waiters. Further, it had come to Savchenko's attention that many of the Americans were referring to him and his staff as "spies." Breen, too, felt that this was "unwarranted and outrageous," and Savchenko, in accepting his apologies, said, "Well, of course, in a company this size, we must expect some who will fall below the mark."

The ballet was at the Mariinsky theatre, which has been renamed, though no one calls it that, the Kirov, after the old revolutionary and friend of Stalin's whose assassination in 1934 is said to have initiated the first of the Moscow trials. Galina Ulanova, the Bolshoi's prima ballerina, made her debut in this theatre, and the Leningrad Opera and Ballet Company, which is now installed there on a repertorial basis, is considered first-class by Soviet critics. Except for the Fenice in Venice, a theatre it somewhat resembles in its eighteenth-century size and style and heating system, I think it the most beautiful theatre I've seen. Unfortunately, the old seats have been replaced by wooden ones, rather like those in a school auditorium, and their harsh, natural color makes too raw a contrast against the subtle grays and silvers of the Mariinsky's simplified rococo interior.

Despite the chilliness of the theatre, everyone, ladies included, were required to leave their coats at the cloakroom; even Mrs. Gershwin was forced to part with her mink, for in Russia it is thought uncultured, *nye kulturni* at its extremest, to enter a theatre, restaurant, museum, any such place, wearing a coat or wrap. At the moment, the principal sufferer from the ruling was Miss Ryan. A tall, striking blonde, Miss Ryan was wearing a low strapless dress that hugged her curves cleverly; and as she swayed down the aisle, masculine eyes swerved in her direction like flowers turning toward the sun. For that matter, the entrance of the entire company was creating a mass stir in the crowded audience. People were standing up to get a better view of the Americans and their black ties, silks and sparkles. Much of the attention was centered on Earl Bruce Jackson and his fiancée, Helen Thigpen. They were sitting in the Royal Box, where a hammer-and-sickle blotted out the Imperial crest. Jackson, lolling his hand over the edge of the box so that his jewelry, a ring on every finger, could be seen to advantage, was slowly inclining his head right and left, like Queen Victoria.

"I'd be freezing, if I weren't so embarrassed," said Miss Ryan, as an usher seated her. "Just look, they think I'm *indecent.*" One couldn't deny that there was a touch of criticism in the glances Miss Ryan's bare shoulders were receiving from surrounding Russian women. Mrs. Gershwin, who was wearing a becoming green cocktail dress, said, "I *told* Wilva Breen we shouldn't get all dressed up. I knew we'd look ridiculous. Well, darling, never again. But really, what *should* we wear?" She asked, looking about as if hunting fashion hints among the audience's melancholy, shapeless attire. "I didn't bring anything that wasn't pretty."

Sitting in the row ahead, there was one girl whose hair was neither plaited nor a sour bundle of string; she had an urchin-cut, which suited her curious, wild-faun face. She was wearing a black cardigan and a pearl necklace. I pointed her out to Miss Ryan.

"But I *know* her," said Miss Ryan excitedly. "She's from Long Island, we went to Radcliffe together! *Priscilla* Johnson," she called, and the girl, squinting near-sighted eyes, turned around. "For God's sake, Priscilla. What are you doing here?"

"Gosh. Gee whiz, Nancy," said the girl, rubbing back her tomboy bangs. "What are *you* doing here?"

Miss Ryan told her, and the girl, who said that she too was staying at the Astoria, explained that she had been granted a lengthy visa to live in the Soviet Union and study Russian law, a subject that had interested her since Radcliffe, where she'd also learned the Russian language.

"But, darling," said Mrs. Gershwin, "how can anyone study Russian law? When it changes so often?"

"Gosh. Ha ha," said Miss Johnson. "Well, that's not the *only* thing I'm doing. I'm making a kind of Kinsey report. It's great fun, gosh."

"I should think," said Miss Ryan. "The research."

"Oh, that's easy," Miss Johnson assured her. "I just keep steering the conversation toward sex; and gee whiz, you'd be surprised what Russians think about it. Gosh, Nancy, the number of men who have mistresses! Or wished they did. I'm sending articles to *Vogue* and *Harper's Bazaar*. I thought they might be interested."

"Priscilla's a sort of genius," Miss Ryan whispered to me, as chandeliers dimmed and the orchestra conductor raised his baton.

The ballet, in three acts with two intermissions, was called *Corsair*. The average Soviet ballet is far less concerned with dancing than with stupendous production, and *Corsair*, though a minor work in their repertory, involves as much change of scenery as the extravagant vaudevilles at Radio City Music Hall or the Folies Bergère, two theatres where *Corsair* would feel quite at home, except that the choreography and its execution are not up to the standards of the former, and the latter would never tolerate a scene of dancing slave girls swathed to the neck. The theme of *Corsair* is very similar to *The Fountains of Bahchisarai*, a poem of Pushkin's that the Bolshoi ballet has taken and swollen into one of its prize exhibits. In *Fountains*, an aristocratic girl is kidnaped by a barbaric Tartar chieftain and hauled off to his harem where, for three hours of playing time, many vile adventures befall her. In *Corsair*, this girl's twin sister undergoes somewhat the same ordeal; here she is the victim of a shipwreck (brilliantly simulated onstage with thunder, lightning, torrents of water crashing against the stricken vessel) who is captured by pirates, after which, for three hours, ditto. Both these tales, and countless like them, reflect a tendency in the contemporary Soviet theatre to rely on fantasy and legend; it would seem that the modern author who wishes to roam beyond the propagandist garden finds that the only safe path is the one that leads him into the forest of fairy stories. But even fantasy needs realistic underpinning, reminders of the recognizable, the human; without them, the power of life is not there, nor is art, a dual absence that occurs too often in the Soviet theatre, whose practitioners appear to believe that trick effects and technical wizardry can be made to supplant them. The Ministry of Culture frequently boasts that Russia is the sole country to have produced an art-culture *en rapport* with its population. The reaction of the audience to *Corsair* was nothing to disprove the claim; every set, every solo brought chandelier-shaking rounds of applause.

The Americans were enthusiastic too. "Magnificent, a dream," Mrs. Breen told Mrs. Gershwin during an intermission spent in the Mariinsky's café-salon. The opinion was seconded by her husband. Yet while praising the ballet, Breen, a dapper man whose facial expressions alternate between boyish beamings and Buster Keaton calm, had a troubled flickering in his eyes, as though perhaps he was comparing the physical elaborateness of *Corsair* with *Porgy and Bess'* three simple changes of scenery; if lavish effects were the criterion, then Soviet audiences were certain to be disappointed with his production.

"Well, *I* don't like it," said Mrs. Gershwin rebelliously, as the Breens moved on to another group. "I can hardly keep awake. And I'm not going to say I like it if I don't. They [the Breens] would put the words in your mouth if they could." That, of course, was the difficulty of the Breens' position. Like parents who have taken their children on a visit to the neighbors, they lived in dreadful anticipation of *gaffes*, of breakage and misconduct.

Refreshments were on sale in the Mariinsky's café-salon: beer, liqueurs, raspberry soda, sandwiches, candy and ice cream. Earl Bruce Jackson said he was starving: "But, man, that ice cream costs a dollar a lick. And guess what they want for a little bitty piece of chocolate not big as your toe? Five-fifty." Ice cream, advertised by the Soviets to be a delicacy of their own contriving, started to become a national passion in the U.S.S.R. in 1939, when American machinery was imported for its making. Most of the customers jammed into the salon stood spooning it out of paper cups while watching the Americans pose for photographs, informal ones, balancing beer bottles on their foreheads, demonstrating the shimmy, doing imitations of Louis Armstrong.

At the second interval I looked for Miss Ryan and found her backed into a corner, haughtily smoking a cigarette in a long holder and trying to pretend she was not the cynosure of puffy girls and leaden-faced women gathered to giggle and comment on her clinging gown and naked shoulders. Leonard Lyons, standing with her, said, "See, now you know how Marilyn Monroe feels. Would she be a wow here! She ought to get a visa. I'm going to tell her."

"Ohhhh," moaned Miss Ryan, "if *only* I could get my coat."

A man in his late thirties, clean-shaven, dignified, an athletic figure with a scholar's face, stepped up to Miss Ryan. "I should like to shake your hand," he said respectfully, "I want you to know how much my friends and I are looking forward to *Porgy and Bess*. It will be a powerful event for us, I can assure you. Some of us have obtained tickets for the first night. I," he said, smiling, "am among the fortunate." Miss Ryan said she was pleased to hear that, and remarked on the excellence of his English, which he explained by saying that he'd spent several of the war years in Washington as part of a Russian Purchasing Commission. "But can you really understand me? It's been so long since I've had the opportunity of speaking—it makes my heart pound." One sensed, in the admiring intensity of his attitude toward Miss Ryan, that the pounding of his heart was not altogether due to the English language. His smile slackened as a fluttering light signaled the end of intermission; and urgently, as though spurred by an impulse he couldn't resist, he said, "Please let me see you again. I'd like to show you Leningrad." The invitation was directed to Miss Ryan, but by polite necessity included Lyons and myself. Miss Ryan told him to call us at the Astoria, and he jotted our names on a program, then wrote out his own and handed it to Miss Ryan.

"Stefan Orlov," Miss Ryan read, as we returned for the last act. "He's quite sweet."

"Yeah," said Lyons. "But he won't call. He'll think it over and get cold feet."

Arrangements had been made for the company to go backstage and meet the ballet artists. The final scene of *Corsair* is partly played on the deck of a ship hung with rope nets, and at the end of the performance, when the Americans came behind the curtain, there was such a congestion onstage that half the dancers had to stand on the ship's deck or climb the rope nets to get a glimpse of the Western colleagues whose entrance they cheered and applauded a full four minutes before enough quiet could be summoned for Breen to make a speech, which began, "It is *we* who should applaud *you*. Your thrilling artistry has produced an evening none of us will ever forget, and we only hope on Monday evening we can a little repay you for the pleasure you have given us." While Breen finished his speech, and the director of the Mariinsky made another, the little ballerinas, sweat seeping through their make-up, crept close to the American performers, and their painted eyes rolled, their lips ohd-ahd as they gazed at the visitors' shoes, shyly, then boldly, touched the dresses, rubbed bits of silk and taffeta between their fingers. One of them reached out and put her arm around a member of the company named Georgia Burke. "Why, precious-child," said Miss Burke, a warm, happy-natured woman, "hug me all you like. It's good to know somebody loves you."

It was nearer one than midnight when the company started the bus ride back to the Astoria. The buses, rolling refrigerators, had the same seating plan as those that operate on Madison Avenue. I sat on the long back seat between Miss Ryan and the interpreter, Miss Lydia. Street lamps, yellowing the snows of empty streets, flashed at the windows like wintry fireflies, and Miss Ryan, looking out, said, "The palaces are so beautiful in the lamplight."

"Yes," said Miss Lydia, stifling a sleepy yawn, "the private homes are beautiful." Then, as though suddenly awake she added, "The *former* private homes."

* * *

The next morning I went shopping on the Nevsky Prospekt with Lyons and Mrs. Gershwin. Leningrad's principal street, the Nevsky is not a third the length of Fifth Avenue, but it is twice as wide; to get across its skidding aisles of traffic is a perilous chore and a rather pointless one, for the stores on either side of the street are all government-owned emporiums selling, in their different classifications, the same stock at the same prices. Bargain hunters, buyers on the lookout for "something a little different" would find shopping on the Nevsky a discouraging experience.

Lyons had set out with starry hopes of picking up "a nice piece of Fabergé" to take home to his wife. After the revolution, the Bolsheviks sold to French and English collectors almost all the jeweled eggs and boxes that Fabergé had created for the royal amusement; the few known examples of his work left in Russia are on display in Leningrad's Hermitage Museum and in the Armory at the Kremlin. Today, on the international market, the beginning price of a small Fabergé box is over two thousand dollars. None of this information impressed Lyons, who felt he was going to locate his Fabergé quickly and quite cheaply at a Commission Shop. Which was right thinking as far as it went, for if such an item existed, then a Commission Shop, a state-controlled pawn brokerage where a comrade can turn the last of his hidden heirlooms into spot cash, is probably the only place you would discover it. We visited several, drafty establishments with the going-gone sadness of auction halls.

In one, the largest, a glass cabinet ran the length of the room, and the spectacle its contents presented, the conglomeration of spookily diverse objects, seemed a dadaist experiment. Rows of secondhand shoes, so worn the spectral shape of the previous owner's foot could be pathetically discerned, were neatly set forth under glass like treasures, which indeed they were at $50 to $175 a pair; a selection of headgear flanked the shoes, flapper cloches and velvet cartwheels; after the hats, the surrealistic variety and value of the cabinet's contents spiraled: a shattered fan ($30), a soiled powder puff ($7), an amber comb with broken teeth ($45), tarnished mesh handbags ($100 and up), a silver umbrella handle ($340), an unexceptional ivory chess set with five pawns missing ($1,450), a celluloid elephant ($25), a pink plaster doll cracked and flaked as though it had been left in the rain ($25). All these articles, and yards more, were placed and numbered with a care that suggested an exhibition of mementos, the possessions of some dead beloved figure, and it was this, the reverence of the display, that made it poignant. Lyons said, "Who do you s'pose *buys* this stuff?" But he had only to look around him to see that there were those who, in lieu of anything else, found the moth-nibbled fan and the silver umbrella handle still fetching, still desirable, quite worth their quoted costs. According to the Russian calendar, Christmas was two weeks off, but Russians prefer to give gifts at New Year's, and the Commission Shops, like all the stores along the Nevsky, were packed with spenders. Though Lyons failed to flush any Fabergé, one pawn-broker came up with a unique nineteenth-century snuffbox, an immense topaz, hollowed and split in half. But the price, $80,000, was more than the customer had in mind.

Mrs. Gershwin, who intended giving a "really good" Christmas present to every member of the *Porgy and Bess* cast ("After all, darling, it's the company's fourth Christmas

together, and I do want to show the darlings my appreciation"), still had a few odds and ends to finish off, though
she'd carted a trunkload of gifts from Berlin. And so, struggling through the Nevsky crowds ("You can't deny there's
a lot of vitality around here," said Lyons), we visited a
furrier where the cheapest sable was a short jacket selling,
or rather not selling, for $11,000. Then we stopped at an
antique shop declared by Intourist to be Leningrad's most
"elegant." The antiques turned out to be used television sets,
an icebox, an old American electric fan, some battered pieces
of Biedermeier and a colossal number of oil paintings depicting scenes of historical event if not value. "What did you
expect, darling?" said Mrs. Gershwin. "There's no such
thing as Russian antiques. If there are, they're French." In-
quiring for caviar, we went to two fancy-food stores, the
local Vendômes; there were pineapples from Africa, oranges
from Israel, fresh lichee nuts from China; but no caviar.
"Where, *where* did I get the idea it was the butter on the
workingman's bread?" lamented Mrs. Gershwin, who said
she'd settle for a cup of tea, a desire that shortly drove us
into a Soviet version of Schrafft's. It was in a cellar, a dun-
geon where waitresses, wearing knee boots and tiaras made
of doily paper, waded across slush-flooded floors carrying
trays of ice cream and improbable pastry to gloomy groups
of middle-aged women. But Mrs. Gershwin had to do without her tea, for there were no tables available, nor even space
to stand.

So far, no one had made a single purchase. Mrs. Gershwin
decided to try a department store. On the way, Lyons, who
had a camera, paused often to take photographs, of match
women and cherry-cheeked girls dragging Christmas trees,
of street-corner flower stalls that in winter sell artificial

roses, paper tulips stuck in flowerpots, as though they were real. Each of his photographic forays caused pedestrian traffic jams, a gallery of silent spectators who smiled, and sometimes scowled, when he took their pictures, too. Presently I noticed that there was one man who continuously showed up among the onlookers, yet did not seem part of them. He always stood at the rear, a chunky man with a crooked nose. He was bundled in a black coat and astrakhan cap and half his face was hidden behind the kind of windshield dark glasses skiers wear. I lost track of him before we reached the department store.

The store was reminiscent of a carnival alley, consisting, as it did, of counters and alcoves whose shelves seemed mostly stocked with shooting gallery prizes, the cheap familiar dolls, ugly urns, plaster animals, the toilette set bedded in a crumpling of white casket silk. Mrs. Gershwin, overcome by an odor of rancid glue, felt swift necessity to leave the "leather-goods" department, a swifter one to flee the perfume counter.

A crowd began trailing us through the store, and when, in an alcove devoted to hats, I started trying on caps of ersatz Persian lamb, a good thirty grinning, jostling Russians ganged around demanding I buy this one, that one, themselves whisking models on and off my head and ordering the clerk to bring more, more, until hats were toppling off the counter. Someone bent to retrieve one from the floor; it was the man wearing ski glasses. The hat I bought, chosen at desperate random, proved later not to fit. A fake astrakhan, it cost $45; and because of the complicated payment system that operates in all Soviet stores, from the humblest grocery to GUM's in Moscow, it required another forty minutes to complete the transaction. First, the clerk gives you a sales slip, which you carry to a cashier's booth, where you cool your heels while the cashier does her computations on an abacus, an efficient method no doubt, still, some clever Soviet should invent the cash register; when the money has been paid, the cashier stamps the sales slip, and this you take back to the clerk, who by now is attending five other people; eventually, though, the clerk will accept the slip, go to check it with the cashier, come back, hand over your purchase, and direct you to a wrapping department, where you join another queue. At the end of this process, I was given my hat in a green box. "Please, darling," Mrs. Gershwin begged Lyons, who was tempted to buy a hat himself. "*Don't* make us go through all that again."

Ski-glasses was nowhere in sight when we left the store. He turned up soon enough, however, at the edge of a group watching Lyons photograph peddlers selling Christmas trees in a snowy courtyard. It was there in the courtyard that I left the hatbox; I must have put it down to slap my numbed hands together. I didn't realize it was missing until many blocks later. Lyons and Mrs. Gershwin were game to go back and look for it. But that wasn't necessary. For as we turned around, we saw Ski-glasses coming toward us, and dangling in his hand was the green hatbox. He gave it to me with a smile that twitched his crooked nose. Before I could think to say thank you, he'd tipped his cap and walked away.

"Well, ho ho—call that a coincidence?" crowed Lyons, a joyous shine livening his shrewd eyes. "Oh, I've had *him* spotted!"

"So have I," admitted Mrs. Gershwin. "But I think it's darling. Adorable. Simply adorable of them to take such good care of us. It makes you feel so protected. Well, darling," she said, as though determined Lyons should be persuaded to adopt her view, "*isn't* it a comfort to know you can't *lose* anything in Russia?"

At the Astoria, after lunch, I rode up in the elevator with Ira Wolfert, the former war correspondent who supposedly intended writing an article on Everyman Opera's tour for the *Reader's Digest*. "But I'm still looking for a story. What it seems to me is, is repetitious," Wolfert told me. "And you can't talk to anybody around here. Russians, I mean. It's giving me claustrophobia, every time I get into a political talk I keep getting the same old line. I was talking to Savchenko, he's supposed to be an intelligent guy, and I said to him, since this is a private talk, do you *honestly* believe all these things you're saying about America? You know, he was saying how Wall Street runs the country. But you can't talk to them. There's no realism in this social realism. Yesterday I was talking to a Russian—I won't define him, one of the guys we've met around here—and he slips me a note. This note asking me to call his sister in New York. He has a sister living there. Later on I see this guy on the street. I pull him down a side street and say, 'What the hell goes on here?' And he says, 'Everything's fine. Only it's better to be careful.' Everything's fine, but the guy's slipping me notes!" Wolfert bit hard on his pipe, and shook his head. "There's no realism. I'm getting claustrophobia."

Upstairs, I could hear the telephone ringing inside my room as I unlocked the door. It was the man I'd met during an intermission at the ballet, Miss Ryan's admirer, Stefan Orlov. He said he'd been calling Miss Ryan but there was no answer. I suggested he try the Breens' suite, one room of which Miss Ryan was using as an office. "No," he said, sounding nervously apologetic. "I must not call again. So soon. But when may I see Nancy? *And* you?" he added, tactfully. I asked him if he would like to come by the hotel for a drink. There was a pause that lasted until I thought we'd been disconnected. Finally he said, "That would not be convenient. But could you meet me, say, in an hour?" I said yes, where? He told me, "Walk around the cathedral. St. Isaac's. Keep walking. I will see you." He rang off without saying good-by.

I went down to the Breens' suite to tell Miss Ryan of the invitation. She was delighted, "I knew he'd call," but crest-fallen, "I'm stuck with six copies of a rush item," she said, inserting layers of paper and carbon into a portable type-writer. The rush item was a two-page letter written by Robert Breen and addressed to Charles E. Bohlen, the American Ambassador to Russia. It began by expressing gratitude over the fact that Ambassador and Mrs. Bohlen were coming to Leningrad for the *Porgy and Bess* première; but the bulk of the letter was in a tone of grieving complaint. Although the production's Soviet tour had the blessings of the U. S. State Department, it was not, contrary to the popular impression, under their official sponsorship. Indeed, the trip had been made financially possible by Russia's own Ministry of Culture. Nevertheless, Breen felt it was "a crying shame" no member of Ambassador Bohlen's staff had been permanently assigned to the company to observe "the day-to-day and minute-to-minute happenings, the individual contacts, and the spontaneous, warm incidents" that Breen considered necessary if the Embassy intended to "prepare properly the sort of full and valid report which rightfully should be expected on this unprecedented project." Breen wrote, "The need for such documentation concerns not only this goodwill tour, important as it is, but also possible future cultural exchanges. No one can imagine the extreme lengths to which we have gone to provide smooth running—or the infinite amount of details which have to be foreseen and arranged if this type of exchange is to bear the fruit of its promise. The documentation should record not only our successes, but also those facets of public relations which might be improved, and the possible failures."

"Give my love to Stefan," Miss Ryan instructed, as I left to keep the appointment. "And if it turns out to be a spontaneous, warm incident be sure and tell me so I can put it in the *Porgy and Bess* log," she said, referring to an official journal of that title maintained by her employers.

It's a stone's throw from the Astoria to the semi-Gothic mass of St. Isaac's Cathedral. I left the hotel at exactly three-thirty, the time Orlov had said he would meet me. But on stepping out the door, I found myself confronting a pair of ski glasses. There was an Intourist Ziv parked at the curb, and the man was sitting in the front seat talking to a chauffeur. For a moment I thought of returning to the hotel; it seemed the sensible course if Orlov was concerned that his rendezvous be off the record. But I decided to stroll past the car and see what happened; as I went by, nerves and an unreliable sense of etiquette prompted me to nod at the man. He yawned and averted his face. I didn't look back until I'd crossed the square and was in the shadows of St. Isaac's. By then, the car was gone. I walked slowly around the cathedral, pretending to admire the architecture, though there was no reason to pretend anything, for the sidewalks were deserted. Still, I felt conspicuous, and not quite lawful. Night swept the sky like the black crows that wheeled and cawed overhead. On the third lap around, I began to suspect Orlov had changed his mind. I tried to forget the cold by counting my steps, and had ticked off two hundred and sixteen when, turning a corner, I came on a scene that made the flow of numbers stop like the hands of a dropped watch.

It was this: four men in black had a fifth man backed against the cathedral wall. They were pounding him with their fists, pushing him forward and hitting him with the full weight of their bodies, like football players practicing on a dummy. A woman, respectably dressed and carrying a pocketbook tucked under her arm, stood on the sidelines as though she were casually waiting while some men friends finished a business conversation. Except for the cawing of crows, it was like an episode from a silent film; no one made a sound, and as the four attackers relinquished the man, leaving him spread-eagled on the snow, they glanced at me indifferently, joined the woman and walked off without a word between them. I went over to the man. He was fat, too heavy for me to lift, and the drink on his breath would have killed scorpions. He was not bleeding and he was not unconscious, but he wanted to speak and couldn't; he gazed up at me like a deaf-mute attempting to communicate with his eyes.

A headlighted car pulled alongside the curb. The strip of black and white checks bordering its frame identified it as a taxi. The rear door opened, and Stefan Orlov called my name. Leaning in the door, I tried to explain what had happened and ask him to help the man, but he was impatient, he didn't want to listen, he kept saying, "Get in," and, "Will you *please* get in"; and at last, with a fury that shocked me, "You're an idiot!" he said, yanking me onto the seat. As the taxi swung in a U-turn, its headlights exposed the man sprawled on the sidewalk, his lifted hands plowing the air, like the claws of an insect cruelly tumbled on its back.

"I'm sorry," said Orlov, regaining a civil voice that also managed to sound sincerely remorseful. "But other people's quarrels. They are not so much interesting, you understand. Now, enjoy yourself. We are going to the Eastern." He commented on Miss Ryan's absence and regretted "deeply" that she'd been unable to accept his invitation. "The Eastern is where you want to take a girl like Nancy. Very good food. Music. A bit of oriental atmosphere." After the clandestine nature of our meeting, it struck me as curious that we were now proceeding anywhere as gay and public as he described; and I said so. He was hurt. "I have no fears, but I'm not an idiot either. The Astoria is a sensitive place. You understand? It's a nuisance to go there. Why shouldn't I see you if I like?" he said, asking himself the question. "You are a singer, I'm interested in music." He was under the impression that both Miss Ryan and myself were singers in the cast of *Porgy and Bess*. When I corrected him, and told him I was a writer, he seemed upset. He had lighted a cigarette, and his lips, pursed to blow out the match, tautened. "Are you a correspondent?" he asked, letting the flame burn. I said no, not what he meant by a correspondent. He blew on the match. "Because I hate correspondents," he said, rather warningly, as though I'd best not be lying to him. "They're filthy. And Americans, it's too bad to say, are the worst. The filthiest." Now that he knew I was a writer, I thought perhaps he saw the situation in a different, less harmless perspective, and so suggested that if the taxi would take me within walking distance of the Asoria, we could amicably part company then and there. He interpreted this as a protest to his opinion of American correspondents. "Please, you misunderstand. I admire so much the American *people*," he said, and told me that the years he'd spent in Washington "were of a happiness I never forget. The Russians who lived in New York were always very snobbish about the Russians who had to live in Washington; they said, 'Oh, my dear, Washington is so *boring* and provincial.'" He laughed at his grande-dame imitation. "But for me, I liked it there. The hot streets in the summer. Bourbon whiskey. I liked so much my flat. I open my windows and pour myself a bourbon," he said, as though reliving these actions. "I sit in my underwear and drink the bourbon and play the Vic loudly as I like. There is a girl I know. Two girls. One of them always comes by."

The so-called Eastern is a restaurant attached to the Hotel Europa, just off the Nevsky Prospekt. Unless a few desiccated potted palms connote the Orient, I am at a loss to explain Orlov's contention that the place had a slant-eyed atmosphere. The atmosphere, if any, was a discouraging one of yellow-walled drabness and sparsely occupied tables. Orlov was self-conscious; he picked at his tie and smoothed his dark hair. While we crossed an empty dance floor, an ensemble, four musicians as spidery as the palms they stood among, were scratching out a waltz. We climbed a flight of stairs that led to a balcony where there were discreet dining booths. "I'm sure you think the Astoria is more elegant," he said, as we were seated. "But that is for foreigners and large snobs. Here is for smaller snobs. I am *very* small snob."

It worried me that he probably couldn't afford the Eastern at all. His overcoat featured a luxurious sable collar and he had a hat of gleaming sealskin. Still, his suit was a poor, thin plaid and the laundered freshness of his white shirt somehow made more apparent its frayed cuffs and collar. But he gave sumptuous instructions to the waiter, who brought us a 400-gram carafe of vodka and a huge helping of caviar heaped in silver ice-cream dishes, toast and slices of lemon on the side. With a passing thought for Mrs. Gershwin, I dispatched every soft, unsalted, gray, pearly bead of it, and Orlov, marveling at the speed of my accomplishment, asked if I would like another serving. I said no, I couldn't possibly, but he saw that I could, and sent the waiter for more.

Meanwhile, he proposed toasts in honor of Miss Ryan. "To Nancy," he said, draining his glass, then, with a refill, "To Nancy. She is a beautiful girl"; and, again pouring, "That beautiful Nancy. Beautiful girl. Beautiful."

The succession of fast-gulped vodka flushed his pale, almost handsome face. He told me he could drink "a fool's fill" and not get drunk, but a gradual dimming of intelligence in his fine blue eyes belied the boast. He wanted to know if I thought Miss Ryan was partial to him. "Because," he said, leaning forward in an attitude of excessive confidence, "she is a beautiful girl, and I like her." I said yes, I gathered he considered her highly. "But you think I'm an idiot? Because I'm nearly forty and I'm married five years?" He spread his hand on the table to show me a plain gold wedding ring. "I would never do harm to my marriage," he said piously. "We have two babies, little girls." He described his wife as "not beautiful, but my principal friend," and told me that aside from the children, the mutual interests they shared made the marriage "a serious composition." Among professional classes in Russia, it can be observed that persons seldom make alliances with anyone outside their own field of work. Doctors marry doctors; lawyers, lawyers. The Orlovs, it seemed, were both mathematicians who taught at the same Leningrad school. Music and the theatre formed their main pleasures; they had taken turns, he said, waiting in line to buy tickets for the *Porgy and Bess* first-night, but in the end they had been allowed just one ticket. "Now my wife pretends she doesn't want to go. That is so I can go." The previous year they had bought a television set as a New Year's present to each other, but now they regretted having spent the money on something "so boring and childish." He expressed himself with equal harshness on the subject of Soviet films. His wife, however, was fond of going to the *kino*, but he himself would only be enthusiastic if ever again they showed American pictures. ("I should like to know. What has happened to that beautiful girl, Joan Bennett? And the other one, Ingrid Bergman? And George Raft? What a wonderful actor! Is he still alive?") Apart from this disagreement on the merits of movie going, his wife's tastes coincided with his at every point; they even, he said, enjoyed the same sport, "boating," and for several years had been saving to buy a small sailboat, which they intended docking at a fishing village near Leningrad where each summer they spent two months' vacation. "That is what I live for—guiding a boat through the poetry of our white nights. You must come back when the white nights are here. They are a true reward for nine months' dark."

The vodka was exhausted, and Orlov, after calling for a replenishment, grumbled that I wasn't keeping pace with him. He said it "disgusted" him to watch me "just tasting," and demanded that I "drink like a decent fellow or leave the table." I was surprised how easy it was to empty a glass in one swallow, how pleasant, and it appeared not to affect me except for a tickling warmth and a feeling that my critical faculties were receding. I began to think that after all Orlov was right, the restaurant did have an oriental atmosphere, a Moorish coziness, and the music of the orchestra, scraping like cicadas among the palms, seemed to acquire a beguiling, nostalgic lilt.

Orlov, at the stage of repeating himself, said, "I'm a good man and I have a good wife," three times before he could reach the next sentence, which was, "But I have strong muscles." He flexed his arms. "I'm passionate. A lusty dancer. On hot nights, with the window open, and the Vic playing loud as we like . . . and the Vic playing loud as we like. One of them always comes by. And we dance like that. With the window open on hot nights. That's all I want. To dance with Nancy. Beautiful. A beautiful girl. You understand? Just to dance. Just to . . . Where is she?" His hand swept the table. Silverware clattered on the floor. "Why isn't Nancy here? Why won't she sing for us?" With his head tilted back he sang, "Missouri woman on the Mississippi with her apron strings Missouri woman drags her diamond rings by her apron strings down the bad Missouri on the Mississippi blues . . ." His voice grew louder, he lapsed into Russian, a hollering still obscurely associated with the tune of "St. Louis Blues."

I looked at my watch. To my astonishment it was nine o'clock. We'd been sitting in the Eastern almost five hours, which meant I couldn't be as sober as I reckoned. The realization and the proof of it struck simultaneously, like a pair of assassins who had been lying in wait. The tables seemed to slide, the lights swing, as though the restaurant were a ship riding a rough sea. At my request, insistence, Orlov asked for the check, but he went on singing while he counted out his rubles, sang his way down the stairs and waltzed by himself across the dance floor, ignoring the orchestra for his own accompaniment, "Missouri woman you're a bad Missouri woman on the Mississippi blues . . ."

In front of the Eastern there was a vendor selling rubber animals. Orlov bought a rabbit and handed it to me. "Tell Nancy from Stefan." Then he pulled me along a street that led away from the Nevsky Prospekt. As mud lanes replaced pavement it became clear that our destination was not the Astoria. For this was no neighborhood of palaces. Instead it was as though I were walking again through the slums of New Orleans, a district of dirt streets and broken fences, sagging wooden houses. We passed an abandoned church where wind wailed round the domes like a widow at the grave. Not far from the church, sidewalks resumed, and, with them, the city's imperial façade. Orlov headed toward the lighted windows of a café. The cold walk had quietened, somewhat sobered him. At the door, he said, "Here it is better. A workingman's place."

It was as if one had fallen into a bear pit. The body heat and beery breath and damp-fur smell of a hundred growling, quarreling, pawing customers filled the bright-lighted café. Ten and twelve men huddled around each of the room's half-dozen tables.

The only women present were three look-alike waitresses, brawny girls, wide as they were tall, and with faces round and flat as plates. In addition to waiting, they did duty as bouncers. Calmly, expertly, with an odd absence of rancor and less effort than it takes to yawn, they could throw a punch that knocked the stuffings out of men double their size. Lord help the man who fought back. Then all three girls

would converge on him, beat him to his knees, literally wipe
the floor with him as they dragged his carcass to the door and
pitched it into the night. Some men, would-be customers
decidedly persona non grata, never got into the café, for as
soon as any of these undesirables appeared at the door the
ladies of the establishment formed a flying, flailing wedge to
drive him out again. Yet they could be courteous. At least
they smiled at Orlov, impressed, I think, by his sable collar
and expensive hat. One of them showed us to a table where
she told two men, young jut-jawed bruisers wearing leather
coats, to get up and give us their chairs. One was willing,
the other argued. She settled his objections by snatching his
hair and twisting his ear.

For the most part, only upper-strata restaurants are li-
censed to sell vodka, and since the café was not in that category, Orlov ordered Russian cognac, a brackish liquid that
came in large tea glasses overflowing their brim. With the
blitheness of a man blowing foam off a beer, he emptied a
third of his glass and asked if the café "pleased" me, or did I
think it "rough." I answered yes, and yes. "Rough, but not
hooligan," he differentiated. "On the waterfront, yes, that
is hooligan. But here is just ordinary. A workingman's place.
No snobs." We had eight companions at the table and they
took an interest in me, picked at me like magpies, plucked a
cigarette lighter out of my hand, a scarf from around my
neck, objects they passed from one to the next, glaring at
them, grinning over them, and showing, even the youngest,
rows of rotted teeth, wrinkles for which age could not account. The man nearest was jealous and wanted all my attention. It was impossible to guess how old he was, anywhere
from forty to seventy. He had an eye missing, and this cir-

cumstance enabled him to do a trick which he kept forcing
me to watch. It was meant to be a parody of Christ on the
Cross. Taking a swallow of beer he would stretch his arms
and droop his head. In a moment a trickle of beer came crying out the gaping redness of his hollow eye socket. His
friends at the table thought it was an uproarious stunt.

Another favorite of the café was a boy who roamed
around with a guitar. If you bought him a drink he'd sing
you a song. He played one for Orlov, who translated it to
me, saying it was the kind of song "we" like. It was the
lament of a sailor longing for the village of his youth and a
lost love called Nina. "The green of the sea is the green of
her eyes." The boy sang well, with plaintive flamenco wav-
erings in his voice. I sensed, though, that he was not concen-
trating on the lyrics. His thoughts and his gaze too were
directed toward me. His white face had a sadness that seemed
to be painted on, like a clown's. But it was his eyes that bothered me. Then I knew why. It was because they reminded me
of the expression, the deaf-mute pleadings, in the eyes of the
man left lying on the cathedral sidewalk. When he stopped
playing, Orlov told him to sing another song. Instead the
boy tried to speak to me.

"I . . . you . . . mother . . . man." He knew about ten words
of English and he struggled to pronounce them. I asked
Orlov to interpret, and as they talked together in Russian it
was as though the boy were singing again. While his voice
wove some sorrowful prose melody, his fingers tinkered with
the strings of the guitar. Tears sprang to his eyes, and he
rubbed them away with the flat of his palm, leaving grimy
smudges like a child. I asked Orlov what he was saying. "It's
not so much interesting. I'm not interested in politics." It

seemed inconceivable the boy was talking politics, and when I persisted, Orlov was annoyed. "It's nothing. A nuisance. He wants you to help him."

Help was a word the boy understood. "Help," he said, nodding vigorously. "Help."

"Isn't he a nuisance?" said Orlov. "He says his father was English and his mother Polish, and because of this he says he's very badly treated in our country. He wants you to write the British Ambassador. Something like that. He wants to go to England."

"English man," said the boy, pointing at himself proudly. "Help." I didn't see how I could, and as he looked at me despair began to shade the hopeful shine of his wet eyes. "Help," he repeated reproachfully. "Help. Help."

Orlov gave him a coin and told him the name of a song he wanted to hear. It was a comedy song with unending choruses, and though the boy drudged through it listlessly, even the waitresses laughed and roared out the key lines, which everybody seemed to know. The one-eyed man, angry that there should be such laughter for anything except his trick, climbed on his chair and stood like a scarecrow Jesus, beer oozing from the empty socket and dribbling down his cheek. At five minutes to midnight, closing time, the waitresses began to switch the lights on and off, warningly. But the customers kept the song going, clung to these last minutes, as though they loathed to trade the café's camaraderie for cold streets, the fierce lonely journeys homeward. Orlov said he'd walk me to St. Isaac's Square. But first, a final toast. He proposed, "To a long life and a merry one. Is that what they say?" Yes, I told him, that's what they say.

The boy with the guitar blocked our path to the door. Exiting customers were still warbling his song; you could hear their voices echoing down the street. And in the café the waitresses were shooing out the last die-hards, darkening the lights in earnest. "Help," said the boy, gently catching hold of my sleeve. "Help," he said, his eyes full on me, as a waitress, at Orlov's request, pushed him aside to let us by. "Help, help," he called after me, a door between us now, and the words a muted sound fading into nothing like the night-falling snow.

"I think he's a crazy person," said Orlov.

"New York could've been bombed, for all we know," said Leonard Lyons to the financier, Herman Sartorius, who was sitting next to him in a bus that was taking the company on a morning visit to the Hermitage Museum. "I've never been in a place I couldn't read a newspaper, find out what's going on in the world. A prisoner, that's how I feel." Sartorius, a tall, graying, solemnly courteous man, confessed that he too missed Western newspapers and wondered aloud if it would seem "not quite the correct thing" if he inquired at a Leningrad bank for the current New York Stock Exchange quotations.

As it happened, there was a passenger seated behind them who could have supplied any information they wanted. It was his business to know what went on beyond the iron curtain, especially in America. A Russian, his name was Josef ("Call me Joe") Adamov, and he was in Leningrad to tape-record interviews with the *Porgy and Bess* cast for Radio Moscow, the station that beams broadcasts to countries outside the Soviet orbit. Adamov's talents are devoted to programs intended for American, or English-speaking, consumption. The programs consist of news reports, music, and soap operas sudsy with propaganda. Listening to one of these plays is a startling experience, not for the content, which is crude, but for the acting, which isn't. The voices pretending to be "average" Americans seem precisely that: one has absolute belief in the man who says he's a Midwest farmer, a Texas cowhand, a Detroit factory worker. Even the voices of "children" sound familiar as the crunch of Wheaties, the crack of a baseball. Adamov bragged that none of these actors had ever left Russia, their accents were manufactured right in Moscow. Himself a frequent actor in the plays, Adamov has so perfected a certain American accent that he fooled a native of the region, Lyons, who said, "Gee, I'm dumfounded, I keep wondering what's he doing so far from Lindy's." Adamov indeed seems to belong on the corner of Broadway and Fifty-first, a copy of *Variety* jammed under his arm. Although his slang needs dusting off, it is delivered with a bizarrely fluent side-of-the-mouth technique. "Me, I'm no museum-type guy," he said, as we neared the Hermitage. "But if you go in for all that creepy stuff, they tell me this joint's okay, really loaded." Swart, moon-faced, a man in his middle thirties with a jumpy, giggling, coffee-nerves animation, his shifty eyes grow shiftier when, under duress, he admits that his English was learned in New York, where he lived from the ages of eight to twelve with an émigré grandfather. He prefers to skate over this American episode. "I was just a kid," he says, as though he were saying, "I didn't know any better."

A foreign resident in Moscow, who knows Adamov well, described him to me as "no fool. An opportunist with two fingers in every pie." And an Italian correspondent, another old Moscow hand, said, "Ah, si. Signor Adamov. The smiler with the knife." In short, Adamov is a successful man, which means, as it does elsewhere, though far more so in Russia, that he enjoys privileges unknown to the ordinary citizen. The one he values most is a two-room bachelor apartment in Moscow's Gorky Street, where he lives, to hear him tell it, the life of a Turk in his seraglio. "Gimme a buzz you come to Moscow, you wanta meet some cute kids." Meanwhile, he thought some members of the *Porgy and Bess* company were "pretty cute kids," particularly the saucer-eyed singer in the chorus named Dolores ("Delirious") Swann. At the museum, when the sightseers were separated into battalions of twelve, Adamov made a point of joining Miss Swann in a group that included, among others, the Wolferts, Mrs. Gershwin, Nancy Ryan, Warner Watson and myself.

The Hermitage is part of the Winter Palace, which in recent years has been repainted the imperial color, a frosty chartreuse-*vert*. Its miles of silvery windows overlook a park and a wide expanse of the Neva River. "The Winter Palace was started working 1764 and took seventy-eight years to finish," said the guide, a mannish girl with a brisk, whip-'em-through attitude. "It consists of four buildings and contains, as you see, the world's greatest museum. This where we are standing is the Ambassadorial Staircase, used by the ambassadors mounting to see the Czar."

In the ectoplasmic wake of those ambassadors our party followed her up marble stairs that curved under a filigree ceiling of white and gold. We passed through a splendid hall of green malachite, like a corridor under the sea, and here there were French windows where a few of us paused to look across the Neva at a misty-hazy view of that celebrated torture chamber, the Peter-Paul fortress. "Come, come," the guide urged. "There is much to see and we will not accomplish our mission if we linger at useless spectacles."

A visit to the treasure vault was the mission's immediate

objective. "That's where they keep the ice, the *real* stuff, crown jools, all that crap," Adamov informed Miss Swann. A dragoon of stunted Amazons, several of them in uniform and wearing pistols strapped round their waists, guard the vault's bolted doors. Adamov, jerking a thumb toward the guards, told Warner Watson, "I'll bet you don't have any female cops in America, huh?"

"Sure," said Watson timidly. "We have policewomen, sure."

"But," said Adamov, his moist moon-face going scarlet with laughter, "not as fat as these, huh?"

While the vault's complicated steel doors were being un-locked, the guide announced, "Ladies will please leave their pocketbooks with the custodians." Then, as though to circum-vent the obvious implication, "It is a matter of ladies causing damage dropping their pocketbooks. We have had that ex-perience."

The vault is divided into three small, chandelier-lighted rooms, the first two entirely occupied by the museum's most unique display, a sophisticated panorama of Scythian gold, buttons and bracelets, cruel weapons, papery leaves and wreath garlands. "First-century stuff," said Adamov. "B.C. A.D. all that crap." The third room is intellectually duller, and much more dazzling. A dozen glass-enclosed cabinets (bearing the metal marker of their maker, Holland and Sons, 23 Mount Street, Grosvenor Square, London) afire with aristocratic souvenirs. Onyx and ivory walking sticks, musical birds that sing with emerald tongues, a lily bouquet made of pearls, another of ruby roses, rings and boxes that give off a trem-bling glare like heat waves.

Miss Swann sang, "But dee-*imonds* are a girl's best friend," and someone who shouted, "Where's that Earl Jackson?"

was told, "Oh, Earl—you know that cat wouldn't be up this hour of the day. But he's sure going to be sorry he missed this. Him feeling the way he does about sparkles."

Adamov planted himself in front of the cabinet containing one of the collection's few examples of Fabergé, a miniature version of the Czar's symbols of power: crown, scepter and orb. "It's gorgeous," sighed Miss Swann. "Don't you think it's gorgeous, Mr. Adamov?" Adamov smiled indulgently. "If *you* say so, kid. Personally, I think it's junk. What good does it do anybody?"

Ira Wolfert, chewing on an unlit pipe, was rather of Adamov's opinion. At least, "I hate jewelry," he said, glowering at a tray of blazing froufrou. "I don't know the difference between a zircon and a diamond. Except I like zircons better. They're shinier." He put an arm around his wife, Helen. "I'm glad I married a woman who doesn't like jewelry."

"Oh, I like *jewelry*, Ira," said Mrs. Wolfert, a comfortable-looking woman prone to expressing decisive notions in a tentative tone. "I like *creations*. But *this*, this is all trickery and show-off. It makes me ill."

"It makes me ill, too," said Miss Ryan. "But in quite a different way. I'd give anything for that ring—the tiger's eye."

"It makes me ill," Mrs. Wolfert repeated. "I don't call these things creations. This," she said, indicating a brooch of her own, a straightforward design in Mexican silver, "is what *I* call a creation."

Mrs. Gershwin was also making comparisons. "I wish I'd *never* come here," she said, forlornly fingering her diamonds. "I feel so dissatisfied, I'd like to go home and crack my husband on the head." Miss Ryan asked her, "If you could have any of this you wanted, what would you take?"

"All of it, darling," replied Mrs. Gershwin.

Miss Ryan agreed. "And when I got it home, I'd spread it on the floor and rip off my clothes and just *roll*."

Wolfert desired nothing, he simply wanted to "get the hell out of here and see something interesting," a wish he conveyed to the guide, who acquiesced by herding everyone to the door and counting them as they left. Some six kilometers later, the group, its ranks thinned by fatigue cases, stumbled into the last exhibit hall, weak-legged after two hours of inspecting Egyptian mummies and Italian Madonnas, craning their necks at excellent old masters excruciatingly hung, poking about the sarcophagus of Alexander Nevsky, and marveling over a pair of Peter the Great's Goliath-large boots. "Made," said the guide, "by this progressive man with his *own* hands." Now, in the last hall, the guide commanded us to "go to the window and view the hanging garden."

"But where," bleated Miss Swann, "where *is* the garden?"

"Under the snow," said the guide. "And over here," she said, directing attention to the final item on the agenda, "is our famous The Peacock."

The Peacock, an exotic mechanical folly constructed by the eighteenth-century clockmaker, James Cox, was brought to Russia as a gift for Catherine II. It is housed in a glass cage the size of a garden gazebo. The focus of the piece is a peacock perched among the gilded leaves of a bronze tree. Balanced on other branches are an owl, a cock rooster, a squirrel nibbling a nut. At the base of the tree there is a scattering of mushrooms, one of which forms the face of a clock. "When the hour strikes, we have here a forceful happening," said the guide. "The peacock spreads her tail, and the rooster cackles. The owl blinks her eyes, and the squirrel has a good munch."

Adamov grunted. "I don't care what it does. It's dopey."
Miss Ryan took him to task. She wanted to know why he
should feel that way about an object of such "imaginative
craftsmanship." He shrugged. "What's imaginative about it?
A lot of jerks going blind so milady can watch a peacock fan
her tail. Look at those leaves. Think of the work went into
that. All for nothing. A nonutilitarian nothing. What'cha up
to, kid?" he said, for Miss Ryan had started scribbling in a
notebook. "What'cha doing? Putting down all the dumb
things I say?" Actually, as Miss Ryan was surprised into explaining, she was writing a description of the clock. "Uh-
huh," he said, his voice not as genial as his smile, "you think
I'm pretty dumb, don't you? Well, put this down. I'll tell
you a good reason I don't like it. Because that peacock's
gonna go on fanning her tail when I'm dust. A man works
all his life, he ends up dust. That's what museums are, reminders of death. Death," he repeated, with a nervous titter
that expanded into mirthless guffaws.

A gang of soldiers, part of another tour, approached The
Peacock just as the hour chimed, and the soldiers, country
boys with their heads shaved bald, their drab uniforms sagging in the seat like diapers, had the double enchantment of
gaping at foreigners and watching the golden-eyed winkings
of an owl, a peacock flash its bronze feathers in the wan
light of the Winter Palace. The Americans and the soldiers
crowded close to hear the rooster crow. Man and art, for a
moment alive together, immune to old mortality.

It was Christmas Eve. The translators from the Ministry
of Culture, under the supervision of their chief, Savchenko,
had personally set up a skinny fir tree in the center of an
Astoria dining room and decorated it with hand-colored pa-

per cards, wisps of tinsel. The members of the company, sentimental over their fourth Christmas together, had gone on spending sprees: a razzledazzle of cellophane and ribbon spread in a knee-deep, twenty-foot circle round the tree. The presents were to be opened at midnight. Long past that hour, Miss Ryan was still in her room wrapping packages and rummaging through suitcases selecting from her possessions trinkets to take the place of gifts she'd neglected to buy. "Maybe I could give the bunny to one of the kids," she said, meaning the rubber rabbit sent her by Stefan Orlov. The rabbit nestled among her bed pillows. She'd inked whiskers on its face and on its side printed, STEFAN—THE BUNNY. "I guess not," she decided. "If I gave him away no one would ever believe I'd snagged a Russian beau. *Almost* did." Orlov had not telephoned again.

I helped Miss Ryan carry her presents down to the dining room, where she was just in time for the end of the gift-distributing. The children had been allowed to stay up for the party, and now, hugging new dolls and squirting water pistols filled with raspberry soda, they cycloned through the gaudy wrapping-paper debris. The grownups danced to the music of the Russian jazz band, which could be heard playing in the connecting main restaurant. Mrs. Breen whirled by, a bit of holiday ribbon floating round her neck. "Isn't it bliss?" she said. "Aren't you happy? After all, we don't spend *every* Christmas in Leningrad!" The waitresses, young English-language students who had volunteered to tend table for the American troupe, demurely refused invitations to dance. "Oh, come on, honey," one waitress was urged, "let's you and me melt that curtain together." Vodka, abetting the spirit of the occasion, had already melted the reserve of the Ministry of Culture representatives. They each had received presents from the company, and Miss Lydia, who had been given a compact, wanted to kiss everyone in sight. "It is too kind, so kind," she said, tirelessly examining her pudgy face in the compact's mirror.

Even the aloof Savchenko, a dour, glacial Santa Claus, or Father Frost, as the fellow is known in Russia, seemed after a while willing to forget his dignity, at any rate was unprotesting when a girl in the cast plumped herself on his lap, threw her arms around him and, between kisses, told him, "How come you want to look like a grumpy old bear when you're just a doll? A living doll, that's what you are, Mr. Savchenko." Breen, too, had affectionate words for the Ministry of Culture executive. "Let's all drink to the man we can thank for this wonderful party," he said, hoisting a tumbler of vodka, "one of the best friends we have in the world, Nikolai Savchenko." Savchenko, wiping away lipstick, responded by proposing another toast. "To the free exchange of culture between the artists of our countries. When the cannons are heard, the muses are silent," he continued, quoting his favorite maxim. "When the cannons are silent, the muses are heard."

The radio man from Moscow, "Joe" Adamov, was busily tape-recording aspects of the party on a portable machine. Eight-year-old Davy Bey, solicited for a comment, said into Adamov's microphone, "Hello, everybody, happy Christmas. Daddy wants me to go to bed, but we're all having a grand time, so I'm not going. Well, I got a gun and a boat, only what I wanted was an airplane and not so many clothes. Any kids would like it, why don't they come over and play with us. We got bubble gum, and I know some good places to hide." Adamov also recorded "Silent Night, Holy Night," which the cast, gathered round the tree, sang with a volume that drowned the next-room thumping of the dance band. Ira Wolfert and his wife added their voices to the choir. The Wolferts, parents of adult children, had booked a telephone call to America. "All our children will be together tonight; tomorrow they go different ways," said Mrs. Wolfert when the caroling ended. "Oh, Ira," she squeezed her husband's hand, "that's the only present I want. For our call to come through." It never did. They waited till two, then went to bed.

After two, the Christmas party infiltrated the adjoining room, the Astoria's "night club," which is permitted to operate later than twelve on Saturdays, the only night of the week when patrons outnumber personnel. The Soviet habit of seating strangers together does not encourage uninhibited conversation, and the cavernous restaurant, occupied to near capacity by Leningrad's elite, was unreasonably subdued, the merest few, mostly young army and naval officers with their sweethearts, taking advantage of the orchestra's respectable rhythms. The rest, artists and theatrical personalities, groups of military Chinese, jowly commissars accompanied by their uncorseted, gold-toothed wives, sat around bored and uncaring as castaways on a Pacific atoll.

Earl Bruce Jackson took one look, and said, "What-cha say, cats, let's get the snakes crawlin', put some hotcha in the pot, skin the beast and sprinkle pepper in his eyes." Whereupon five members of the company commandeered the bandstand. The hotel musicians had not the least objection to being ousted. They all were fans of American jazz, and one of them, a devotee of Dizzy Gillespie, had accumulated a large record collection by listening to foreign broadcasts and recording the music on discs made from old x-ray plates.

Junior Mignatt spit into a trumpet, banana-fingered Lorenzo Fuller struck piano chords. Moses Lamar, a powerhouse with sandpaper lungs, stomped his foot, opened his mouth wide as an alligator. "Grab yo' hat 'n grab yo' coat, leave yo' worry on de do'step . . ." It was as though the castaways had sighted rescue on the horizon. Smiles broke out like an unfurling of flags, tables emptied onto the dance floor. ". . . just direct yo' feet . . ." A Chinese cadet tapped his foot, Russians packed close to the bandstand, riveted by Lamar's scratchy voice, the drumbeat riding behind it. ". . . to de sunny *sunny* SUNNY . . ." Couples rocked, swayed in each other's arms. ". . . side ah de streeeet!"

"Look at them zombies go!" said Jackson, and shouted to Lamar, "They're skinned, man, skinned. Throw on the gasoline and burn 'em alive. Ooble-ee-do."

Mrs. Breen, a smiling shepherd gazing at her flock, turned to Leonard Lyons. "You see. We've broken through. Robert's done what the diplomats couldn't." A skeptical Lyons replied, "All I say is fiddles play while Rome burns."

At one of the tables I noticed Priscilla Johnson, the college friend of Miss Ryan's who was studying Russian law, and writing, so she said, articles on Soviet love life. She was sitting with three Russians, one of whom, a gnarled unshaven gnome with frothy black hair, splashed champagne into a glass and thrust it at me. "He wants you to sit down, and, gosh, you'd better," Miss Johnson advised. "He's a wild man, sort of. But fascinating." He was a Georgian sculptor, responsible for the heroic statuary in the new Leningrad subway, and his "wild man" quality came out in sudden rash assertions. "You see that one with the green tie?" he asked in English, pointing at a man across the room. "He's a rotten coward. An MVD. He wants to make me trouble." Or, "I like the West. I have been to Berlin, and met Marlene Dietrich. She was in love with me."

The other couple at the table, a man and wife, were silent until Miss Johnson and the sculptor left to dance. Then the woman, a death-pale brunette with Mongolian cheekbones and green almond eyes, said to me, "What an appalling little man. So dirty. A *Georgian*, of course. These people from the South!" She spoke English with the spurious elegance, the strained exactness of Liza Doolittle. "I am Madame Nervitsky. You of course know my husband, the crooner," she said, introducing me to the gentleman, who was twice her age, somewhere in his sixties, a vain, once-handsome man with an inflated stomach and a collapsing chin line. He wore make-up—powder, pencil, a touch of rouge. He knew no English, but told me in French, "*Je suis* Nervitsky. Le Bing Crosby de Russie." His wife was startled that I'd never heard of him. "No? *Nervitsky? The famous crooner?*"

Her surprise was justified. In the Soviet Union, Nervitsky is a considerable celebrity, the idol of young girls who swoon over his interpretations of popular ballads. During the twenties and thirties he lived in Paris, enjoying a minor vogue as a cabaret artist. When that faltered, he went on a honkytonk tour of the Far East. Though of Russian parentage, his wife was born in Shanghai, and it was there that she met and married Nervitsky. In 1943 they moved to Moscow, where she launched a not too prosperous career as a film actress. "I am a painter really. But I can't be bothered ingratiating all the right people. That is necessary if you want your pictures shown. And painting is so difficult when one travels." Nervitsky spends most of the year making personal appearances throughout Russia. He was currently engaged for a series of concerts in Leningrad. "Nervitsky is more sold out than the Negroes," his wife informed me. "We are going to the Negro première," she said, and added that she was sure it would be a "delightful" evening because "the Negroes are so amusing and there is so little amusing here. Nothing but work, work. We're all too tired to be amusing. Don't you find Leningrad absolutely dead? A beautiful corpse? And Moscow. Moscow is not quite as dead, but so ugly." She wrinkled her nose and shuddered. "I suppose, coming from New York, you find us very shabby? Speak the truth. You think *me* shabby?" I didn't think that, no. She wore a simple black dress, some good jewelry, there was a mink stole slung over her shoulders. In fact, she was the best-dressed, best-looking woman I'd seen in Russia. "Ah, you're embarrassed to say. But I know. When I look at your friends, these American girls, I *feel* shabby. There are no nice things next to my skin. It isn't that I'm poor. I have money . . ." She hesitated. Miss Johnson and the sculptor were returning to the table. "Please," she said, "I would like to say something to you privately. Do you dance?"

The band was smooching its way through "Somebody Loves Me," and the crowd on the floor listened to Lamar rasp out the lyrics with transfixed, transfigured faces. ". . . who can it be oh *may*-be *ba*-by *may*-be it's you!" Madame Nervitsky danced well, but her body was tense, her hands icy. "*J'adore le musique des Negres.* It's so wicked. So vile," she said, and then, in the same breath, began to whisper rapidly in my ear, "You and your friends must find Russia very expensive. Take my advice, don't change your dollars. Sell your clothes. That is the way to get rubles. Sell. Anyone will buy. If it can be done discreetly. I am here in the hotel, Room 520. Tell your friends to bring me shoes, stockings, things for close to the skin. Anything," she said, digging her nails into my sleeve, "tell them I will buy *anything*. Really," she sighed, resuming a normal voice and raising it above the shriek of Mignatt's trumpet, "the Negroes are so delightful."

Somewhat set back from the Nevsky Prospekt, there is an arcaded building bearing a marked resemblance to St. Peter's. This is the Kazin Cathedral, Leningrad's largest antireligious museum. Inside, in an atmosphere of stained-glass gloom, the management has produced a Grand Guignol indictment against the teachings of the church. Statues and sinister portraits of the Popes follow each other down the galleries like a procession of witches. Everywhere ecclesiastics leer and grimace, make, in captioned cartoons, satyr suggestions to nunlike women, revel in orgies, snub the poor to cavort with the decadent rich. Ad infinitum the museum demonstrates its favorite thesis: that the church, the Roman Catholic in particular, exists solely as a protection to capitalism. One caricature, an enormous oil, depicts Rockefeller, Krupp, Hetty Green, Morgan and Ford plunging ferocious hands into a mountainous welter of coins and blood-soaked war helmets.

The Kazin Cathedral is popular with children. Understandably so, since the exhibition is liberally sprinkled with horror-comic scenes of brutality and torture. The schoolteachers who herd daily swarms of pupils through the place have difficulty dragging them away from such attractions as The Chamber of the Inquisitors. The Chamber is a real room peopled with the life-sized wax figures of four Inquisitors relishing the agonies of a heretic. The naked victim, chained to a table, is being branded with hot coals by a pair of masked torturers. The coals are electrically lighted. Children, even when pulled away, keep sneaking back for a second look.

Outside the cathedral, on the many columns supporting its arcades, there is another kind of display. Coarse chalk drawings, the usual men's room graffiti, scarcely worth mentioning, except that it seems on first thought an odd place to find it; and on second it doesn't. In a way it belongs.

Antireligious museums were not among the sightseeing projects their hosts had lined up for the *Porgy and Bess* cast. Quite the contrary, on Sunday, Christmas Day, the Soviets provided the choice of attending a Catholic Mass or a Baptist service. Eleven members of the company, including Rhoda Boggs, a soprano playing the part of the Strawberry Woman, went to the Baptist Evangelical Church, whose Leningrad parishioners number two thousand. Afterward I saw Miss Boggs sitting alone in the Astoria dining room. She is a round, honey-colored, jolly-faced woman, always carefully groomed, but now her little Sunday best hat was slightly askew, the handkerchief she kept dabbing at her eyes was wet as a washcloth.

"I'm tore to pieces," she told me, her breasts heaving. "I've been going to church since I can walk, but I never felt Jesus like I felt Jesus today. Oh, child, he was *there*. He was out in the open. He was plainly written on every face. He was singing with us, and you never heard such beautiful singing. It was old people mostly, and old people can't sing like that without Jesus is helping them along. The pastor, there was a sweet old man, he asked us colored people would we render a spiritual, and they listened so quiet, all those rows and rows and rows of old faces just looking at us, like we were telling them nobody's alone when Jesus is everywhere on this earth, which is a fact they know already, but it seemed to me like they were glad to hear it. Anybody doubts the presence of Our Saviour, he should've been there. Well, it came time to go. To say good-by. And you know what happened? They stood up, the whole congregation. They took out white hankerchiefs and waved them in the air. And they sang, 'God Be With You Till We Meet Again.' The tears were just pouring down our faces, them and ours. Oh, child, it churned me up. I can't keep nothing on my stomach.''

That evening, with the première less than twenty-four hours away, the windows of the Astoria stayed lighted late. All night footsteps hurried along the corridors, doors slammed and telephones rang, as though a calamity were happening.

In Suite 415, Ambassador Bohlen and his wife entertained a small group of aides and friends who had just arrived with them by train from Leningrad. The gathering, which included Roye L. Lowry, Second Secretary at the Embassy and one of the two diplomats who had "briefed" the company in Berlin, was exceptionally quiet, since the Bohlens didn't want their presence in the hotel known until the last possible moment. They concealed themselves so successfully that the next morning Warner Watson, believing the diplomatic contingent were coming by plane, set out for the Leningrad airport with a bouquet for Mrs. Bohlen. Directly below the ambassadorial apartment, in Suite 315, Mrs. Breen was see-sawing on a Relaxer Board, while her husband polished the precurtain speech he planned to deliver. It had been suggested to him that he might circumvent the Communist propaganda potential in *Porgy and Bess* by pointing out that its picture of American Negroes concerned the long ago, not today, and so he added the line, "*Porgy and Bess* is set in the past.

It no more reflects the present than if it were about life under the Czars in Russia." In Room 223, Leonard Lyons was at his typewriter outlining the opening-night column he intended cabling his newspaper, the *New York Post*. "On stage were the flags of both nations, the U.S.S.R. and the U.S.A." he wrote, previewing the event. "The last time an American flag was displayed here was when there were only forty-five states in the union. A representative of the Ministry of Culture phoned to inquire how many states are united now. Yesterday a wardrobe mistress sewed three more stars on the old flag." The item finished a page. Lyons inserted a new sheet with fresh carbons. Instead of throwing the old carbon in a wastebasket, he took it to the bathroom and flushed it into oblivion. It was safer, he felt, to destroy used carbons, otherwise the Soviets, or perhaps rival correspondents, might ferret them out and decipher what he was writing. And indeed, the hotel was seething with journalistic competitors. The *Saturday Evening Post* was there in the person of Charles R. Thayer, Ambassador Bohlen's brother-in-law. Thayer, and C. L. Sulzberger of the *New York Times*, had arrived with the Bohlen party. The *Saturday Review* was sending Horace Sutton, *Time* and *Life* already had a photographer-reporting team on hand, and Mrs. Richard O'Malley, of AP's Moscow bureau, was speeding toward Leningrad aboard the crack Red Arrow Express, the same train which had, the night before, brought CBS correspondent Dan Schorr.

Now, on the second floor, in Room 111, Schorr, a heavyset bachelor in his middle thirties, was simultaneously trying to correct a manuscript, keep a pipe lighted and dictate on the telephone to a stenographer in Moscow. "Okay. Here's the story. You put in the slugs. Let's go," he barked, and began to read from typed pages. "*The Porgy and Bess Company comma believed to be the first American theatrical troupe ever to appear in Russia comma will open its Soviet engagement tomorrow night before a selected audience of two thousand two hundred I* repeat two two oh oh *at Leningrad's Palace of Culture comma but off-stage the Negro actors and singers have already scored a smash hit period The sixty members of the cast comma just by being themselves comma have had a tremendous impact on this comma the second largest city in the Soviet Union* ... that's right, isn't it? It is the second largest?" For twenty minutes more Schorr droned out anecdotes and fact. Long lines of Leningraders had waited all night in the snow to buy tickets at a top-scale of sixty rubles ($15), a price doubled and tripled on the black market. "Hey, what's a synonym for black market that we can get past the censors? Okay, make it curb price." Toward the end, he was saying, "*They have given Leningrad a Christmas probably unlike any in history period Until four o'clock this morning they gathered around a Christmas tree dash provided by a solicitous Soviet government dash and sang carols and spirituals period.* Yeah, I know I'm overfiling this story. But I got excited. Real excited. You can see it. The impact of one culture on another culture. And by the way, listen, I'm having a helluva time. They're a great bunch, these *Porgy and Bess* people. Like living with a circus."

On Monday morning, the day of the première, the cast met at Leningrad's Palace of Culture for a final dress rehearsal with full orchestra. Orginally the Soviets had intended housing the production in the attractive Mariinsky theatre, but the demand for tickets convinced them they could double their profit by transferring the opera to the huge Palace of Culture. The Palace, a pile of muddy-orange concrete, was slapped together in the thirties. From the outside it is not unlike one of those decaying examples of supermarket architecture along Hollywood and Vine. Several things about the interior suggest a skating rink. Its temperature, for one. But Davy Bey, and the other children in the company, thought it was "a grand place," especially the vast backstage with its black recesses for hiding, its fly ropes to swing on, and where the tough backstage crew, strong men and stronger women, caressed them, gave them candy sticks and called them "*Aluchka*," a term of affection.

I rode over to the rehearsal in a car shared by two of the Ministry's interpreters, Miss Lydia and the tall, personable youth named Sascha. Miss Lydia, a woman who enjoys her food, was in a fine state of excitement, as though she were about to sit down to a delicious meal. "We will see it, no? Now we will *see* this *Porgy-Bess*," she said, wiggling on the seat. And then it occurred to me that yes, of course, at last Miss Lydia and her Ministry colleagues would be able to judge for themselves "this *Porgy-Bess*," the myth that had for so long consumed their hours and energy. Even Savchenko would be having his first glimpse. Here and there along the route, Miss Lydia happily pointed at street placards advertising the show. Breen's name, repeated often, was in bigger, bolder type than Gershwin's, and the name of his absent co-producer, Blevins Davis, was omitted altogether. The day before, Mrs. Gershwin had observed to Warner Watson that in Russia the name Gershwin seemed to be "riding in the rumble seat"; to which Watson had replied, "Look, Lee, it's got to be Robert's show this time. He wants it that way. He's just got to have it."

"How do you sit that still?" Miss Lydia inquired of Sascha. "Now we *see* it. Before the ordinary people." Sascha *was* still. He had a seasick, stricken look, and not without reason. That morning Savchenko had thrown Breen into a tailspin by telling him that the production's theatre programs were still at the printer and would not be obtainable for another few days. It was an authentic crisis because the programs contained a synopsis of the opera's plot, and Breen was afraid that without this guide the audience would have difficulty following the action. Savchenko offered a solution. Why not have one of the Ministry's translators come before the curtain and, prior to each act, outline the plot? Sascha had been chosen for the task. "How will I handle my feet?" he said, his eyes hypnotized with stage fright. "How will I speak when there is no water in my mouth?" Miss Lydia tried to soothe him. "Think only what an honor! Many important people will be present. You will be noticed. If you were *my* son, Sascha, I would be very proud."

Inside the Palace of Culture's darkened auditorium, Sascha and Miss Lydia found seats in the fourth row. I sat down behind them, between Savchenko and "Joe" Adamov, both of whom were exploring their mouths with toothpicks. Other Russians, some thirty-odd who had finagled invitations to watch the run-through, were scattered around in the first several rows. Among them were Moscow journalists and photographers who had come to cover the première. The orchestra in the pit, an importation from Moscow's Stanislavski theatre, was winging through the overture with confident ease. The conductor, Alexander Smallens, a Russian-born American who has made rather a life's work of *Porgy and Bess*, having maestroed its every incarnation, including the original 1935 production, said the Stanislavski was the sixty-first orchestra under his command and the best of the lot. "Superb musicians, and a joy to work with. They love the score, and they have the tempo, the rhythm. All they need now is a little more the *mood*."

On stage, Breen, wearing a beret, a windbreaker, and a pair of close-fitting frontier pants, motioned the cast into place for the first scene. Flat overhead rehearsal lights shadowed the actors' faces, drained the color from the scenery and accentuated its wrinkled wornness. The set, a simple functional job, depicts a corner of Catfish Row with its balconied houses and shuttered windows. Presently, responding to a signal from Breen, a soprano leaned over a balcony and began to sing the opening song, "Summertime." Miss Lydia recognized the melody. She swayed her head and hummed with the music until Savchenko tapped her on the shoulder and growled an admonition that made her shrink in her seat. Midway through the performance, Adamov dug me with his elbow and said, "I speak pretty good English, right? Well *I* can't figure what the hell they're yelling about. All this dialect crap! I think . . ." but I never heard what he thought, for Savchenko turned round with a look that strangled Adamov. Most of the Russians were as silent as Savchenko could have wished. The rows of profiles, silhouetted in the glow from the stage, remained as severely unmarred by expression as coin engravings. At the end, with the last aria sung, there was a quiet drifting off to the cloakrooms. Savchenko and Miss Lydia, Sascha and two other young men from the Ministry, Igor and Henry, waited together while an attendant brought their coats. I walked over and asked Miss Lydia her opinion of what she'd seen. She bit her lower lip, her eyes darted toward Savchenko, who said firmly, "Interesting. Most interesting." Miss Lydia nodded, but neither she nor Sascha, Igor nor Henry, would venture a different adjective. "Yes," they all said, "interesting. Most interesting."

The average playing time of *Porgy and Bess* is approximately two and a half hours, but this final run-through, involving many pauses for corrections, lasted from 10 A.M. until two in the afternoon. The cast, edgy with hunger and anxious to return to the hotel, were annoyed when, after the theatre had emptied of Russian spectators, Breen informed them that the rehearsal was not yet over. He wanted to restage the curtain calls.

As matters stood, and though only the two players in the title roles took individual bows, the pattern of calls already established required six minutes to complete. Not many productions can expect an audience to sustain six minutes of applause. Breen now proposed extending these six minutes indefinitely by contriving what amounted to "a separate little show. Just," he said, "an impromptu thing. Sort of like an encore." It consisted of having a drummer beat a bongo while, one at a time, every winking, waving member of the company sashayed across the stage inviting individual applause. Even the stage manager, the wardrobe mistress, the electricians, and naturally the director himself, were set to receive homage from the audience. One had the choice of two conclusions: either Breen was counting on an ovation of volcanic vigor, or he feared the reverse, and so was insuring prolonged applause by staging this "impromptu" extra curtain call. Obviously, under the delicate diplomatic circumstances, no audience would walk out while the performers were still, in a sense, performing.

Private limousines had been put at the disposal of the leading players. Martha Flowers, who alternates with Ethel

Ayler in the role of Bess, and who had been assigned to sing
the part that evening, offered me a return ride to the Astoria. I asked if she were nervous about the première. "Me?
Uh-uh. I've been doing this show two years. The only thing
makes me nervous is, maybe I'm ruining my voice for serious
work." Miss Flowers, a young Juilliard graduate, is ambitious to make a reputation as a concert recitalist. She is small
and perky. Whether smiling or not, her lips are always pursed
downward, as though she'd just tasted a green persimmon.
"I'm tired, though. I sure am that. This kind of climate's
no good for a singer. You've really got to watch your throat,"
she said, massaging her own. "The other Bess, you know—
Ethel, she's in bed with a bad cold. Got a temperature and
everything. So I'll have to sing the matinée tomorrow and
maybe the evening, too. Well, a person could ruin their voice
forever, carrying on like that." She described her schedule
between now and curtain time. "I ought to eat something.
But first I'll take a bath. Can you float in your tub? Mine's
so big I can float. I'll take a nap, too. We start for the theatre
at six. Maybe six-thirty I'll be slipping into my costume and
pinning that old red flower in my hair. Then I guess I'll have
a long sit."

At six-thirty, the hour when Miss Flowers was presumably
in her dressing room pinning on a paper rose, Mrs. Breen
and Mrs. Gershwin were in the Bohlens' suite, where they
had been asked to have drinks prior to leaving for the Palace
of Culture. Breen himself, too busy to accept the Ambassador's hospitality, had already gone to the theatre.

The drinks, Scotch and tap water, were being served by
Bohlen's aide, Roye L. Lowry, and Mrs. Lowry, a couple
harmoniously matched in their conservative, schoolteacherish

demeanor. Mrs. Bohlen's close friend, Marina Sulzberger, the quick-witted wife of the *Times* man, was also present to provide the hostess with conversational assistance. Not that Mrs. Bohlen, a serenely efficient woman with a dairymaid complexion and sensible blue eyes, gives an impression of being unable to keep any conversation afloat, however awkward. But there was, if one remembers the exceedingly reproachful letter Breen had dispatched to Bohlen a few days earlier, a certain awkwardness inherent in this meeting between representatives of Everyman Opera and the U. S. State Department. As for the Ambassador, one would not suppose, from his amiable manner, that he'd ever received such a letter. A career diplomat for more than twenty-five years, a large percentage of them spent at the Moscow Embassy, where he first held Lowry's present post, Second Secretary, and where he was ultimately appointed Ambassador in 1952, Bohlen still resembles a photograph taken the year (1927) he graduated from Harvard. Experience has harshened his sportsman's handsomeness, salted his hair and reduced, rather obliterated, a dreaming naïveté around the eyes. But the direct look of youth, of rugged stamina, has stayed with him. He lounged in his chair, sipping Scotch and talking to Mrs. Breen as though they were in a country room with a warm hearth and lazing dogs on the floor.

But Mrs. Breen couldn't relax. She sat on the edge of her seat, like an applicant for a job. "It's so sweet of you to have come. Just dear of you," she told Bohlen in a small-girl voice that was somehow not quite her own. "It means so much to the cast."

"You don't think we would've *missed* it?" said Bohlen, and his wife added, "Not for anything in the world! It's the high point of the winter. We've thought of nothing else, have we, Chip?" she said, using the Ambassador's nickname.

Mrs. Breen modestly lowered her eyes, a touch of color tinged her cheeks. "It means so much to the cast."

"It means so much to *us*," said Mrs. Bohlen. "Our life isn't so amusing that we could afford to miss something like this. Why, we'd have got here if we'd had to walk the whole way. Crawled on our hands and knees."

Mrs. Breen raised her eyes for an instant and glanced sharply at the Ambassador's wife, as though half suspecting her of satiric intent; then, reassured by Mrs. Bohlen's straight, clear face, she dropped her gaze again. "It's just dear of you," she whispered. "And of course we're all thrilled about the party in Moscow."

"Oh, yes . . . the party," said Mrs. Bohlen, with detectable resignation. In honor of the company's Moscow première, two weeks hence, the Bohlens had promised to give an official reception at their residence, Spaso House.

"Robert and I do hope Mr. Bulganin will be there. We want to thank him personally for all the courtesy we've received. The Ministry of Culture paid Robert a lovely tribute. Seven ivory elephants." Mrs. Breen was referring to a mantelpiece parade of plastic elephants that Savchenko had presented as a gift to Breen.

"How very nice," said Mrs. Bohlen dimly, as though she'd lost the conversational thread. "Well, of course, we can't be quite sure *who's* coming to the party. We're sending out two hundred invitations, more or less, but since Russians never answer an R.S.V.P., we never know who to expect or how many."

"That's right," said the Ambassador. "You don't count on

these fellows until they walk in the door. Any of them. And when they give a party themselves they almost never invite you until the last minute. Everyone in the diplomatic corps keeps the evening free when we know there's going to be a big affair at the Kremlin. We just sit around, hoping the phone will ring. Sometimes we're in the middle of dinner before they invite us. Then it's a rush. Fortunately, you never have to dress for these things," he said, reverting to a previous topic, and a painful one for Mrs. Breen, who, earlier in the day, had been chagrined to learn that Bohlen was unwilling to attend the opening in black-tie. Indeed, driven by her determination to "make everything gala," she had gone a step further and envisioned the Ambassador wearing white tie and tails, which is what her husband planned to do. But, "It never occurred to me to bring a dinner jacket," said Bohlen, fingering a button of the dark gray suit he considered proper to the occasion. "No one wears them here. Not even for a première."

Over in a corner, Mrs. Gershwin and Mrs. Sulzberger were elaborating on the same sartorial theme. "Of *course* we shouldn't dress up. That's what I've told Wilva all along. We went to a ballet the other night and looked perfectly ridiculous. Oh, there's too much fuss around here. I don't know what the fuss is all about. After all, it's *only* little old *Porgy*."

"Actually," said Mrs. Sulzberger, a Greek-born woman whose clever eyes sparkle with Mediterranean mischief, "it might not be a bad thing for the Russians to see people dressed. There's no excuse to go about looking the way they do. When we first came here, I felt sorry for them," she said, and added that she and her husband had been in the Soviet Union two weeks, staying as house guests of the Bohlens.

"I thought the way they dressed, the dreariness of it all, I imagined it was because they were terribly poor. But really, you know, that's not true. They look this way because they want to. They do it on purpose."

"Yes," said Mrs. Gershwin, "that's what I think."

"I wonder," mused Mrs. Sulzberger. "I wonder. Do you suppose the Russians are so awful because they've always been beaten? Or have they always been beaten because they're so awful?"

"Yes," said Mrs. Gershwin, "that's what I think."

Lowry caught the Ambassador's eye, and glanced significantly at his watch. Outside the hotel a limousine was purring its engine, preparing to carry the Bohlens to the theatre. Other Zivs, a street-long gleam of them, waited for Mrs. Breen and Mrs. Gershwin, for Savchenko and Adamov and the employees of AP, Time-Life, CBS. Soon the cars would start slithering across the square, like a funeral cortege.

Bohlen swallowed his Scotch and accompanied his guests to the door of the suite. "I don't think you have any thing to worry about," he told Mrs. Breen. "The Russians are very musical people. You'll have rubles coming out of your ears."

"Adorable man. And she's charming, too," Mrs. Gershwin remarked to Mrs. Breen, as the two ladies descended the stairs.

"Adorable. But," said Mrs. Breen, her shy little-girl voice suddenly maturing, "Robert and I *did* want it to be gala."

"Well, darling, we can't be gala if we're going to be conspicuous," observed Mrs. Gershwin, whose diamonded decorations made her look as though she were moving in a spotlight. "Frankly, myself, I think it would do the Russians a world of good to see people dressed up. There's no excuse for them to go around looking the way they do. When we first came here, I felt sorry for them, but now . . ."

Across town, at the Palace of Culture, snow-sprinkled crowds were massing on the sidewalk to watch the ticket holders arrive, and inside the theatre a sizable number, baking in a blaze of newsreel and television arc lights, were already seated. Baskets of flowers, yellow and white, flanked the stage, and crossed flags, an entwining of stars and stripes and hammer and sickle, floated above the proscenium. Backstage, where the tuning orchestra's chirping flutes and moaning oboes echoed like forest sounds, Martha Flowers, costumed and completely calm, despite the distant, rising audience-roar, was having, as she'd predicted, "a long sit."

And it was very long. The curtain, announced for eight, went up at nine-five and came down at eleven-forty. By midnight I was back at the Astoria waiting for a call from Henry Shapiro, the UP correspondent in Moscow, who'd said he would telephone me after the première to find out "how it went. What really happened." There is no absolute truth in these matters, only opinion, and as I attempted to formulate my own, tried to decide what I was going to tell Shapiro, I stretched on the bed and switched out the light. My eyes smarted from the recent glare of flash bulbs, I seemed still to hear the soft clickety noise of newsreel cameras. And indeed, lying in the dark, it was as though a film were rushing through my head, a disconnected rampage of pictures: Martha Flowers tripping to the footlights to throw the audience a kiss, Savchenko striding through the lobby listening for comments, the terror in Sascha's eyes, Miss Ryan covering her face with her hands. I made a conscious effort to slow the film down, let it start at the beginning.

It began with the audience, an army standing at solemn attention while the orchestra played the national anthems of the two countries: Savchenko had courteously insisted that "The Star Spangled Banner" should be heard first. Then individual faces came into focus: Ambassador and Mrs. Bohlen, the Sulzbergers, the Lowrys, Miss Ryan and Leonard Lyons, all together in a front row. Near them, on a platform extending from the side of the stage, a squadron of photographers waited impatiently until the anthems ended: then the platform resembled a besieged fortress, photographers firing away while assistants reloaded their cameras. Some, like CBS's Dan Schorr, desperately alternated between cameras and tape recorders as they went to work documenting the precurtain ceremonies. There was no need for such haste. The speeches, and their translations, lasted an hour.

The Russians were brief enough. Konstantin Sergeev, the dapper young ballet master of the Leningrad Theatre, shook hands with Breen and, speaking into a microphone, said, "Dear Brothers in art, welcome. We in the Soviet Union have always paid attention and tribute to the art of the United States. We know and cherish the works of such fine artsits as Mark Twain, Walt Whitman, Harriet Beecher Stowe, Jack London, and Paul Robeson. We appreciate the talents of George Gershwin, and that is why this meeting is so joyous." Afterward, apropos of this speech, Mrs. Gershwin said, "I thought I'd faint when I heard the name Gershwin being lumped in with all those Communists."

Breen bowed to Sergeev, and stepped up to the microphone, a preening, impeccable figure in his trim tuxedo and starched shirt. "He just lost his nerve," said Miss Ryan, explaining why at the last minute her employer had abandoned the idea of wearing white tie and tails. But now, watching Breen react to the applause that greeted him, one wouldn't have guessed there was a nerve in his system. His smooth blond face, bleached by the strong lights and exploding flash bulbs, possessed an inward-gazing remoteness, as though he had for so long dreamed the scene before him that it was still a dream; and when he spoke, the measured, sepulchral timbre of his actor's voice strengthened the impression that he thought himself alone on an empty stage addressing an imaginary audience, practicing, as it were, for an ego-satisfying moment that would someday come true. Imaginary audiences are notoriously submissive; but the Palace of Culture assemblage began to grow talkative themselves as Breen rambled on, the Russian translator trailing behind him. With graceful, *grand seigneur* sweepings of the hand, he introduced Ambassador and Mrs. Bohlen, who rose in their seats to acknowledge applause. The Ambassador had been expected to deliver a speech, but much to Bohlen's relief, and Breen's regret, the Soviets, extremely sensitive to protocol, had asked that this part of the program be deleted because they had no one of "comparable eminence" to make, on the Russian behalf, a rejoinder. Mrs. Gershwin was also introduced, and the conductor, Alexander Smallens, who received a sumptuous hand when Breen announced that Smallens was "born right here in Leningrad." The introductions continued as Breen presented members of the cast who were not performing that evening: Ethel Ayler, the alternate Bess, sufficiently recovered from her cold to have climbed out of bed and into a skimpy, strapless blue gown. And Lorenzo Fuller, the alternate Sportin' Life. Fuller had a "few" words to say, among them a Russian phrase he'd memorized, *"Dobro poshlavat, druzya,"* which means "Welcome, friends." The audience roared approval. But as clock hands crept toward nine, even the frenzied photographers paused to consult watches. "Jesus," said one correspondent, "they ought to have a gong around here. Like Major Bowes." It was as though Breen had overheard him, for abruptly the ceremonial group vacated the stage.

The theatre grew quieter than a hens' roost at sunset as the audience settled back, confident that now the curtain would rise and reveal what they'd paid their rubles to see, *Porgy and Bess*. Instead, Sascha appeared. He crossed the stage stiff-legged and wobbly, as though he were walking a plank. A sheaf of typewritten pages quivered in his hands, and his face, bloodlessly pallid, was drenched with sweat. The instant the audience caught wind of why he was there, to read them the opera's plot, the hens' roost turned into a hornets' nest. They couldn't tolerate another syllable *about* the show, they simply wanted to see it; and a mutiny that broke out in the balcony, where rude voices started shouting, spread to the orchestra: the patrons clapped, whistled, stamped their feet. "Poor Sascha, oh, poor boy," said Miss Ryan, covering her face with her hands. "It's too terrible. I can't bear to watch." Several rows back of Miss Ryan, Sascha's two friends, Igor and Henry, slumped on their spines, but Miss Lydia, less squeamish, glared round at her neighbors, as though she'd like to crack them with her pocketbook. On stage, Sascha went on reading, mumbling, as if he were whispering a prayer against the deafening tumult; like Breen before him, he seemed locked in a dream, a numbing, naked-in-the-street nightmare. Smallens flicked his baton, and the overture sounded as Sascha retreated into the wings.

It was soon evident that the audience regretted not having paid more attention to Sascha's résumé of the two-act tale the opera tells. In skeleton, the story is this: a crippled begger, Porgy, falls in love with a Charleston tart, Bess. Alas, this neurotic young woman is under the wicked influence of two other gentlemen. One, the devilish dope peddler, Sportin' Life, has enticed her into drug addiction, while the second, an alluringly muscular criminal named Crown, monopolizes the heroine's libidinous impulses. Porgy dispenses of the latter rival by killing him, and when he is sent to jail for the deed, Bess alleviates her woes by going on a dope binge, during which Sportin' Life persuades her to forget Porgy and traipse off with him to New York: "That's where we belong, sister" he sings as they head for the sugary lights of Harlem. In the last scene, Porgy, acquitted of Crown's murder, sets out for the North in a goat-drawn cart, believing, and leaving the spectator to believe, that he will find Bess and bring her home. Although this narrative line seems straight as a ruler, the intricate vocal-choreographic terms in which it is developed would confuse any audience where the language barrier is present, particularly if the music, the style of dancing, the directorial approach are each and all virgin territory, as they were to the overwhelming majority of those assembled in the Palace of Culture.

"Summertime" ended, and there was no applause. The entrance of Porgy went unheralded. Leslie Scott, playing the part, finished "A Woman Is a Sometimes Thing," and paused for the acclaim the number ordinarily arouses. The fact that none came caused a temporary lapse of stage action. Recovering, the cast launched into a jazzy crap-game sequence: whispering ran through the audience, as though they were asking each other what it meant, these excited men tossing dice? The whispering gathered momentum and turned into gasps, a tremor of shock, when Bess, making her initial appearance, hiked up her skirt to adjust her garter. Miss Ryan observed to Mrs. Lowry, "If they think *that's* so daring, just wait." The words weren't out of her mouth before Sportin' Life's witty, lascivious gyrations ignited fresh fire-crackers of audible astonishment. The crap game concludes with Crown killing one of Porgy's neighbors; a funeral scene follows: while the murdered man's widow sings a lament, "My Man's Gone Now," the mourning inhabitants of Cat-fish Row sway in a tribal circle around the corpse. At this point, an important Soviet dignitary turned to a correspond-ent and said in Russian, "Ah, now I see! They are going to *eat* him." The deceased, undevoured, was trundled off to his grave, and the opera progressed to Porgy's optimistic "I've Got Plenty of Nothin'." Scott, a big and solidly con-structed baritone, belted it across the footlights with a fervor that should've stopped the show. It didn't.

The audience's persistent silence seemed not altogether at-tributable to apathy; rather, for the most part, it appeared to be the result of troubled concentration, an anxious desire to understand; and so, fearful of missing the essential phrase, the significant clue that would unmask the mysteries con-fronting them, they listened and watched with the brooding intentness of students in a lecture hall. But the first act was almost over before the warmth that comes with comprehen-sion wafted through the theatre. It was created by "Bess, You Is My Woman Now," a duet sung by the two principals: suddenly it was clear that Porgy and Bess were in love, that their song was a tender rejoicing, and the audience, rejoic-ing too, deluged the performers with applause that was brief but heavy, like tropic rain. However, the drought set in again as the music segued into the jamboree fanfare of "I Can't Sit Down," the first-act finale. The scene is peppered with folklorish humor; and, occasionally, isolated chuckles, lonely-sounding patches of laughter, indicated there were persons who appreciated it. The curtain descended. Silence. The house lights began to come up; the audience blinked, as though until this instant they hadn't known the act was over. They caught their breath, like passengers at the end of a roller-coaster ride, and began to applaud. The applause lasted thirty-two seconds.

"They're stunned," said Lowry, parroting the words, though somehow transforming the spirit, of Breen's prophecy. "They've never seen anything like it."

If the Russians were stunned, they were not alone. Several of the American journalists huddled together, comparing notes. "It's not going over," a baffled Dan Schorr complained to a bewildered Time-Life photographer. And Mrs. Bohlen, following her husband up the aisle, was poignantly pensive. Later she told me the thought behind the expression: "I was thinking—well, we've laid an egg. Now what are we going to do about it?"

Out in the crowded lobby, Mrs. Breen smilingly expressed sentiments of a sunnier nature; according to her, the performance was going "beautifully." A correspondent interposed to ask why, in that case, the Russians were "sitting on their hands." Mrs. Breen stared at the questioner as though she thought him certifiable. "But they aren't *supposed* to applaud," she said. "Robert *planned* it that way. So that there wouldn't *be* any applause. It interrupts the mood."

The Wolferts agreed with Mrs. Breen; they felt the première was turning out a triumph. "First time we've seen the show," said Wolfert. "I don't like musicals. Got no use for them. But this one's pretty good."

Another American, the Russian-speaking Priscilla Johnson, spent the intermission eavesdropping on the customers. "They're quite shocked," she reported. "They think it's awfully immoral. But gosh, you can't blame them for not liking it. It's such a second-rate production. That's what makes me sad. If only it were *really* good, then you could blame them. Too bad, too bad," she said, ruffling her bangs, shaking her head. "This whole setup: the Breens, the publicity and all—gosh, it's just not geared for failure."

Like Miss Johnson, Savchenko and Adamov circulated about sampling opinions. "It's a very big success" was all Savchenko would admit; but Adamov, whose slang was growing richer under the company's tutelage, said, "So a lot of squares don't dig it. They don't flip. So is that big news? You got squares in New York, ain'tcha, man?"

Madame Nervitsky and her crooner-husband passed by. "Oh, we're amazed," she told me, flourishing a sword-length cigarette holder. "Nervitsky thinks it *très dépravé*. Not I. I adore the vileness of it all. The rhythm, the sweat. Really, the Negroes are too amusing. And how wonderful their teeth!" Moving closer, she said, "You did tell your friends? Room 520. Don't telephone, come quietly, bring anything. I will pay very well."

Stefan Orlov was standing at a refreshment counter, a glass of mineral water in his hand. "My friend," he said, clapping me on the shoulder. "What a night we had, yes? The next morning, my wife, she had to beat me out of bed. Tie my shoes and knot my tie. Not angry, you understand: laughing at me." He produced a pair of opera glasses, and peered through them. "I saw Nancy. I wondered if I should try to speak to her. But I said to myself no, Nancy is sitting with fashionable people. Will you tell her that I saw her?" I said I would, and asked if he was enjoying *Porgy and Bess*. "I wish I had a ticket for every night. It's an experience. Powerful! Like Jack London. Like Gogol. I will never forget it," he said, pocketing the opera glasses. A frown creased his forehead, he opened his mouth to speak, changed his mind, took a swallow of water instead, then changed his mind again, and decided to tell me. "The question isn't whether I forget. Or what we old ones think. It's the young people who matter. It matters that they have new seeds planted in their hearts. Tonight," he said, looking around the lobby, "all these young people will stay awake. Tomorrow, they'll be whistling the music. A nuisance, humming in the class-rooms. And in the summer, that's what you'll hear: young people whistling along the river. They won't forget."

Backstage, a tranquil climate prevailed as the performers readied themselves for the second act. Leslie Scott, not the least unnerved by the reception of the previous stanza, grinned and said, "Sure, they're kinda slow. But most audiences don't warm up until the duet ["Bess, You Is My Woman Now"], and that went over okay. From here on out, we'll sail." Martha Flowers, freshening her make-up in front of a mirror, said, "This audience, that audience, I don't know the difference. You wouldn't either, you been doing this show two years." But Sascha, lacking Miss Flowers' professional *savoir*, was an alarming sight as he waited in the wings to repeat his role of plot narrator: head bowed, and holding to a dancer's practice bar like a fighter on the ropes, he listened dazedly while his seconds, Igor and Henry, whispered encouragement.

To Sascha's surprise, his return bout was victorious. The audience was eager to hear what would happen in the next act, and Sascha, who two weeks later applied to the Moscow Art Theatre for a drama student fellowship, ecstatically recounted Crown's murder and Porgy's imprisonment. He walked off to one of the largest hands of the evening; Miss

Lydia was still clapping after the house lights had dimmed.

The element in the opera which seemed most to disturb the Soviets, its sensuality, reaches a peak of Himalayan proportions in the opening twenty minutes of Act Two. A song "I Ain't Got No Shame" ("doin' what I likes to do"), and the shake-that-thing brand of choreography accompanying it, proved too aptly titled, too graphically illustrated, for Russian comfort. But it was the ensuing scene which contained, from a prudish viewpoint, the real affront. The scene, a favorite of the director's and one he'd kept heightening in rehearsal, begins with Crown's attempting to rape Bess—he grips her to him, gropes her buttocks, her breasts; and ends with Bess raping him—she rips off his shirt, wraps her arms around him and writhes, sizzles like bacon in a skillet; blackout. Areas of the audience suffered something of a blackout, too. "Christ," said one correspondent, his voice carrying in the hush, "they wouldn't get away with that on Broadway!" To which another American journalist, a woman, replied, "Don't be silly. It's the best thing in the show."

Leslie Scott had predicted the second act would "sail"; his forecast was almost verified during the opera's remaining forty minutes. The street-cry song of the Strawberry Woman started favorable winds blowing. Again, like the love duet, the melody and the situation, simply a peddler selling strawberries, was one the Russians could grasp, be charmed by. After that, every scene seemed to be accepted; and though the performance did not sail, perhaps because too much water had already been shipped, at least it floated, wallowed along in a current of less frigid temperature.

As the curtain fell, and the calls commenced, cameramen, scooting up and down the aisles, divided their shots between applauding Russians and salaaming actors. "They're stunned,"

Lowry once more pronounced, and his wife tacked on the
inevitable "They've never seen anything like it." The applause, which one experienced witness described as "nothing
compared to an opening night at the Bolshoi," sustained a
logical number of curtain calls, then swiftly declined. It was
now, when people were leaving their seats, that Breen made
his bid for a more impressive demonstration by unleashing
the extra-added "impromptu" curtain call he'd rehearsed that
afternoon. On came the cast, one by one, each of them ca-
vorting to the beat of a bongo drum. "Oh, no," groaned Miss
Ryan. "They shouldn't do this. It's just begging." In the en-
durance test that followed, the audience compromised by
substituting a chantlike pattern of clapping for authentic applause. Three minutes passed; four, five, six, seven. At last,
when Miss Flowers had blown a final kiss across the footlights, and the electricians, et al., had been acknowledged,
Breen, taking the ultimate bow, permitted the curtain to be
lowered.

Ambassador and Mrs. Bohlen, and various Soviet officials,
were ushered backstage to shake hands with the cast. "I
don't know what all the fuss is about," Mrs. Gershwin gaily
cried as she squeezed through the backstage pandemonium.
"It's *only* little old *Porgy*." Savchenko pushed toward Mrs.
Breen; stiffly offering his hand, he said, "I want to congratu-
late you on a very big success." Mrs. Breen dabbed at her
eyes, as though drying phantom tears. "That ovation. Wasn't
it glorious?" she said, turning to gaze at her husband, who
was posing for a photograph with Bohlen. "Such a tribute to
Robert."

Outside, I had to walk some distance before finding a taxi.
A threesome, two young men and a girl, walked ahead of
me. I gathered they'd been part of the *Porgy and Bess* audi-

ence. Their voices reverberated down the shadowed, snow-silent streets. They were all talking at once, an exhilarated babble now and again mixed with humming: the strawberry street cry, a phrase of "Summertime." Then, as though she had no true understanding of the words but had memorized them phonetically, the girl sang, "There's a boat that's leavin' soon for New York, come with me, that's where we belong, sister . . ." Her friends joined in, whistling. Orlov had said, "And in the summer, that's what you'll hear: young people whistling along the river. They won't forget."

The promise of these young people who wouldn't forget, who'd been stimulated into new visions: surely, I thought, that was enough to justify my telling Henry Shapiro the première was a success. Not the "bomb-shell" conquest the proprietors of Everyman Opera had expected; but a victory of finer significance, one that would mature and matter. And yet, as I lay in my room thinking it over, qualms seized me when eventually the telephone rang. "How did it go? What really happened?" were questions to be answered on journalism's unsubtle level. Could I, with any honesty, give Shapiro a radiant account of the opera's overall reception? I preferred to; and suspected that it was what he, quite naturally, wanted to hear. But I let the telephone ring while a plethora of *ifs* plunged around in my head: if the Russians had been able to consult a printed program, if the fanfare and ceremonial aspects had been curtailed, if less had been demanded of the audience, if . . . I quit stalling and picked up the receiver. But the person on the line was Miss Lydia, who said she was sorry, someone had called me from Moscow and been disconnected. I had no more calls that evening.

Reviews of the production were published by two of the city's leading papers, *Smena* and *Evening Leningrad*. In Ambassador Bohlen's opinion, the articles were "By and large, really excellent. Very thoughtful. It shows they took it seriously."

The *Evening Leningrad* critic wrote, "*Porgy and Bess* is a work stamped with brilliant talent and unusual mastery . . . warmly received by the audience." A further fifteen hundred words elaborated on that statement. He praised the score ("Gershwin's music is melodic, sincere, intentionally suffused with Negro musical folklore. There are plenty of really expressive and contrasting melodies"), Breen's direction ("The show is directed with great mastery and rivets one's attention with its dynamic sweep"), the conductor ("The musical part of the performance is on a very high level"), and the cast (". . . plays together with a harmony rarely to be seen . . ."). The libretto, however, provoked a gentle reprimand, for the writer noticed in it "some elements of expressionism and melodrama, an abundance of the customary details regarding criminal investigation." Nor did *Evening Leningrad* forget to press the political pedal: "We, Soviet spectators, realize the corrosive effect of the capitalistic system on the consciousness, the mentality and the moral outlook of a people oppressed by poverty. This lifts Heyward's play, as set to music by Gershwin, into the realms of social drama." But such comments seemed a mere pianissimo compared to the loud chords of propaganda that opponents of the *Porgy and Bess* tour had anticipated.

The second critic, U. Kovalyev, writing in *Smena*, mentioned a factor ignored by *Evening Leningrad*: "The astoundingly erotic coloring of some of the dancing scenes is unpleasant. And it is hard to lay the blame on a specific national dance. It is more the taste of the director and perhaps his kind of 'tradition' stemming from Broadway 'burlesques' and 'revues.' But on the whole," continues Kovalyev, "*Porgy and Bess* presents one of the most interesting events of this theatrical season. It is an excellently performed production, colorful, full of movement and music. It testifies to the high talent of the Negro people. Very possibly not all of the music and the staging will be approved by the Soviet audiences and everything will not necessarily be understandable to them. We are not used to the naturalistic details in the dance, to the excessive jazz sound of the symphony orchestra, etc. Nevertheless the performance broadens our concept of the art of contemporary America, and familiarizes us with thus far unknown facets of the musical and theatrical life of the United States."

These reviews did not appear until Thursday, three days after the opening. By then, their publication was rather an anticlimax and the company was inclined to regard them with a yawn. "Sure it's nice they write okay things, but who cares?" said one member of the cast, expressing a prevalent attitude. "It's not what the Russians think. It's the stuff they're hearing about us back home. *That's* what counts."

The company was already aware of what America was hearing, for late Tuesday afternoon, the day following the première, Breen received a cable on the subject from Everyman Opera's New York office. Miss Ryan typed copies of it, and she was about to put one of them on the company's bulletin board when we met in the lobby. "Hi," she said. "Guess what? Stefan the Bunny called. He wants to take me dancing. Do you think it'll be all right? I mean, as long as he just wants to dance? Anyway, I don't care. I'd go dancing with Jack the Ripper, anything to get away from *Porgy and Bess*," she said, and thumbtacked her type-written version of the cable to the bulletin board.

LT ROBERT BREEN HOTEL ASTORIA LENINGRAD USSR

WONDERFUL ARTICLES HERE ALL DECEMBER 27 PAPERS
STOP ALL MENTION TEN MINUTES STANDING OVATION STOP

JOURNALS HEADLINE—"LENINGRAD GOES WILD OVER PORGY
AND BESS" STOP

AP FACTUAL RELEASE INCLUDES GREAT TICKET DEMAND
AND SIZE AUDIENCE STOP

TRIBUNE STESSES WARM AUDIENCE RECEPTION STOP

TELEGRAM HEADLINE—"PORGY WINS PRAISE FROM RUSSIA"
OVER AP RELEASE STOP

MIRROR EDITORIAL "HEART TO HEART DIPLOMACY—CAST
TAKING LENINGRAD BY SONG WE ARE PROUD OF THEM"
STOP

AP RELEASE IN SOME PAPERS SAYS MOSCOW RADIO TERMED
PREMIERE GREAT SUCCESS STOP

TIMES EDITORIAL TODAY BY SULZBERGER "PORGY BESS
OPENING ANOTHER WINDOW TO WEST"

JOURNAL EDITORIAL TODAY—"MADE TREMENDOUS HIT"

NBC CBS NEWSCASTS FABULOUS

CONGRATULATIONS TO EVERY SINGLE SOUL WITH YOU

"Of course," remarked Miss Ryan, perusing the cable,
"that's not *exactly* how it arrived. The Breens did a little
adding and editing. There was one line: '*Times* says scored
moderate success.' You can bet Wilva cut that out! Well,"
she said with a smile, a sigh, "why not make a good thing

better? Wilva just wants everybody to feel wonderful, and I think that's kind of endearing."

All afternoon members of the company, passing through the lobby, stopped to read the message from New York. It made them grin; they walked away with lightened steps. "What'cha say, man?" said Earl Bruce Jackson to Warner Watson as they stood reading the cable. "We're making history!" And Watson, rubbing his hands together, replied, "Yep, uh-huh. I guess we've got *history* fenced in."

The Duke
in His Domain

(*1956*)

M OST JAPANESE GIRLS GIGGLE. The little maid on the fourth floor of the Miyako Hotel, in Kyoto, was no exception. Hilarity, and attempts to suppress it, pinked her cheeks (unlike the Chinese, the Japanese complexion more often than not has considerable color), shook her plump peony-and-pansy-kimonoed figure. There seemed to be no particular reason for this merriment; the Japanese giggle operates without apparent motivation. I'd merely asked to be directed toward a certain room. "You come see Marron?" she gasped, showing, like so many of her fellow-countrymen, an array of gold teeth. Then, with the tiny, pigeon-toed skating steps that the wearing of a kimono necessitates, she led me through a labyrinth of corridors, promising, "I knock you Marron." The "l" sound does not exist in Japanese, and by "Marron" the maid meant Marlon—Marlon Brando, the American actor, who was at that time in Kyoto doing location work for the Warner Brothers-William Goetz motion-picture version of James Michener's novel *Sayonara*.

My guide tapped at Brando's door, shrieked "Marron!" and fled away along the corridor, her kimono sleeves fluttering like the wings of a parakeet. The door was opened by another doll-delicate Miyako maid, who at once succumbed to her own fit of quaint hysteria. From an inner room, Brando called, "What is it, honey?" But the girl, her eyes squeezed shut with mirth and her fat little hands jammed into her mouth, like a bawling baby's, was incapable of reply. "Hey, honey, what is it?" Brando again inquired, and appeared in the doorway. "Oh, hi," he said when he saw me. "It's seven, huh?" We'd made a seven-o'clock date for dinner; I was nearly twenty minutes late. "Well, take off your shoes and come on in. I'm just finishing up here. And, hey, honey," he told the maid, "bring us some ice." Then, looking after the girl as she scurried off, he cocked his hands on his hips and, grinning, declared, "They kill me. They really kill me. The kids, too. Don't you think they're wonderful, don't you love them—Japanese kids?"

The Miyako, where about half of the *Sayonara* company was staying, is the most prominent of the so-called Western-style hotels in Kyoto; the majority of its rooms are furnished with sturdy, if commonplace and cumbersome, European chairs and tables, beds and couches. But for the convenience of Japanese guests, who prefer their own mode of décor while desiring the prestige of staying at the Miyako, or of those foreign travelers who yearn after authentic atmosphere yet are disinclined to endure the unheated rigors of a real Japanese inn, the Miyako maintains some suites decorated in the traditional manner, and it was in one of these that Brando had chosen to settle himself. His quarters consisted of two rooms, a bath and a glassed-in sun porch. Without the overlying and underlying clutter of Brando's personal belongings, the rooms would have been textbook illustrations of the Japanese penchant for an ostentatious barrenness. The floors were covered with tawny *tatami* matting, with a discreet scattering of raw-silk pillows; a scroll depicting swimming golden carp hung in an alcove, and beneath it, on a stand, sat a vase filled with tall lilies and red leaves, arranged just so. The larger of the two rooms—the inner one—which the occupant was using as a sort of business office where he also dined and slept, contained a long, low lacquer table and a sleeping pallet. In these rooms, the divergent concepts of Japanese and Western decoration—the one seeking to impress by a lack of display, an absence of possession-exhibiting, the other intent on precisely the reverse—could both be observed, for Brando seemed unwilling to make use of the apartment's storage space, concealed behind sliding paper doors. All that he owned seemed to be out in the open. Shirts, ready for the laundry; socks, too; shoes and sweaters and jackets and hats and ties, flung around like the costume of a dismantled scarecrow. And cameras, a typewriter, a tape recorder, an electric heater that performed with stifling competence. Here, there, pieces of partly nibbled fruit; a box of the famous Japanese strawberries, each berry the size of an egg. And books, a deep-thought cascade, among which one saw Colin Wilson's *The Outsider* and various works on Buddhist prayer, Zen meditation, Yogi breathing and Hindu mysticism, but no fiction, for Brando reads none. He has never, he professes, opened a novel since April 3, 1924, the day he was born, in Omaha, Nebraska. But while he may not care to read fiction, he does desire to write it, and the long lacquer table was loaded with overfilled ashtrays and piled pages of his most recent creative effort, which happens to be a film script entitled *A Burst of Vermilion*.

In fact, Brando had evidently been working on his story at the moment of my arrival. As I entered the room, a subdued-looking, youngish man, whom I shall call Murray, and who had previously been pointed out to me as "the fellow that's helping Marlon with his writing," was squatted on the matting, fumbling through the manuscript of *A Burst of Vermilion*. Weighing some pages on his hand, he said, "Tell ya, Mar, s'pose I go over this down in my room, and maybe we'll get together again—say, around ten-thirty?"

Brando scowled, as though unsympathetic to the idea of resuming their endeavors later in the evening. Having been slightly ill, as I learned later, he had spent the day in his room, and now seemed restive. "What's this?" he asked, pointing to a couple of oblong packages among the literary remains on the lacquer table.

Murray shrugged. The maid had delivered them; that was all he knew. "People are always sending Mar presents," he told me. "Lots of times we don't know who sent them. True, Mar?"

"Yeah," said Brando, beginning to rip open the gifts, which, like most Japanese packages—even mundane purchases from very ordinary shops—were beautifully wrapped. One contained candy, the other white rice cakes, which proved cement-hard, though they looked like puffs of cloud. There was no card in either package to identify the donor. "Every time you turn around, some Japanese is giving you a present. They're crazy about giving presents," Brando observed. Athletically crunching a rice cake, he passed the boxes to Murray and me.

Murray shook his head, he was intent on obtaining Brando's promise to meet with him again at ten-thirty. "Give me a ring around then," Brando said, finally. "We'll see what's happening."

Murray, as I knew, was only one member of what some of the *Sayonara* company referred to as "Brando's gang." Aside from the literary assistant, the gang consisted of Marlon Brando, Sr., who acts as his son's business manager; a pretty, dark-haired secretary, Miss Levin; and Brando's private make-up man. The travel expenses of this entourage, and all its living expenses while on location, were allowed for in the actor's contract with Warner Brothers. Legend to the contrary, film studios are not usually so lenient financially. A Warner man to whom I talked later explained the tolerance shown Brando by saying, "Ordinarily we wouldn't put up with it. All the demands he makes. Except—well, this picture just *had* to have a big star. Your star—that's the only thing that really counts at the box office."

Among the company were some who felt that the social protection supplied by Brando's inner circle was preventing them from "getting to know the guy" as well as they would have liked. Brando had been in Japan for more than a month, and during that time he had shown himself on the set as a slouchingly dignified, amiable-seeming young man who was always ready to co-operate with, and even encourage, his co-workers—the actors particularly—yet by and large was not socially available, preferring, during the tedious lulls between scenes, to sit alone reading philosophy or scribbling in a schoolboy notebook. After the day's work, instead of accepting his colleagues' invitations to join a group for drinks, a plate of raw fish in a restaurant and a prowl through the old geisha quarter of Kyoto, instead of contributing to the one-big-family, houseparty bonhomie that picture-making on location theoretically generates, he usually returned to his hotel and stayed there. Since the most fervent of movie-star fans are the people who themselves work in the film industry, Brando was a subject of immense interest within the ranks of the *Sayonara* group, and the more so because his attitude of friendly remoteness produced, in the face of such curiosity, such wistful frustrations. Even the film's director, Joshua Logan, was impelled to say, after working with Brando for two weeks, "Marlon's the most exciting person I've met since Garbo. A genius. But I don't know what he's like. I don't know anything about him."

The maid had re-entered the star's room, and Murray, on his way out, almost tripped over the train of her kimono. She put down a bowl of ice, and with a glow, a giggle, an elation that made her little feet, hooflike in their split-toed white socks, lift and lower like a prancing pony's, announced, "Appapie! Tonight on menu appapie."

Brando groaned. "Apple pie. That's all I need." He stretched out on the floor and unbuckled his belt, which dug too deeply into the swell of his stomach. "I'm supposed to be on a diet. But the only things I want to eat are apple pie and stuff like that." Six weeks earlier, in California, Logan had told him he must trim off ten pounds for his role in *Sayonara*, and before arriving in Kyoto he had managed to get rid of seven. Since reaching Japan, however, abetted not only by American-type apple pie but by the Japanese cuisine, with its delicious emphasis on the sweetened, the starchy, the fried, he'd regained, then doubled this poundage. Now, loosening his belt still more and thoughtfully massaging his midriff, he scanned the menu, which offered, in English, a wide choice of Western-style dishes, and after reminding himself "I've *got* to lose weight," he ordered soup, beefsteak with French-fried potatoes, three supplementary vegetables, a side dish of spaghetti, rolls and butter, a bottle of *sake*, salad, and cheese and crackers.

"And appapie, Marron?"

He sighed. "With ice cream, honey."

Though Brando is not a teetotaler, his appetite is more frugal when it comes to alcohol. While we were awaiting the dinner, which was to be served to us in the room, he supplied me with a large vodka on the rocks and poured himself the merest courtesy sip. Resuming his position on the floor, he lolled his head against a pillow, dropped his eyelids, then shut them. It was as though he'd dozed off into a disturbing dream; his eyelids twitched, and when he spoke, his voice—an unemotional voice, in a way cultivated and genteel, yet surprisingly adolescent, a voice with a probing, asking, boyish quality—seemed to come from sleepy distances.

"The last eight, nine years of my life have been a mess," he said. "Maybe the last two have been a little better. Less rolling in the trough of the wave. Have you ever been analyzed? I was afraid of it at first. Afraid it might destroy the impulses that made me creative, an artist. A sensitive person receives fifty impressions where somebody else may only get seven. Sensitive people are so vulnerable; they're so easily brutalized and hurt just because they *are* sensitive. The more sensitive you are, the more certain you are to be brutalized, develop scabs. Never evolve. Never allow yourself to feel anything, because you always feel too much. Analysis helps. It helped me. But still, the last eight, nine years I've been pretty mixed up, a mess pretty much . . ."

The voice went on, as though speaking to hear itself, an effect Brando's speech often has, for like many persons who are intensely self-absorbed, he is something of a monologuist —a fact that he recognizes and for which he offers his own explanation. "People around me never say anything," he says. "They just seem to want to hear what I have to say. That's why I do all the talking."

Watching him now, with his eyes closed, his un-lined face white under an overhead light, I felt as if the moment of my initial encounter with him were being re-created. The year of that meeting was 1947; it was a winter afternoon in New York, when I had occasion to attend a rehearsal of Tennessee Williams' *A Streetcar Named Desire*, in which Brando was to play the role of Stanley Kowalski. It was this role that first brought him general recognition, although among the New York theatre's cognoscenti he had already attracted attention, through his student work with the drama coach Stella Adler and a few Broadway appearances—one in a play by Maxwell Anderson, *Truckline Café*, and another as Marchbanks opposite Katharine Cornell's Candida, in which he showed an ability that had been much praised and discussed. Elia Kazan, the director of *A Streetcar Named Desire*, said at that time, and has recently repeated, "Marlon is just the best actor in the world." But ten years ago, on the remembered afternoon, he was still relatively unknown; at least, I hadn't a clue to who he might be when, arriving too early at the *Streetcar* rehearsal, I found the auditorium deserted and a brawny young man stretched out atop a table on the stage under the gloomy glare of work lights, solidly asleep. Because he was wearing a white T shirt and denim trousers, because of his squat gymnasium physique—the weight-lifter's arms, the Charles Atlas chest (though an opened *Basic Writings of Sigmund Freud* was resting on it)—I took him for a stagehand. Or did until I looked closely at his face. It was as if a stranger's head had been attached to the brawny body, as in certain counterfeit photographs. For this face was so very untough, superimposing, as it did, an almost angelic refinement and gentleness upon hard-jawed good looks: taut skin, a broad, high forehead, wide-apart eyes, an aquiline nose, full lips with a relaxed, sensual expression. Not the least suggestion of Williams' unpoetic Kowalski. It was therefore rather an experience to observe, later that afternoon, with what chameleon ease Brando acquired the character's cruel and gaudy colors, how superbly, like a guileful salamander, he slithered into the part, how his own persona evaporated—just as, in this Kyoto hotel room nine years afterward, my 1947 memory of Brando receded, disappeared into his 1956 self. And the present Brando, the one lounging there on the *tatami* and lazily puffing filtered cigarettes as he talked and talked, was, of course, a different person—bound to be. His body was thicker; his forehead was higher, for his hair was thinner; he was richer (from the producers of *Sayonara* he could expect a salary of three hundred thousand dollars, plus a percentage of the picture's earnings); and he'd become, as one journalist put it, "the Valentino of the bop generation"—turned into such a world celebrity that when he went out in public here in Japan, he deemed it wise to hide his face not only by wearing dark glasses but by donning a surgeon's gauze mask as well. (The latter bit of disguise is not so *outré* in Japan as it may sound, since numerous Asians wear such masks, on the theory that they prevent the spreading of germs.) Those were some of the alterations a decade had made. There were others. His eyes had changed. Although their *caffè-espresso* color was the same, the shyness, any traces of real vulnerability that they had formerly held, had left them; now he looked at people with assurance, and with what can only be called a pitying expression, as though he dwelt in spheres of enlightenment where they, to his regret, did not. (The reactions of the people subjected to this gaze of constant commiseration range from that of a young actress who avowed that "Marlon is really a very *spiritual* person, wise and very sincere; you can see it in his eyes" to that of a Brando acquaintance who said, "The way he looks at you, like he was so damn sorry for you—doesn't it make you want to cut your throat?") Nevertheless, the subtly tender character of his face had been preserved. Or almost. For in the years between he'd had an accident that gave his face a more conventionally masculine aspect. It was just that his nose had been broken. And maneuvering a word in edge-wise, I asked, "How did you break your nose?"

". . . by which I don't mean that I'm *always* unhappy. I remember one April I was in Sicily. A hot day, and flowers everywhere. I like flowers, the ones that smell. Gardenias. Anyway, it was April and I was in Sicily, and I went off by myself. Lay down in this field of flowers. Went to sleep. That made me happy. I was happy *then*. What? You say something?"

"I was wondering how you broke your nose."

He rubbed his nose and grinned, as though remembering an experience as happy as the Sicilian nap. "That was a long time ago. I did it boxing. It was when I was in *Streetcar*.

We—some of the guys backstage and me—we used to go
down to the boiler room in the theatre and horse around,
mix it up. One night I was mixing it up with this guy and—
crack! So I put on my coat and walked around to the nearest hospital—it was off Broadway somewhere. My nose was
really busted. They had to give me an anesthetic to set it,
and put me to bed. Not that I was sorry. *Streetcar* had been
running about a year and I was sick of it. But my nose healed
pretty quick, and I guess I would've been back in the show
practically right away if I hadn't done what I did to Irene
Selznick." His grin broadened as he mentioned Mrs.
Selznick, who had been the producer of the Williams play.
"There is one shrewd lady, Irene Selznick. When she wants
something, she wants it. And she wanted me back in the play.
But when I heard she was coming to the hospital, I went to
work with bandages and iodine and mercurochrome, and—
Christ!—when she walked in the door, I looked like my head
had been cut off. At the least. And *sounded* as though I
were dying. 'Oh, Marlon,' she said, 'you poor, *poor* boy!'
And I said, 'Don't you worry about anything, Irene. I'll be
back in the show tonight!' And she said, 'Don't you dare!
We can manage without you for—for—well, a *few* days
more.' 'No, no,' I said. 'I'm okay. I want to work. Tell them
I'll be back tonight.' So she said, 'You're in no condition, you
poor darling. I *forbid* you to come to the theatre.' So I stayed
in the hospital and had myself a ball." (Mrs. Selznick, recall-
ing the incident recently, said, "They didn't set his nose
properly at all. Suddenly his face was quite different. Kind
of tough. For months afterward I kept telling him, 'But
they've *ruined* your face. You must have your nose broken
again and reset.' Luckily for him, he didn't listen to me. Because I honestly think that broken nose made his fortune as

far as the movies go. It gave him sex appeal. He was too beautiful before.")

Brando made his first trip to the Coast in 1949, when he went out there to play the leading role in *The Men*, a picture dealing with paraplegic war veterans. He was accused, at the time, of uncouth social conduct, and criticized for his black-leather-jacket taste in attire, his choice of motorcycles instead of Jaguars and his preference for obscure secretaries rather than movie starlets; moreover, Hollywood columnists studded their copy with hostile comments concerning his attitude toward the film business, which he himself summed up soon after he entered it by saying, "The only reason I'm here is that I don't yet have the moral courage to turn down the money." In interviews, he repeatedly stated that becoming "simply a movie actor" was the thing furthest from his thoughts. "I may do a picture now and then," he said on one occasion, "but mostly I intend to work on the stage." However, he followed *The Men*, which was more of a *succès d'estime* than a commercial triumph, by re-creating Kowalski in the screen treatment of *A Streetcar Named Desire*, and this role, as it had done on Broadway, established him as a star. (Defined practically, a movie star is any performer who can account for a box-office profit regardless of the quality of the enterprise in which he appears; the breed is so scarce that there are fewer than ten actors today who qualify for the title. Brando is one of them; as a box-office draw, male division, he is perhaps outranked only by William Holden.) In the course of the last five years he has played a Mexican revolutionary (*Viva Zapata!*), Mark Antony (*Julius Caesar*) and a motorcycle-mad juvenile delinquent (*The Wild One*); earned an Academy Award in the role of a dockyard thug (*On the Waterfront*); impersonated Napoleon (*Désirée*);

sung and danced his way through the part of an adult delinquent (*Guys and Dolls*); and taken the part of the Okinawan interpreter in *The Teahouse of the August Moon*, which, like *Sayonara*, his tenth picture, was partly shot on location in Japan. But he has never, except for a brief period in summer stock, returned to the stage. "Why should I?" he asked with apathy when I remarked on this. "The movies have a greater potential. They can be a factor for good. For moral development. At least some can—the kind of movies I want to do." He paused, seemed to listen, as though his statement had been tape-recorded and he were now playing it back. Possibly the sound of it dissatisfied him; at any rate, his jaw started working, as if he were biting down on an unpleasant mouthful. He looked off into space suddenly and demanded, "What's so hot about New York? What's so hot about working for Cheryl Crawford and Robert Whitehead?" Miss Crawford and Whitehead are two of New York's most prominent theatrical producers, neither of whom has had occasion to employ Brando. "Anyway, what would I be in?" he continued. "There aren't any parts for me."

Stack them, and the playscripts offered him in any given season by hopeful Broadway managements might very well rise to a height exceeding the actor's own. Tennessee Williams wanted him for the male lead in each of his last five plays, and the most recent of these, *Orpheus Descending*, which was pending production at the time of our talk, had been written expressly as a co-starring vehicle for Brando and the Italian actress Anna Magnani. "I can explain very easily why I didn't do *Orpheus*," Brando said. "There are beautiful things in it, some of Tennessee's best writing, and the Magnani part is great; she stands for something, you can understand her—and she would wipe me off the stage. The char-

acter I was supposed to play, this boy, this Val, he never
takes a stand. I didn't really know what he was for or against.
Well, you can't act a vacuum. And I told Tennessee. So he
kept trying. He rewrote it for me, maybe a couple of times.
But—" He shrugged. "Well, I had no intention of walking
out on any stage with Magnani. Not in that part. They'd
have had to mop me up." Brando mused a moment, and
added, "I think—in fact, I'm sure—Tennessee has made a
fixed association between me and Kowalski. I mean, we're
friends and he knows that as a person I am just the opposite of
Kowalski, who was everything I'm against—totally insensi-
tive, crude, cruel. But still, Tennessee's image of me is confused with the fact that I played that part. So I don't know if
he could write for me in a different color range. The only
reason I did *Guys and Dolls* was to work in a lighter color—
yellow. Before that, the brightest color I'd played was red.
From red down. Brown. Gray. Black." He crumpled an
empty cigarette package and bounced it in his hand like a
ball. "There aren't any parts for me on the stage. Nobody
writes them. Go on. Tell me a part I could do."

In the absence of vehicles by worthy contemporaries,
might he not favor the work of older hands? Several responsible persons who appeared with him in the film had admired his reading of Mark Antony in *Julius Caesar*, and
thought him equipped, provided the will was there, to essay
many of the Mount Everest roles in stage literature—even,
possibly, Oedipus.

Brando received reminders of this praise blankly—or,
rather, he seemed to be indulging his not-listening habit. But
sensing silence again, he dissolved it: "Of course, movies
date so quickly. I saw *Streetcar* the other day and it was already an old-fashioned picture. Still, movies do have the

greatest potential. You can say important things to a lot of people. About discrimination and hatred and prejudice. I want to make pictures that explore the themes current in the world today. In terms of entertainment. That's why I've started my own independent production company." He reached out affectionately to finger *A Burst of Vermilion*, which will be the first script filmed by Pennebaker Productions—the independent company he has formed.

And did *A Burst of Vermilion* satisfy him as a basis for the kind of lofty aims he proposed?

He mumbled something. Then he mumbled something else. Asked to speak more clearly, he said, "It's a Western."

He was unable to restrain a smile, which expanded into laughter. He rolled on the floor and roared. "Christ, the only thing is, will I ever be able to look my friends in the face again?" Sobering somewhat, he said, "Seriously, though, the first picture *has* to make money. Otherwise, there won't be another. I'm nearly broke. No, no kidding. I spent a year and two hundred thousand dollars of my own money trying to get some writer to come up with a decent script. Which used my ideas. The last one, it was so terrible I said I can do better myself. I'm going to direct it, too."

Produced by, directed by, written by, and starring. Charlie Chaplin has managed this, and gone it one better by composing his own scores. But professionals of wide experience —Orson Welles, for one—have caved in under a lesser number of chores than Brando planned to assume. However, he had a ready answer to my suggestion that he might be loading the cart with more than the donkey could haul. "Take producing," he said. "What does a producer do except cast? I know as much about casting as anyone does, and that's all producing is. Casting." In the trade, one would be hard put to it to find anyone who concurred in this opinion. A good producer, in addition to doing the casting—that is, assembling the writer, the director, the actors, the technical crew, and the other components of his team—must be a diplomat of the emotions, smoothing and soothing, and above all, must be a skilled mechanic when it comes to dollars-and-cents machinery. "But seriously," said Brando, now excessively sober, "*Burst isn't* just cowboys-and-Indians stuff. It's about this Mexican boy—hatred and discrimination. What happens to a community when those things exist."

Sayonara, too, has moments when it purports to attack race prejudice, telling, as it does, the tale of an American jet pilot who falls in love with a Japanese music-hall dancer, much to the dismay of his Air Force superiors, and also to the dismay of her employers, though the latter's objection is not the racial unsuitability of her beau but simply that she has a beau at all, for she is a member of an all-girl opera company—based on a real-life counterpart, the Takarazuka Company—whose management promotes a legend that off-stage its hundreds of girls lead a conventlike existence, unsullied by male presences of any creed or color. Michener's novel concludes with the lovers forlornly bidding each other *sayonara*, a word meaning farewell. In the film version, however, the word, and consequently the title, has lost significance; here the fadeout reveals the twain of East and West so closely met that they are on their way to the matrimonial bureau. At a press conference that Brando conducted upon his Tokyo arrival, he informed some sixty reporters that he had contracted to do this story because "it strikes very precisely at prejudices that serve to limit our progress toward a peaceful world. Underneath the romance, it attacks prejudices that exist on the part of the Japanese as well as on our part," and also he was doing the film because it would give him the "invaluable opportunity" of working under Joshua Logan, who could teach him "what to do and what not to do."

But time had passed. And now Brando said, with a snort, "Oh, *Sayonara*, I love it! This wondrous hearts-and-flowers nonsense that was supposed to be a serious picture about Japan. So what difference does it make? I'm just doing it for the money anyway. Money to put in the kick for my own company." He pulled at his lip reflectively and snorted again. "Back in California, I sat through twenty-two hours of script conferences. Logan said to me, 'We welcome any suggestions you have, Marlon. Any changes you want to make, you just make them. If there's anything you don't like—why, rewrite it, Marlon, write it your own way.'" Brando's friends boast that he can imitate anybody after fifteen minutes' observation; to judge by the eerie excellence with which he mimicked Logan's vaguely Southern voice, his sad-eyed, beaming, aquiver-with-enthusiasm manner, they are hardly exaggerating. "*Rewrite?* Man, I rewrote the whole damn script. And now out of that they're going to use maybe eight lines." Another snort. "I give up. I'm going to walk through the part, and that's that. Sometimes I think nobody knows the difference anyway. For the first few days on the set, I tried to act. But then I made an experiment. In this scene, I tried to do everything wrong I could think of. Grimaced and rolled my eyes, put in all kinds of gestures and expressions that had no relation to the part I'm supposed to be playing. What did Logan say? He just said, 'It's wonderful! Print it!'"

A phrase that often occurs in Brando's conversation, "I only mean forty percent of what I say," is probably applicable here. Logan, a stage and film director of widely recognized and munificently rewarded accomplishments (*Mister Roberts, South Pacific, Picnic*), is a man balanced on enthusiasm, as a bird is balanced on air. A creative person's need to believe in the value of what he is creating is axiomatic; Logan's belief in whatever project he is engaged in approaches euphoric faith, protecting him, as it seems designed to do, from the nibbling nuisance of self-doubt. The joy he took in everything connected with *Sayonara*, a film he had been preparing for two years, was so nearly flawless that it did not permit him to conceive that his star's enthusiasm might not equal his own. Far from it. "Marlon," he occasionally announced, "says he's never been as happy with a company as he is with us." And "I've never worked with such an exciting, inventive actor. So pliable. He takes direction beautifully, and yet he always has something to add. He's made up this Southern accent for the part; I never would have thought of it myself, but, well, it's exactly right—it's perfection." Nevertheless, by the night I had dinner in Brando's hotel room Logan had begun to be aware that there was something lacking in his rapport with Brando. He attributed it to the fact that at this juncture, when most of the scenes being filmed concentrated on Japanese background (street crowds, views, spectacles) rather than actors, he had not yet worked with Brando on material that put either of them to much of a test. "That'll come when we get back to California," he said. "The interior stuff, the dramatic scenes. Brando's going to be great—we'll get along fine."

There was another reason for Logan's inability, at that point, to give his principal player the kind of attention that might have established closer harmony: he was in serious disharmony with the very Japanese elements that had con-

tributed most to his decision to make the picture. Long in-
fatuated with the Japanese theatre, Logan had counted
heavily on interlacing *Sayonara* with authentic sequences
taken from the classic Kabuki theatre, the masked Nō dra-
mas, the Bunraku puppet plays; they were to be, so to say,
the highbrow-lights of the film. And to this end Logan,
along with William Goetz, the producer, had been in negotiation for over a year with Shochiku, the gigantic film company that controls a major part of Japan's live theatrical
activities. The ruler of the Shochiku empire is a small, unsmil-
ing eminence in his eighties, known as Mr. Otani; he has a
prénom, Takejiro, but there are few men alive on such familiar terms that they would presume to use it. The son of a
butcher (and therefore, in Japan's Buddhist society, a member of the outcast group), Otani, together with a brother
now dead, founded Shochiku and nurtured it to the point
where, for the last four years, its payroll has been the biggest of any single company in Japan. A tycoon to rival Ko-
kichi Mikimoto, the late cultured-pearl potentate, Otani casts
a cloaklike shadow over the entire Japanese entertainment industry; in addition to having monopolistic control of the
classic theatre, he owns the country's most extensive chain
of movie houses and music halls, produces many films, and
has a hand in radio and television. From Otani's vantage point,
any transactions with the Messrs. Logan and Goetz must
have looked like very small *sake*. However, he was at first in
sympathy with their project, largely because he was impressed by the fervor of Logan's veneration for Kabuki, Nō,
and Bunraku, the three unquestionably genuine gems in the
old man's crown, and the ones closest to his heart. (According to some specialists, these ancient arts owe their continued
health mainly to his generosity.)

But Otani is not all philanthropist; when Shochiku's negotiations with the *Sayonara* management were supposedly
concluded, the former had given the latter, for a handsome
price, franchise to photograph scenes in Tokyo's famed Kabuki Theatre, and, for a still handsomer honorarium, permission to make free use of the Kabuki troupe, the Nō
plays and players, and the Bunraku puppeteers. Shochiku had
also agreed to the participation of its own all-girl opera company—a necessary factor in the production of the film, since
the Takarazuka troupe depicted in the novel had deeply resented Michener's "libel" and refused any co-operation whatever. Logan, leaving for Japan, was so elated he could have
flown there under his own power. "Otani's given us carte
blanche, and this is going to be it, the real thing," he said.
"None of that fake Kabuki, that second-rate stuff, but the
real thing—something that's never been put in a picture before." And was not destined to be; for, across the wide Pacific, Logan and his associates had a personal Pearl Harbor
awaiting them. Otani is seldom seen; he usually appears in
the person of bland assistants, and as Logan and Goetz dis-
embarked from their plane, a group of these informed the
film makers that Shochiku had made an error in its financial
reckoning; the bill was now much higher than the initial esti-
mate. Producer Goetz objected. Otani, certain that he held
the stronger cards (after all, here were these Hollywood people in Japan, accompanied by an expensive cast, an expensive
crew, and expensive equipment), replied by raising the tab
still more. Whereupon Goetz, himself a businessman as tough
as tortoise shell, ended the negotiations and told his director
they would have to make up their own Kabuki, Nō, Bunraku, and all-girl opera company from among unattached,
free-lancing artists.

Meanwhile, the Tokyo press was publicizing the contretemps. Several papers, the *Japan Times* among them, implied that Shochiku was to be censured for having "acted in bad faith"; others, taking a pro-Shochiku, or perhaps simply an anti-*Sayonara*, line, expressed themselves as delighted that the Americans would not have the opportunity to "degrade our finest artistic traditions" by representing them in a film version of "a vulgar novel that is in no way a compliment to the Japanese people." The papers antagonistic to the *Sayonara* project especially relished reporting the fact that Logan had cast a Mexican actor, Ricardo Montalban, in the part of a ranking Kabuki performer (Kabuki is traditionally an all-male enterprise; the grander, more difficult roles are those of women, played by female impersonators, and Montalban's assignment was to portray one such) and then had had the "effrontery" to try and hire a genuine Kabuki star to substitute for Montalban in the dance sequences, which, one Japanese writer remarked, was much the same as "asking Ethel Barrymore to be a stand-in."

All in all, the local press was touchily interested in what was taking place down in Kyoto—the city, two hundred and thirty miles south of Tokyo, in which, because of its plethora of historic temples, its photogenic blue hills and misty lakes, and its carefully preserved old-Japan atmosphere, with elegant geisha quarter and paper-lantern-lighted streets, the *Sayonara* staff had decided to take most of their location shots. And, all in all, down in Kyoto the company was encountering as many difficulties as its ill-wishers could have hoped for. In particular, the Americans were finding it a problem to muster nationals willing to appear in their film —an interesting phenomenon, considering how desirous the average Japanese is of having himself photographed. True, the movie makers had rounded up a ragbag-picking of Nō players and puppeteers not under contract to Shochiku, but they were having the devil's own time assembling a presentable all-girl opera company. (These peculiarly Japanese institutions resemble a sort of single-sex, innocent-minded Folies Bergère; oddly, few men attend their performances, the audiences being, on the whole, as all-girl as the cast.) In the hope of bridging this gap, the *Sayonara* management had distributed posters advertising a contest to select "the one hundred most beautiful girls in Japan." The affair, for which they expected a big turnout, was scheduled to take place at two o'clock on a Thursday afternoon in the lobby of the Kyoto Hotel. But there were no winners, because there were no contestants; none showed up.

Producer Goetz, one of the disappointed judges, resorted next, and with some success, to the expedient of luring ladies out of Kyoto's cabarets and bars. Kyoto—or, for that matter, any Japanese city—is a barfly's Valhalla. Proportionately, the number of premises purveying strong liquor is higher than in New York, and the diversity of these saloons— which range from cozy bamboo closets accommodating four customers to many-storied, neon-hued temples of fun featuring, in accordance with the Japanese aptitude for imitation, cha-cha bands and rock 'n' rollers and hillbilly quartets and *chanteuses existentialistes* and oriental vocalists who sing Cole Porter songs with American Negro accents—is extraordinary. But however low or however deluxe the establishment may be, one thing remains the same: there is always on hand a pride of hostesses to cajole and temper the clientele. Great numbers of these sleekly coifed, smartly costumed, relentlessly festive *jolies jeunes filles* sit sipping Parfaits d'Amour (a syrupy violet-colored cocktail currently fashionable in these surroundings) while performing the duties of a poor man's geisha girl; that is, lightening the spirits, without necessarily corrupting the morals, of weary married men and tense, anxious-to-be-amused bachelors. It is not unusual to see four to a customer. But when the *Sayonara* officials began to try to corral them, they had to contend with the circumstance that nightworkers, such as they were dealing with, have no taste for the early rising that picture-making demands. To acquire their talents, and see that the ladies were on the set at the proper hour, certain of the film's personnel did everything but distribute engagement rings.

Still another annoyance for the makers of *Sayonara* involved the United States Air Force, whose co-operation was vital, but which, though it had previously promised help, now had fits of shilly-shallying, because it gravely objected to one of the basic elements of the plot—that during the Korean War some American Air Force men who married Japanese were shipped home. This, the Air Force complained, may have been the *practice*, but it was not official Pentagon policy. Given the choice of cutting out the offending premise, and thereby removing a sizable section of the script's entrails, or permitting it to remain, and thereby forfeiting Air Force aid, Logan selected surgery.

Then, there was the problem of Miss Miiko Taka, who had been cast as the Takarazuka dancer capable of arousing Air Force Officer Brando's passion. Having first tried to obtain Audrey Hepburn for the part, and found that Miss Hepburn thought not, Logan had started looking for an "unknown," and had come up with Miss Taka, poised, pleasant, an unassuming, quietly attractive nisei, innocent of acting experience, who stepped out of a clerking job with a Los Angeles travel bureau into what she called "this Cinderella fantasy." Although her acting abilities—as well as those of another *Sa-yonara* principal, Red Buttons, an ex-burlesque, ex-television jokester, who, like Miss Taka, had had meager dramatic training—were apparently causing her director some concern, Logan, admirably undaunted, cheerful despite all, was heard to say, "We'll get away with it. As much as possible, I'll just keep their faces straight and their mouths shut. Anyway, Brando, he's going to be so great *he'll* give us what we need." But as for giving, "I give up," Brando repeated. "I'm going to give up. I'm going to sit back. Enjoy Japan."

At that moment, in the Miyako, Brando was presented with something Japanese to enjoy: an emissary of the hotel management, who, bowing and beaming and soaping his hands, came into the room saying "Ah, Missa Marron Brando—" and was silent, tongue-tied by the awkwardness of his errand. He'd come to reclaim the "gift" packages of candy and rice cakes that Brando had already opened and avidly sampled. "Ah, Missa Marron Brando, it is a missake. They were meant for derivery in another room. Aporogies! Aporogies!" Laughing, Brando handed the boxes over. The eyes of the emissary, observing the plundered contents, grew grave, though his smile lingered—indeed, became fixed. Here was a predicament to challenge the rightly renowned Japanese politeness. "Ah," he breathed, a solution limbering his smile, "since you rike them very much, you muss keep one box." He handed the rice cakes back. "And they"—apparently the rightful owner—"can have the other. So, now everyone is preased."

It was just as well that he left the rice cakes, for dinner was taking a long while to simmer in the kitchen. When it arrived, I was replying to some inquiries Brando had made about an acquaintance of mine, a young American disciple of Buddhism who for five years had been leading a contemplative, if not entirely unworldly, life in a settlement inside the gates of Kyoto's Nishi-Honganji Temple. The notion of a person's retiring from the world to lead a spiritual existence —an oriental one, at that—made Brando's face become still, in a dreaming way. He listened with surprising attention to what I could tell him about the young man's present life, and was puzzled—chagrined, really—that it was not at all, or at all, a matter of withdrawal, of silence and prayer-sore knees. On the contrary, behind Nishi-Honganji's walls my Buddhist friend occupied three snug, sunny rooms brimming with books and phonograph records; along with attending to his prayers and performing the tea ceremony, he was quite capable of mixing a martini; he had two servants, and a Chevrolet in which he often conveyed himself to the local cinemas. And speaking of that, he had read that Marlon Brando was in town, and longed to meet him. Brando was little amused. The puritan streak in him, which has some width, had been touched; his conception of the truly devout could not encompass anyone as *du monde* as the young man I'd described. "It's like the other day on the set," he said. "We were working in a temple, and one of the monks came over and asked me for an autographed picture. Now, *what* would a monk want with my autograph? A picture of me?"

He stared questioningly at his scattered books, so many of which dealt with mystical subjects. At his first Tokyo press conference, he had told the journalists that he was glad to be back in Japan, because it gave him another chance to "investigate the influence of Buddhism on Japanese thought, the determining cultural factor." The reading matter on display offered proof that he was adhering to this scholarly, if somewhat obscure, program. "What I'd like to do," he presently said, "I'd like to talk to someone who *knows* about these things. Because—" But the explanation was deferred until the maid, who just then skated in balancing vast platters, had set the lacquer table and we had knelt on cushions at either end of it.

"Because," he resumed, wiping his hands on a small steamed towel, the usual preface to any meal served in Japan, "I've seriously considered—I've very *seriously* thought about—throwing the whole thing up. This business of being a successful actor. What's the point, if it doesn't evolve into anything? All right, you're a success. At last you're *accepted*, you're welcome everywhere. But that's it, that's all there is to it, it doesn't lead anywhere. You're just sitting on a pile of candy gathering thick layers of—of *crust*." He rubbed his chin with the towel, as though removing stale make-up. "Too much success can ruin you as surely as too much failure." Lowering his eyes, he looked without appetite at the food that the maid, to an accompaniment of constant giggles, was distributing on the plates. "Of course," he said hesitantly, as if he were slowly turning over a coin to study the side that seemed to be shinier, "you can't *always* be a failure. Not and survive. Van Gogh! There's an example of what can happen when a person never receives any recognition. You stop relating; it puts you outside. But I guess success does that, too. You know, it took me a long time before I was aware that that's what I was—a big success. I was so absorbed in myself, my own problems, I never looked around, took account. I used to walk in New York, miles and miles, walk in the streets late at night, and never *see* anything. I was never sure about acting, whether that was what I really wanted to do; I'm still not. Then, when I was in

Streetcar, and it had been running a couple of months, one night—dimly, dimly—I began to hear this roar. It was like I'd been asleep, and I woke up here sitting on a pile of candy."

Before Brando achieved this sugary perch, he had known the vicissitudes of any unconnected, unfinanced, only partly educated (he has never received a high-school diploma, having been expelled before graduation from Shattuck Military Academy, in Faribault, Minnesota, an institution he refers to as "the asylum") young man who arrives in New York from more rural parts—in his case, Libertyville, Illinois. Living alone in furnished rooms, or sharing underfurnished apartments, he had spent his first city years fluctuating between acting classes and a fly-by-night enrollment in Social Security; Best's once had him on its payroll as an elevator boy.

A friend of his, who saw a lot of him in those pre-candy days, corroborates to some extent the rather somnambulistic portrait Brando paints of himself. "He was a brooder, all right," the friend has said. "He seemed to have a built-in hideaway room and was always rushing off to it to worry over himself, and gloat, too, like a miser with his gold. But it wasn't all Gloomsville. When he wanted to, he could rocket right out of himself. He had a wild, kid kind of fun thing. Once he was living in an old brownstone on Fifty-second Street, near where some of the jazz joints are. He used to go up on the roof and fill paper bags with water and throw them down at the stiffs coming out of the clubs. He had a sign on the wall of his room that said 'You Ain't Livin' If You Don't Know It.' Yeah, there was always something jumping in that apartment—Marlon playing the bongos, records going, people around, kids from the Actors' Studio, and a lot of down-and-outers he'd picked up. And he could be sweet. He was the least opportunistic person I've ever known. He never gave a damn about anybody who could help him; you might say he went out of his way to avoid them. Sure, part of that—the kind of people he didn't like and the kind he did, both—stemmed from his insecurities, his inferiority feelings. Very few of his friends were his equals—anybody he'd have to *compete* with, if you know what I mean. Mostly they were strays, idolizers, characters who were dependent on him one way or another. The same with the girls he took out. Plain sort of somebody's-secretary-type girls—nice enough but nothing that's going to start a stampede of competitors." (The last-mentioned preference of Brando's was true of him as an adolescent, too, or so his grandmother has said. As she put it, "Marlon always picked on the cross-eyed girls.")

The maid poured *sake* into thimble-sized cups, and withdrew. Connoisseurs of this palely pungent rice wine pretend they can discern variations in taste and quality in over fifty brands. But to the novice all *sake* seems to have been brewed in the same vat—a toddy, pleasant at first, cloying afterward, and not likely to echo in your head unless it is devoured by the quart, a habit many of Japan's *bons vivants* have adopted. Brando ignored the *sake* and went straight for his filet. The steak was excellent; Japanese take a just pride in the quality of their beef. The spaghetti, a dish that is very popular in Japan, was not; nor was the rest—the conglomeration of peas, potatoes, beans. Granted that the menu was a queer one, it is on the whole a mistake to order Western-style food in Japan, yet there arise those moments when one retches at the thought of more raw fish, sukiyaki, and rice with seaweed, when, however temptingly they may be prepared and

however prettily presented, the unaccustomed stomach re-
volts at the prospect of eel broth and fried bees and pickled
snake and octopus arms.

As we ate, Brando returned to the possibility of renouncing
his movie-star status for the satisfactions of a life that "led
somewhere." He decided to compromise. "Well, when I get
back to Hollywood, what I *will* do, I'll fire my secretary and
move into a smaller house," he said. He sighed with relief,
as though he'd already cast off old encumbrances and entered upon the simplicities of his new situation. Embroidering on its charms, he said, "I won't have a cook or maid.
Just a cleaning woman who comes in twice a week. But"—
he frowned, squinted, as if something were blurring the bliss
he envisioned—"wherever the house is, it has to have a
fence. On account of the people with pencils. You don't know
what it's like. The people with pencils. I need a fence to keep
them out. I suppose there's nothing I can do about the
telephone."

"Telephone?"

"It's tapped. Mine is."

"Tapped? Really? By whom?"

He chewed his steak, mumbled. He seemed reluctant to
say, yet certain it was so. "When I talk to my friends, we
speak French. Or else a kind of bop lingo we made up."

Suddenly, sounds came through the ceiling from the room
above us—footfalls, muffled voices like the noise of water
flowing through a pipe. "Sh-h-h!" whispered Brando, listening intently, his gaze alerted upward. "Keep your voice
down. *They* can hear everything." They, it appeared, were
his fellow actor Red Buttons and Buttons' wife, who occupied the suite overhead. "This place is made of paper," he
continued in tiptoe tones, and with the absorbed countenance

of a child lost in a very earnest game—an expression that half explained his secretiveness, the looking-over-his-shoulder, coded-bop-for-telephones facet of his personality that occasionally causes conversation with him to assume a conspiratorial quality, as though one were discussing subversive topics in perilous political territory. Brando said nothing; I said nothing. Nor did Mr. and Mrs. Buttons—not anything distinguishable.

During the siege of silence, my host located a letter buried among the dinner plates, and read it while he ate, like a gentleman perusing his breakfast newspaper. Presently, remembering me, he remarked, "From a friend of mine. He's making a documentary, the life of James Dean. He wants me to do the narration. I think I might." He tossed the letter aside and pulled his apple pie, topped with a melting scoop of vanilla ice cream, toward him. "Maybe not, though. I get excited about something, but it never lasts more than seven minutes. Seven minutes exactly. That's my limit. I never know why I get up in the morning." Finishing his pie, he gazed speculatively at my portion; I passed it to him. "But I'm really considering this Dean thing. It could be important."

James Dean, the young motion-picture actor killed in a car accident in 1955, was promoted throughout his phosphorescent career as the all-American "mixed-up kid," the symbol of misunderstood hot-rodding youth with a switchblade approach to life's little problems. When he died, an expensive film in which he had starred, *Giant*, had yet to be released, and the picture's press agents, seeking to offset any ill effects that Dean's demise might have on the commercial prospects of their product, succeeded by "glamorizing" the tragedy, and in ironic consequence, created a Dean legend of rather necrophilic appeal. Though Brando was seven years

older than Dean, and professionally more secure, the two actors came to be associated in the collective movie-fan mind.
Many critics reviewing Dean's first film, *East of Eden*, remarked on the well-nigh plagiaristic resemblance between
his acting mannerisms and Brando's. Off-screen, too, Dean
appeared to be practicing the sincerest form of flattery; like
Brando, he tore around on motorcycles, played bongo
drums, dressed the role of rowdy, spouted an intellectual rig-
marole, cultivated a cranky, colorful newspaper personality
that mingled, to a skillfully potent degree, plain bad boy and
sensitive sphinx.

"No, Dean was never a friend of mine," said Brando, in
response to a question that he seemed surprised to have been
asked. "That's not why I may do the narration job. I hardly
knew him. But he had an *idée fixe* about me. Whatever I
did he did. He was always trying to get close to me. He used
to call up." Brando lifted an imaginary telephone, put it to
his ear with a cunning, eavesdropper's smile. "I'd listen to
him talking to the answering service, asking for me, leaving
messages. But I never spoke up. I never called him back. No,
when I—"

The scene was interrupted by the ringing of a real telephone. "Yeah?" he said, picking it up. "Speaking. From
where? . . . Manila? . . . Well, I don't know anybody in Manila. Tell them I'm not here. No, when I finally met Dean,"
he said, hanging up, "it was at a party. Where he was throwing himself around, acting the madman. So I spoke to him.
I took him aside and asked him didn't he know he was sick?
That he needed help?" The memory evoked an intensified
version of Brando's familiar look of enlightened compassion. "He listened to me. He knew he was sick. I gave him
the name of an analyst, and he went. And at least his *work*

improved. Toward the end, I think he was beginning to find his own way as an actor. But this glorifying of Dean is all wrong. That's why I believe the documentary could be important. To show he wasn't a hero; show what he really was —just a lost boy trying to find himself. That ought to be done, and I'd like to do it—maybe as a kind of expiation for some of my own sins. Like making *The Wild One*." He was referring to the strange film in which he was presented as the Führer of a tribe of Fascistlike delinquents. "But. Who knows? Seven minutes is my limit."

From Dean the conversation turned to other actors, and I asked which ones, specifically, Brando respected. He pondered; though his lips shaped several names, he seemed to have second thoughts about pronouncing them. I suggested a few candidates—Laurence Olivier, John Gielgud, Montgomery Clift, Gérard Philipe, Jean-Louis Barrault. "Yes," he said, at last coming alive, "Philipe is a good actor. So is Barrault. Christ, what a wonderful picture that was—*Les Enfants du Paradis!* Maybe the best movie ever made. You know, that's the only time I ever fell in love with an actress, somebody on the screen. I was mad about Arletty." The Parisian star Arletty is well remembered by international audiences for the witty, womanly allure she brought to the heroine's part in Barrault's celebrated film. "I mean, I was really in *love* with her. My first trip to Paris, the thing I did right away, I asked to meet Arletty. I went to see her as though I were going to a shrine. My ideal woman. Wow!" He slapped the table. "Was that a mistake, was that a disillusionment! She was a tough article."

The maid came to clear the table; *en passant*, she gave Brando's shoulder a sisterly pat, rewarding him, I took it, for the cleaned-off sparkle of his plates. He again collapsed on the floor, stuffing a pillow under his head. "I'll tell you," he said, "Spencer Tracy is the kind of actor I like to watch. The way he holds back, *holds* back—then darts in to make his point, darts back. Tracy, Muni, Cary Grant. They know what they're doing. You can learn something from them."

Brando began to weave his fingers in the air, as though hoping that gestures would describe what he could not precisely articulate. "Acting is such a tenuous thing," he said. "A fragile, shy thing that a sensitive director can help lure out of you. Now, in movie-acting, the important, the *sensitive* moment comes around the third take of a scene; by then you just need a whisper from the director to crystallize it for you. Gadge"—he was using Elia Kazan's nickname—"can usually do it. He's wonderful with actors."

Another actor, I suppose, would have understood at once what Brando was saying, but I found him difficult to follow. "It's what happens inside you on the third take," he said, with a careful emphasis that did not lessen my incomprehension. One of the most memorable film scenes Brando has played occurs in the Kazan-directed *On the Waterfront*; it is the car-ride scene in which Rod Steiger, as the racketeering brother, confesses he is leading Brando into a death trap. I asked if he could use the episode as an example, and tell me how his theory of the "sensitive moment" applied to it.

"Yes. Well, no. Well, let's see." He puckered his eyes, made a humming noise. "That was a seven-take scene, and I didn't like the way it was written. Lot of dissension going on there. I was fed up with the whole picture. All the location stuff was in New Jersey, and it was the dead of winter—the cold, Christ! And I was having problems at the time. Woman trouble. That scene. Let me see. There were seven takes because Rod Steiger couldn't stop crying. He's one of those actors loves to cry. We kept doing it over and over. But I can't remember just when, just how it crystallized itself for me. The first time I saw *Waterfront*, in a projection room with Gadge, I thought it was so terrible I walked out without even speaking to him."

A month earlier, a friend of Brando's had told me, "Marlon always turns against whatever he's working on. Some element of it. Either the script or the director or somebody in the cast. Not always because of anything very rational—just because it seems to comfort him to be dissatisfied, let off steam about something. It's part of his pattern. Take *Sayonara*. A dollar gets you ten he'll develop a hoss on it somewhere along the line. A hoss on Logan, maybe. Maybe against Japan—the whole damn country. He loves Japan *now*. But with Marlon you never know from one minute to the next."

I was wondering whether I might mention this supposed "pattern" to Brando, ask if he considered it a valid observation about himself. But it was as though he had anticipated the question. "I ought to keep my mouth shut," he said. "Around here, around *Sayonara*, I've let a few people know the way I feel. But I don't always feel the same way two days running."

It was ten-thirty, and Murray called on the dot.

"I went out to dinner with the girls," he told Brando, his telephone voice so audible that I could hear it, too; it spoke above a blend of dance-band rumble and barroom roar. Obviously he was patronizing not one of the more traditional, cat-quiet Kyoto restaurants but, rather, a place where the customers wore shoes. "We're just finishing. How about it? You through?"

Brando looked at me thoughtfully, and I, in turn, at my coat. But he said, "We're still yakking. Call me back in an hour."

"Okay. Well ... okay. Listen. Miiko's here. She wants to know did you get the flowers she sent you?"

Brando's eyes lazily rolled toward the glassed-in sun porch, where a bowl of asters was centered on a round bamboo table. "Uh-huh. Tell her thanks very much."

"Tell her yourself. She's right here."

"No! Hey, wait a minute! Christ, *that's* not how you do it." But the protest came too late. Murray had already put down the phone, and Brando, reiterating "*That's* not how you do it," blushed and squirmed like an embarrassed boy.

The next voice to emanate from the receiver belonged to his *Sayonara* leading lady, Miss Miiko Taka. She asked about his health.

"Better, thanks. I ate the bad end of an oyster, that's all. Miiko? ... Miiko, that was very *sweet* of you to send me the flowers. They're beautiful. I'm looking at them right now. Asters," he continued, as though shyly venturing a line of verse, "are my favorite flowers ..."

I retired to the sun porch, leaving Brando and Miss Taka to conduct their conversation in stricter seclusion. Below the windows, the hotel garden, with its ultra-simple and *soigné* arrangements of rock and tree, floated in the mists that crawl off Kyoto's waterways—for it *is* a watery city, criss-crossed with shallow rivers and cascading canals, dotted with pools as still as coiled snakes and mirthful little waterfalls that sound like Japanese girls giggling. Once the imperial capital and now the country's cultural museum, such an aesthetic treasure house that American bombers let it go unmolested during the war, Kyoto is surrounded by water, too;

beyond the city's containing hills, thin roads run like cause-
ways across the reflecting silver of flooded rice fields. That
evening, despite the gliding mists, the blue encircling hills
were discernible against the night, for the upper air had
purity; a sky was there, stars were in it, and a scrap of moon.
Some portions of the town could be seen. Nearest was a
neighborhood of curving roofs, the dark façades of aristocratic houses fashioned from silky wood yet austere, northern, as secret-looking as any stone Siena palace. How brilliant
they made the street lamps appear, and the doorway lanterns
casting keen kimono colors—pink and orange, lemon and
red. Farther away was a modern flatness—wide avenues and
neon, a skyscraper of raw concrete that seemed less endur-
ing, more perishable, than the papery dwellings stooping
around it.

Brando completed his call. Approaching the sun porch, he
looked at me looking at the view. He said, "Have you been
to Nara? Pretty interesting."

I had, and yes, it was. "Ancient, old-time Nara," as a local cicerone unfailingly referred to it, is an hour's drive from
Kyoto—a postcard town set in a show-place park. Here is
the apotheosis of the Japanese genius for hypnotizing nature
into unnatural behavior. The great shrine-infested park is a
green salon where sheep graze, and herds of tame deer wander under trim pine trees and, like Venetian pigeons, gladly
pose with honeymooning couples; where children yank the
beards of unretaliating goats; where old men wearing black
capes with mink collars squat on the shores of lotus-quilted
lakes and, by clapping their hands, summon swarms of fish,
speckled and scarlet carp, fat, thick as trout, who allow their
snouts to be tickled, then gobble the crumbs that the old men
sprinkle. That this serpentless Eden should strongly appeal

to Brando was a bit surprising. With his liberal taste for the off-trail and not-overly-trammeled, one might have thought he would be unresponsive to so ruly, subjugated a landscape. Then, as though apropos of Nara, he said, "Well, I'd like to be married. I want to have children." It was not, perhaps, the *non sequitur* it seemed; the gentle safety of Nara just could, by the association of ideas, suggest marriage, a family.

"You've got to have love," he said. "There's no other reason for living. Men are no different from mice. They're born to perform the same function. Procreate." ("Marlon," to quote his friend Elia Kazan, "is one of the gentlest people I've ever known. Possibly the gentlest." Kazan's remark had meaning when one observed Brando in the company of children. As far as he was concerned, Japan's youngest generation—lovely, lively, cherry-cheeked kids with bowlegs and bristling bangs—was always welcome to lark around the *Sayonara* sets. He was good with the children, at ease, playful, appreciative; he seemed, indeed, their emotional contemporary, a co-conspirator. Moreover, the condoling expression, the slight look of dispensing charitable compassion, peculiar to his contemplation of some adults was absent from his eyes when he looked at a child.)

Touching Miss Taka's floral offering, he went on, "What other reason is there for living? Except love? That has been my main trouble. My inability to love anyone." He turned back into the lighted room, stood there as though hunting something—a cigarette? He picked up a pack. Empty. He slapped at the pockets of trousers and jackets lying here and there. Brando's wardrobe no longer smacks of the street gang; as a dresser, he has graduated, or gone back, into an earlier style of outlaw chic, that of the prohibition sharpie—black snap-brim hats, striped suits and somber-hued George

Raft shirts with pastel ties. Cigarettes were found; inhaling, he slumped on the pallet bed. Beads of sweat ringed his mouth. The electric heater hummed. The room was tropical; one could have grown orchids. Overhead, Mr. and Mrs. Buttons were again bumping about, but Brando appeared to have lost interest in them. He was smoking, thinking. Then, picking up the stitch of his thought, he said, "I can't. Love anyone. I can't trust anyone enough to give myself to them. But I'm ready. I want it. And I may, I'm almost on the point, I've really got to . . ." His eyes narrowed, but his tone, far from being intense, was indifferent, dully objective, as though he were discussiong some character in a play—a part he was weary of portraying yet was trapped in by contract. "Because—well, what else is there? That's all it's all about. To love somebody."

(At this time Brando was, of course, a bachelor, who had, upon occasion, indulged in engagements of a quasi-official character—once to an aspiring authoress and actress, by name Miss Blossom Plumb, and again, with more public attention, to Mlle. Josanne Mariani-Bérenger, a French fisherman's daughter. But in neither instance were banns ever posted. One day last month, however, in a sudden and somewhat secret ceremony at Eagle Rock, California, Brando was married to a dark, sari-swathed young minor actress who called herself Anna Kashfi. According to conflicting press reports, either she was a Darjeeling-born Buddhist of the purest Indian parentage or she was the Calcutta-born daughter of an English couple named O'Callaghan, now living in Wales. Brando has not yet done anything to clear up the mystery.)

"Anyway, I have *friends*. No. No, I don't," he said, verbally shadowboxing. "Oh, sure I do," he decided, smoothing the sweat on his upper lip. "I have a great many friends. Some I don't hold out on. I let them know what's happening. You have to trust somebody. Well, not all the way. There's nobody I rely on to tell *me* what to do."

I asked if that included professional advisers. For instance, it was my understanding that Brando very much depended on the guidance of Jay Kanter, a young man on the staff of the Music Corporation of America, which is the agency that represents him. "Oh, Jay," Brando said now. "Jay does what I tell *him* to. I'm alone like that."

The telephone sounded. An hour seemed to have passed, for it was Murray again. "Yeah, still yakking," Brando told him. "Look, let *me* call *you* ... Oh, in an hour or so. You be back in your room? ... Okay."

He hung up, and said, "Nice guy. He wants to be a director—eventually. I was saying something, though. We were talking about friends. Do you know how I make a friend?" He leaned a little toward me, as though he had an amusing secret to impart. "I go about it very gently. I circle around and around. I circle. Then, gradually, I come nearer. Then I reach out and touch them—ah, so gently . . ." His fingers stretched forward like insect feelers and grazed my arm. "Then," he said, one eye half shut, the other, à la Rasputin, mesmerically wide and shining, "I draw back. Wait awhile. Make them wonder. At just the right moment, I move in again. Touch them. Circle." Now his hand, broad and blunt-fingered, traveled in a rotating pattern, as though it held a rope with which he was binding an invisible presence. "They don't know what's happening. Before they realize it, they're all entangled, involved. I have them. And suddenly, sometimes, I'm all *they* have. A lot of them, you see, are people who don't fit anywhere; they're not accepted, they've been hurt, crippled one way or another. But I want to help them, and they can focus on me; I'm the duke. Sort of the duke of my domain."

(A past tenant on the ducal preserve, describing its seigneur and his subjects, has said, "It's as though Marlon lived in a house where the doors are never locked. When he lived in New York, the door always *was* open. Anybody could come in, whether Marlon was there or not, and everybody did. You'd arrive and there would be ten, fifteen characters wandering around. It was strange, because nobody seemed to really know anybody else. They were just there, like people in a bus station. Some type asleep in a chair. People reading the tabs. A girl dancing by herself. Or painting her toenails. A comedian trying out his night-club act. Off in a corner, there'd be a chess game going. And drums—bang, boom, bang, boom! But there was never any drinking— nothing like that. Once in a while somebody would say, 'Let's go down to the corner for an ice-cream soda.' Now, in all this Marlon was the common denominator, the only connecting link. He'd move around the room drawing individuals aside and talking to them alone. If you've noticed, Marlon can't, *won't*, talk to two people simultaneously. He'll never take part in a *group* conversation. It always has to be a cozy tête-à-tête—one person at a time. Which is necessary, I suppose, if you use the same kind of charm on everyone. But even when you know that's what he's doing, it doesn't matter. Because when *your* turn comes, he makes you feel you're the only person in the room. In the world. Makes you feel that you're under his protection and that your troubles and moods concern him deeply. You have to believe it; more than anyone I've known, he radiates *sincerity*. Afterward you may ask yourself, 'Is it an act?' If so, what's the point? What have you got to give him? Nothing except—and this *is* the point—affection. Affection that lends him authority over you. I sometimes think Marlon is like an orphan who later on in life tries to compensate by becoming the kindly head of a huge orphanage. But even outside this institution he wants everybody to love him." Although there exist a score of witnesses who might well contradict the last opinion, Brando himself is credited with having once informed an interviewer, "I can walk into a room where there are a hundred people— if there is *one* person in that room who doesn't like me, I know it and have to get out." As a footnote, it should be added that within the clique over which Brando presides he is esteemed as an intellectual father, as well as an emotional big brother. The person who probably knows him best, the comedian Wally Cox, declares him to be "a creative philosopher, a very deep thinker," and adds, "He's a real liberating force for his friends."

Brando yawned; it had got to be a quarter past one. In less than five hours he would have to be showered, shaved, breakfasted, on the set, and ready for a make-up man to paint his pale face the mulatto tint that Technicolor requires.

"Let's have another cigarette," he said as I made a move to put on my coat.

"Don't you think you should go to sleep?"

"That just means getting up. Most mornings, I don't know why I do. I can't face it." He looked at the telephone, as though remembering his promise to call Murray. "Anyway, I may work later on. You want something to drink?"

Outside, the stars had darkened and it had started to drizzle, so the prospect of a nightcap was pleasing, especially if I should have to return on foot to my own hotel, which was a mile distant from the Miyako. I poured some vodka; Brando declined to join me. However, he subsequently reached for my glass, sipped from it, set it down between us, and suddenly said, in an offhand way that nonetheless conveyed feeling, "My mother. She broke apart like a piece of porcelain."

I had often heard friends of Brando's say, "Marlon worshiped his mother." But prior to 1947, and the première of *A Streetcar Named Desire*, few, perhaps none, of the young actor's circle had met either of his parents; they knew nothing of his background except what he chose to tell them. "Marlon always gave a very colorful picture of home life back in Illinois," one of his acquaintances told me. "When we heard that his family were coming to New York for the opening of *Streetcar*, everybody was very curious. We didn't know what to expect. On opening night, Irene Selznick gave a big party at '21.' Marlon came with his mother and father. Well, you can't imagine two more attractive people. Tall, handsome, charming as they could be. What impressed me—I think it amazed everyone—was Marlon's attitude toward them. In their presence, he wasn't the lad we knew. He was a model son. Reticent, respectful, very polite, considerate in every way."

Born in Omaha, Nebraska, where his father was a salesman of limestone products, Brando, the family's third child and only son, was soon taken to live in Libertyville, Illinois. There the Brandos settled down in a rambling house in a countrified neighborhood; at least, there was enough country around the house to allow the Brandos to keep geese and hens and rabbits, a horse, a Great Dane, twenty-eight cats and a cow. Milking the cow was the daily chore that belonged to Bud, as Marlon was then nicknamed. Bud seems to have been an extroverted and competitive boy. Everyone who came within range of him was at once forced into some variety of contest: Who can eat fastest? Hold his breath longest? Tell the tallest tale? Bud was rebellious, too; rain or shine, he ran away from home every Sunday. But he and his two sisters, Frances and Jocelyn, were devotedly close to their mother. Many years later Stella Adler, Brando's former drama coach, described Mrs. Brando, who died in 1954, as "a very beautiful, a heavenly, lost, girlish creature." Always, wherever she lived, Mrs. Brando had played leads in the productions of local dramatic societies, and always she had longed for a more brightly footlighted world than her surroundings provided. These yearnings inspired her children. Frances took to painting; Jocelyn, who is at present a professional actress, interested herself in the theatre. Bud, too, had inherited his mother's theatrical inclinations, but at seventeen he announced a wish to study for the ministry. (Then, as now, Brando searched for a belief. As one Brando disciple once summed it up, "He needs to find something in life, something in himself, that is permanently true, and he needs to lay down his life for it. For such an intense personality, nothing less than that will do.") Talked out of his clerical ambitions, expelled from school, rejected for military service in 1942 because of a trick knee, Brando packed up and came to New York. Whereupon Bud, the plump, towheaded, unhappy adolescent, exits, and the man-sized and very gifted Marlon emerges.

Brando has not forgotten Bud. When he speaks of the boy he was, the boy seems to inhabit him, as if time had done little to separate the man from the hurt, desiring child. "My father was indifferent to me," he said. "Nothing I could do interested him, or pleased him. I've accepted that now. We're

friends now. We get along." Over the past ten years the
elder Brando has supervised his son's financial affairs; in addition to Pennebaker Productions, of which Mr. Brando, Sr.,
is an employee, they have been associated in a number of ven-
tures, including a Nebraska grain-and-cattle ranch, in which
a large percentage of the younger Brando's earnings was in-
vested. "But my mother was everything to me. A whole
world. I tried so hard. I used to come home from school . . ."
He hesitated, as though waiting for me to picture him: Bud,
books under his arm, scuffling his way along an afternoon
street. "There wouldn't be anybody home. Nothing in the
icebox." More lantern slides: empty rooms, a kitchen. "Then
the telephone would ring. Somebody calling from some bar.
And they'd say, 'We've got a lady down here. You better
come get her.'" Suddenly Brando was silent. In the silence
the picture faded, or, rather, became fixed: Bud at the telephone. At last the image moved again, leaped forward in
time. Bud is eighteen, and: "I thought if she loved me enough,
trusted me enough, I thought, then we can be together, in
New York; we'll live together and I'll take care of her.
Once, later on, that really happened. She left my father and
came to live with me. In New York, when I was in a play.
I tried so hard. But my love wasn't enough. She couldn't care
enough. She went back. And one day"—the flatness of his
voice grew flatter, yet the emotional pitch ascended until
one could discern, like a sound within a sound, a wounded be-
wilderment—"I didn't care any more. She was there. In a
room. Holding on to me. And I let her fall. Because I
couldn't take it any more—watch her breaking apart, in front
of me, like a piece of porcelain. I stepped right over her. I
walked right out. I was indifferent. Since then, I've been
indifferent."

The telephone was signaling. Its racket seemed to rouse him from a daze; he stared about, as though he'd wakened in an unknown room, then smiled wryly, then whispered, "Damn, damn, damn," as his hand lurched toward the telephone. "Sorry," he told Murray. "I was just going to call you ... No, he's leaving now. But look, man, let's call it off tonight. It's after one. It's nearly two o'clock ... Yeah ... Sure thing. Tomorrow."

Meanwhile, I'd put on my overcoat and was waiting to say good night. He walked me to the door, where I put on my shoes. "Well, *sayonara*," he mockingly bade me. "Tell them at the desk to get you a taxi." Then, as I walked down the corridor, he called, "And listen! Don't pay too much attention to what I say. I don't always feel the same way."

In a sense, this was not my last sight of him that evening. Downstairs, the Miyako's lobby was deserted. There was no one at the desk, nor, outside, were there any taxis in view. Even at high noon the fancy crochet of Kyoto's streets had played me tricks; still, I set off through the marrow-chilling drizzle in what I hoped was a homeward direction. I'd never before been abroad so late in the city. It was quite a contrast to daytime, when the central parts of the town, carousel by crowds of fiesta massiveness, jangle like the inside of a *pachinko* parlor, or to early evening—Kyoto's most exotic hours, for then, like night flowers, lanterns wreathe the side streets, and resplendent geishas, with their white ceramic faces and their ballooning lacquered wigs strewn with silver bells, their hobbled wiggle-walk, hurry among the shadows toward meticulously tasteful revelries. But at two in the morning these exquisite grotesques are gone, the cabarets are shuttered; only cats remained to keep me company, and drunks and red-light ladies, the inevitable old beggar-bundles in doorways, and, briefly, a ragged street musician who followed me playing on a flute a medieval music. I had trudged far more than a mile when, at last, one of a hundred alleys led to familiar ground—the main-street district of department stores and cinemas. It was then that I saw Brando. Sixty feet tall, with a head as huge as the greatest Buddha's, there he was, in comic-paper colors, on a sign above a theatre that advertised *The Teahouse of the August Moon.* Rather Buddha-like, too, was his pose, for he was depicted in a squatting position, a serene smile on a face that glistened in the rain and the light of a street lamp. A deity, yes; but more than that, really, just a young man sitting on a pile of candy.

Style:
and the Japanese

(*1955*)

�✷

T HE FIRST PERSON WHO EVER IMPRESSED ME, beyond the
reaches of my family, was an elderly Japanese gentleman
called Mr. Frederik Mariko. Mr. Mariko ran a florist shop
in New Orleans. I met him when I was perhaps six, just
wandered into his shop, you might say, and during the ten
years of our friendship, or until he quite suddenly died on a
steamboat trip to St. Louis, he made me with his own hands
a score of toys—flying fish swung on wires, a maquette garden filled with dwarf flowers and feathery medieval animals, a dancer with a wind-up fan that fluttered for three
minutes; and these toys, much too exquisite to be *played*

with, were my original aesthetic experience—they made a world and set a standard of taste. There was such mystery about Mr. Mariko, not as a man (he was simple and alone and hard-of-hearing, which emphasized his apartness) but because one could never decide, watching him work at his arrangements, what made him choose between those brown leaves and that green vine so sophisticated, so accurate an effect. Years later, reading the novels of Lady Murasaki or *The Pillow-Book of Sei Shonagon*, and then, later still, seeing the Kabuki dancers and those three astonishing films (*Rashomon*, *Ugetsu* and *Gates of Hell*), the memory of Mr. Mariko loomed, but the mystery of his luminous toys and dwarf bouquets somewhat subsided in a realization that his gifts were the extension of an entire national sensibility: like visual musicians, the Japanese seem to have perfect pitch in areas of shape and color.

Perfect: when the curtain rises on a performance of the Kabuki dancers, a premonition of the entertainment, the *frisson* it will ultimately achieve, is already there in the severely rich patterns of color, exotically solemn postures of the dancers kneeling in their robes like porcelain figurines. Or again, a scene, a pantomime, from *Rashomon*: the young bride, traveling in a veiled sedan chair and attended by her husband, sways slowly through the forest, the camera creating a rapturous menace out of leaves and sunlight and the sleepy, seducing eyes of a watching bandit. Of course, *Rashomon* was filmed in black and white; it was not until *Gates of Hell* that the complete palette came into view, the colors like new inventions: absinthe, and browns that sparkle like sherry. It is all a ceremony of Style, a phenomenon that seems to rotate, in a manner quite separate from emotional content, on absolute style alone.

High style has never been a forte of the Western theatre; at any rate, we have not developed anything so chemically pure and self-contained as this. A half-comparison might be made with Restoration comedy: there is at least the same appreciation of the artificial; and it is true that in the gangster thriller and cowboy genre Americans have produced a classically stylized form of code and behavior. But these are snappy fragments, outbursts; the Japanese sense of style is the accumulation of long and seriously beautiful aesthetic thought. Although, as Arthur Waley has mentioned, a principal basis of this thought is dread—dread of the explicit, the emphatic—hence the single blade of grass describing a whole universe of summer, the slightly lowered eyes left to suggest the deepest passion.

In ninth-century Japan, and indeed earlier, most correspondence was conducted in poetry: a cultivated Japanese knew several hundred poems and scriptures from which he could quote lines suitable to any idea or occasion—if not, he contrived his own, for poetry was the entertainment of the day. Judging from what we have seen of their entertainment recently, their dances and their films, the custom still prevails; certainly what we have received have been poems of communication.

Observations

(1959)

Isak Dinesen

R UNGSTED IS A SEA TOWN on the coast road between
Copenhagen and Elsinore. Among eighteenth-century travelers the otherwise undistinguished village was well known
for the handsomeness of its Inn. The Inn, though it no longer
obliges coachmen and their passengers, is still renowned: as
the home of Rungsted's first citizen, the Baroness Blixen,
alias Isak Dinesen, alias Pierre Andrezel.

The Baroness, weighing a handful of feathers and fragile
as a *coquillage* bouquet, entertains callers in a sparse, spar-
kling parlor sprinkled with sleeping dogs and warmed by a
fireplace and a porcelain stove: a room where she, an impos-

ing creation come forward from one of her own Gothic tales, sits bundled in bristling wolfskins and British tweeds, her feet fur-booted, her legs, thin as the thighs of an ortolan, encased in woolen hose, and her neck, round which a ring could fit, looped with frail lilac scarves. Time has refined her, this legend who has lived the adventures of an iron-nerved man: shot charging lions and infuriated buffalo, worked an African farm, flown over Kilimanjaro in the perilous first planes, doctored the Masai; time has reduced her to an essence, as a grape can become a raisin, roses an attar. Quite instantly, even if one were deprived of knowing her dossier, she registers as *la vraie chose*, a true somebody. A face so faceted, its prisms tossing a proud glitter of intelligence and educated compassion, which is to say wisdom, cannot be an accidental occurrence; nor do such eyes, smudges of kohl darkening the lids, deeply set, like velvet animals burrowed in a cave, fall into the possession of ordinary women.

If a visitor is invited to tea, the Baroness serves a very high one: sherry before, afterward a jamboree of toast and varied marmalades, cold pâtés, grilled livers, orange-flavored crêpes. But the hostess cannot partake, she is unwell, she eats nothing, nothing at all, oh, perhaps an oyster, one strawberry, a glass of champagne. Instead, she talks; and like most artists, certainly all old beauties, she is sufficiently self-centered to enjoy herself as conversational subject.

Her lips, just touched with paint, twist in a sideways smile of rather paralytic contour, and speaking an English brushed with British inflections, she might say, "Ah, well, yes, what a lot of stories this old Inn could tell. It belonged to my brother, I bought it from him; *Last Tales* paid the last installment. Now it is mine, absolutely. I have plans for it after I die. It will be an aviary, the grounds, the park, will be

a bird sanctuary. All the years in Africa, when I had my
highland farm, I never imagined to make my home again in
Denmark. When I knew, was certain, the farm was slipping
away, saw I'd lost it, that is when I began writing my stories:
to forget the unendurable. During the war, too; the house
was a way station for Jews escaping to Sweden. Jews in the
kitchen and Nazis in the garden. I had to write to save my
mind, I wrote *The Angelic Avengers*, which was not a political parable, though it amused me how many decided it to
be so. Extraordinary men, the Nazis. I often argued with
them, spoke back very sharply. Oh, don't think I mean to
seem brave, I risked nothing; they were such a masculine society, they simply didn't care what a woman thought. Another muffin? Please do. I enjoy dining vicariously. I waited
for the postman today; I'd hoped he'd bring a new parcel of
books. I read so quickly, it's difficult to keep me supplied.
What I ask of art is air, an atmosphere. That is very meager
on the menu nowadays. I never weary of books that I like,
I can read them twenty times—can, and have. *King Lear*.
I always judge a person by what he thinks of *King Lear*. Of
course, one does want a new page; a different face. I have a
talent for friendship, friends are what I have enjoyed most:
to stir, to get about, to meet new people and attach them."

Periodically the Baroness does stir. Leaning on the affectionate arm of forlornly cheerful Miss Clara Svendsen, her
long-in-service secretary-companion ("Dear Clara. Orginally
I hired her as a cook. After three wretched meals I accused
her, 'My dear, you are an imposter. Speak the truth!' She
wept, and told me she was a schoolteacher from the north
of Denmark who loved my books. One day she'd seen an
advertisement I'd placed for a kitchen wench. So she came;
and she wanted to stay. Since she couldn't cook, we arranged

she should be secretary. I regret the decision exceedingly. Clara is an appalling tyrant"), she sets forth for Rome or London, going usually by ship ("One does not travel in a plane; one is merely sent, like a parcel"). Last January, the winter of 1959, she made her initial visit to America, a country to which she is grateful because it provided the first publisher and audience for her work. Her reception was comparable to Jenny Lind; at least out-distanced anything accorded a literary dignitary since Dickens and Shaw. She was televised and *Life*ized, the one public "reading" for which she was scheduled developed into a marathon of ticket-scalper, standing-ovation events, and no one, heaven knows, has ever been guest of honor at so numbing a number of parties ("It was delicious. New York: ah! *That* is where things are happening! Lunches and dinners, champagne, champagne; everyone was too kind. I arrived weighing sixty-five pounds and came home an even fifty-three; the doctors didn't know why I was alive, they insisted I ought to be dead, but oh, I've known that for years, Death is my oldest flirt. No, we *lived*, and Clara—Clara gained a stone").

Her acceptance of immense age and its consequences is not stoically final; notes of healthy hope intrude: "I want to finish a book, I want to see next summer's fruit, and Rome again, Gielgud at Stratford, perhaps America. If only. *Why* am I so weak?" she asks, twitching at her lilac scarves with a brown bony hand; and the question, accompanied by the chimings of a mantel clock and a murmur from Miss Svendsen, invites the guest to depart, permitting the Baroness to doze on a couch next to the fire.

As the visitor goes he may be presented a copy of her favorite of her books ("Because it is about real things"), the beautiful *Out of Africa*. A souvenir inscribed "*Je responde-ray*—Karen Blixen."

"*Je responderay*," she explains, standing at the door and, in farewell, offering her cheek to be kissed, "I answer—a lovely motto. I borrowed it from the Finch-Hatton family. I like it because I believe every one of us has an answer in him."

Her own answer has been a yes to life, an affirmation her art echoes with an echo that will echo.

Mae West

ONCE UPON A TIME an outrageous young man of wide acquaintance thought to give an unusual tea party. It was to honor Miss Mae West, then appearing in a Manhattan night club. Dame Edith Sitwell was invited to pour, a task the Dame, always a devotee of *outré* incident, accepted. New York illuminati, titillated at the prospect of an interview between two ladies of such differently composed distinction, begged bids.

"My dear," the young man was congratulated in advance, "it's *the* camp of the season."

But—everything went awry. At four the Dame, pleading laryngitis, telephoned her regrets. By six, with the party at midpoint, it seemed Miss West would disappoint, too. Muttering guests mentioned hoax; at seven the host retired to a private chamber. Ten minutes later the guest of honor arrived, and what remained of the assemblage were not sorry they had waited. Not sorry, but strangely confused. The familiar appurtenances were there: the brass wig, the scimitar eyes with sword-length lashes, the white skin, white as a cottonmouth's mouth, the shape, that Big Ben of hour-glass figures, that convict's dream—nothing was absent; except Miss West.

For surely this was not the real Mae. Yet it was indeed Miss West: an uneasy, a shy and vulnerable, an unclassifiably virginal woman whose tardy entrance was conceivably due to having lingered on the street before summoning the courage to ring the bell. As one watched her, a jittery moth of a smile leaping about her lips but never alighting, huskily whisper "Sopleastameetya," and, as though too bashful to proceed, at once abandon her seat on the seesaw of any potential conversation, the tour de force nature of her theatre-self, its eerie and absolute completeness, struck with force. Removed from the protecting realm of her hilarious creation, her sexless symbol of uninhibited sexuality, she was without defense: her long lashes fluttered like the feelers of a beetle on its back.

Only once did the tougher Mae reveal herself. The display was occasioned by an intense young girl who, approaching the actress, announced, "I saw *Diamond Lil* last week; it was wonderful."

"Didja, honey? Wheredja see it?"

"At the Museum. The Modern Museum."

And a dismayed Miss West, seeking shelter in the sassy drawl of her famous fabrication, inquired, "Just whaddya mean, honey? A *museum*?"

Louis Armstrong

❦

Surely the satch has forgotten, still, he was one
of this writer's first friends, I met him when I was four, that
would be around 1928, and he, a hard-plump and belligerently
happy brown Buddha, was playing aboard a pleasure steamer
that paddled between New Orleans and St. Louis. Never
mind why, but I had occasion to take the trip very often,
and for me the sweet anger of Armstrong's trumpet, the
froggy exuberance of his come-to-me-baby mouthings, are a
piece of Proust's madeleine cake: they make Mississippi moons
rise again, summon the muddy lights of river towns, the
sound, like an alligator's yawn, of river horns—I hear the

rush of the mulatto river pushing by, hear, always, stomp! stomp! the beat of the grinning Buddha's foot as he shouts his way into "Sunny Side of the Street" and the honeymooning dancers, dazed with bootleg brew and sweating through their talcum, bunny-hug around the ship's saloony ballroom. The Satch, he was good to me, he told me I had talent, that I ought to be in vaudeville; he gave me a bamboo cane and a straw boater with a peppermint headband; and every night from the stand announced: "Ladies and gentlemen, now we're going to present you one of America's nice kids, he's going to do a little tap dance." Afterward I passed among the passengers, collecting in my hat nickels and dimes. This went on all summer, I grew rich and vain; but in October the river roughened, the moon whitened, the customers lessened, the boatrides ended, and with them my career. Six years later, while living at a boarding school from which I wanted to run away, I wrote my former, now famous, benefactor, and said if I came to New York couldn't he get me a job at the Cotton Club or somewhere? There was no reply, maybe he never got the letter, it doesn't matter, I still loved him, still do.

*

Jean Cocteau
and André Gide

❧

ANDRÉ GIDE, THAT MORALIZING IMMORALIST, a writer favored with sincerity but denied imagination, quite disapproved of Jean Cocteau, whose gifts the mischievous muses had reversed, making of him, both as man and artist, a creature vastly imaginative but vivaciously insincere. It is interesting, then, that Gide should have authored the most accurate, and for that reason most sympathetic, description of our eldest terrible child.

Gide is writing in his journal; the time is August 1914. "Jean Cocteau had arranged to meet me in an 'English tearoom' on the corner of the rue de Ponthieu and the avenue

d'Antin. I had no pleasure in seeing him again, despite his
extreme kindness; but he is incapable of seriousness, and all
his thoughts, his witticisms, his sensations, all the extraordinary brilliance of his customary conversation shocked me
like a luxury article displayed in a period of famine and
mourning. He is dressed almost like a soldier, and the fillip
of the present events has made him look healthier. He is
relinquishing nothing, but simply giving a martial twist to
his usual liveliness. When speaking of the slaughter of Mul-
house he uses amusing adjectives and mimicry; he imitates
the bugle call and the whistling of the shrapnel. Then, changing subjects since he sees he is not amusing me, he claims to
be sad; he wants to be sad with the same kind of sadness as
you, and suddenly he adopts your mood and explains it to
you. Then he talks of Blanche, mimics Mme. R. and talks
of the lady at the Red Cross who shouted on the stairway, 'I
was promised fifty wounded men for this morning; I want
my fifty wounded men.' Meanwhile he is crushing a piece of
plum cake in his plate and nibbling it; his voice rises suddenly
and has odd twists; he laughs, leans forward, bends toward
you and touches you. The odd thing is that I think he would
make a good soldier. He asserts that he would and that he
would be brave too. He has the carefree attitude of the street
urchin; it is in his company that I feel the most awkward, the
most heavy, the most gloomy."

In the spring of 1950, in the piazza of a Sicilian town
where Gide was vacationing (it was the last year of his life),
he had another meeting with Cocteau, a farewell encounter
which the writer of these notes happened to observe. It
was Gide's custom to dream away the morning hours propped
in the piazza sun; there he sat sipping from a bottle salt-
water brought fresh from the sea, a motionless mandarin

shrouded in a woolly wintry black cape and with a wide-
brimmed dark fedora casting a shadow the length of his
stern, brimstone countenance: an idle idol-saint (of sorts)
unspeaking and unspoken to except for occasional consulta-
tions with those of the village Ganymedes who snagged his
fancy. Then one morning Cocteau, whirling a cane, sauntered upon the piazza scene and proceeded to interrupt the
steely-eyed reveries of Il Vecchio (as the local *ragazzi* called
the distinguished octogenarian). Thirty-four years had gone
by since the wartime tea party, yet nothing in the attitude of
the two men toward each other had altered. Cocteau was
still anxious to please, still the rainbow-winged and dancing
dragonfly inviting the toad not merely to admire but perhaps devour him. He jigged about, his jingling merriment
competed with the bell-music of passing donkey carts, he
scattered rays of bitter wit that stung like the Sicilian sun,
he effused, enthused, he fondled the old man's knee, caressed
his hands, squeezed his shoulders, kissed his parched Mongolian cheeks—nay, nothing would awaken Il Vecchio: as
though his stomach turned at the thought of digesting such
fancy-colored fodder, he remained a hungerless frog upon a
thorny frond; until at last he croaked, "Do be still. You are
disturbing the view."

Very true: Cocteau was disturbing the view. He has been
doing so since his debut as an opium-smoking prodigy of seventeen. For more than four decades this eternal gamin has
conducted a fun-for-all vaudeville, with many flashing
changes of attire: poet, novelist, playwright, journalist, designer, painter, inventor of ballets, film maker, professional
conversationalist. Most of these costumes have fit well, a
few brilliantly. But it is in the guise of catalytic agent that
he has been most capable: as an innovator for, and propa-

gandist of, other men's ideas and gifts—from Radiguet to
Genet, Satie to Auric, Picasso to Bérard, Worth to Dior.
Cocteau has lived absolutely inside his time, and more than
anyone else, formed French taste in the present century. It
is Cocteau's kinship with his own epoch, his exclusive concern with the modern, that lay at the root of Il Vecchio's
aversion. "I do not seek to be of my epoch; I seek to overflow my epoch" was Gide's declared ambition; a commend-
able one, too. But isn't it possible that a man who has so en-
livened our today will, if not overflow, at least trickle into
somebody's tomorrow?

Humphrey Bogart

IF ONE LISTENS ATTENTIVELY to any man's vocabulary, it will be noticed that certain key-to-character words recur. With Bogart, whose pungent personal thesaurus was by and large unspeakably unprintable, "bum" and "professional" were two such verbal signposts. A most moral—by a bit exaggerating you might say *"prim"*—man, he employed "professional" as a platinum medal to be distributed among persons whose behavior he sanctioned; "bum," the reverse of an accolade, conveyed, when spoken by him, almost scarifying displeasure. "My old man," he once remarked of his father, who had been a reputable New York doctor, "died ten thousand dollars in debt, and I had to pay off every cent. A guy who doesn't leave his wife and kids provided for, he's a bum." Bums, too, were guys who cheated on their wives, cheated on their taxes, and all whiners, gossipists, most politicians, most writers, women who Drank, women who were scornful of men who Drank; but the bum true-blue was any fellow who shirked his job, was not, in meticulous style, a "pro" in his work. God knows he was. Never mind that he might play poker until dawn and swallow a brandy for breakfast: he was always on time on the set, in make-up and letter-perfect in his part (forever the same part, to be sure, still there is nothing more difficult to interestingly sustain than repetition). No, there was never a mite of bum-hokum about Bogart; he was an actor without theories (well, one: that he should be highly paid), without temper but not without temperament; and because he understood that discipline was the better part of artistic survival, he lasted, he left his mark.

Ezra Pound

B ORN 1885, AN IDAHO BOY. Taught school; was tossed out for being "too much the Latin Quarter type." Soon sought solace amid similar souls abroad. Aged twenty-three, while starving himself fat on a potato diet in Venice, he published *A Lume Spento*, a first book of poems which instigated a fierce friendship with Yeats, who wrote of him: "A rugged and headstrong nature and he is always hurting people's feelings, but he has I think some genius and great goodwill." Goodwill: to say it slightly!—between 1909 and 1920, while living first in London, then Paris, he steadily championed the careers of others (it was to Pound that

Eliot dedicated *The Wasteland*; it was Pound who raised the money that enabled Joyce to complete *Ulysses*). His generosity in this sphere is a matter on which even Hemingway, who does not often celebrate the kindness of others, has offered testimony: "So then, so far," he wrote, writing in 1925, "we have Pound the major poet devoting, say, one fifth of his time to his poetry. With the rest of his time he tries to advance the fortunes, both material and artistic, of his friends. He defends them when they are attacked, he gets them into magazines and out of jail. He loans them money. He sells their pictures. He arranges concerts for them. He writes articles about them. He introduces them to wealthy women. He gets publishers to take their books. He sits up all night with them when they claim to be dying and witnesses their wills. He advances them hospital expenses and dissuades them from suicide. And in the end a few of them refrain from knifing at the first opportunity."

Nevertheless, he managed to regularly issue pamphlets, roar out his Cantos ("the epic of the farings of a literary mind," so Marianne Moore, evidencing her customary exactness, defined them) and to give both sculpture and painting a serious if unavailing try. But it was the study of economics that became increasingly his intensest interest ("History that omits economics is sheer bunk"); he developed odd notions on the subject, and some of them led to his ruin: in 1939, by now a long-term mussolinized Italophile, he began broadcasting via Rome radio a sequence of Fascist-tempered discourses which culminated in his being indicted as an American traitor; units of the American army advancing into Italy caught up with him in 1945. For several weeks, like a zoo-beast mangy and rabid, he was imprisoned in an open-air cage at Pisa. Some months later, on the eve of his treason trial, he was declared insane, as might be any poet in his right artistic mind; and so he spent the next twelve years sealed away in the District of Columbia's St. Elizabeth Hospital. While there, he published *The Pisan Cantos* and won the Bollingen Prize, an award excessively censured in dough-headed circles.

However, one rainy Washington April day in 1958, Pound, an old man of seventy-two, his once flaming beard gone ashen and his satyr-saint's face scribbled with lines that spelled out a disconsolate tale, stood before a certain Judge Bolitha J. Laws and heard himself declared "incurably insane." Incurable, but "harmless" enough to go free. Whereupon Pound announced, "Any man who could live in America is insane," and prepared to depart for Italy.

Photographs were taken of him a few days before he sailed. Arrogant, mocking, his eyes squeezed shut as he burst into snatches of senseless song, he strode back and forth, as though still pacing a Pisan cage; or, rather, a cage that had become life itself.

Marilyn Monroe

❈

M ONROE? Just a slob, really, an untidy divinity—in the sense that a banana split or cherry jubilee is untidy but divine.

Her slippery lips, her overspilling blondness and sliding brassiere straps, the rhythmic writhing of restless poundage wriggling for room inside roomless décolletage—such are her emblems, those caricaturable flauntings that, one would have supposed, made her at once world-recognizable. However, in what is said to be real life, the Monroe is not easily identified. She maneuvers New York streets unmolested by stares, signals for taxis that do not stop, is served orange juice at a sidewalk Nedick's by an attendant unaware that the customer is the subject of some of his more ambitious ambitions: indeed, more often than otherwise one has to be *told* Monroe is Monroe, for she seems, casually glanced, merely another specimen of the American geisha, the expense-account darling, those cabaret-cuties whose careers progress from tinted hair at twelve to a confiscated husband or three at twenty.

But true to type as aspects of the Monroe are, she is not genuinely of the genre, she is too untough to be; moreover, she is capable of sensitive concentration always the secret of making any talent work, which hers does: the character she performs, a waif-figure of saucy pathos, is sound and of convincing charm: very understandably so, since there is small difference between her screen image and the impression she privately conveys—the appeal of both personalities stems from the same circumstance: that she is an orphan, in spirit and actually; she is stained, and illuminated by, the stigmata of orphan-thinking: while trusting no one, not very much, she labors like a fieldhand to please everybody, she wants to make of each of us an affectionate protector, and consequently we, her audience, her acquaintances, are flattered, pitying, aroused. The depth of her anxiety (anyone never less than an hour late for any appointment is detained by uncertainty and *angst*, not vanity; it is *angst*, too, a tension developed by the continuous need to please, that a good deal causes her frequent sore-throated indispositions, her nibbled nails, her damp palms, her Japanese-like fits of giggling) induces a butter-hearted sympathy that the dazzle of her overall demeanor does nothing to dissipate: what could be more potent, beguiling, more disarming, than a fanfared person for whom one is asked, and is able, to feel sorry; in such a situation all participants may wolf their cake and keep it, too.

Over and again we read that the Monroe is an "institution," a "symbol"; even her present husband, playwright Arthur Miller, has written an article to thus inform us. However, institutions tend to be things of gloom, and symbols are more bloodless still: it will be a dour day if this so alively lovely lass ever accepts seriously such dank verbal imprisonment.

Jane Bowles

(1966)

I T MUST BE SEVEN OR EIGHT YEARS since I last saw the
modern legend named Jane Bowles; nor have I heard from
her, at least not directly. Yet I am sure she is unchanged; indeed, I am told by recent travelers to North Africa, who
have been or sat with her in some dim Casbah café, that
this is true, and that Jane, with her dahlia-head of cropped,
curly hair, her tilted nose and mischief-shiny, just a trifle mad
eyes, her very original voice (a husky soprano), her boyish
clothes and schoolgirl's figure and slightly limping walk, is
more or less the same as when I first knew her more than
twenty years ago: even then she had seemed the eternal

urchin, appealing as the most appealing of nonadults, yet with some substance cooler than blood invading her veins and with a wit, an eccentric wisdom no child, not the strangest *Wünderkind*, ever possessed.

When I first met Mrs. Bowles (1944? 1945?), she was already, within certain worlds, a celebrated figure: though only in her twenties, she had published a most individual and much remarked novel, *Two Serious Ladies*; she had married the gifted composer and writer, Paul Bowles, and was, together with her husband, a tenant in a glamorous boarding house established on Brooklyn Heights by the late George Davis. Among the Bowleses' fellow boarders were Richard and Ellen Wright, W. H. Auden, Benjamin Britten, Oliver Smith, Carson McCullers, Gypsy Rose Lee and (I seem to remember) a trainer of chimpanzees who lived there with one of his star performers. Anyway, it was one hell of a household. But even amid such a forceful assembly, Mrs. Bowles, by virtue of her talent and the strange visions it enclosed, and because of her personality's startling blend of playful-puppy candor and feline sophistication, remained an imposing, stage-front presence.

Jane Bowles is an authoritative linguist; she speaks, with the greatest precision, French and Spanish and Arabic—perhaps this is why the dialogue of her stories sounds, or sounds to me, as though it has been translated into English from some delightful combination of other tongues. Moreover, these languages are self-learned, the product of Mrs. Bowles's nomadic nature: from New York she wandered on to and all over Europe, traveled away from there and the impending war to Central America and Mexico, then alighted awhile in the historic ménage on Brooklyn Heights. Since 1947 she has been almost continuously resident abroad: in

Paris or Ceylon, but largely in Tangier—in fact, both Jane and Paul Bowles may now safely be described as permanent Tangerinos, so total has their adherence become to that steep, shadowy-white seaport. Tangier is composed of two mismatching parts, one of them a dull, modern area stuffed with office buildings and tall, gloomy dwellings, and the other a Casbah descending through a medieval puzzlement of alleys and alcoves and kif-odored, mint-scented piazzas down to the crawling-with-sailors, ship-horn-hollering port. The Bowleses have established themselves in both sectors—have a sterilized, *tout confort* apartment in the newer quarter and also a refuge hidden away in the darker Arab neighborhood: a native house that must be one of the city's tiniest habitations—ceilings so low that one had almost literally to move on hands and knees from room to room; but the rooms themselves are like a charming series of postcard-sized Vuillards— Moorish cushions spilling over Moorish-patterned carpets, all cozy as a raspberry tart and illuminated by intricate lanterns and windows that allow the light of sea-skies and views that encompass minarets and ships and the blue-washed roof-tops of native tenements, receding like a ghostly staircase to the clamorous shoreline. Or that is how *I* remember it on the occasion of a single visit made at sunset on an evening, oh, fifteen years ago.

A line from Edith Sitwell: *Jane, Jane, the morning light creaks down again*—This from a poem I've always liked without, as so often with the particular author, altogether understanding it. Unless "morning light" is an image signifying memory(?). My own most satisfying memories of Jane Bowles revolve around a month spent in side-by-side rooms in a pleasantly shabby hotel on the rue du Bac during an icy Paris winter—January, 1951. Many a cold evening was spent in Jane's snug room (fat with books and papers and food-stuffs, and a snappy white Pekingese puppy bought from a Spanish sailor); long evenings spent listening to a phonograph and drinking warm apple-jack while Jane built sloppy, marvelous stews atop an electric burner: she is a good cook, yes-sir, and kind of a glutton, as one might suspect from her stories, which abound in accounts of eating and its artifacts. Cooking is but one of her extracurricular gifts; she is also a spooky accurate mimic, and can re-create with nostalgic admiration the voices of certain singers—Helen Morgan, for example, and her close friend, Libby Holman. Years afterward I wrote a story called *Among the Paths to Eden*, in which, without realizing it, I attributed to the heroine several of Jane Bowles's characteristics: the stiff-legged limp, her spectacles, her brilliant and poignant abilities as a mimic. ("She waited, as though listening for music to cue her; then, *'Don't ever leave me, now that you're here! Here is where you belong. Everything seems so right when you're near. When you're away it's all wrong.'* And Mr. Belli was shocked, for what he was hearing was exactly Helen Morgan's voice, and the voice, with its vulnerable sweetness, refinement, its tender quaver toppling high notes, seemed not to be borrowed, but Mary O'Meaghan's own, a natural expression of some secluded identity.") I did not have Mrs. Bowles in mind when I invented Mary O'Meaghan—a character she in no essential way resembles; but it is a measure of the potent impression Jane has always made on me that some fragment of her should emerge in this manner.

That winter Jane was working on *In the Summer House*, the play that was later so sensitively produced in New York.

I'm not all that keen on the theatre: cannot sit through most plays once; nevertheless, I saw *In the Summer House* three times, and not out of loyalty to the author, but because it had a thorny wit, the flavor of a newly tasted, refreshingly bitter beverage—the same qualities that had initially attracted me to Mrs. Bowles's novel *Two Serious Ladies*.

My only complaint against Mrs. Bowles is not that her work lacks quality, merely quantity. The volume in hand constitutes her entire shelf, so to say. And grateful as we are to have it, one could wish that there was more. Once, while discussing a colleague, someone more facile than either of us, Jane said, "But it's so easy for him. He has only to turn his hand. Just *turn* his hand." Actually, writing is never easy: in case anyone doesn't know, it's the hardest work around, and for Jane, I think it is difficult to the point of true pain. And why not?—when both her language and her themes are sought after along tortured paths and in stony quarries: the never-realized relationships between her people, the mental and physical discomforts with which she surrounds and saturates them—every room an atrocity, every urban landscape a creation of neon-dourness. And yet, though the tragic view is central to her vision, Jane Bowles is a very funny writer, a humorist of sorts—but *not*, by the way, of the Black School. Black Comedy, as its perpetrators label it, is, when successful, all lovely artifice and lacking any hint of compassion. Her subtle comprehension of eccentricity and human apartness as revealed in her work require us to accord Jane Bowles high esteem as an artist.

Cecil Beaton

(1969)

✥

To call a book *The Best of Beaton* is catchy enough, but inaccurate—unless some one book could contain fine specimens of Beaton's many facets: his stage décors, his costume designs, sketches and paintings, pages reprinted from his very remarkable journals and at least several verbatim samples of his conversational gifts, for surely Cecil is one of the few surviving artists in this increasingly obsolete area.

I don't know, I've never asked him, but I suspect Cecil would prefer to be remembered for his talents in mediums other than photography—a phenomenon quite common with persons who develop multiple gifts: they often prefer to rather slight the original one. It might be said that Beaton was without any central talent until, as a very ambitious but unsensible young man of great sensibility, he started using a camera: it was the camera, curiously enough, that released all the subtler creative strains.

And for all the documented brilliance of his other muses, it is as a photographer that Beaton attains cultural importance—not only because of the individual excellence of his own work, but because of its influence on the work of the finest photographers of the last two generations: whether or not they admit it, or are even conscious of it, there is almost no first-rate contemporary photographer of any nationality who is not to some degree indebted to Cecil Beaton. Why? Look at the pictures. Even the earliest ones presage future influence on a multitude of camera-artists. For instance, the portraits of Lady Oxford and Edith Sitwell made in the twenties: no one had photographed faces in quite this manner before, surrounded them with such neo-romantic, stylized décor (spun glass, masked statues, pastry molds and extravagant costumes: all the appurtenances of Beaton's own surrealism) or lighted them with such lacquered luminosity. And the thing is, these portraits have not "dated," not even, in a technical sense, the so-called "fashion" photographs. (The attitude of photographers toward fashion photography, and the position it holds in their careers, is an ambiguous business. With the exception of Cartier-Bresson, a man of independent means, I can't offhand recall a single photographer seriously making a livelihood out of his trade who doesn't work extensively for either fashion magazines or advertising agencies. And why not? It disciplines the artist and forces his invention. Beaton, like many others, owes a number of his most interesting photographs to the limitations imposed by purely commercial factors. But photographers as a breed seem not to gain much satisfaction from their labors in such vineyards—I don't mean Beaton: he is too much a craftsman and too unpretentious not to be grateful for the merit of his work in whatever style.)

But again, this question of unyellowing, of the timeless quality in these pictures. Of course, in some instances Beaton has already pre-aged his portraits by setting them in the past—for example, the various pastiche of Victorian daguerreotype: the combination of modern with long-ago creates its own time—suspension. But when one speaks of the timeless, this is not what one means. Then what *does* one mean? Well, any in the series Beaton calls Time Sequences—subjects he has had the opportunity to photograph over periods extending as much as four decades. One observes a slowly thickening, but ever lustrous, rather maniacal-eyed Picasso; an Auden, starting off like a duly wrinkled bloodhound pup and ending looking like the hound's sagging, tobacco-stained sire; or Cocteau, fragile and fresh and expensive as a sprig of muguet in January, then later, with his jeweled fingers, seeming an animated Proustian souvenir. None of these studies is dependent for its effect upon its relation to the rest of the sequence; separated, any one of them seems an ageless and definitive image of the man. Yet how eerie, and sad, yet how exhilarating to see these faces as they flow through time —frozen by sensitively manipulated light and shadow.

It is not difficult to discern Beaton's influence in the work of others: a harder task is to identify those who have influenced him. Obviously he is indebted to Baron de Meyer, that original and tragic artist who contributed photographs of a pioneer stylishness to the earlier issues of *Vanity Fair*. Beaton, with his own sense of elegance, was the first direct descendant of the late Baron. And Beaton admired Steichen; but name a photographer not obliged to Steichen. To my mind, Beaton's work does not reflect artistic sources as much as it does his private social interests and the temperaments of his times. For example, in 1938 and 1939 Beaton photographed a contingent of personalities not amid flowers and the sleek apparatus of the studios, but through the broken windows of abandoned sinister houses and factories. These photographs are like fever charts of the future, a prediction of the bombs soon to explode.

Speaking of which, one of Beaton's most distinguished and versatile achievements are his war photographs, these smoky pictures of London asunder, of violent skies and bandaged children: here the artist produces a brutal poignance, a harsher color, than the viewer usually associates with his photographic palette. This is also true of Beaton's photographs of India and China, countries in which he served during the war. A pity, for though these are not military pictures in the sense that Cim's or Capa's were, they are nevertheless war documents of painful poetic insight which illustrate a side of Beaton insufficiently recognized. Nowadays a professional photographer is by necessity almost a professional traveler: editors with commissions hustle them on to jets that hustle them around the world in pursuit of Lord knows what. Even the feeblest talents are subsidized in this manner (and may I say in passing that ninety percent—make that ninety-five—of fully employed photographers are feeble indeed: an amazing racket, really, and even a few of the very few genuinely gifted photographers secretly consider themselves racketeers). But Cecil has always been a determined roamer, and as a youth wandered by cargo boat from Haiti to Morocco. Myself, also a footloose fellow, I've run into Mr. B.

in the damndest places. On the beach at Waikiki—with hula music in the background. In a Sicilian olive grove, in a Greek monastery, in the lobby of the Barcelona Ritz, by the pool at the Bel Air Hotel, at a café table in the Tangier Casbah, on a junk in the Hong Kong bay, backstage at a Broadway musical, on a *téléphérique* climbing a Swiss alp, in a geisha house in Kyoto, among the ruins of Angkor Wat, the temples of Bangkok, aboard Daisy Fellowes' yacht *Sister Ann*, in a Harlem night club, a Venetian palazzo, a Parisian *antiquaire*, a London shoeshop, and so forth on and on. The point is, I've observed Beaton in all climates, mental and otherwise, and have often had the privilege of watching him work with a camera—actually, we have once in a while collaborated: my text accompanying his photographs. I've had that sort of experience with other photographers, particularly Henri Cartier-Bresson and Richard Avedon—both of whom I respect extremely: with Beaton added, I consider that they ought to occupy the first three places in any list of the world's superior photographers. But how differently each man operates! Avedon is primarily a studio photographer; at any rate, he seems at his most creative ease in the midst of perfectly functioning machinery and attentive assistants. Rather recently I worked with Avedon, under primitive conditions, on a story in the American Midwest; he had no assistant and was using a new-fangled Japanese camera that was capable of taking a hundred-odd exposures before the film needed changing. We slaved the whole of one morning, drove many a mile through heat and dust, and then, when we returned to the motel where we were staying, Avedon, with a jittery little laugh, suddenly announced that all our labor was for naught: it had been so many years since he had worked without assistants, who always prepared his cameras, that he had forgot to put any film in the Japanese job.

Cartier-Bresson is another *tasse de thé* entirely—self-sufficient to a fault. I remember once watching Bresson at work on a street in New Orleans—dancing along the pavement like an agitated dragonfly, three Leicas swinging from straps around his neck, a fourth one hugged to his eye: click-click-click (the camera seems a part of his own body), clicking away with a joyous intensity, a religious absorption. Nervous and merry and dedicated, Bresson is an artistic "loner," a bit of a fanatic.

But not Beaton. This man, with his cool (sometimes cold) blue eyes and palely lifted eyebrows, is as casual and detached as he seems: with a camera in his hand, he just knows what he is doing, that's all, has no need for a lot of temper and attitudinizing. Unlike many of his colleagues, I've never heard Cecil talk about Technique or Art or Honesty. He simply takes pictures and hopes to be paid for them. But the way in which he works is very special to him. One of the immediately striking things about Beaton's personal behavior is the manner in which he creates an illusion of time-without-end. Though he is apparently always under the pressure of a disheartening schedule, one would never suppose he wasn't a gentleman of almost tropical leisure: if he has ten minutes to catch a plane, and yet is speaking with you on the telephone, he does nothing to shorten the call but continues to indulge in a luxury of marvelous manners. Nevertheless, you can be damn sure he will make that plane. As with the caller, so it is with the sitter: a person sitting for Beaton has a sense of slightly drifting in space—of not being photographed but painted, and painted by a casual, barely visible presence.

But Beaton is there, oh yes. For all his quiet tread he is one of the most on-the-spot people alive: his visual intelligence is genius—the camera will never be invented that could capture or encompass all that he actually sees. To listen to Beaton describe in strictly visual terms a person or room or landscape is to hear a recitation that can be hilarious or brutal or very beautiful, but will always certainly be brilliant. And that—the remarkable visual intelligence infiltrating his pictures, however diluted—is what makes Beaton's work unusually separate, the preservative for which our next-century historians will be even more grateful than we are now.

❋

Ghosts in Sunlight: the Filming of In Cold Blood

(1967)

❊

ONE HOT AFTERNOON LAST MARCH in a courthouse on the high wheat plains of western Kansas, Richard Brooks turned to me, between takes of the movie he was directing, and rather reproachfully asked, "What are you laughing at?"

"Oh, nothing," I said, but the truth was that I'd remembered a long-ago question by Perry Smith, one of the two murderers whose trial was being re-enacted here. He had been captured a few days before, and his question was, "Were there any representatives of the cinema there?" I wondered what he would have thought of the present scene: the huge arc lights arranged inside the courtroom where he and

Richard Hickock had been tried, the jury box filled with the very same men who had convicted them, the purring generators, whirring cameras, the whispering technicians dancing in and out among thick coils of electric cable.

The first conversation I ever had with Perry Smith was at the beginning of January, 1960. It was a cold day, glittery as an icicle; Smith and I talked together at the sheriff's office in a room where prairie winds pressed against the windows, sucked the glass, rattled it. I was fairly rattled myself, for I had been working for more than a month on a book about the murder of Herbert Clutter and his family, *In Cold Blood*, and unless I could establish close contact with this half-Irish, half-Indian young man, I would have to abandon the project. His court-appointed attorney had persuaded him to speak to me; but it was soon obvious that Smith regretted having granted the interview. He was remote, suspicious, sullenly sleepy-eyed: It took years, hundreds of letters and conversations, before I slipped all the way past this façade. At the moment, nothing I said interested him. He rather arrogantly began to question my credentials. What kind of writer was I, and what had I written? Well, he said, after I'd provided a dossier, he'd never heard of me or any of my books; but—had I written any movies? Yes, one: *Beat the Devil*. Now the sleepy eyes somewhat wakened. "Uh-huh. I remember. Only saw it because Humphrey Bogart was in it. Did you, uh, uh, *know* Bogart? Personally?" When I answered that Bogart had been a close friend of mine, he smiled in the flustered, fragile way I came to know very well. "Bogart," he said, his voice so soft one could scarcely hear it above the wind. "I've always had this thing about him. He was my favorite actor. I saw *Treasure of the Sierra Madre*—oh, over and over. One of the reasons I liked that

picture so much was—the old man in it, Walter Huston?
that played the crazy gold prospector?—he was just like my
father. Tex Smith. *Just* like him. I couldn't get over it. It
really hit me." Then he said, "Were you there last night?
When they brought us in?"

He was referring to the previous evening when the two
handcuffed murderers, escorted by a regiment of state troop-
ers, had arrived by car from Las Vegas, where they were
arrested, to be arraigned at the Finney County courthouse
in Garden City, Kansas. Hundreds of people had waited for
hours in the dark and zero-cold to glimpse them; the crowd,
orderly, almost awesomely hushed, had filled the square.
The press, too, had been heavily represented by newsmen
from all over the West and Midwest; there were also several
television crews.

I told him yes, I'd been present—and had minor pneumonia to prove it. Well, he said, he was sorry about that:
"Pneumonia is nothing to fool around with. But tell me—I
was so scared I couldn't see what was happening. When I
saw that crowd, I thought, Jesus, these people are going to
tear us limb from limb. To hell with the public hangman.
They were going to hang us on the spot. Which maybe
wouldn't have been the worst idea. I mean, what's the use
of going through this whole ordeal? Trial and everything.
It's such a farce. These prairie-billies, they'll hang us in the
long run." He chewed his lip; something shy and bashful
happened to his face—the aw-gee expression of a kid digging
his toe into the ground. "What I wanted to know is—were
there any representatives of the cinema there?"

This was typical of Perry—of his pathetic linguistic pre-
tensions (the careful insertion of words like "cinema"), and
of the kind of vanity that made him welcome "recognition"

regardless of its nature. He tried to disguise it, shrug it off, but nevertheless he was undeniably gratified when I informed him that indeed the event had been recorded by motion-picture cameras.

Now, seven years later, I laughed to myself at the recollection, but I avoided answering Brooks's query because the young men who were playing Perry and Dick were standing nearby, and I felt extremely uneasy in their presence. Self-conscious. I had seen photographs of Robert Blake (Perry) and Scott Wilson (Dick) before they were selected for the roles. But it wasn't until I went to Kansas to follow the progress of the film that I met them. And meeting them, having to be around them, was not an experience I care to repeat. This has nothing to do with my reaction to them as private individuals: they both are sensitive, seriously gifted men. It's simply that despite the clear physical resemblance to the original pair, their photographs had not prepared me for the mesmerizing reality.

Particularly Robert Blake. The first time I saw him I thought a ghost had sauntered in out of the sunshine, slippery-haired and sleepy-eyed. I couldn't accept the idea that this was someone pretending to be Perry, he was Perry—and the sensation I felt was like a free fall down an elevator shaft. Here were the familiar eyes, placed in a familiar face, examining me with the detachment of a stranger. It was as though Perry had been resurrected but was suffering from amnesia and remembered me not at all. Shock, frustration, helplessness—these emotions, combined with impending flu, sent me home to a motel on the outskirts of Garden City. The Wheat Lands Motel, a place I had often stayed during the years I worked on *In Cold Blood*. An accumulated remembrance of those years, the loneliness of the endless wintry nights with forlorn salesmen coughing next door, seized me like a sudden Kansas cyclone and threw me on the bed.

To quote from my day-to-day journal: "Presently passed out, having drunk a pint of Scotch in less than thirty minutes. Woke in the morning with fever, television still going and total lack of knowledge of where I was or why. All unreal because too real, as reality's reflections tend to be. Called Dr. Maxfield, who gave me an injection and several prescriptions. But the trouble is in my mind (?)."

That phrase "reality's reflections" is self-explanatory, but perhaps I ought to clarify my own interpretation of it. Reflected reality is the essence of reality, the truer truth. When I was a child I played a pictorial game. I would, for example, observe a landscape: trees and clouds and horses wandering in grass; then select a detail from the overall vision—say, grass bending in the breeze—and frame it with my hands. Now this detail became the essence of the landscape and caught, in prismatic miniature, the true atmosphere of a panorama too sizable to encompass otherwise. Or if I was in a strange room, and wanted to understand the room and the nature of its inhabitants, I let my eye wander selectively until it discovered something—a shaft of light, a decrepit piano, a pattern in the rug—that seemed of itself to contain the secret. All art is composed of selected detail, either imaginary or, as in *In Cold Blood*, a distillation of reality. As with the book, so with the film—except that I had chosen my details from life, while Brooks had distilled his from my book: reality twice transposed, and all the truer for it.

As soon as the book was published, many producers and directors expressed a desire to make a film of it. Actually, I had already decided that if a film was to be made, I wanted the writer-director Richard Brooks to act as intermediary be-

tween book and screen. Aside from my long-standing respect
for his imaginative professionalism, he was the only director
who agreed with—and was willing to risk—my own concept of how the book should be transferred to film. He was
the one person who entirely accepted two important points:
I wanted the film made in black and white, and I wanted it
played by a cast of unknowns—that is, actors without "public" faces. Although Brooks and I have different sensibilities,
we both wanted the film to duplicate reality, to have the actors resemble their prototypes as much as possible, and to
have every scene filmed in its real locale: the house of the
murdered Clutter family; the same Kansas variety store where
Perry and Dick bought the rope and tape used to bind their
four victims; and certain courthouses, prisons, filling stations,
hotel rooms and highways and city streets—all those places
that they had seen in the course of their crime and its after-
math. A complicated procedure, but the only possible one by
which almost all elements of fantasy could be removed and
reality thereby achieve its proper reflection.

I felt this particularly strongly when Brooks and I went
into the Clutter house while Brooks was preparing to film
the murder sequence. To quote from my journal again:
"Spent the afternoon at the Clutter farm. A curious experience to find myself once more in this house where I have so
often been, and heretofore under such silent circumstances:
the silent house, the plain rooms, the hardwood floors that
echo every footstep, the windows that look out on solemn
prairies and fields tawny with wheat stubble. No one has
really lived there since the murders. The property was
bought by a Texan who farms the land, and who has a son
who occasionally stays there. Certainly it has not gone to
ruin; nevertheless it seems abandoned, a scarecrow without

crows to frighten. The present owner gave Brooks permission to film there; a considerable amount of the original furniture was still on hand, and Brooks's chief assistant, Tom Shaw, has done an extraordinary job of tracking down and retrieving the departed pieces. The rooms looked precisely the same as they had when I examined them in December, 1959—that is, soon after the crime was discovered. Mr. Clutter's Stetson hanging on a wall hat rack. Nancy's sheet music open at the piano. Her brother's spectacles resting on a bureau, the lenses shimmering in sunlight.

"But it was the Venetian blinds that I noticed—that I, as it were, 'framed.' The blinds cover the windows of Mr. Clutter's office, the room by which the murderers entered the house. Upon entering, Dick had parted the Venetian slats and peered through them to see if any witnesses were lurking in the moonlit night; again, on departing, and after the immense noise of the shootings, Dick's eyes had explored the landscape through the slats, his heart pounding for fear that the crash of four shotgun blasts might have roused the countryside. And now the actor who is impersonating Dick, and who is so uncannily like Dick, is on the verge of repeating these actions. Yet eight years have passed, the Clutter family are gone and Dick is dead, but the Venetian blinds still exist, still hang at the same windows. Thus reality, via an object, extends itself into art; and that is what is original and disturbing about this film: reality and art are intertwined to the point that there is no identifiable area of demarcation.

"Almost the whole of the murder sequence is being photographed in total darkness—except for the use of flashlights. This has never been done before, because ordinarily a flashlight is incapable of producing light sufficiently powerful to register a scene without the aid of extra illumination. In the present case, however, the production's technicians have invented flashlights fixed with special batteries that generate solid shafts of white blaze—extremely effective as the beams wander in the darkness, crossing and crisscrossing.

"Brooks's attention to detail can occasionally be comic. Today he noticed that between takes inside the Clutter house several of the crew were smoking cigarettes. Suddenly he clapped his hands and shouted, 'All right! Cut that out! Mr. Clutter never allowed anyone to smoke in this house, so I'm not going to allow it either.'"

Presently undermined by flu and the strain of reliving painful events, I left Brooks and his company to get on with their work free of my critical surveillance. No director can abide an author staring over his shoulder; and, agreeable as our relationship was, I sensed that Brooks felt my presence made everyone edgy, himself included. He was not unhappy to see me go.

Returning to New York, I was surprised to find that few people asked me how the film was progressing. Rather, they were curious to know what the reaction of the townspeople was to the fact of the film's being made in their midst: Was the atmosphere antagonistic? Cooperative? What? To answer the question, I have to refer to my own experiences during the years I spent roaming around Finney County, accumulating material.

When I arrived there in 1959 I knew no one, and no one, except the local librarian and several schoolteachers, had ever heard of me. As it happened, the first person I interviewed turned out to be the only genuine enemy I made there—at least the only one both openly and covertly hostile (a contradiction in terms, but nevertheless accurate). This fellow was, and is, the editor of the local daily paper, the Garden City *Telegram*, and therefore in a position to constantly publicize his belligerent attitude toward me and the work I was attempting to do. His columns are signed Bill Brown, and he is as plain as his name: a thin, rumpled man with mud-colored eyes and a beige complexion. Of course, I understood his resentment, and at first sympathized with it: here was this "New York" writer, as he often drawlingly described me, invading his terrain and presuming to write a book about a "sordid" subject that was best swept away and forgotten. His continuous theme was: "We want to forget our tragedy, but this New York writer isn't going to let us." Therefore, it came as no surprise when Brown started a campaign to prevent Brooks from filming the Kansas scenes in Garden City and Holcomb. Now his theme was that the advent of these "Hollywood people" would attract "undesirable elements," and everything in Finney County would go to hell. Huffed and puffed, did Mr. Brown, but his efforts failed. For the simple reason that most of the people I met in western Kansas are reasonable and helpful; I couldn't have survived if it hadn't been for their consistent kindness, and I made friends among them that will last a lifetime.

That was in March of last year. In September, I traveled to California to see a rough cut of the finished film. On arrival, I had a meeting with Brooks, who was screening the picture for me the following day. Brooks is a very secretive man; he hoards his scripts, locks them up at night and never lets anyone read a complete version. Shooting on *In Cold Blood* had ended in June, and since that time Brooks had worked only with a cutter and a projectionist, not allowing anyone else to view a foot of the film. As we talked he

seemed under the kind of whitened strain one does not asso-
ciate with so assertive and vigorous a man. "Of course I'm
nervous," he said. "Why shouldn't I be? It's *your* book—
and suppose you don't like it?"

And suppose you don't like it? Excellent question; and,
strangely, one I'd never asked myself, principally because I
had chosen the ingredients, and I always have faith in my
own judgment.

The next day, when I arrived at Columbia studios around
noon, Brooks was even more nervous. My God, he was
glum! He said, "I've had some rough moments with this
picture. But today's the roughest." On that note we walked
into the screening room, and the sensation was not unlike
entering a death cell.

Brooks picked up a telephone connected with the projectionist's booth. "All right. Let's go."

The lights dimmed. The white screen turned into a highway at twilight: Route 50 winding under draining skies
through a countryside empty as a cornhusk, woebegone as
wet leaves. In the far horizon a silvery Greyhound bus appears, enlarges as it hummingly approaches, streaks by. Music: solitary guitar. Now the credits start as the image
changes, dissolves into the Greyhound's interior. Slumber
hangs heavily. Only a weary little girl roams the aisle, gradually wandering toward the darkened rear, lured there by the
lonely, disconnected plunk-plunk-plunk of a guitar. She finds
the player, but we do not see him; she says something to
him, but we cannot quite hear what it is. The guitarist strikes
a match to light a cigarette, and the flame partially illumi-
nates his face—Perry's face, Perry's eyes, sleepy, remote. Dis-
solve to Dick, then to Dick and Perry in Kansas City, then

to Holcomb, and Herbert Clutter breakfasting on the final day of his life, then back to his future executioners: the contrapuntal technique I used in writing the book.

The scenes move with striking fluidity, but I am increasingly gripped by a sense of loss; and a ring forms around my heart, like the frosty haze around a harvest moon. Not because of what is on the screen, which is fine, but because of what isn't. Why has such-and-such been omitted? Where is Bobby Rupp? Susan Kidwell? The postmistress and her mother? In the midst of my dilemma of not being able to concentrate appreciatively on what was there because of what wasn't, the film caught fire—literally. One could see the tiny fire burning on the screen, a zipper of flame that separated the images and crisped them. In the silence following the abrupt halt, Brooks said, "Nothing serious. Just an accident. It's happened before. We'll have it fixed in a minute."

A lucky accident, for during the time it took the projectionist to repair the damage and resume the screening, I managed to resolve the quarrel I was having with myself. Look, an inner voice said, you're being unrealistic, unfair. This picture is two hours long, and that is as long as it can reasonably be. If Brooks included everything you would like to have shown, every nuance you're grieving over, it would last nine hours! So stop worrying. Watch it for what it is: judge from that.

I did, and it was like swimming into a familiar sea only to be surprised by a muscular wave of sinister height, trapped in a hurtling current that carried me downward to ocean-floor depths, escorted me, pummeled raw and groggy, onto a beach uniquely desolate—not, unfortunately, the victim of a bad dream, or of "just a movie," but of reality.

The screen returned to its pristine state; overhead lighting resumed. But again, as in the motel room in Garden City, I seemed to wake up not knowing where I was. A man was sitting near me. Who was he, and why did he look at me so intently, as if expecting me to say something? Ah, Brooks. Finally I said, "By the way, thank you."

Self-Portrait

(1972)

Q: IF YOU HAD TO LIVE in just one place—without ever leaving—where would it be?

A: Oh, dear. What a devastating notion. To be grounded in just one place. After all, for thirty years I've lived everywhere and had houses all over the world. But curiously, no matter where I lived, Spain or Italy or Switzerland, Hong Kong or California, Kansas or London, I *always* kept an apartment in New York. That must signify something. So, if really forced to choose, I'd say New York.

Q: But *why?* It's dirty. Dangerous. In every way difficult.

A: Hmmm. Yes. But though I can live for long stretches in

mountainous or seaside solitude, primarily I am a city fellow. I like *pavement*. The sound of my shoes on pavement; stuffed windows; all-night restaurants; sirens in the night—sinister but alive; book and record shops that, on impulse, you can visit at midnight.

And in that sense, New York is the world's only city *city*. Rome is noisy and provincial. Paris is sullen, insular, and, odd to say, extraordinarily puritanical. London? All my American friends who have gone to live there bore one so by saying, "But it's so civilized." I don't know. To be totally dead, utterly dull—is that civilized? And to top it all, London is also highly provincial. The same people see the same people. Everybody knows your business. At most, it is only possible to lead *two* separate lives there.

And that is the great advantage of New York, why it is *the* city. One can be a multiple person there: ten different people with ten different sets of friends, none overlapping.

Q: Do you prefer animals to people?

A: I like them about equally. Still, I've usually found there is something secretively cruel about people who really feel more warmly toward dogs and cats and horses than people.

Q: Are *you* cruel?

A: Occasionally. In conversation. Let's put it this way: I'd rather be a friend of mine than an enemy.

Q: Do you have many friends?

A: About seven or so whom I can entirely rely upon. And about twenty more I more or less trust.

Q: What qualities do you look for in friends?

A: Firstly, they mustn't be stupid. I've once or twice been in love with persons who were stupid, indeed very much so; but that is another matter—one can be in love with someone without feeling the least in communication with that person. God, that's how most people get married and why most marriages are unhappy.

Usually, I can tell quite early on whether it is possible for someone and myself to be friends. Because one doesn't have to finish sentences. I mean, you start to say something, then realize, midway, that he or she has already understood. It is a form of mental-emotional conversational shorthand.

Intelligence apart, attention is important: I pay attention to my friends, am concerned about them, and expect the same in return.

Q: Are you often disappointed by a friend?

A: Not really. I've sometimes formed dubious attachments (don't we all?); I've always done it with my eyes open. The only hurt that hurts is one that takes you by surprise. I am seldom surprised. Though I have a few times been outraged.

Q: Are you a truthful person?

A: As a writer—yes, I think so. Privately—well, that is a matter of opinion; some of my friends think that when relating an event or piece of news, I am inclined to alter and overelaborate. Myself, I just call it making something "come alive." In other words, a form of art. Art and truth are not necessarily compatible bedfellows.

Q: How do you like best to occupy your spare time?

A: Not sexually, though I have had my enthusiastic periods. But, as more than a casual pastime, it is too heart-scalding and costly, however you interpret the latter adjective.

Really, I like to read. Always have. There are not many contemporary writers I like too well. Though I have admired, among our own Americans, the late Flannery O'Connor, and Norman Mailer, William Styron, Eudora Welty, Katherine Anne Porter, the early Salinger. And oh, really, a number of others. I've never liked Gore Vidal's fiction, but I think his nonfiction is first-class. James Baldwin, ditto. But for the last decade or so I prefer to read writers I've already read. Proven wine. Proust. Flaubert. Jane Austen. Raymond Chandler (one of the *great* American artists). Dickens (I had read all of Dickens before I was sixteen, and have just now completed the full cycle again).

I am partial to films, too—though I leave in the middle quite a lot. But I only like to go to films alone, and only in the daytime when the theatre is mostly empty. That way I can concentrate on what I'm seeing, and depart when I feel like it without having to discuss the merits of the project with someone else: with me, such discussions always lead to argument and irritation.

I prefer to work in the mornings, usually for about four or five hours, and then, if I'm alone in a city, any city, I meet a friend for lunch at some favorite restaurant (in New York: Lafayette, La Côte Basque, Orsini's, the Oak Room at The Plaza, and, until its unhappy demise, the Colony). Many people say they hate to lunch; it fattens them, fatigues them, altogether spoils their day. It makes mine. There are some men I enjoy lunching with, but by and large I prefer beautiful, or at least extremely attractive, alert, and *au courant* women. I count in this category several very young ladies (Lally Weymouth, Amanda Burden, Penelope Tree, Louise Melhado —the latter, alas, married to a very square stockbroker). But I don't consider that any woman deserves full marks until she attains and maintains qualities of style and appearance and amusing good sense beyond the point of easy youthful beguilement: this, a partial list, and a prejudicial one, would have to include Barbara Paley, Gloria Guinness, Lee Radziwill, Oona Chaplin, Gloria Cooper, Slim Keith, Phyllis Cerf,

Kay Meehan, Viola Loewy, D. D. Ryan, Evelyn Avedon, Pamela Harriman, Kay Graham—well, one could go on for quite a while, though certainly the names would not top fifty. Notice, the persons I mention are private citizens, not public; after all, for certain public characters—Garbo (an ultimately selfish and tiresome woman) or Elizabeth Taylor (a sensitive, self-educated lady with a tough but essentially innocent attitude—if you sleep with a guy, gosh, that means you have to marry him!)—*allure* is their trade.

Though I know I'm supposed to be very sociable, and though some of the above statements would seem to testify to that, I like to be alone. I like fast, finely made cars, I like lonely motels with their ice machines and eerie anonymity; so sometimes I get behind the wheel and, without warning, without particular destination, drive all alone as far as a thousand miles. I've only once consulted a psychiatrist; instead, I should have gone for a drive with the top down and a wind blowing and a sun shining.

Q: Of what are you most afraid?

A: Not death. Well, I don't want to *suffer*. But if one night I went to sleep and failed to wake, that thought doesn't trouble me much. At least it would be something different. In 1966 I was nearly killed in an auto accident—was flung through the windshield head-on, and though seriously wounded and certain that what Henry James called The Distinguished Thing (death) was nearby, lay fully conscious in pools of blood reciting to myself the telephone numbers of various friends. Since then, I've had a cancer operation, and the only altogether upsetting part was that I had to loiter around an aimless week between the day of diagnosis and the morning of the knives.

Anyway, it strikes me as absurd and rather obscene, this

whole cosmetic and medical industry based on lust for youth,
age-fear, death-terror. Who the hell wants to live forever?
Most of us, apparently; but it's idiotic. After all, there *is*
such a thing as life-saturation: the point when everything is
pure effort and total repetition.

Poverty? Fanny Brice said, "I've been rich and I've been
poor. Believe me, rich is better." Well, I disagree; at least
I don't think money makes any ultimate difference to anyone's personal adjustment or (moronic word) "happiness."
I know very well a considerable number of very rich people (I don't count anyone rich who can't quite quickly summon up fifty million dollars in hard currency); and there are
some who say, when feeling in a bitchy mood, that I don't
know anybody else (to which one can best reply, at least
they sometimes pick up the check, and never ask for a loan).
But the point is: I can't think of a single rich person who, in
terms of contentment, or a lessening of the general human
anxiety, has it easier than the rest of us. As for me, I can accept it either way: a furnished room on some side street in
Detroit or Cole Porter's old apartment in the Waldorf Towers, which the decorator Billy Baldwin transformed into such
an island of sublime and subtle luxury. What I couldn't survive is the middle ground: the sound of lawn mowers and
water sprinklers outside a two-car-garage ranch split-level in
Scarsdale or Shaker Heights. Well, I never said I wasn't a
snob. I only said I wasn't afraid of being poor.

Failure? Failure is the condiment that gives success its flavor. No, I've drunk that special hemlock, bit that bullet (especially working in the theatre) enough to now scorn it.
Honestly, I don't give a damn what anybody says about me,
either privately or in print. Of course, that was not true when
I was young and first began to publish. And it is not true now

on one count—a betrayal of affection can still traumatically disturb me. Otherwise, defeat and criticism are matters of indifference, remote as the mountains of the moon.

Q: Then what does frighten you?

A: The thought that I might lose my sense of humor. Become a mind without a soul, start down the path to madness, and thereby, as the Zen riddle runs, spend the rest of a ruined life listening to the sound of one hand clapping.

Q: What shocks you? If anything?

A: Deliberate cruelty. Cruelty for its own sake, verbal or physical. Murder. Capital punishment. Child-beaters. Animal-baiters.

Once, long ago, I discovered that my best friend, aged eighteen, was having a fully realized love affair with his stepmother. At the time I was shocked; needless to add, I'm not now, and thinking back, can see that it was probably a positive benefit to them both. Since then, I've never been surprised, not to say shocked, by any sexual-moral arrangement. If so, I'd have to lead the parade of our nation's million-upon-million hypocrites.

Q: It is now six years since you published *In Cold Blood.* What have you been working on since then?

A: Published as a book a long short story, "The Thanksgiving Visitor." Collaborated on a film, *Trilogy,* based on three of my short stories ("A Christmas Memory," "Miriam," "Among the Paths to Eden"); made a documentary film about capital punishment, *Death Row U.S.A.,* which was commissioned by ABC but never shown in this country (others, yes; Canada, for one) for reasons still mysterious and unexplained. Have also recently completed a screenplay of Fitzgerald's *The Great Gatsby*—a nearly perfect short novel (or, really, long short story), but hell to dramatize because it consists almost entirely of long-ago exposition and, as it were, offstage scenes. Personally, I like my adaptation, but the producers, Paramount Pictures, are of a different opinion; my pity to whoever attempts a rewrite.

It took five years to write *In Cold Blood*, and a year to recover—*if* recovery is the word; not a day passes that some aspect of that experience doesn't shadow my mind.

However, prior to beginning *In Cold Blood*, in fact soon after finishing *Breakfast at Tiffany's* in 1957, I began to prepare the notes and structure for an ambitious novel then entitled, and entitled now, *Answered Prayers*, which derives from a remark of St. Theresa's: "More tears are shed over answered prayers than unanswered ones." I think that's true: no matter what desires are requited, they are always replaced by another. It's like those racing greyhounds and the mechanical rabbit—one can never catch it. It makes for the worst and best in life. I remember a friend at Robert Kennedy's funeral, someone very close to him, and she said: "It was such a hot day. Sweltering. And there was the grave waiting in the grass under this great cool green tree. And suddenly I envied him. Envied him all that green peacefulness. I thought, Bless you, Bobby, you don't have to fight any more. You're safe."

Answered Prayers is complicated technically and much the longest work I've done—indeed, triple the length of all my other books combined. During the past year or so I've been under great pressure to finish it; but literature has its own life, and insists on dancing to its own measure. *Answered Prayers* is like a wheel with a dozen spokes; the fuel that spins the wheel is an extraordinary young woman who has had fifty affairs, could have married virtually anyone, but for twelve years has loved an "older" man who can't marry because he is married, and *won't* divorce because he expects, with reasonable cause, to be the next President of the United States.

Q: If you hadn't decided on writing, a creative life, what would you have done?

A: Become a lawyer. I often considered it, and many lawyers, including one attorney general and a Supreme Court justice, have told me I would have made a first-class trial lawyer, though my voice, often described as "high and childish" (*among* other things), might have been a detriment.

Also, I wouldn't have minded being kept, but no one has ever wanted to keep me—not more than a week or so.

Q: Do you take any form of exercise?

A: Yes. Massage.

Q: Can you cook?

A: Not for company. For myself, I always dish up the same cuisine. Crackers and cream of tomato soup. Or a baked potato stuffed with fresh caviar.

Q: If *Reader's Digest* ever commissioned from you an "Unforgettable Character" article, whom would you write about?

A: God forbid that such a degrading assignment should ever come my way. But if it did—ahem, let's see. Robert Frost, America's Poet Laureate, was fairly memorable. An old bastard, if ever there was one. I met him when I was eighteen; apparently he didn't consider me a sufficiently humble worshiper at the altar of his ego. Anyway, by writing a scurrilous letter to Harold Ross, the late editor of *The New Yorker*, where I was then employed, he got me fired from my first and last time-clock job. Perhaps he did me a favor; because then I sat down and wrote my first book, *Other Voices, Other Rooms*.

As a child, I lived until I was ten or so with an elderly spinster relative in a rural, remote part of Alabama. Miss Sook Faulk. She herself was not more than twelve years old mentally, which is what accounted for her purity, timidity, her strange, unexpected wisdom. I have written two stories about her, "A Christmas Memory" and "The Thanksgiving Visitor"—both of which were filmed for television with Geraldine Page portraying Miss Faulk with an uncanny beauty and accuracy.

Miss Page is rather unforgettable, come to consider: a Jekyll and Hyde; Dr. Jekyll on stage, Mr. Hyde off. It is purely a matter of appearance; she has better legs than Dietrich and as an actress can project an illusion of infinite allure—but in private she insists, Lord knows why, in disguising herself under witchlike wigs and costumes of consummate eccentricity.

Of course, I don't care much for actresses *or* actors. A friend, I can't remember just now who, said, "All actresses are more than women, and all actors are less than men. A half-true observation; still, true enough to be, in my opinion, the root cause of the prevailing theatrical neurosis. But the trouble with most actors (*and* actresses) is that they are dumb. And, in many instances, the dumbest are the most gifted. Sir John Gielgud, the kindest man alive, an incomparable technician, brilliant voice; but, alas, all his brains are in his voice. Marlon Brando. No actor of my generation possesses greater natural gifts; but none other has transported intellectual falsity to higher levels of hilarious pretension. Except, perhaps, Bob Dylan: a sophisticated musical (?) con man pretending to be a simple-hearted (?) revolutionary but sentimental hillbilly.

But enough of this question. It was stupid to start with.

Q: What is the most hopeful word in any language?

A: Love.

Q: And the most dangerous?

A: Love.

Q: Have you ever wanted to kill anybody?

A: Haven't you? No? Cross your heart? Well, I still don't believe you. Everybody at one time or another has wanted to kill someone. The true reason why many people commit suicide is because they are cowards who prefer to murder themselves rather than murder their tormentor. As for me, if desire had ever been transferred into action, I'd be right up there with Jack the Ripper. Anyway, it's amusing to think about: the plotting, the planning, the surprise and regret imprinting the face of the villain-turned-victim. Very relaxing. Better than counting sheep.

Not long ago my doctor suggested that I adopt some healthier hobby other than wine-tasting and fornication. He asked if I could think of anything. I said, "Yes, murder." He laughed, we both did, except I wasn't laughing. Poor man, little did he know what a painful and perfect demise I'd planned for him when, after eight days abed with something closely resembling black cholera, he still refused to pay me a house call.

Q: What are your political interests?

A: I've known a few politicians whom I liked, and a more surrealist montage could not be imagined. Adlai Stevenson was a friend, and always a generous one; we were staying as guests in the same house when he died, and I remember watching a manservant pack his belongings, and then, when the suitcases were so pathetically filled, but still unclosed, I walked in and helped myself to one of his ties—a sort of sentimental theft, because the night before I'd complimented him on the tie and he'd promised to give it to me. On the other hand, I like Ronald Reagan, too. Many of my friends think I'm teasing them when I say that. I'm not. Though Governor Stevenson and Governor Reagan are quite different spirits, the latter shares with the former a modesty, an "I'm looking you in the eye and I mean what I say" directness that is rare enough among us folk, not to mention politicians. I suppose New York's Senator Jacob Javits and Governor Reagan, for purely reflex reasons, feel antipathetical toward each other. Actually, I think they would get along fine, and would make an interesting political combination. (Of course, the real reason I always speak well of Governor Reagan and Senator Javits is that I like both their wives, though they are even less alike than their husbands, Mrs. Javits being a lacquered but still untamed city urchin, a smoochy-voiced and sexy-eyed child-woman with a vocabulary as fresh and salty and Brooklyn-bred as the waves that spank the beaches at Coney Island. As for Mrs. Reagan—I don't know, there is about her something so small-town American and nostalgia-making: the homecoming queen riding past on a throne of roses.)

The two politicians I've known best were President Kennedy and his brother Robert. They, too, were quite unalike, and not as close as generally believed; at any rate, the younger brother was very much afraid of the elder—

Q: Do we really have to hear *any* more about *any* Kennedy? Moreover, you're sidestepping the question, which wasn't about politicians but your own interest in politics.

A: I have none. I've never voted. Though, if invited, I suppose I might join almost anyone's protest parade: Antiwar, Free Angela, Gay Liberation, Ladies' Lib, etc.

Q: If you could be anything, what would you most like to be?

A: Invisible. To be visible or invisible at will. I mean, think of the possibilities: the power, the riches, the constant erotic amusement.

Q: What are your chief vices? And virtues?

A: I have no vices. The concept doesn't exist in my vocabulary. My chief virtue is gratitude. So far as I know, I've never betrayed anyone who was kind to me. But as art is life's compensation for the flawed delights of living, I reserve my greatest gratitude for those poets, painters, composers who have compensated me most. A work of art is the one mystery, the one extreme magic; everything else is either arithmetic or biology. I think I understand a considerable lot about writing; nevertheless, when I read something good, in fact, a work of art, my senses sail away into a universe of wonder: How did he do it? How is it possible?

Q: Looking back, it would seem as though some of your answers are rather inconsistent. Deliberate cruelty, you say, is the one unforgivable sin. Then you confess to occasional verbal cruelty, and later on admit that you have contemplated prepared murder.

A: Anyone consistently consistent has a head made of biscuit. My head, the interior, may be made of something odd, but it isn't biscuit.

Q: Suppose you were drowning. What images, in the classic tradition, do you envision rolling across your mind?

A: A hot Alabama day in, oh, 1932, so I must be eight, and I am in a vegetable garden humming with bees and heat waves, and I am picking and putting into a basket turnips and slushy scarlet tomatoes. Then I am running through a pine and honeysuckle woods toward a deep cool creek, where I bathe and wash the turnips, the tomatoes. Birds, bird-music, leaf-light, the stringent taste of raw turnip on my tongue: pleasures everlasting, hallelujah. Not far away a snake, a cotton-mouth moccasin, writhes, ripples across the water; I'm not afraid of it.

Ten years later. New York. A wartime jazz joint on West 52nd Street: The Famous Door. Featuring my most beloved American singer—then, now, forever: Miss Billie Holiday. *Lady Day*. Billie, an orchid in her hair, her drug-dimmed eyes shifting in the cheap lavender light, her mouth twisting out the words: *Good mornin', Heartache—You're here again to stay—*

June, 1947. Paris. Having a *fine l'eau* at a sidewalk café with Albert Camus, who tells me I must learn to be less sensitive to criticism. (Ah! If he could have lived to see me now.)

Standing at the window of a *pension* on a Mediterranean island watching the afternoon passenger boat arrive from the mainland. Suddenly, there on the wharf carrying a suitcase is someone I know. Very well. Someone who had said good-by to me, in what I took to be final tones, not many days prior. Someone who had apparently had a change of mind. So: is it the real turtle soup?—or only the mock? Or is it at long last love? (It was.)

A young man with black cowlicked hair. He is wearing a leather harness that keeps his arms strapped to his sides. He is trembling; but he is speaking to me, smiling. All I can hear is the roar of blood in my ears. Twenty minutes later he is dead, hanging from the end of a rope.

Two years later. Driving down from the April snows of the Alps into the valleys of an Italian spring.

Visiting, at Père-Lachaise in Paris, the grave of Oscar Wilde—overshadowed by Epstein's rather awkward rendition of an angel; I don't think Oscar would have cared for it much.

Paris. January, 1966. The Ritz. An unusual friend comes to call, bringing as gifts masses of white lilac and a baby owl in a cage. The owl, it seems, must be fed live mice. A waiter at the Ritz very kindly sent it to live with his farm-family in Provence.

Oh, but now the mental slides are moving very fast. The waves are closing over. Picking apples on an autumn afternoon. Nursing to life a bulldog puppy ill-to-death with distemper. And she lives. A garden in the California desert. The surf-sound of wind in the palm trees. A face, close by. Is it the Taj Mahal I see? Or merely Asbury Park? Or is it at long last love? (It wasn't—God no, was it ever not.)

Suddenly, everything is again spinning backward; my friend Miss Faulk is making a scrap-quilt, the design is of roses and grapes, and now she is drawing the quilt up to my chin. There is a kerosene lamp by the bed; she wishes me happy birthday, and blows out the light.

And at midnight when the church-bell chimes I'm eight.

Once more, the creek. The taste of raw turnip on my tongue, the flow of summer water embracing my nakedness. And there, *just* there, swiveling, tangoing on the sun-dappled surface, the exquisitely limber and lethal cotton-mouth moccasin. But I'm not afraid; am I?

℗

The Best in Fiction from PLUME